Under the Moon

a Goddesses Rising book

Under the Moon

a Goddesses Rising book

Natalie J. Damschroder

Entangled Publishing, LLC
2614 South Timberline Road
Suite 109
Fort Collins, CO 80525
Visit our website at www.entangledpublishing.com.

Edited by Kerri-Leigh Grady
Cover design by Heather Howland and Hot Damn Designs

Ebook ISBN   978-1-62061-216-3
Print ISBN   978-1-62061-215-6

Manufactured in the United States of America

First Edition December 2011

The author acknowledges the copyrighted or trademarked status and trademark owners of the following wordmarks mentioned in this work of fiction: AC/DC, American Medical Association, Band-Aids, Boston Landing, Camaro, Charger, Crocs, Daddy Warbucks, Dean Koontz, Dumpster, Fairfield Inn, Fairfield University, Federal Bureau of Investigation, Formica, Henley, Hoyer, J. Crew, Jetway, Lexus, Metallica, Metro Cab, Mustang, NFL Network, Ohio State University, Plexiglas, Prius, Romance Writers of America, Samuel Adams Beer, Sarett Nature Center, Taser, Taurus, Toyota, Vulcan, Walmart, Westminster, X-Men.

This book is dedicated to Jim, who taught me what falling in love was all about in the first place, and made sure I never had to face the despair of hard choices.

CHAPTER ONE

*Society views goddesses the same way they view psychics—
most people don't believe in us, and since there are only about a
hundred goddesses in the United States, skeptics rarely have occasion
to be proven wrong. Some people have open minds but still no
reason to seek to use a goddess's talents. If you choose a public career
as a goddess, you join in the responsibility for image maintenance.
Help us keep public opinion positive.*

—The Society for Goddess Education and Defense,
Public Relations Handbook

When Quinn Caldwell's cell phone rang, she assumed one of her clients needed an appointment or a Society member had a question about next week's annual meeting. It took her a second to pull her attention from the paperwork on her desk, another three to register the name on the screen.

Nick Jarrett.

Her spark of joy at seeing his name quickly changed to concern. He wouldn't be calling for anything good. Quinn plugged her ear against the noise from the bar outside her office door, held her breath, and flipped open the phone. "Nick?"

"Quinn." The rumble of his vintage Charger's engine harmonized with Nick's voice. "Service isn't good out here so just listen."

She knew it. "What's wrong?"

"We have a problem. I'm coming early. I'll explain when I get there. I won't have a very good cell signal most of the time. I'm at least a day away, so stay close to Sam, and don't…" His voice cut in and out before disappearing altogether.

Quinn's skin prickled. She closed the phone, frowning. Nick never came until at least the week before new moon, when she was most vulnerable. In the fifteen years of their relationship, he'd never come a whole week early.

Something big had to be happening.

Quinn was the only goddess whose power source was the full moon, which meant she was only fully able to use her abilities for the seven days around it. As the month waned, she grew more "normal" until the new-moon period, when she had no ability to tap the power. That was when Nick appeared. Never now.

"Who was that?" Sam's solid, warm hand landed on her shoulder, and he dropped a pile of papers on the desk in front of her. Quinn blinked at the shift from the surreal nature of the phone call to the mundane clutter of her narrow office at the back of Under the Moon, the central-Ohio bar she'd inherited from her father. It was her main business, a connection to the parents who died within months of each other twelve years ago, leaving her without any real family. It also kept her connected to the public between power cycles. The goddesses who made a living with their abilities mostly relied on word of mouth to find clients, and Quinn's bar, centrally located for locals and travelers, had enough people channeling through it to give her customers for both businesses.

"Nobody," she said, still lost in thought. She shook off the fog. "I mean, Nick."

Sam's eyebrows disappeared under his dark, shaggy bangs. He crossed to his smaller but far more organized desk near the office door. His chair squeaked when he dropped into it. "Nick called you?"

"Yeah. He's coming early."

"Great." Sam glowered and mumbled something under his breath. "Why? The moon is barely waning gibbous."

"I don't know. The signal dropped." She worried her lower lip. *Stay close to Sam.* Why? The order was protective—and after all, Nick was her protector, so that was his default mode—but what did she need protection from? She rubbed her right forearm, the phantom ache a reminder of the first time Nick had been assigned to her, that "goddess" wasn't a synonym for "invincible."

Sam sighed. "When is he getting here?"

"I don't know that, either." She rested her head on her hand, her elbow on a pile of folders on her worn oak desktop. The full moon would completely wane by tomorrow, taking most of her power with it, so she'd worked steadily for the last week, using mostly telekinesis and her healing ability to help her clients. She hadn't slept enough to balance the depletion of her normal energy, and her sluggish brain resisted the apprehension buzzing in her now.

"We'll have to wait until he shows up, I guess." She shook off the mental fuzzies and focused on Sam. He watched her, longing mixing with concern in his light brown eyes.

"How long did you sleep?" he asked.

She stifled a yawn. "Seven hours, six minutes."

He shook his head. "That's not enough."

"Gonna have to be. It sounds like we have a full house tonight."

"It's busy for a Tuesday," he acknowledged. Murmurs and laughter mixed with the jukebox music filtering in from the main room. It was still early, too.

"Bets and Katie are both sick, so they probably need us out there." She stood and stretched, closing her eyes briefly and arching with her arms high. He didn't answer. "Sam?" She caught him staring at the stretch of skin bared by her sweatshirt and tugged it over the waistband of her jeans. Heat seeped through her, dragging tingles in its wake. Did he notice her skin flush?

He gave himself a little shake and pulled his gaze away. "Yeah. Yeah, I guess." But he scowled.

Quinn propped her hands on her hips. "What's wrong?"

"Nothing." He sat up and shifted papers on his desk, but she knew it wasn't "nothing."

"Sam."

He sighed. "We need to talk. You've put me off all week, and now we've got Nick…"

Shit. She had hoped Nick coming early would put an end to this debate. She dragged her cotton apron off the back of her chair and busied herself tying it. "I'd better get to work."

But Sam didn't get up. His voice was low and deep when he said, "Why didn't you come to me?"

Her hands stilled, and she avoided his steady gaze by checking for her order pad and pen. "You know why."

"I'm still here." He stood and came around the desk, and she couldn't help but look at him now. He dwarfed her, filling her vision, his scent flooding her senses, feeding the grinding need she'd battled for weeks. She kept her lids shuttered so he couldn't see the inevitable dilation of her pupils and take the reaction the wrong way. Her moon lust knew what Sam could give her, her body giving a Pavlovian response to his nearness.

Tapping her power source had a price. As energy flowed through her, it depleted her resources like exercise depleted an athlete. Instead of needing water and vitamins to balance her body, Quinn needed sex. She'd never understood why, but her body had always been recharged by that primal connection to another human being. She hadn't had that for three months now, and the longer she resisted, the more difficult it got.

So Sam's long legs, ridged stomach, and broad chest all called to her. Quinn's hands flexed, anticipating the silk of his shaggy hair bunched in them. *Only a few minutes*, a voice whispered in her head. *That's all it will take. For balance.* A moment of thought, of remembering the heat between them, was enough to make her crave it again. Her mouth watered as she watched Sam's long-fingered hand track up his chest and around the back of his neck, a move she knew was calculated.

That didn't matter. She took a step toward him, then forced herself to stop. She'd told Sam three months ago that she wouldn't use him anymore and had held fast to the decision no matter how willing he was. It had been six years since she'd first had sex with him, and she'd only recently understood the damage they were doing to each other. Sam didn't believe she could stop, but she *had* fought the moon lust for nearly twelve weeks. Tomorrow would end this full-moon cycle; she'd have it completely under control, and it would get easier next month. It had to. *Yeah, because it's been a cakewalk so far.* But she didn't have to convince herself—she had to convince Sam.

"I've told you. What we're doing isn't fair. You've stopped dating, stopped even looking for—" She hesitated, uncertain how to phrase it.

"I don't need to look for it." His tone was hard with conviction, and Quinn closed her eyes, despairing.

"That's my point," she said. "I'm tying you up, and you deserve better."

"That's a matter of debate, and you don't have to suffer because of it."

Her laugh didn't need to be forced. "Not having sex isn't suffering."

"For you it is."

He'd closed the distance between them, and though Quinn

knew she didn't move, her body seemed to surge toward him in agreement. She breathed in the remains of the aftershave he'd used this morning and wavered. He smelled so *good*.

A shout came from the other side of the paneled door, jerking Quinn out of her trance and replacing it with guilt. She couldn't give in. Sam cared too much. And so did she, but not in the way he wanted.

"We'll talk about this later," she said as the racket outside the door escalated.

"You bet we will." He set his jaw and opened the door, striding out ahead of her.

Quinn followed, her heart and body aching. She immersed herself in taking drink and snack orders from the bikers crowding around four-tops and stroking cues around the two pool tables, but being busy didn't distract her mind. When she wasn't detouring every trip around the room to peer out the front door to see if Nick had arrived, she was fretting over Sam.

He was her best friend and more. The son of a goddess, he'd been fresh out of college when he came to her six years ago looking for a job. He'd designed his education around becoming his mother's assistant, but she'd died soon after graduation. Sam believed she'd put too much wear and tear on her body using her power to help others. Since he couldn't save her, he'd found Quinn.

She poured a pitcher of light beer for a group of Tuesday regulars and watched Sam help Katie deliver a full tray to a celebrating bowling team. He'd become indispensable within three months of her hiring him. He did research for the full-moon jobs on topics as wide-ranging as agriculture, medicine, geometry, and psychology. He also managed the bar and her schedule—managed *her* so she didn't deplete her resources too fast or take on jobs she shouldn't.

He caught her watching as he carried the tray back behind the bar and flashed a dimple. She couldn't help smiling back, but then quickly bent to wipe down an empty table.

When she needed to recharge during the full moon, he volunteered. He joked that it was the best perk of the job, but they never discussed a long-term plan, assuming they'd take things as they came. Like Sam would meet someone he wanted to be with, and they'd stop.

But it hadn't happened. Quinn realized that Sam didn't flirt with any of the women who came through the bar, and he kept his relations with her staff professional. He never pushed her when it wasn't full moon. There was only one reason a guy would settle for that, and she couldn't give him what he needed.

She considered and discarded a dozen speeches as she drew ale, poured whiskey, and brushed up against Sam whenever she had to get to the register. She was acutely aware of the tightness of her nipples, the sensitivity between her legs that grew whenever their bodies were near. As the moon rose, even as weak as it was, it tugged on her like the tides. Desire surged and ebbed, but it took concentration on her lingering guilt to force the latter.

The bikers, transients who'd been well behaved and heavy tippers, waved as they left at twelve thirty. To Quinn's relief, the place was empty of customers within fifteen minutes. For a moment, she watched the waitresses and busboy wiping down tables and flipping chairs while Sam counted cash at the old-fashioned register.

Resigned to the coming confrontation and wanting to get it over with, she said, "Why don't you guys go home? We can handle the rest of this." No one argued. As they filed out, chorusing their good nights, Quinn braced herself for Sam's first salvo.

"Did you talk to Nick again?" he asked, surprising her.

"No." She ducked under the bar pass-through and crossed to the door to lock it, peering out the small pane of glass onto the gravel lot for the millionth time. "I tried to call, but I still can't get through."

"He's never come this early before." Sam flipped one of the heavy oak chairs up onto a hewn and polished tabletop. "What do you think is going on?"

"There's no point speculating." She went to the other side of the room to help him. "Let's not start listing all the possible reasons. That's too stressful." She didn't want to tell Sam that Nick had told her to stay close to him. That would increase his worry and maybe keep him from going home. She desperately needed some space to get through the next few hours without giving in to the moon lust.

"Okay. So we'll talk about us." Sam pulled down a chair and sat in front of her.

"Can I say no?"

He just looked at her.

"Fine." She sighed and half sat on a nearby table. Sam waited, his eyebrows raised, his mouth cocked, as if he already knew what she was going to say and found it absurd.

"You're twenty-eight, Sam."

"I know how old I am."

Quinn folded her arms. "I'm ten years older than you."

"I know how old you are, too."

"I don't want to keep you from fulfilling your destiny."

He chuckled, shaking his head. "And what's my destiny?"

"It doesn't matter." She steeled herself, ignoring the slow roll of need in her gut. "It's not me."

He sobered. "Quinn…"

"No, Sam." She made an effort to keep her voice steady. "You deserve a chance to find someone right for you. But that's not the main issue." She sighed. "It's time."

She didn't want to talk about the way he'd been watching her. She recognized something in him that she'd buried deep inside herself, didn't even acknowledge anymore. The belief that there was nothing else out there that could give him what he was missing. She'd tried to fill a hole in herself with Sam, using the moon lust as an excuse, not realizing it or seeing that she was creating a matching hole in him. And now she couldn't believe she'd been so blind and selfish.

"I don't get it." He spread his arms wide. "I'm not looking for someone else!"

"That's the problem!" she shot back. "I'm holding you back from finding something real and lasting. A relationship with a woman who won't relegate you to one week every month, for one thing."

A muscle in his jaw twitched. "You need me."

He meant it in a general sense, but it resonated physically. Need of the more carnal variety pulsed in half a dozen places. Quinn clenched her thighs, shifted her folded arms, and fought the impulse to reassure him. She'd told him the first week he worked for her that she would never lie to him. If she said she didn't need him, he'd recognize the deception, and that would hurt him more than not being needed would.

"I'm not going to die if I don't have sex," she said instead. "I've managed three months already."

"Yeah, and it took its toll. You had to work harder to do the same things this month, didn't you?"

"No." That wasn't a lie, but it wasn't completely true, either. When Sam raised his eyebrows, she said, "I got tired faster. But I need more sleep, that's all. I should be able to manage this another way." Frustrated, she pulled the bar towel off her shoulder and slapped it on the tabletop behind her.

"You've tried," Sam said. "You told me so, back when you first hired me. It never worked, and the need grew. So why do you think it will be different now?"

"Because I'm older."

"And more powerful. Wouldn't that make the need worse?"

Damn him, he had an answer for everything. "I'll find someone else." Her gut twisted. The consequence of her heritage would be much easier to deal with if she didn't care whom she slept with, but she always had. As much as it balanced her physically, sex with strangers or acquaintances left her more emotionally bereft, especially after her parents died.

Then came Sam. He'd filled so many holes in her life. Business manager, friend, family. Quinn knew that if she let him, he'd take that even further, marry her and raise children with her, and as blissful as the fantasy was, it would never be as perfect as he wanted it to be. She couldn't love him the way he deserved to be loved.

"Who else?" He spread his hands and looked around. "Where are you going to find a guy like me? Available whenever you need him, able to take what you give—and give what you demand—and be safe? Not in here, I'll tell you that much."

Quinn didn't respond. He was right. She'd tried before. She'd figured one-night stands were every guy's dream, so it would be easy. But too much got in the way. Locals wanted her to do it on their schedule. Basic standards, like avoiding disease and not having sex with attached men, were impossible if she targeted travelers. Most of all, though, was the compulsion that grew as she got older and used more power. The sexual need for mental and physical balance wasn't something she could rein in once unleashed. Sam was the only man who had managed to withstand the intensity long-term. The only one who hadn't called her a freak.

Sam sprawled in his chair in front of her, his long legs so close, the frayed cuff of his jeans brushed her ankle. To keep from moving away, she gripped the edge of the table until her knuckles cracked. Retreat would be an admission that she couldn't handle it. "I've managed fine so far."

"Have you?" He held out a hand, a knowing in his eyes that she couldn't refute. The moon had risen hours ago, close enough to last quarter that she could do only the smallest tasks, but it fed her passion.

I have. The words caught in her throat. Her palms itched, wanting her to reach out and touch him. Take in the smoothness of his hot skin, get her close enough to breathe him in again. She'd climb onto his lap with the friction of denim on denim, his hard thighs between her legs, the rails of the chair digging into her knees. For an instant, the image was so real she thought she'd done it, given in. She blinked and found herself still standing, the involuntary ache almost unbearable. She curled her fists harder around the table edge until her knuckles ached, determined not to make the hallucination reality. She finally managed a nod to answer his question.

"Really." He pushed out of the chair and slowly unfolded his body to stand inches away, deliberately testing her. She held herself still, hoping he couldn't see the pounding of her heart beneath her white button-down shirt. She closed her eyes as he gathered her in to him, his arms loose around her back.

Her hands rose to rest against his chest. Her fingertips dug in to the resistant muscle, and her breath came out almost as a groan. Tension eased out of him as her body gave in, relief sending tingles head to toe as it curved toward him. "Dammit, Sam." Her thoughts blurred under the intensity of Sam's body heat. She couldn't fight it anymore. Fight him.

"Tell me what you want, Quinn." His voice rumbled through the swishing, thumping pulse in her ears. She dragged her focus back from the soft fabric beneath her palms, the delicious pressure of his hardness against her belly.

"What?" she managed to gasp.

"I'll do what you want. Whatever you want." His lips brushed her ear. Tingles erupted and danced across her skin, but what he'd said, what he was doing, penetrated. The offer wasn't just for wild sex. Though he could take advantage of the lust raging through her, he respected her decision. Which brought home all the reasons he didn't deserve the wrong choice.

She leaned back, unable to look at him, her arms trembling with the effort of denying them both. The guilt almost overwhelmed the need. "I'm sorry, Sam."

He eased away, his hands sliding from her back to her upper arms, making sure she was steady, and then dropping when he'd put a foot of space between their bodies. "You're sure." Not a question.

Quinn nodded and finally met his eyes, regretting the sorrow she'd put there. "I have to do this. Please, please understand."

He sighed and twisted to replace his chair on the tabletop. He stood with his back to her for a long moment, one hand still on the leg of the chair, before facing her again. "I won't push anymore. Just…promise me you won't…" He waved a hand. "You know. Get yourself into trouble."

Her voice squeezed past the burning thickness in her throat. "I promise."

They worked in silence to finish closing, their usual easy tandem punctuating the finality of her decision.

When they were done, Sam nodded and looked around, hands on his hips, clearly at a loss. "Okay. I guess I'm going home, then. You're all right?"

Nick had told her to stick close to Sam, but there was no way she could ask him to stay now. She wished she knew how much longer Nick would be.

"I'm fine," she lied. "Thanks." She nudged him toward the door, turning him away from her so he couldn't see the tears filling her eyes. "I'll see you tomorrow."

"Lock up after I leave."

She closed the door hard behind him and twisted the lock so he'd hear it, then pulled down the blind. Sobs pushed upward from deep within her and she sank to the floor, covering her mouth to keep the sound from reaching Sam, whose presence she still felt on the other side of the wood. Finally, his boots crunched on the gravel, growing fainter with each step. When the familiar hum of his Camaro faded, she allowed herself to break down.

• • •

Quinn slept late the next morning. Her night had been full of erotic dreams, interrupted by abrupt waking to check the clock and try to call Nick, to no avail. Hoping some combination of rest, nutrition, and physical exertion would purge her system of the moon lust, she followed a workout with oatmeal and a shower. She was relieved, when she was done, to find herself less *hungry*. It wasn't gone, but she could distract herself with work and by this time next week, maybe she'd be back to normal.

She took a deep breath before heading down the rickety staircase hugging the side of the building. Sam's schedule had him there by ten or eleven most mornings, but she wasn't sure what to expect after last night. Maybe he'd call in sick, or have cleaned out his things and left a letter of resignation on her desk. Maybe, in trying to preserve the most valuable thing in her life, she'd destroyed it.

Bracing one hand on the rough wood planks of the outer wall, Quinn yanked on the warped back door, taking a moment to prop it wide and let in the sunlight and crisp October breeze. Not stalling. Just…setting up.

She paused on the threshold to let her eyes adjust to the dim office. Her desk was how she'd left it the night before, with piles of invoices and orders to approve, checks to sign, and client files to review. Dust floated in the beam of sunlight that hit the floor in front of her feet. Quinn forced herself to look deeper into the room to Sam's desk, usually as full as hers, if more neatly organized. She held her breath as her vision sharpened, and movement turned into Sam's hand making sharp notations on a printed spreadsheet. He flipped open a file and tapped a few keys on his keyboard without looking up at her.

"How long did you sleep?" he asked.

Breathing was suddenly easier than anything she'd done so far today. Sam asked her that every damned morning. "Eight hours, thirty-three minutes." Her perfect internal clock had amused and delighted him at first, then became nagging when he used it to manage her, whether over how long she'd slept, gone without eating, or focused on a client. But that was what he was paid for, after all, and she welcomed the symbol of normalcy. He nodded his approval and kept working. Quinn went to her desk and booted up her computer.

Sam said, "You hear from Nick?"

"No." The ongoing lack of contact after the urgency of his call scared her. "Sam, I—"

He shoved to his feet and headed out front. "We're low on vodka. I'll pull some up."

Quinn sighed and slumped. So much for normalcy.

It didn't get better. Sam worked out front while she stayed in the office. When she went into the bar, he retreated to the back. She stopped trying to talk to him, hoping the space would be a buffer both for their personal and professional relationships, and for her fading moon lust.

There was still no word from Nick.

Finally, Quinn settled herself in a corner of the bar with her laptop to handle stuff that had piled up over the week, hoping her full e-mail in-box and the routine work, the easy decisions, would keep her eyes off the clock. Requests for appointments and vendor info she forwarded to Sam. Most of the rest was related to the Society. Quinn served as the board's secretary, and many of her personal e-mails were about the annual Society meeting next week. Those she moved into a folder to address later. The official Society list e-mail was full of political posts, with elections coming up in November, but she skimmed and deleted most of them.

She'd gotten into such a rhythm that when Nick's name appeared, it was a moment before her reaction caught up. The words were innocuous at first, so she didn't understand the fear filling her until it merged with her ongoing low-level anxiety over last night's phone call.

I plan to ask Quinn to put this on the agenda for the meeting, but I thought you should all know ahead of time, so you can be careful.

Nick Jarrett's gone rogue.

Quinn pulled her cell phone out of her pocket to try to reach Nick yet again. This had to be why he was coming here—but what the hell did it mean and what did it have to do with her?

A crash on the other side of the room redirected her alarm. She was on her feet before she'd even spotted the source of the disruption.

"I'll goddamn keep drinking if I wanna keep drinking!" An old man, greasy gray hair hanging below a dingy trucker cap, wobbled in front of his overturned chair, arms flailing. Despite his obvious intoxication, his aim was good enough to hit Katie's tray and send glasses flying. Quinn stormed across the room, glaring at anyone who looked like they might want to join the fight. None of her regulars moved. Most had seen her in action, and they didn't want to get involved. A few strangers half rose but subsided when they saw her striding to the rescue.

Not that Katie needed rescuing. Nearly as tall as Quinn's five feet ten, the young woman had honed her manner and strength in New York City. By the time Quinn reached them, Katie was quietly telling the drunk how he was expected to behave in Under the Moon.

Quinn's heart rate and footsteps slowed, ready to back up her waitress but also willing to let her handle it. Then the drunk fumbled a switchblade out of his pocket and flicked it open.

Shit. She lurched forward, but she was still too far away to do anything, and Katie hadn't noticed the knife. Reacting on instinct rather than thought, Quinn snapped her fingers and opened her hand as the knife soared to it. Relief flooded her. *Concentrate. This isn't over yet.* She squeezed the handle of the knife so no one could see her shaking.

The drunk waved his hand, then frowned when he realized it was empty. "What the—" He looked up and blinked at Quinn. "How'd you do that?"

Quinn signaled a white-faced Katie to step away. She glanced around to be sure everyone was out of reach and then faced the drunk.

"You want to leave my establishment," she told him with forced calm.

He scowled. "T'hell I do. I ordered a beer! And I'm not leavin' till I get it!"

"Yes you are." She jerked back as the man lunged at her, flicking her fingers at him. He slammed into an invisible wall but only grew angrier. Quinn swallowed hard. She didn't have the power for more than this, and she couldn't risk her staff getting hurt. Summoning the knife and stopping the drunk's movement required only a little access to the waning moon. But because it had already passed the zenith of its arc, even this drained her.

She had enough for one more act. *Please let it be enough.* She thought *heat* and pointed at the sleeve of the man's denim jacket. A second later it caught fire. He yelled and slapped at it, extinguishing the flame almost immediately, but it had done its job.

His eyes wide, he tried to back away. The overturned chair tripped him up and he stopped. "What are you?" His voice quavered.

Electric awareness alerted Quinn to the presence of the man two feet behind her before she heard his voice, a slight Texas drawl mellowing the deep rumble that always made her think of his perfectly tuned muscle car.

"She's a goddess."

"Goddess," the drunk scoffed. "Them's just a myth."

Nick Jarrett stepped past Quinn, standing between her and the drunk without making it look like he was getting in her way. The hunger that had been easing all day flared, but because she'd never recharged with Nick, she was able to stamp it down more easily than she had last night.

"You don't believe your own eyes?" Nick said to the drunk.

The drunk scowled at them, then at the tiny wisp of smoke rising from his sleeve. He blinked blearily and stumbled toward the door, grumbling under his breath.

"That's what I thought." Nick swung around to look at her, a hint of a smile on his full lips and welcome in his green eyes. "Nice parlor tricks."

Quinn snorted, covering how happy and relieved she was to see him, and turned to her busboy. "Catch that guy and call Charlie to pick him up in his cab, will you?"

"Sure." He pulled out his cell phone and hit speed dial on his way out. Everyone else dispersed, leaving Quinn relatively alone with Nick. Adrenaline drained out of her, and she would have sat, if showing weakness in front of him wasn't so unappealing.

"So what's going on?" She tucked her fingertips into her jeans pockets. The anxiety buzzing in her all day disappeared, allowing the alarm triggered by the e-mail to resurge. "You're never early."

"We've got a problem."

Quinn watched him scan the room, cataloging her customers and staff, lingering on her computer in the far corner and the closed door to her office. His face tightened, and he moved a step closer.

"I know we do," she said.

He whipped his head around, his eyes sharp. "You do?"

"I just found out. Come here." She led him to the table where her computer slept, its screen dark. "I read this e-mail not five minutes ago." They sat down, and she tapped a key to wake the computer while Nick signaled for a beer.

They waited for the wireless connection to reestablish. "You getting a lot of trouble like that guy?" he asked.

"No more than usual." She glanced at him. "Why? Is someone else?"

"Nah." He stood to pull off his battered, hip-length brown leather coat and hang it over the back of the chair, then rolled the sleeves of his flannel shirt up strong forearms. A waitress sashayed over to set an amber bottle on their table. She looked at Quinn, who shook her head, but Nick made a face and dropped the money on her tray. "Don't listen to her."

Quinn didn't bother to argue. They had the same argument every time he came. Sometimes she won, sometimes he did. It balanced in the end.

Nick sat back down and took a pull of the beer, his strong throat working with the swallow. Light from a nearby candle picked up glints of gold in his short-cropped, dark blond hair. "Where's Sam?"

Quinn cleared her throat. "In the office." She diverted her eyes to the computer screen but heard his small snort of derision. "I had it under control, Nick."

"The moon's waning, Quinn. I don't care how powerful you are at peak, you're tapped out by this time—"

"Not completely. And protecting me isn't Sam's job." She winced, realizing too late it might sound like criticism of Nick, and she hadn't meant it to be.

He froze, the bottle halfway to his mouth, then set it down. "I told you to stick close. He should be out here. Or you shouldn't. And I'm not listening to you argue with me. What have you got?" He turned the computer toward him, ignoring her exasperation.

She twisted to read the e-mail with him, now more confused by the words on the screen than anything else. "Well?"

Seconds passed while his eyes tracked over the words. "Fuck me," he said softly. "That's not the problem I was talking about at all."

CHAPTER TWO

The power harnessed by goddesses is a connection to the energy
generated by all life in this world—energy that is absorbed by,
altered by, or resonating in non-living objects, as well. A goddess's
power is capacity. She is like a vessel, using her source to access,
manipulate, and channel energy into and through herself.
This ability allows her to do amazing things.

—The Society for Goddess Education and Defense,
New Member Brochure

Quinn dropped back against her chair, staring at Nick. Being accused of going rogue wasn't what had brought him here? "What's the other problem?"

His eyes flicked toward her, then back to the screen. He scrolled down to read the signature on the e-mail, then back up to the top. "There's a leech out there. He's hit two goddesses already."

Fear twanged deep inside her, like a plucked cello string—a completely different kind of fear than the routine rush of facing a drunk with a switchblade and more concrete than an undefined "rogue" accusation. "So when you said 'we,' you meant me."

His mouth curved on one side. "Well, yeah." He waggled a finger at the laptop. "This, though, this is definitely 'we.'"

"Who did he hit?" she asked, and his smirk dropped.

"Tanda and Chloe."

She closed her eyes, her heart weeping for her friends. Why hadn't she heard about this before? It hadn't been that long since they talked, or at least e-mailed. She didn't see them often, living so far apart, but she had been looking forward to getting together at the upcoming Society meeting.

She couldn't imagine how they must be feeling right now. "Goddess" wasn't only a job description—it was a state of being. When the leech took that away, he would have destroyed their essence.

Quinn clenched her fist and let heat coalesce in her palm, just to connect to her source, to her core. It came slowly, the moon nearly out of her reach, and panic flirted at the edges of her consciousness until her fingers flinched open, stung.

Stop it. She wasn't a hand wringer. She was a problem solver. She asked questions and set a plan based on the answers. Never mind that a leech was a whole lot different from retrieving lost wedding rings and helping the corn crop flourish. "They're on opposite coasts," she pointed out.

"I know."

"When?"

"Not long ago. Four days apart."

That wasn't much time. Leeching was hard. It took preparation. Travel wouldn't be an obstacle—Oregon to Rhode Island was still less than a day, even with layovers. But for someone to have leeched two of them that close together…

"We have to be talking about two people," she said, the fear doubling until Nick shook his head.

"They say it was the same guy. They'd know."

Of course, Tanda and Chloe would know. It wasn't like a murder, the victims unable to describe their attacker. Leeching left the goddess alive but powerless. Bile crept up the back of Quinn's throat. She didn't ask about protectors. Her friends both had regular power sources and had never come under threat, as far as she knew, so they wouldn't have had one.

She swallowed hard. "Do you think he's moving this way? Is that why you came?"

He lifted a shoulder. "No one knows where he's going next. It's a sure bet he's going somewhere, though. Here is as likely as anywhere else."

So there was no concrete reason Nick was here. Not an external one, anyway. Logically, she didn't need him now, but something deeper, more visceral was fiercely glad he'd come. The part of her that she'd closed up tight, determined not to allow light and hope that didn't exist, cracked open.

She reached for Nick's beer and took a long swallow, forcing herself to concentrate on the practical. "He won't be after me yet. Not if he's doing any kind of research on us. And he has to be, to get two in four days."

Nick made a half-agreeing motion with his head. "Tanda and Chloe both use their abilities commercially. It wouldn't be hard to collect information on them, especially if he's a computer geek like your guy in there." He indicated the closed office door.

"Well, their websites, sure."

"And their customer bases," Nick said.

The population at large ignored the hundred or so goddesses in the United States. Most people had never met a goddess or seen one at work. It made sense that the leech would target ones who operated publicly. Which Quinn did, so Nick was right, she was a potential target.

She grimaced at his raised eyebrows. "My point is, if I am a target, he'd have to be studying me." Her body shuddered when she resisted the urge to look over her shoulder. "And if he's studying me, he knows when I have access to power. He'd be foolish to try to leech me when it's not the full moon. " She lifted his bottle toward her mouth again, but he grabbed it away and drained it.

Quinn continued. "A leech would have to get close to his target, tune into the energies she uses before he can take her power. If she's away from her source—or if the source is away from her— there's no power to take. Right?"

"Right," Nick acknowledged. He raised his hand to signal for another beer.

"So let's table that and discuss this." She jabbed a finger at the screen. "Do you know what it's about?"

Nick slowly shook his head, studying the words as if they were a code.

"What does it mean?" she demanded. "Rogue from what?" The word still made the back of her neck prickle, even though it had no support. Not like "murderer" or "rapist" did. It taunted with its intangibility. How could they fight a threat they didn't understand?

He shrugged. "No idea. Never heard it used like that before. Any responses to the e-mail?" He closed it and opened her incoming mailbox. Though Quinn doubted there was anything private in there, she pulled the computer back around anyway.

"No," she said after a minute of scanning. "Nothing. That's odd, since this came in last night. And I didn't get a separate message about putting it on the agenda."

"You know her?"

She opened the e-mail again. She hadn't even noticed who sent it, but she knew almost everyone in the Society. The message was signed, "Jennifer in Mississippi."

"Not well. You?"

He shook his head. "She's not one of mine."

"Whose, then?"

"You know it doesn't work like that." He rubbed his hand over his mouth and shadowed jaw. "I don't know who's where, unless it directly affects one of my assignments."

"Which makes this kind of thing a helluva lot easier."

Nick grinned at Quinn's annoyance. "What kind of thing?"

"You know." She floundered for a second before pointing at the word "rogue" on the screen. "That. It's…unsettling."

He blew out a breath. "Well, nothing we can do about it now. I guess we wait for the meeting and see what's what."

She rebelled at the idea of sitting back and doing nothing, but there was a more immediate concern. She raised her eyebrows at him. "You're coming to the meeting?"

"If you are, of course I am."

"But why?"

He looked at her, something churning deep in his eyes that she hadn't seen there before. "Leech, Quinn."

"I told you, he won't come now." She moved to shut down the computer, unsure why she was so agitated about him being here that long. He usually stayed for only a week at a time, close to the new moon. She could handle being with him for a week, since he was more of a constant presence than an interference. But clearly that wasn't going to be the case this time.

"I don't care. He could capture you now, hold you until the moon's full again. I'm not taking a chance." Nick stood to pull on his jacket. "I have to drive to Marion to pick up a few things. Don't look at me like that," he said when she frowned. "It wasn't on the way, and I had to stop here and see you. I'll be back before you close. Stay around people and don't lock me out."

Quinn wasn't sure which was stronger, her annoyance at his high-handedness or the warmth of knowing he'd been in such a rush to check on her in person. "I'll have your room made up for you." Her dad had always kept a couple of rooms above the bar ready in case of severe weather or stranded motorists, but to save money when he died, Quinn had made them into her personal living space. When Nick was here, he stayed in the room farthest from hers and closest to the outside door.

"Stay around people," he ordered again, and she rolled her eyes.

"I promise, Dad."

His glower made her grin, but it fell as soon as he disappeared through the rough wooden door into the darkness outside. The noise and movement in the bar faded around her, and she slipped back to when they'd first met. She was twenty-three, Nick twenty-one and fresh from Protectorate training. Quinn had just helped a friend escape from an abusive boyfriend. She'd been pretty cocky back then, high on exploring the extent of her abilities. Using shields and telekinesis, Quinn protected the friend and her kids when the boyfriend tried to stop them, so they were able to collect all their things and get away without him following. Quinn remained behind as the friend fled to a shelter. Turning the tables on the bully had been fun. She'd tested the limits of her element control, setting him on fire without letting him actually burn and sucking enough air out of the room to make him think he was going to suffocate.

But of course, she'd been stupid and arrogant. Her friend disappeared into the system, so the boyfriend came after Quinn. He was smart enough and knew enough about her to wait until the new moon, when her only defense was physical. She hadn't seen it coming, foolishly closing the bar alone while her father was away at a convention. The boyfriend had shoved through the door as Quinn was locking it, knocking her back onto the floor. She'd stared up past his passionless face at the rage in his eyes, and cold, foreign fear paralyzed her. Somehow, when he reached to grab her shirt, his fist cocked, she'd dredged up the strength to fight back. The fiasco had earned her a broken arm.

Nick arrived a few days later, informing her that her mother had called the Society, who contacted the Protectorate. Quinn wanted to be furious, but she wasn't stupid. Besides the fact that vulnerability and nervousness had become her companions, she was a young, unattached woman. Why would she fight having a hot, rugged, mysterious guy at her side? Especially one who drove a muscle car and wore a beat-up leather jacket, trappings she knew were meaningless, but damn, they were hot.

At first, Nick stayed until the boyfriend was arraigned for the assault charges and released on bail. He'd been spotted lurking once, but Nick's presence kept him away. Nick spent some time training Quinn in self-defense, and when the threat appeared averted, the Protectorate moved him on to another assignment.

Quinn had hated the cold pit of fear the incident had left in her, and she refused to do nothing when there were so many people she could help. They'd established a system to help abused women get out of their situations, and Nick's assignment turned permanent. He set a random schedule to deter anyone who might be planning an attack, always overlapping with the new moon. When Quinn's father had his fourth, fatal heart attack and her mother died from an infection a few months later, Quinn took over the bar and her goddess business grew naturally into other, less directly dangerous work. Her reputation included the presence of a badass protector, so the threat against her became dormant, and their working relationship became routine.

Their friendship had started with their first words. Quinn couldn't remember them now, only that whatever Nick said had snagged a connection inside her with the strength of platinum. He wasn't a silent, lurking presence like a normal bodyguard. They debated physical versus energy-sourced protection. The defensive perspective he provided gave her a new way of looking at the world, and it made her stronger. And even though he was never there to see it, she was better able to serve her clients during the week around the full moon.

They enjoyed the same TV shows and movies and even shared political and social opinions. Quinn would have called them soul mates, but the one time they'd seemed to be venturing over that line, Nick had made it clear he wouldn't go there. Month by month their friendship had deepened, as had both her feelings and Nick's determination.

Shaking off the melancholy, she spent some time clearing tables and shooting the shit with her regulars. She needed to put a buffer between her unsettling moments with Nick and talking to Sam. He was so sensitive to her moods he'd instantly know what she was feeling, and things were bad enough between them without pulling Nick into the mix. Eventually, she felt clear enough to go bring Sam up to date.

This time when she entered the office, instead of pretending he hadn't noticed her, he eyed her carefully from head to toe.

"You're okay?"

"Yeah, why?" She set the laptop on her desk.

"I heard the commotion. I was on the phone, and by the time I came out, everything looked fine."

"Just a drunk. We got rid of him." She shoved her hair back and leaned against the side of her desk. "We have a problem, Sam."

He stared at the pencil he was twirling between his hands. "I don't think we do." He seemed to steel himself and looked up. Hurt flickered in his eyes before a wall went up. Quinn forgot what she'd been about to say. "We settled everything last night. I've been your employee, and a tool—"

Appalled, she cut in. "You're not a tool, Sam, you're my friend. My *family*. I can't—"

"Will you shut up and listen?" He stood, the pain replaced by anger and determination. "I don't want this to change anything."

Quinn opened her mouth, sorrow and regret surging, but he

stopped her with a sweep of his hand.

"You are my best friend. I understand that you can't care about me the way I'd hoped. But you still need me. I don't want you to send me away. I can—"

Someone knocked on the door and opened it without waiting for a response. Katie came through and zeroed in on Quinn, apparently not noticing their tension. "Nick's here."

Sam threw up his hands and let them slap down onto his thighs. "Great. Perfect timing."

The women, used to the friction between the two men, ignored him. "Thanks, Katie. Can you please tell him his room's ready?"

"Sure." Katie closed the door behind her.

Sam paced across the few feet behind his desk, muttering something about competition.

"He's—" Quinn stopped her automatic protest. It wouldn't do any good to say that Nick wasn't competition, since it wasn't exactly true and Sam might take it the wrong way. She bit her lip. Did he still hope she'd change her mind?

He halted, obviously making an effort to rein himself in. "So what's he doing here now, anyway?"

Quinn didn't have time to respond before Nick sauntered in.

"Hey, Sam." He eyed the other man, his brow creasing when he sensed Sam's hostility. "You tell him?" he asked Quinn.

"I didn't get a chance to yet."

Nick dropped into a chair in front of Quinn's desk, turning it to make a triangle among the three of them. She stood frozen, her body practically vibrating with the friction filling the room. Sam stuck his hands on his hips, the move widening his body, and she would have sworn he stretched to his full height to tower over Nick. Not intimidated, Nick propped his work boot on the edge of Quinn's desk and tilted his chair back, a smug smile flickering at the corners of his mouth.

"Tell me what?" Sam demanded.

"I've gone rogue," Nick declared at the same time Quinn said, "We've got a leech."

Sam looked from one to the other. Nick's grin had expanded to fully cocky. Quinn, no doubt, looked grim. The room filled with implications, too many questions to be asked, and a metallic tang of fear from all three of them. Quinn could almost see Sam's brain sorting through the mess to find the most immediate concern. Of course, that was the one sitting in front of him.

"Rogue? What does that mean?"

Nick shrugged and filched a peppermint from the bowl on Quinn's desk. "No idea. And I haven't. But some people seem to think I have, which will make the other problem worse. Raise your hand if you think *that's* coincidence."

No one did.

"The leech." Sam stuck his hands on his hips and looked at Quinn again, concern and accusation on his face. "*That's* the problem you came in here to tell me about. Not—"

She nodded, wishing she didn't feel so relieved about the distraction from their discussion.

"Fuck." He dropped into his chair. "That's, like, a crisis, not a problem."

"Not for us," Nick said. "Not yet. But it will be. Quinn's got a lot of power, and she's public about it, so it's a sure bet he'll be after her."

"Not until the moon's full again. So we have some time." Sam grabbed a pad out of a drawer and started writing. "Where's he hit so far?"

"Tanda and Chloe."

He stopped writing, and his sadness fed Quinn's. Where were they right now? Had the leeching done physical damage as well as taking their power? Who was looking after them? She checked her watch. It was too late in the night to call Chloe in Rhode Island, but maybe Tanda was still up. Assuming she wanted to accept phone calls.

Sam went back to his notes. "They both draw their power from water."

"They do?" Nick dropped his foot and the chair legs to the floor with a *thump*.

Quinn nodded. "Chloe from the ocean, Tanda from rain."

"I wonder if that's all he wants," Nick said.

"I doubt it." Quinn sat down and pulled out her cell phone. "It might explain why he could leech Chloe so soon after Tanda, if his preparation was similar. So he might hit another goddess whose power source is a form of water, but it won't be where he stops."

Nick frowned. "What's that woman in Mississippi's source? The one who said I'd gone rogue?"

"Jennifer." She stiffened. "Flowing water. That's why she's near the river. Do you think—"

"She's been hit already?" Nick dialed his cell phone. "There's a chance."

While he waited for his call to be answered, Quinn scrolled to find Tanda's number. The line barely rang once before it went to voice mail. Quinn didn't know what to say, so she hung up and listened to Nick's side of his own conversation.

"Hey, it's Nick. Jarrett. Yeah, you too. Hey, you know who's got Jennifer…" He raised his eyebrows at Quinn.

"Hollinger," she said, the name popping into her head. "Jennifer Hollinger. She's in Vicksburg, Mississippi."

Nick repeated the information and waited. "Okay, thanks anyway. Let me know if you find out." He snapped the phone closed and shook his head. "We don't cover her much. She stays by the river most of the time. Can you contact her?" he asked Quinn. "Find out if she's okay? It's only been two days since Chloe, but with the power he got from her, he could make it quicker."

Quinn nodded and went to her file cabinet to pull out the Society roster. She found Jennifer's phone number and left a message for her, but a bad feeling grew the more she considered what they knew. She went online and checked messages again. There was still nothing else from Jennifer, and no responses on the Society e-mail loop. In fact, there was no discussion on the Society loop at all, and given the news about the leech alone, there should be dozens of messages. She checked the group settings, but everything looked okay. After a moment, she typed: *I haven't heard anything from Jennifer about Nick, and she doesn't answer her phone. Anyone know what's going on?*

Before she sent the e-mail, she told Nick what she was doing and asked, "Should I mention the leech?"

He shrugged one shoulder. "Up to you. Anyone mention it yet?"

"No. Strange."

"John said the Society doesn't want to start a panic. They've assigned a security team to investigate it, and the Protectorate has mobilized protectors for goddesses they think might be vulnerable." He reached for another mint, avoiding her eyes, and she wondered if that meant he was supposed to be protecting someone else. Something warm flared low in her abdomen, but she frowned.

"I get not wanting to start a panic, but they can't sit on the knowledge. People have to know. It's bad enough Tanda and Chloe had no warning."

"They're probably trying to avoid being bombarded," Sam said. "They've got to have their hands full. This is way beyond pamphlets and PR."

"I guess." But Quinn still didn't agree with their methods. After a moment of hesitation, she added a line to the e-mail asking if anyone had heard about a leech and clicked send.

Sam bounced his pen against his pad. "How does someone become a leech, anyway?" He directed the question at Nick. "I mean, not just anyone can do it, right? Or everyone would."

"Not a lot of people know goddesses," Nick said. "So not *everyone* would." He crossed a leg over his knee and stretched his arms over his head before bracing his hands behind his neck. The heat in Quinn's belly spread and added bite. She stared at the computer screen and clicked refresh on her e-mail in-box, waiting for her body to subside so she could tune back into the guys' conversation.

"When was the last time a leech actually existed?"

Sam's question was rhetorical. There hadn't been a leech in their lifetime. Goddess fairy tales abounded with leeches instead of trolls and witches or the specter of nuclear war. Parents lumped leeches in with child abductors, piggybacking warnings with lessons about not talking to strangers. But they never discussed how a leech came to be. Quinn hadn't even known until she met Nick. As a protector, he had extensive training in all possible threats.

"So?" Sam scowled at Nick, then at Quinn. "Why are you avoiding the question?"

Nick raised one eyebrow at Quinn. She sighed. "A leech can only exist if a goddess bestows power on him."

"What?" Sam sat up sharply. "They can do that? *You* can do that?"

"Yeah, but…no, not me. But some goddesses, yes." Quinn hunched her shoulders a little. "Not like donating blood or something. It's tied into her abilities, I guess, and the recipient has to be male and receptive."

"Who wouldn't be receptive?" Sam asked. When Nick and Quinn both looked at him, he made an "oh, come on" face. "I'm not saying *I* would. I mean—"

"Receptive as in physically capable," Quinn said. "And there's no way to test for that or anything. Right?" she confirmed with Nick.

"As far as I know. But it's not like anyone teaches this stuff. No one *wants* it to happen. The legend is that she can only give power to a man, and since he won't be a natural vessel, he'll have to constantly reacquire it. So he becomes—"

"A leech." Sam blew out a breath. "Okay. So a goddess had to have started this."

Quinn didn't say anything. She had no idea of the actual process involved and wasn't sure she'd understand it if she did. Goddesses were vessels for energy, similar to batteries but with only short-term storage. Each goddess had a different capacity and manifestation, so she supposed some had the ability to transfer power to a vessel with the capacity to receive it.

She hated the idea of any goddess she knew doing such a thing. They didn't come into their power or even know what would feed it until they hit age twenty-one. Because their life expectancy was higher than a normal human's, they weren't fully mature, and fully connected to the world's energy, until then. The whole process of determining the source and training to channel the energy was different for every person and meant a long learning curve. Who would go through all of that and then give some of it up? Who wouldn't care about the damage they could do if they created a leech?

The more immediate concern, she decided, was determining who was next so they could prevent it. Stop the leech, then find who'd created him.

Sam seemed to be going down the same road she was. "Quinn, does the roster list details about the goddesses? Like power source, age, stuff like that?"

She shook her head. "That's kept in a database at headquarters in Boston, but general members don't have access."

"You're the board's secretary, though, not a general member."

"Good point." Quinn leaned over to access the computer. "I'll see what I can get."

"Tanda's your age, right, Quinn?" Nick drummed his fingers on the desk.

"A year younger." She entered her officer code and password to access the Society's protected web pages. "Chloe's older than us, by maybe six or seven years." Midthirties to maybe fiftyish would be the ideal age span for leeching. Leeching a young goddess would be like eating celery to put on weight—more effort was expended than benefit gained.

Quinn logged into the live forums and saw that Alana, the Society's executive director, was online. She IMed her a request for access to the database. Alana responded immediately.

ED: Why do you need it?

QUINN C: We're trying to track the leech.

She watched the screen for a few minutes. Alana didn't respond. She felt Nick and Sam looking at her and glanced up. "I'm working on it."

The computer chimed.

ED: The board and security team are in charge of the investigation. Your assistance is not required.

There was the sound of a door closing and the screen read, *ED has gone offline, 11:22 p.m.*

"Shit." Quinn stared at the screen, stunned and a little hurt at the abrupt cut-off.

"Well?"

She slapped the lid down and bounced back in her chair. "Nothing. She said the board and security team are investigating and they don't need our assistance." She busied herself crumpling up scrap paper, but Nick guessed what she was thinking anyway.

"They heard about me going rogue and know you're mine."

"Tell me again what that means?" Sam sounded exasperated.

"We don't know!" Quinn and Nick said together.

Sam shook his head, looking disgusted. "Don't you think we'd better figure it out? Or why this goddess you've never met would say it?"

"I dunno, maybe she's got a hard-on for Quinn." Nick swung to face her. "Maybe she's the one who created the leech, and she wants to get rid of me so you're vulnerable. Which *would* make you an immediate target."

It was too logical to refute. "Maybe."

Sam, who'd been packing his computer into his tote, paused. "I should stay here tonight, then."

"Hell, no." Nick swung himself upright and clapped a hand on Sam's shoulder. "You know I've got it covered. Besides, you two keep saying she can't be leeched until full moon."

He slid out from under Nick's hand. "It can't hurt to have another set of eyes and ears here."

"It's okay," Quinn said to stave off a fight. "I really believe nothing's going to happen tonight. Go home and get some sleep."

Sam slung his bag over his shoulder, looking unhappy. "I'll make sure they don't need me out front. Let me know tomorrow if you come up with anything brilliant." He didn't look back as he left.

Nick flashed his crooked grin at her. "Alone at last."

"Shut up." Her fatigue had grown exponentially over the last hour. The only blessing was that it overwhelmed the residual hunger. Sam's exit had deflated all the tension, too, and the relief left Quinn's muscles as lax as her brain.

Well, she didn't know everyone's age or power source, but she knew some. It wouldn't hurt to write those, at least. She picked up the roster to make notes in each record.

Nick watched her for a few minutes. "You look exhausted."

Quinn shot him a glare. "That's probably because I am. It's the end of the cycle," she reminded him. "I'll be okay."

"Why didn't you recharge?" He toed off his boots, the action serving to add casualness to the question. "Isn't that part of Sam's job?"

"No," she snapped. "It's not."

Nick didn't move, but Quinn swore his entire body had tightened. "Since when?"

"Why do you want to know?"

"Why won't you answer me?"

Both their tones remained mild, but undercurrents surged. Quinn couldn't face this now, not after last night's emotional turmoil and today's revelations.

"It's none of your business, Nick."

He drew in a breath. "Yeah, you're right." With a groan, he stretched until his fingers scraped the low ceiling. "I'm beat. You mind if I head to bed?"

"No, go ahead. You know where things are."

"Yeah."

She flipped a page, skimmed the list, and made a couple more notes. Nick didn't leave. She waited, but he just stood, the air heavy with everything he didn't say.

Finally, he moved away. "Good night, Quinn."

"Night, Nick."

When he closed the office door, she laid the roster on her desk and drew a deep breath of her own.

She hadn't wanted to admit it, but Alana's response rattled her as much as everything else tonight. Maybe more. The leech threat was general, and even the "Nick is rogue" thing wasn't about her. But Quinn was used to being in the midst of everything the Society did. Barbara Valiant, the president—who Quinn suspected was over a hundred years old—often consulted with her to get the "younger generation's perspective." Quinn had served on a dozen national committees since she'd turned twenty-one, ran the Ohio chapter for four years, and was finishing her second term on the board. When she went to meetings in Boston, she always had dinner with Alana, whom she'd thought was a friend. Her abrupt dismissal didn't compute.

Unless they'd not only heard Nick had gone rogue, they believed it.

And they thought Quinn was involved.

CHAPTER THREE

*Fear and ignorance have always put Society members in danger.
This reality spawned the Protectorate, an ancient organization
of bodyguards, discrete from the Society, self-governed and
autonomous and funded by a centuries-old wealth managed in trust.
Any goddess away from the source of her power who may be a
target of those who want to do harm will be assigned a protector.*

—The Society for Goddess Education and Defense,
New Member Brochure

Quinn tried, but despite her exhaustion, she couldn't sleep very
long. There had never been any question that they would try to stop
this guy. Nick hadn't bothered to suggest they hole up so he could
bar the door and keep her safe. Sam had automatically gone into
investigative mode. She knew their priority was still keeping the
leech away from her, but none of them wanted anyone else to be
harmed.

Every time she started to doze, her brain woke her with a new
angle, so finally she got up and returned to the computer. She spent
hours doing research, both online and in some of the historical
archives on the Society website, trying to figure out what "rogue"
meant in the context of either goddesses or protectors. There
wasn't much about rogue goddesses. They documented the birth
and progress of every known goddess and, since one was born

an average of once every year and a half, it wasn't difficult to do. Lineages made it unlikely that a new goddess would escape the notice of the Society. If a goddess was unable to pay her Society dues, a sustenance fund covered it.

Quinn knew a few goddesses who disdained the politics of the organization, and a few more who preferred a freer existence, but they all still maintained minimum levels of membership to stay part of the Society's community. In the last hundred years, three goddesses who had problems with the Society had been labeled rogue. Only one had gone on to do things that went against their general moral code.

Quinn supposed that would be hard for regular people to believe. Goddesses were all about power, after all, and power corrupts. But as far back as goddess history went, the abilities that came with their heritage had been accompanied by compassion and wisdom. Goddesses were rare; goddesses doing harm even more so, and those that did were quickly taken care of. Gods were nonexistent. Some claimed men hadn't learned the lessons of corruption and therefore eliminated their line of descent long ago. Quinn didn't quite believe that. Goddesses were still human, and there were plenty of normal women who were corrupt.

Others thought one or more of the "original" goddesses, who'd had much greater abilities in a world unpolluted and not yet depleted of resources, had deliberately eliminated the gods' ability to procreate. No one knew for sure.

Regardless, even in the information Quinn had found about the rogue goddesses, there'd been no mention of rogue protectors. Maybe the Protectorate archives contained something, but of course Quinn didn't have access. She wasn't sure if Nick did, but he was treating the whole thing so lightly, she didn't trust him to check.

She needed to go to Boston.

• • •

"I don't know why we can't take the Charger, that's all." Nick slammed the driver's door and unlocked the trunk. After handing Quinn her duffel, he unloaded his pockets into the trunk's storage case. She counted two pistols and three knives.

"Because I don't want to take three days to travel," she said. Again.

"*You* wouldn't be driving. It would be no more than twelve hours there, twelve back, tops. That's barely a day."

"I'm in a hurry." She swung her bag over her shoulder and headed toward the terminal. "What's your problem with flying, anyway?"

"It's not the being-in-the-air part—"

"Let me guess. It's takeoffs and landings."

"Nope. It's the lack of viable escape routes." He held out a hand to stop a cab so they could cross to the terminal. "Kinda hard to protect you when there's nowhere to go."

Quinn smiled. "Great, you can relax. There won't be anything to protect me from."

"Never let down your guard." He moved ahead of her to scope out the counters. Midafternoon, midweek, the crowd wasn't too bad. Nick stood watch while Quinn used their e-tickets to check them in at the self-service kiosk, and he maintained his vigilance through security and down the concourse.

"Nick, please," Quinn protested after he made yet another three-hundred-and-sixty-degree spin. "I feel like we're on a stealth attack for the U.S. military."

He glared at her but settled down. "I have a bad feeling about this."

"I know. But I have to go." She slowed as they approached

their gate, noting the line of people stretching away from the boarding pass scanner and spilling out onto the main concourse. The gate attendant announced boarding for their flight, all rows, and they joined the line, slowly moving forward.

Quinn handed over her boarding pass, waited for the attendant to run it through the scanner, and continued down the Jetway. She was on the plane before she realized Nick wasn't right behind her. The attendant glared when she tried to go back, so she found her seat, stowed her carry-on bag, and settled in, feeling the seconds tick by into minutes before he appeared at the front of the plane.

"Problem?" she asked when Nick appeared, scowling, three disgruntled-looking passengers following him down the aisle.

"Damned pass wouldn't scan." He zipped his duffel, tossed a book onto his seat next to Quinn, and straightened. "I'm gonna do a quick walk-through. Stay here."

"Will do."

She picked up his book, surprised to see an old Dean Koontz horror novel. Nick wasn't the reading-for-pleasure type. She tried to think of what he usually did during downtime, but there hadn't been much. When he was with her he was always on alert, always engaged either with her or the people around them. The realization that after so many years there might still be things she didn't know about Nick Jarrett was unnerving.

As soon as the thought crossed her mind, she rejected it. Reading preferences aside, he was no stranger to her. She knew well his need to be in control, his surface amusement at everyone and everything around him, his snap judgments about people. She understood his compassion, the legacy he followed. He did the job he did because of a deep nobility, something he'd deny but that had been the foundation of the wall they'd set between them. A wall introduced by his words but bricked by her own distance.

A few moments later, he dropped into his seat and held out his hand for the book. "Full flight."

"Anything suspicious?"

"Nope. Ninety percent business people, ten percent frazzled families."

"Exactly what I would pretend to be, were I after me." She handed him the book. "I don't think I've ever seen you read."

"You're gonna sleep most of the flight. I need something to do." He tucked the book into the pocket in front of him, then tilted toward her to dig underneath him for his seat belt. His scent rushed through her, spiking her in place with his hard chest and broad shoulders only inches away. The burn faded slowly after he sank into his seat.

"So." He turned his attention back to her. "Who are we seeing in Boston?"

Quinn had spent the day shopping, packing, and leaving instructions for her staff. "I thought Sam would have told you."

Nick snorted. "Sam doesn't tell me squat. What?" He shrugged at her disbelief. "I'm competition. Guys don't help the competition."

"You're not," Quinn said without thinking. Nick's mouth quirked in his familiar half smile, but before he could say anything more on the topic, she changed it. "I need to see Alana in person. Something's up, and she won't tell me online or over the phone."

"Aren't you going to see her next week for the meeting?"

"We can't wait until next week." She didn't tell him about her growing uneasiness. He'd think it was fear of the leech, and it wasn't, really. The leech was frightening on the level of hurricanes and car crashes—he may never come after her. But Jennifer's e-mail and Alana's IM blow-off were more personal, the reasons more unknown, and that was scarier. Quinn was afraid waiting a week would allow the chasm the Society was building around her and Nick to be too deep to overcome.

The attendant began her demonstration while the plane

backed from the gate and taxied to the runway. A few minutes later they were taking off. Quinn watched the world zip by, conscious of Nick's tension. Sure, he wasn't afraid. But teasing him about his reasons for hating flying didn't seem fair at the moment.

As soon as they were airborne, Nick opened his book. "Nighty-night."

Annoying as he was, he was right. She hated the boredom of travel and always fell asleep, no matter how hard she tried not to. The drone of the engine and general white noise of the cabin helped her doze until they approached Logan Airport two hours later. Her dreams were vague and jumbled, but all of them incorporated an awareness of Nick's proximity. She knew when he stood to remove and stow his coat overhead, when he ordered orange juice from the attendant. She sensed when he watched her sleep, and she tightened her arms around herself when he got up to go to the restroom or do another walk-through.

She kept her eyes closed when she reached full awareness, not wanting to leave the state of comfort being near Nick gave her. A simple state that would disappear as soon as he knew she was awake, old barriers going up automatically.

He touched her arm. "Quinn. We're about to land."

She lifted her head and yawned. "You sleep at all?"

"Yeah, right." He drew the blanket off her to fold it. "You drooled on my shirt, you know."

"I did…not." There was a wet spot on his shoulder. Her cheeks flamed with embarrassment. "Sorry."

The captain announced preparation for landing, and they lapsed into silence. They didn't say much until they were in the rental car, a Taurus Nick wrinkled his nose at.

"Where to?" he asked, starting the engine.

Quinn rolled down her window an inch to let in the crisp evening breeze. "Sam booked us rooms at—"

"Rooms? Plural? No." He shook his head. "We'll have to change that."

"Fine." She wasn't going to argue with him, plus it would be cheaper. "We'll get a suite. Turn up here." Half an hour later, Nick left the car with the hotel valet and followed Quinn inside. She signed for the new room and handed Nick his key card.

Once they were alone in the elevator, she said, "I want to freshen up and then head over to the Society to see if I can catch Alana."

Nick glanced at his watch. "It's after seven."

"She might still be there. If not, we can try her at home."

"You could call first."

"I don't want to alert her." The way she'd acted, she was likely to run and hide if she knew Quinn was coming.

When they arrived at the brick building housing the Society office, Quinn used her officer ID card to activate the elevator. When they got upstairs and emerged in the main reception area, she turned off the alarm with the code given to all board members and staff. The light flashed green.

"They haven't locked you out yet."

She shrugged to hide her relief. "I guess they didn't expect me to fly here." She surveyed the dark reception area and looked down the hall. With the exception of a small lamp behind the front desk, no lights were visible, not even cracks under doors.

"Doesn't look like she's here." Nick opened the door to leave. "How far's her house?"

"Hang on." Quinn went to the wide white desk and sat down at the computer.

"What are you doing?"

"They leave the computers on for backup. Or they did the last time I was here." She flipped on the monitor, which faded into a desktop image of a white-robed ancient goddess with dark hair down to her ankles.

"She's hot." Nick leaned over her shoulder.

Quinn ignored him. She accessed the hard drive and skimmed through the contents until she found the main database and opened it. With a few clicks, she sorted for the information she needed, hit print, and exited out of the server.

"Sweet." Nick pulled the first pages off the printer. "You don't think she'd give you this if you asked in person?"

Quinn didn't want to find out. "Just a precaution." She glanced through the files and folders again but found nothing with a label as obvious as "leech" or "Quinn Caldwell." She closed all the open windows onscreen, found an empty file folder on the shelf beneath the printer, and took the sheets Nick had gathered.

Nick checked his watch as they exited the building. "Still want to go to Alana's now? It's getting late."

"She's not far, and we won't stay long. She should be home, at least."

They drove in silence the few miles to Cambridge. It was nearly nine o'clock, but when they pulled up in front of Alana's condo, lights shone in the front window.

Nick parked at the curb, his gaze on the house. "One car in the driveway, garage closed. Company?"

"Maybe. I don't know anything about her social life, except she's not married."

"Okay." He pulled the keys from the ignition and opened his door. "I'll let you do the talking."

"Gee, thanks."

The neighborhood was quiet. No traffic, no movement. Most windows had lights shining behind drapes or sheers, some flickering with changing TV imagery. A dog barked somewhere down the block. It was the type of idyllic scene Quinn hadn't been a part of since her parents died and she moved in to the bar. A pulse of longing took her by surprise. *Sam could have given you this.*

She banished the insidious whisper as Nick's strong hand rested on the small of her back. They went up the short walkway together, and Quinn's longing twisted into something deeper, more intense, and less attainable.

Quinn skipped the bell and used the knocker on the red-painted door. Less than a minute later, Alana yanked it open. When she saw Quinn, her eyes widened, and she backed up a few steps before she caught herself.

"Do you know what time it is?" she barked, but Quinn wasn't fooled.

"Why are you afraid of me?" Quinn stayed on the step, not wanting to provoke her. But anger quickly overshadowed hurt feelings.

"I'm— I'm not afraid of you."

"Yeah, that's why you're stuttering," Nick scoffed from behind Quinn, who shushed him.

Alana shifted sideways and angled the door in front of her. "You flew seven hundred miles and are knocking on my door at nine o'clock at night. Why wouldn't I be afraid?"

Quinn sighed. "I have no idea. Can I come in? I just want to talk to you."

Alana stared at the floor a minute. The muscle in her forearm stood out as her grip on the doorknob tightened. But finally she nodded. "For a minute."

"That's all I want."

Alana backed up a few inches and Quinn stepped into the ceramic-tiled foyer, but when Nick made to follow, Alana blocked him.

"Not you."

"She doesn't leave my sight." His voice was a low growl, his amusement gone.

But Alana had recovered herself and held firm. "And you don't come in my house."

"It's all right," Quinn told him. "If I'm not out in three minutes or signal that I'm okay, you can bust in."

He compressed his lips and narrowed his eyes but gave a short nod. "Three minutes." He took his cell phone out of his pocket and held it up. Quinn nodded, and Alana shut the door.

"What do you want, Quinn?"

"Can we sit?" She looked down to set her watch timer, and when she looked up, Alana had folded her arms and leaned against the simple white wall.

"Why bother? We might as well stay by the door your watchdog is itching to break down." Her animosity was palpable. "Let's get it over with."

"Okay. You said the board was taking care of the leech. But I'm on the board."

"So?"

"So why did I have to hear about this from Nick?"

Alana's chin came up, and her mouth stayed closed.

"Is Barbara upset with me about something?"

"Not exactly."

"Well then what, exactly?"

No response.

Dammit. Quinn loosened her jaw and tried a different angle. "Has anyone checked on Jennifer Hollinger?"

Alana's eyebrows rose. "Checked on her for what?"

"She sent a message to the loop and said she was going to follow up directly with me and didn't."

Alana shook her head. "So?"

"The leech has gone after two goddesses who draw from water. Jennifer draws from water. Now she's not answering her phone or checking messages."

"It's only been four days…" Alana trailed off. Quinn knew she didn't need to point out that it had only been four days between Tanda and Chloe.

There was a subtle shift in the air. "I'll call Barbara in the morning," Alana said, her tone softer. "The security team may already be down there. I don't know what they're doing. But thanks for pointing it out."

That wasn't the reason Quinn was here, though. "I don't know what everyone thinks, but the goddesses are as important to me as they are to anyone."

"It's not that." Alana's demeanor was more sympathetic than antagonistic now, but she wasn't any more forthcoming.

"Then what? Why do I feel ostracized?"

Alana looked torn. "I can't—"

"Can't *what*?" Quinn ground her teeth in frustration. "What is going *on*?"

Her watch beeped. She crossed the few feet to the door and opened it. Nick faced her, leaning one arm against the jamb, his jaw tight and his eyes blazing.

"I'm fine," she told him.

"I'm not. I don't like this, Quinn."

"I know. A few more minutes, I promise."

"Hurry."

Quinn smiled. Nick waited a few beats, then smiled back. "Get outta here."

She closed the door and turned back to Alana.

"I think we're done," the other woman said.

"No, we're not. Not until you tell me why the board is marginalizing me."

"Quinn, I can't. I'm not even supposed to talk to you or Nick. Please stop pushing me."

"Why?"

"Because it's not polite?"

"Tell me something. With all I've given to this organization, I deserve a little consideration."

Alana bit her lip.

Encouraged, Quinn pushed a little harder. "I've sacrificed a lot and never asked for anything. And with the meeting next week—"

"Stop it!" Alana launched herself away from the wall. "I know it's not fair, but they have to protect the Society. Family ties are always stronger than—" She stopped, looking stricken.

Quinn leaned toward her, almost holding her breath. "Family ties? What family ties?"

"Nothing. Please go. I'll check on Jennifer tomorrow." She turned Quinn and pushed her toward the door. "We'll see you at the meeting next week, if you decide to come. No one will blame you if you don't." She yanked open the door and shoved Quinn hard.

"*Oof.*" Nick caught her. The door slammed behind them. They stood, Nick looking wry, Quinn stunned. *Family?* She had no family. Her parents had been only children and…

Oh my god. The thought struck her hard enough to leave her breathless again. But the implications were too complicated to consider, and her brain pulled up another, even more wrenching possibility.

"What happened?"

"I have no idea," Quinn managed to answer.

Nick hooked her elbow with his hand and strode them to the car. "That whole thing was weird. She was scared of me."

"Yeah."

"No one's been scared of me before." He half shrugged. "You know, who wasn't supposed to be."

"She wasn't scared of me." Quinn slipped into her seat and closed the car door. Nick roared away from the curb before she even had her seat belt on. "But she was scared of something that has to do with me."

"Like what?" He braked at the stop sign but didn't stop. She wanted to tell him to slow down, but she shared his desperation, the need to get away. It didn't make sense—no one was chasing them, and it was a sharp contrast to her eagerness when Alana had first mentioned family—but she felt it nonetheless. She'd assume Alana's fear was infectious, but the last person Quinn would ever be afraid of was Nick.

"Could we be related?" she blurted.

Nick slammed on the brakes. The tires screeched.

Quinn flew forward and caught herself on the dash. "What the hell?"

"What makes you think we're related?" Nick's eyes blazed.

Had she just thought she'd never be afraid of him? "Nothing."

"Bullshit."

"No, but—" She took a deep breath. This was what she was trying to run from. It threatened to skew their entire relationship. "Let's get back to the hotel, okay? I want to be inside. Then we'll talk. Don't worry, I don't keep secrets from you."

"Damn right, you don't." He accelerated again, his speed and abrupt movements telegraphing his impatience.

As soon as they were inside the hotel room, Nick cornered her.

"What makes you think we're related?"

Quinn didn't intend to stall, exactly, but his reaction gave her the excuse. She circled him and backed toward the sitting area. "Why does it bother you so much that we might be?"

He hesitated. Then his shoulders relaxed. He tossed the keys into a thick glass dish on the spindly table behind the couch. "It doesn't."

"Nick."

"C'mon, Quinn, tell me what's going on."

Quinn removed her jacket and dropped it onto a narrow stuffed chair, then dropped herself onto the hard cushions of the ultra-modern couch. Muscles all over her body protested, then eased out their knots and tension. "Alana said something about family ties. That seems to be the reason the board is keeping me out of the loop on the leech. Since there's the whole thing about you going rogue…" God, what if he was her brother? She pressed a hand to her stomach as nausea churned.

"It's logical they wouldn't trust the goddess related to the rogue protector." Nick pulled two beers from the minibar next to the particleboard dresser, popped the tops, and sat on the couch with her, handing her one. "But I guarantee you, we aren't related."

Quinn took a pull of the ice-cold beer. "How do you know?"

Pink flared across his cheekbones, subtle but there. "I checked."

"You checked?" she repeated, incredulous. "What, you hired a PI to make sure we weren't secretly brother and sister?"

"Not exactly." The flush faded and he grinned with his usual cockiness. "I had an aunt into genealogy. She made this big book that goes back, like, twelve generations. I looked for your name."

That didn't ease her mind, the reason for her shock rolling over her again. "I'm adopted, Nick. Caldwell is my adoptive name."

His expression didn't change. "I know."

"You know my original name?"

"I do."

She stared at him, caught in that numb state when something so surprises you, your emotional center can't react. He didn't seem to notice.

"And I looked for both. By the time we met I had nephews in the book. Aunt Phyllis was thorough. There's no one in there who could have been you or your blood family." He drank, and Quinn watched his Adam's apple bob as he swallowed. After he wiped the sleeve of his flannel shirt across his mouth, he continued. "I memorized six pages of the damned book, okay?"

"How did you know who my birth family was?"

Nick leaned forward and set his bottle onto the glass coffee table. "It was part of my training."

She raised one eyebrow. "To investigate me?"

"Of course not. It was investigation in general. You were one of my study assignments."

Now that Nick had put to rest the horrifying possibility that they were related, she needed to accept that Alana had to have meant her birth family. But Quinn had decided, long before her adoptive parents died, that she wouldn't dishonor them by seeking her birth parents. After they died, being alone was less painful than being rejected. She lived her life as if they didn't exist, but now she was being forced to acknowledge them, and maybe more.

It was far easier to talk about Nick.

"What did you learn?" Almost out of habit, she swallowed some more beer before setting her bottle down, too. She didn't need a fuzzy head, and she was already tired after being up all night and getting less than two hours of sleep on the plane.

"Surface stuff. The names of your birth parents, adoptive parents, *their* parents, where you grew up, went to school, worked. You know." He twisted to lean against the arm of the couch. Quinn kicked off her shoes, pulled her legs up onto the couch, and faced him from the opposite end.

"Did you get assigned to me later because I'd been a training assignment already?" Her heart thumped a little harder as she waited for his answer. It came in a curl of his lips, a tenderness she'd rarely detected in his eyes.

"Something like that," he said, the curl lifting into a smile. "We get info for every goddess we're assigned to. When your mother called for a protector, I was available and they knew I already had the background on you."

Quinn watched her knee rock back and forth, a little lost in the past. He'd been so confident and strong, even as new as he was to the Protectorate, and that had allowed her to turn away from her fear and be strong, herself. Maybe he'd been that confident because he already knew her. Maybe he'd even cared about her.

Dangerous territory. Nick watched her steadily, as if he knew what she was thinking and wanted her to think it. But why? She already knew she meant more to him than a standard assignment. He didn't talk about his other goddesses much. She knew he traveled all over the country to be wherever he was needed, and he protected other goddesses not even half as often as he protected her. But she also knew he wouldn't take his relationship with her any deeper because his duty to those goddesses was just as strong as his personal feelings. No, stronger.

Quinn had settled for what they had because it was so much better than not having him at all. She'd always believed that was also Nick's motivation. But now that she recognized the same pattern with Sam, she had to see her relationship with Nick differently, too.

The familiar ache of longing sharpened enough to make her turn away from that line of thought and face the other. Family ties. Alana could have meant only one thing.

"What—" She swallowed, but the rest of the question still came out raspy. "What did you learn about my birth parents?"

Nick's tone was gentle when he asked, "What do you know about them?"

She folded her arms and lifted her shoulders. "Not much. I met them once, when I was about eight. They were still together, but they were only twenty-three. They told me they'd given me up for adoption because they were too young to take care of me."

"Did your birth mother tell you what you were?"

"Not really, but she didn't have to. I was too young to

understand the whole genetic thing, but I believed I was a goddess because my real mother—my adoptive mother, I mean—was a goddess. But they had different sources and skills." She remembered the small tricks her birth mother had done and how awed Quinn had been. "My birth mother snapped her fingers and made a hair ribbon appear. I thought it was out of thin air, but it was probably from her pocket. My hair was frizzy beyond belief, and I hated it, but she smoothed her hand down it and tied it with the ribbon, and it was perfect after that."

"Still is."

He said it so low Quinn wasn't sure she'd heard him. She hesitated before going on. "She left a box for me, some things her mother had handed down to her, things to help me focus my power and learn how to use it. But my mom was the one who actually taught me."

"Did you ever look for your birth parents once you were an adult?"

She shook her head. "Of course I thought about it, all adopted kids do, but I decided not to. At first, I didn't want to hurt my parents." They'd been a close-knit family, especially after her father quit the corporate world to open the bar. Her mother was a traditional housewife who didn't use her power for commercial use. Seeking her other parents had seemed insulting, and then Quinn's father had his first heart attack when she was nineteen. He stayed fragile until he died seven years later, leaving her the bar she'd renamed Under the Moon. Her mother suffered so much with his death that Quinn hadn't even considered adding to it.

"After Mom died, I was so lonely it was easy to spin fantasies about reconnecting with my birth family. But I decided there were more reasons I'd be sorry than glad if I tried."

Nick shifted closer on the cushions and lifted her feet into his lap, stretching out her legs. He rubbed her arch, like he often did after she'd worked a long shift at the bar—with care and skill and no awareness he was doing it. Warmth blossomed where he touched her and seeped up through her muscles. The banked hunger glowed a little, but she was so tired and so distracted by their conversation it remained low, present but ignorable.

"What kind of reasons?" he asked.

"The usual. However young they'd been, they were still together eight years later. What if it hadn't worked out after that and they were both miserable and blamed me? Or it could have been the opposite, and they had a great life together I wasn't a part of."

"But you had a good life without them, too." He pressed his thumb deep into her arch, stroking upward, and she shivered.

"Yes, and being sorry I wasn't part of their life would have been disloyal to Mom and Dad." She'd still had to work hard to fight the disappointment when they never tried to contact her again. "Mom wasn't a very powerful goddess. She derived her power from plant energy but couldn't draw enough to do spectacular things. I was afraid if my birth mother was as powerful as I can be, especially if she had a constant source, that would make Mom feel bad, too."

"Not after she was gone," Nick pointed out.

Quinn shook her head. "No, the only real risk after they'd both died was that I'd be rejected. Whatever I found couldn't hurt Mom and Dad, then. But my birth parents didn't want me when I was born, and they didn't want me when I was eight, so why would they want me at twenty-six?" Her throat tightened, the vulnerability of being left behind returning. "Or what if they welcomed me at first but decided they didn't like me? I was already in too much pain to face that."

Nick nodded and slid his hand from the top of her foot to her ankle, resting it there. His heat seeped through her sock, relaxing her even more. But god, it was easy to remember that pain. Only the bar and Nick's visits had given her anything to be happy about at first. Slowly, she'd built her own independent life. And then Sam came along, and the pain had faded.

"I don't know much more than that," Nick told her. "Just that they're from New England and were still here fifteen years ago."

His gaze went distant and Quinn wondered if he was thinking of his own family. His parents had both been protectors, two strong legacies who went back to the origin of the Protectorate. Nick had wanted to be a protector since he was a little boy, but then his parents had been injured in a mundane car accident and forced to retire. His two older brothers had nothing to do with goddesses, so it was up to Nick to carry on the family legacy. It drove every choice he made.

"How often do you see your family?" she asked, stifling a yawn. Her eyelids had gained a few pounds.

"The usual. Holidays and stuff. We get together in the summer sometimes. You know, family vacations."

"I can't picture you with them."

His smile was sad. "I don't exactly fit. Six or eight families, all with spouses and kids. Even the divorced ones get along. Stepparents and real parents in one big, chaotic, mostly happy group." He framed a space with his hands. "And then there's me." He stuck his fist out to the side. "The kids climb all over me, their parents braced to snatch them to safety. At night, once the kids are asleep, they want me to tell exciting stories, because I'm the freedom and adventure they want but will never risk." His tone had gone bitter at the end, an edge of resentment at the burden he'd taken on but no one else would share.

Quinn hesitated over whether or not to pry open that crack. "Wow." She eyed his beer. "I thought you only had one of those."

He chuckled. "It's not some big secret. I like my life. I love my family. It's balanced."

Her yawn caught up to her, and she tilted her head sideways against the back of the couch. "You don't feel like something's missing?" Like she did. It was harder and harder to keep it buried.

"Sometimes." He shifted again, tugging her down so her head rested on the pillow behind her, her neck more comfortable. She lost the battle against her heavy eyelids.

"Do you?" he countered.

Quinn shook her head and tried to make her tongue work. "Rarely." She didn't have the energy to correct the lie, and somewhere in the very small part of her brain that was still awake, she knew she wasn't ready to go down that road, with or without Nick. She let herself continue to drift until she fell asleep.

Only to wake a short time later with the world exploding around them.

CHAPTER FOUR

Each goddess has a specific source that serves as a conduit between her and the energy. She also has a unique combination of abilities that we like to compare to talents. Just as one child in a family might have an affinity for playing music while another can fix any mechanical item or perform complex mathematical equations in his or her head, so can each goddess have a unique combination of talents.

— The Society for Goddess Education and Defense,
Goddess Source/Ability Catalog

Quinn shot off the couch so fast she nearly tumbled to the floor, her heart slamming in her chest, gushing aimless adrenaline through her. Nick caught her before she landed in the shards of glass that were all that remained of the coffee table next to them. The air vibrated with a ringing noise so loud she could see Nick's mouth moving but couldn't hear his voice. For a few seconds, the room swam and Quinn was barely capable of covering her ears to muffle the noise. He impatiently swung her up and over to a clear patch of floor, running his hands all over her, and she realized he was checking for glass. The noise must have shattered it, because no one else was in the room.

"I'm fine," she tried to tell Nick, but she couldn't hear her own voice, either. She tugged on his arm and he straightened, angling his body in front of hers.

Quinn couldn't see the source of the sound, like a wet finger circling the rim of a crystal goblet, but far louder. Her chest heaved, and she searched the room wildly, desperate for a clue of what to do, how to act. Something black and hard flew toward them, propelled by nothing. Nick shoved her toward the floor, and it smashed against the wall over their heads before dropping a few inches away. A Bible. Someone had thrown a Bible at them. *Telekinesis.* The leech must have found them.

Nick grabbed her hand and pulled her toward the open bedroom door, away from attack. Quinn managed to grab her bag off the bed when Nick released her to sling his duffel across his body. He went straight to the window and began shoving it open.

Quinn slammed the door behind them, flinching as if something would hit it as she did. If this was the leech, where was he? In the hall or outside the building? Were they running into a trap?

It was a little quieter in here, and nothing else in the room moved. She stood, trying to catch her breath, to think. Nick said something, motioning, but she still couldn't hear him over the roaring in her ears. The horrible ringing grew louder again, as if it had followed them. But there was still nothing to see or defend against. They had to get out.

Nick grabbed a chair from the corner and shoved it under the window. He grabbed Quinn's elbow and dragged her to the chair. When he held up a hand, she nodded and watched him step up on it, push backward through the narrow opening and onto something she couldn't see, and reach for her hand. She leaned out to look and saw scaffolding against the side of the building. She twisted to look up. There was nothing above them.

The ringing stopped abruptly. Quinn glanced back as the bedroom door flew open and smacked the wall behind it, but no one entered. She jumped onto the chair to follow Nick out.

"Let me go first." Even in the sudden quiet, his voice was muffled through her closed ears. He motioned to illustrate his words. "We're going to climb down the side, but some of the distances between holds are long. I'll guide you."

She nodded, impatient. He swung over the side and climbed down while Quinn scanned the area, even though Nick had to have already checked to be sure it was clear. She struggled to regulate her breathing and watched where Nick put his hands and feet before she followed.

She swung a leg through the window and grabbed the sill to lower herself to the scaffold. Pain shot through her right forearm. She gasped and let go. Blood oozed from a two-inch cut over the muscle, deep enough to hurt when she tried to use it. She couldn't let it hamper her and grit her teeth as she began to climb down the side. At the *X*s between levels, she shifted to the left and slid down the sloping tubes, her palms stinging from the friction on the cold metal.

A few steps later, they were on the sidewalk. Both looked up, but the scaffolding was clear of forms or moving shadows. Her body sagged, her breathing and heart rate easing, and the sensation of something chasing them faded. Her ears were still closed in protection, but even that was easing.

"Nice job. Let's go." Nick ran down the alley, away from the front of the hotel. Quinn followed without question, pressing the hem of her shirt against her wound. The rental car was probably being watched. The attacker knew what room they were in, so he might know more. Even though someone could be in the back of the hotel as easily as the front, there were Dumpsters and pallets and darkness that offered more protection than the bright lights and tiny valet stand on the main road.

Nick let her catch up to him before they reached the back of the building. "Time?" he whispered into her ear. It was too dark for him to see his watch.

"Eight past two," she whispered back. Nick's arm around her waist tightened when her lips touched his ear. He turned his head back to whisper to her again.

"We'll run, few blocks, cab, airport."

Quinn nodded. Nick leaned to peer around the corner, then signaled her to move. They dashed across the rear alley and continued on to the next main street. After looking both ways, they turned to the right, which was better lit and had a bit of traffic. Dodging black iron lampposts and street signs, they ran, sometimes single file, down the narrow concrete-and-brick sidewalk for three blocks before they slowed to a walk. Quinn realized they were still—or again—holding hands, and she didn't want to let go.

"You're limping."

She looked down. The toes of her socks were flopping. She paused and bent to pull them on tighter. "I didn't have time to get my shoes."

A car approached behind them. Quinn's pulse sped up, and she braced to run again until she saw the green Metro Cab logo on the white sedan. Nick flagged it down, and they got inside practically before it came to a complete stop. As soon as her butt hit the vinyl seat, her body started to shake from the adrenaline ebb, the kind of deep shudders that weren't visible from the outside. She imagined her face was as white as the moon, though.

"Where to?" The cabbie yawned, which wasn't very reassuring, but the streets, while not empty, didn't require rush-hour alertness, either.

"You need shoes," Nick said to Quinn.

"Nothing's going to be open around here. I'll get something at the airport."

"Airport?" Cabbie asked.

"Airport," Nick answered, and he turned back to Quinn, immediately spotting the blood on her arm. "What the hell?" He grabbed her arm quickly but gently, lifting it to see better. "Why didn't you say something?"

"It's not bad." But she hissed when he probed it.

"You have a first-aid kit?" he asked the cabbie, who tossed back a white plastic box with a red plus on it.

"It'll need better cleaning and a proper bandage." Nick used a few antiseptic wipes to clean the cut and cursed when he could only find small Band-Aids to cover it. "I'm sorry."

"Don't be silly." He looked so upset, even in the darkness, that she didn't tell him about the deep throbbing pain. She'd get some painkillers at the airport.

"Did we luck into that scaffolding?" Quinn tried to keep her voice low enough not to be overheard.

"Sam may not be a protector," Nick admitted, "but he knows what he's doing."

"But I changed the room."

He shrugged. "He left instructions. Did you notice the room numbers?"

"No."

"The ones she crossed off were one floor below the suite. I spotted the scaffolding when we first got in." He looked down at her bag on the floor next to her feet. "What did you manage to rescue out of there?"

"Everything." Thank god. "I only had the one bag, and we never got around to talking about the printout. It's still in there."

"Next time, bring extra shoes."

"Yeah right." She watched lights flash past for a few minutes. When Nick didn't bring up the details of the attack, she guessed he didn't want to talk about it in front of strangers.

The cabbie dropped them in front of their terminal. Quinn paid him, and they went inside. She dug into her bag to find the e-tickets for their return flight Nick kept his hand on her uninjured arm while he took the tickets from her, scanned them, and pulled off the boarding passes after they printed. "Where to?"

"Boston Landing has shops. I should be able to get some shoes once stores open." Their flight out was early, but still hours away.

"All right." Nick scrubbed his hands over his face. "Let's use the bathroom and get some coffee."

Quinn grinned. "You gonna follow me into the ladies' room?"

"Don't tempt me. Keep your phone ready to beep me." He watched her go into the restroom. Quinn would have been amused if it hadn't been so reassuring.

She used the much-needed facilities first, then washed her arm without removing the Band-Aids. The cut looked raw and fresh but didn't bleed again. She took the time to brush her teeth, wash her face, and comb her hair, which didn't look even close to perfect, no matter what Nick had said last night. With the travel and the sweat from running, not to mention sleeping on it twice, her hair had become lank and uncooperative. She twisted it on top of her head and anchored it with a clip. It didn't help much. It was oh-god-thirty in the morning, and she looked like death, but she had no power to fix it, not even the mundane cosmetic kind. Her head throbbed in time with her arm, from the combined aftermath of the high-pitched scream and the emotions of fight-or-flight.

She braced her hands on the sink top and blew out a long breath. She was avoiding the important thing, which was that in all the years Nick had been her protector, this was the first time since her parents died that she felt like she needed one. She didn't like it. Whoever had attacked them, whatever their goal, they'd made her a target. Worse, everyone around her was now in danger. All from asking a few questions. It could be the leech, but that didn't make sense. No matter what he could have wanted from tonight's attack, these methods wouldn't have gotten him any power.

Maybe she wasn't the target. It could have been someone hunting Nick because of the rogue thing, but that didn't make much more sense. Which brought her back to the questions they were asking. They had to be getting too close to something. How far would this person go to stop them or get what they wanted from her? And who was it? The Society? They wouldn't want the public to find out about the leech, increasing the danger to their goddesses. But it wasn't like Quinn had threatened to go to the media. She was just trying to help.

No, the only thing that did make sense was family. Alana's comments assured her of that much.

Quinn raised her head to face her reflection. Her mouth firmed and her eyes hardened. The vibrations inside her, generated now by tension, subsided under the pressure of resolve. She didn't care what they wanted or who they were. They weren't going to get it, and there would be no collateral damage. Sam's face flashed into her mind, followed by her staff at the bar. Her clients.

Nick.

No, she wouldn't allow the leech or the Society or *anyone* to harm the people she cared about.

She tossed her stuff back into her bag and strode onto the concourse. Nick stopped midpace, his glower fading as she neared. Okay, so maybe Nick would do the not-allowing. That was his job. But she wouldn't play the helpless female. She was a goddess, for cripes sake.

They found a small table outside a coffee shop with no other customers and very sparse foot traffic. Nick allowed Quinn to sit a few feet away while he bought lattes at the counter. His movements smooth and easy, he pulled money out of his wallet and said something that made the barista laugh, but he never stopped surveying the area, shifting his weight to give him different views of the concourse and the sitting area.

Nick lifted his loose flannel shirt to tuck his wallet back in his pocket, and Quinn's mouth went dry. His ass was as spectacular as Sam's, in jeans loose enough to run in but tight enough not to snag on anything. Desire, sweet and pure and *normal*, eased through her. She licked her lips, savoring the burn, the pleasurable ache. The moon lust had ruled her for so long, she'd forgotten what it was like to want someone because he was hot, not because she had to.

Nick chose that moment to check on her. Quinn ducked her head, not wanting him to see, because the last time she'd shown him her feelings, it had been a disaster. She pulled the printout from her bag to examine and managed to refocus by the time Nick set the paperboard cups on the shiny laminate table. It was only about two feet square, so when he sat perpendicular to her, their legs touched. She didn't move away.

"Any idea who that was back there?" Nick asked.

Quinn sighed. "It had to be a goddess. I can't see how technology could have been responsible for scream tones like that. There was no one inside the suite."

"Could have been the leech."

"I suppose." She grimaced in doubt. "It doesn't jive. What was his goal?"

Nick nodded his agreement.

"I don't know who they represented." She relayed her thoughts from the bathroom. "Could it have been the Protectorate?"

"Again, why?" Nick spread his hands. "We haven't learned anything they'd want to cover up."

"I know."

Nick assessed her for a minute while she read some of the data, then shrugged. "Okay, so who can create scream tones?"

She sighed and flipped a page. "Unfortunately, it's not that easy. Our abilities aren't limited like that. We're not X-Men."

"What's that mean?"

She opened her mouth to explain, then saw his face and realized he wasn't asking for a definition. "It means I know half a dozen goddesses who could probably do it, and I'm sure there are many, many more."

He frowned. "Could you have done it? Like, in your sleep?"

"Nope. Not even at full moon."

He leaned his arms on the table. "So we need to look at this another way."

"Not who could, but who *would*. Even if they're working for someone else."

"Any ideas?" he asked again, and she wished she could be as coolly rational about it as he was. They were talking about people she was friendly with, if not true friends.

She flipped another page. The printout held names, contact information, ages, power sources, levels of ability, and cycles. There were only about a hundred in-power goddesses in the country and she knew most of them, at least in passing. But as she skimmed the information, questions raging through her head, she couldn't connect who might have the ability—power level, source, and cycle—with who might have a motive. Her tired brain couldn't keep anything together.

"No." She slammed the folder closed and cupped her coffee between her hands. "I can't think. We'll have to figure it out when we get home."

"Can I look?"

Irritated, she shoved the folder at him. He ignored her burst of attitude, which made her feel petty. If he'd had more sleep than she had over the last couple of days, maybe he could come up with something.

A few minutes later, though, he looked disgusted and handed her the folder.

"I can't make any sense of it. We'll have Sam dig into it. He's the analytical one. Maybe he can set up a program or something."

"Okay."

"Did you hear or see anything besides the noise and the book flying around?"

She closed her eyes to remember. She'd been dreaming, something vague and not restful. Then the glass shattering snapped her awake to the scream. Nick caught her. The book flew across the room, barely missing them. She'd looked for shadows or shapes that didn't belong, but there'd been no way to hear anything over the noise.

"Nothing," she said. "Do you think we got away too easily?"

"Sure felt like it."

That only made it more confusing, but she couldn't argue. "Someone strong enough to do multiple things, even as limited as that was—"

"That was limited?"

"A little noise, tossing a couple of objects around?" She paused when Nick shot her a look at her mocking tone. "Sorry, I forget you don't see any of us with full access to our sources."

"That's kind of the whole point of my job," he said. "If you can attack people, you don't need us."

"My point is, it takes a lot of effort to maintain the tone and still move things around. Someone that strong could have gotten into the suite without us knowing, instead of throwing out all those warnings."

"So why didn't they?"

"Good question." She drained her cooled coffee and tossed the cup into a nearby trash can. "Because their intent wasn't to harm?"

Nick didn't look like he bought that, but he let it go. "How many goddesses can sustain a number of things at once?"

"More than half."

"Still narrows it down a little. We'll look at the list when we get back."

A couple entered the sitting area, followed by a man in a suit talking on a cell phone. As early as it still was, the airport was filling up, and it looked like they'd have to wait until they got home to talk more. They went back to the shops and found one that carried Crocs. Quinn rolled her eyes but felt less conspicuous once she had them on and wasn't walking around in filthy socks anymore. Then they found a drugstore for supplies and Nick cleaned and re-bandaged her arm and, without her saying anything, got her a bottle of painkillers.

They made their way to their terminal, and then the gate. Quinn was so tired by the time they sat down, she could barely keep her eyes open, despite the coffee.

"Come here." Nick put his arm around her shoulder again and nudged her down onto his chest. "We've got a while yet before our flight."

"What about you?" she murmured.

"I'm an expert at sleeping sitting up."

She felt a soft pressure on the top of her head, breathed deeply the scent of warm man with a hint of leather, and relaxed. It should have been less comfortable than any other place she'd dozed over the last thirty-six hours, but she found that it topped the list.

Still, she couldn't seem to fall asleep. She nuzzled into his chest a little. The heartbeat beneath her ear was solid and steady, his breathing so deep and slow it barely moved her head. A little while later, his voice rumbled as he called to arrange pickup of the rental car back at the hotel, then to update Sam.

"We'll be landing around nine thirty, I think. Naw, the Charger's in the lot. That's not a problem. She's exhausted. I'm okay. Can't say I won't crash when we get in. Did you find anything? Yeah, I know. We've got some information, might give us a little bit of direction, but not much. She's being stonewalled. No idea. I think it bothers her a lot more than she's letting on. Hey, are you related to Quinn at all? Cousin, even? Not even distantly? Hey, chill, I'll tell you when we get there. Just trying to cover all the angles, dude. I will. See ya soon." He shifted under her to replace his phone in his pocket, then stroked his hand across the nape of her neck. Her headache began to fade.

The next thing she knew, he said her name, a gentle murmur, an urge to wake up, and her consciousness rose to answer it. But she didn't want to move. Her hand rested on his flat abdomen, her head in the hollow of his shoulder, with his palm on her waist. He surrounded her in a cocoon of warmth and musk. It might not be the only place she'd felt safe over the last few days, but it was definitely her favorite.

"C'mon, Quinn, they're boarding first class. The sooner we get on the plane, the sooner we can get home."

She smiled and opened her eyes. "That makes no sense."

"I know, but my arm's asleep." He unwrapped his arm from around her and stood while she stretched and yawned. She reached for her bag, but he'd already picked up both.

"Homestretch," he encouraged.

Quinn pushed to her feet with a groan. "Unless they're waiting for us at the other end."

His expression told her he'd thought the same thing. They joined the line and inched toward the gate, but now Quinn wished she'd planned ahead, preparing for the *what* instead of trying to figure out the *who*. Her little bit of rest was enough to get her brain working again. She snapped her phone open and hit the speed dial for Sam's cell. He answered right away.

"It's Quinn. I don't have much time, so please don't question or argue. Close the bar. Make the deposit and notify the staff they're on leave with pay until I call them. Pack me a bag like I'm going on a long trip, then grab the schedule for the month and all your contact information. We're going to have to cancel every appointment for the full moon." He made a noise like he was about to interrupt, but he held his silence. She could hear his pen scratching. "Pack for yourself, too, and please get my flash drive out of the safe." She tried to think of anything she'd missed. They reached the agent at the gate, who glared at her. "Go somewhere no one will expect. We'll call you when we land. I'm sorry. I've got to hang up." She disconnected and handed her pass to the agent with a weak smile. "Sorry."

The sour woman dismissed her. "Next, please."

They hurried down the Jetway and caught up to the line at the entrance to the plane.

"I planned to hit the road as soon as we got home, but this way is definitely better," Nick said.

"Thank god for Sam." She nodded at the attendant at the plane door, who smiled as brightly as the ticket taker had scowled.

"With luck," Nick continued once they were seated, "the Charger will be where we left it, and no one will have tampered with it."

Three hours later, they exited the warm terminal and stepped into the cool fall day. He stopped her as they approached the car, parked alone at the back of the short-term lot. The empty space made it impossible for anyone to hide or sneak up on them. It looked unharmed, but plenty could have been done to it without being visible.

"Hold this." Nick handed Quinn his duffel and circled the car, peering through the windows and examining the chassis. Then he lay down and wiggled underneath, making his way up the undercarriage. Quinn kept watch across the lot, listening to the scrape of Nick's boots on the asphalt, random *clink*s and *clunk*s, and his occasional curse. After eight and a half minutes he dragged himself out the other side and dusted off his hands.

"Looks fine. Let me pop the hood."

He took the keys from Quinn, unlocked the driver's door, and pulled the hood release. Though he inspected the engine and checked all the hoses, belts, and lines, she could tell he remained aware of their surroundings. She probably should have been concerned about what he might find, but instead, she appreciated the curve of his torso over the engine block, the flex of his thigh muscles when he bent or leaned. For a brief moment, she considered dragging him into the backseat. The slam of the hood killed the fantasy.

Nick motioned for her to get in the car. "This looks okay, too. Let's roll."

A few minutes later they were on the road, heading north on I-71 away from Columbus.

"Where do you want to go?" Quinn asked.

He shook his head. "All the safe houses I know of are on the grid. We need something none of the goddesses or protectors know about."

She hated that they had to cut themselves off from their main support system. That the system could even be their enemy. But since he didn't have a place for them to go, she did. "Okay. Go west on Thirty-three." She pulled out her cell and dialed Sam's number.

He answered on the second ring. "You're all right?"

"We're fine." The Camaro's engine hummed in the background. "You're out?"

"Yeah. I got everything we should need. Where are we going?"

"Benton Harbor."

"'Nuff said. See you in a few hours."

She turned off the phone to conserve the battery and slid down until her head rested on the back of the seat. "Take Thirty-three to Seventy-five north. Wake me when you need me to drive." She fell asleep smiling at Nick's snort.

• • •

Quinn woke when the car slowed. Less than four hours had passed, and Nick was pulling into a gas station off the highway. The windshield wipers flapped at top speed, sweeping waves of water off the window. The rain pounded on the roof, and Quinn wondered how she could have slept through it.

"We near Sturgis?" she asked, rubbing her eyes and pushing up in the seat, recognizing the wide, flat terrain as Northern Ohio. Her neck hurt, but she felt more rested than she had in two days. Nick looked weary but alert, and she wondered how he'd managed to keep going so long.

"Angola. Rain slowed us down some." He pulled under the pump overhang and the noise disappeared. "You hungry?"

"I'll go in." She looked toward the convenience store. "What do you want?"

He narrowed his eyes at the store entrance a few feet away, taking a moment to study the interior and sweep the area before nodding. "Whatever looks halfway decent. Large coffee." He leaned to dig his wallet from his back pocket.

Quinn waved him off. "I've got it." She eased herself out of the car and stretched, reaching high and arching her back as far as she could without falling over. Her arm twinged, but the pain was minor. She relaxed and tugged her shirt down over her jeans, then glanced back at Nick, who watched her as avidly as Sam had the other day. A flush raced over her body, tightening her nipples. She spun away and hurried toward the little store. She'd better stop stretching with them around.

The store was crowded with people taking a break from the intense rain. There was a line for the microwave, so Quinn selected a few sandwiches that looked halfway fresh from the cooler, added two bags of chips and a can of nuts to her basket, and went to stand in another line for coffee. She hoped it didn't run out before she got to it.

The man in front of her glanced back when she shifted her weight to look past him. After the first quick, casual glance, he took another, longer look, and his demeanor changed. She sighed inwardly. Working in a bar, a woman got a good education on the body language of flirtatious men. And sure enough, the words that came out of his mouth were, "Have I seen you here before?"

"Absolutely not." She tried to hide her amusement. She had to look atrocious.

They moved forward. "I'm sure I have. I wouldn't forget a face like yours." Of course, he wasn't looking at her face. She wished guys like him thought harder about this stuff. Standing here would be less tedious if he had a unique line.

"You're up," she said. He glanced down at himself, then frowned quizzically at her. She jerked her chin toward the coffee. "Your turn."

"Darn, our fun is over."

Quinn rolled her eyes and said nothing, standing back while he filled two cups. A woman by the front counter caught her eye. She glared at Quinn, who shrugged. It wasn't her fault this guy was an ass, and an idiot to boot if he had a girlfriend or wife nearby.

"All yours," he said, grinning wide. Quinn shook her head in disgust. He joined the woman at the counter, who laid into him. His voice rose in defense, and they were so engrossed in their argument as they went out the door that they almost knocked Nick over.

He stared after them, then narrowed his eyes at Quinn as she approached and handed him his large dark roast, black.

"You do that?"

"Hardly." She set the basket on the counter. "And both coffees, please," she told the cashier, who nodded and rang everything up. "All I did was stand there and try not to hurl." She paid the cashier and accepted the bag. "I can't help it if men are scum."

"You don't have to wear those sexy tops."

She barked a laugh and went out the door Nick held for her. "My one-hundred-percent-cotton Walmart special?" She plucked at the loose fabric. "The one that comes all the way up to my neck? Yeah, real sexy."

Nick opened the car door. Quinn slid in. He bent down and said, "Walmart knows how to do clothes that cling in all the right places." Then he winked and slammed the door, leaving her laughing.

A moment later they merged back onto the four-lane divided highway, sliding between a couple of Toyotas. The one behind them zipped into the outer lane to pass, causing an approaching semi to lay on the horn.

Quinn jerked around to look when the truck honked, but Nick never flinched. "Traffic's usually a lot lighter through here," she commented.

"The rain always fucks everybody up." He checked the side mirror and blind spot and pulled out around the car in front of them, which had reacted to the horn by slowing to forty miles an hour. The rain was still coming down so hard, Quinn could barely see the farmland on either side of the highway. She was glad Nick was driving.

She waited until they'd gone a few miles and traffic thinned out away from the exit. The rain had lightened a little, too, so she opened the bag and offered Nick a sandwich. "Ham and cheese, turkey, or PB and J."

"Ham. Thanks." He set it on his thigh. Quinn pulled out the PB and J for herself and flipped up the little tab on her coffee lid to drink. Nick stopped unwrapping his sandwich and looked around, sniffing. "What the hell is that smell?"

"What smell?" She picked up the sandwich and sniffed it. "Seems okay to me." She unwrapped half and handed it back to him. He smelled it.

"No, not that. Smells…sweet. Like an air freshener." He looked at her incredulously, then quickly back at the road. Taillights flashed ahead of them. "You didn't."

"Didn't what?" She lifted her coffee cup to her mouth again and realized what he'd smelled. "Oh, my coffee."

"What the hell? Did you get one of those powdered mix things?"

"No! I drained the dark roast for you. All that was left was decaf or French vanilla."

He made a gagging noise. "Well, drink it fast. That crap lingers."

"Yes, sir."

Nick tore into the sandwich, devouring the first half in three bites. "How long did you sleep?" he asked.

"Three hours, fifty-eight minutes." She opened both bags of chips and set one against Nick's hip. "Why? You need to nap?"

"Hell no. But you're not the most fun traveling companion." He leaned forward and squinted into the rain. "Let's play the alphabet game or something."

Quinn finished her sandwich and balled the wrapper. "I'm going to check in with Sam." She turned on her phone and waited for it to acquire a signal, then a little longer to see if she had any messages. There were two.

Sam had called two hours ago. "Quinn, call me as soon as you get this. It's important." He sounded upset.

The other message had been received right after Sam's. "Quinn, it's Alana. I heard about the…disturbance at your hotel last night. I wanted to make sure you're okay. Call me."

"Huh."

Nick didn't take his eyes off the now-crowded road ahead. "What?"

She told him about the messages. "How would she have heard about the disturbance? Or known it was our hotel?" They were rhetorical questions, so she dialed Sam.

"You didn't tell her where we were staying?" Nick asked.

"I don't think so. Hi, Sam, it's me. Sorry I took—"

He cut her off. "Why didn't you tell me you were attacked in Boston?"

Taken aback, she stuttered. "I—we—there wasn't time. And it wasn't really an *attack*."

"Put it on speaker," Nick urged.

She hated the way speakerphone made the phone mute whenever one side was talking, but she did as he'd asked.

"—inn, your hotel suite was destroyed. They called the bar. Katie put on call forwarding to her home phone in case some of the clients I canceled called back. She said they're charging you several thousand dollars for damage to the walls and furniture. So unless you and Nick were partying hard, you were attacked."

"Why else would we be on the run, Sam?" Nick interjected. "This can't be a surprise."

"I thought you learned something. I didn't know you were in immediate danger. Why didn't you go to the police?"

Quinn and Nick exchanged a look. "When we left the hotel, it was mostly noise," she said. "I thought they'd know we left and stop. What was damaged?"

"The sofa in the outer room and the bed."

"They were shooting blind," Nick murmured. "Probably assumed we'd be sleeping that way."

"And they didn't have enough power to strike both simultaneously," Quinn added, "because the bedroom was clear when we went in."

"Not enough power," Nick mused, "or inexperience using it?"

"You still should have gone to the authorities," Sam insisted. "Someone should know what's going on."

"And tell them what?" Nick asked. "There was a poltergeist with a crystal voice? They'd never buy it."

"They—"

"He's right, Sam. The authorities aren't comfortable with the whole goddess thing. The Society handles stuff like this internally whenever they can."

"Except they're not exactly on your side right now, are they?"

No one answered. He was right, and if there really had been damage in the hotel, it meant Quinn and Nick's assumption that the attacker hadn't wanted to harm them was wrong. She hoped her staff would be safe away from the bar.

"All right." Sam still sounded disgruntled. "I just wanted you to know what was going on. Where are you?"

"A couple of hours out, with this rain. Are you there?"

"Not yet. I think I'm a little ahead of you. I'll stop for supplies when I get to town. Any requests?"

"No."

"Yes!" Nick shouted. "Something hearty! None of your roots-and-berries crap. I want— Jesus!" He wrenched the wheel to swerve around a tire flying out of the rain straight at them.

Quinn screamed and lost her grip on the phone, her hands flying to brace on the dash and the door beside her, the tire's tread pattern burning itself into her brain before the Charger responded and skidded left. Horns blared and tires screeched as the cars in the left lane tried to avoid them and the ones behind responded to the tire. Metal crunched and Quinn twisted to look back. The tire had disappeared behind the sprawled vehicles, but a minivan was crumpled against the median. No one was in danger of rear-ending the Charger, and Quinn's heart resumed its normal rate.

"What the hell?" She turned back to face front, swallowing against the metallic tang in the back of her throat while Nick slowed even more, taillights still flashing ahead of them, though traffic hadn't stopped completely.

"Look." Nick pointed at the source of the tire, an overturned Camaro half on the shoulder, half blocking the right lane. They stared at the smashed passenger side door and front quarter panel, the steam rising from the undercarriage, as they rolled by.

"Oh my god."

"Is that—?" Nick started.

"Yes." Quinn's body had turned to ice, and she became intensely aware of the silent phone at her feet. "Pull over."

It was Sam's car.

CHAPTER FIVE

The true origin of our ancestry has been lost to time and secrecy. Very little is known about our beginnings, but it is believed we are descended from the lines of powerful humans who spawned the tales of the Greek, Roman, and Norse goddesses. Because our heritage is stuff of legend rather than true history, how we use our abilities is of utmost importance.

— The Society for Goddess Education and Defense *booklet,*
"From Isis to Freya"

Quinn shoved her door open before Nick finished swinging the car to the shoulder in front of the overturned vehicle. *Nonononono. Not Sam not Sam not Sam.* She leapt out, skidding on the loose gravel, shouting his name as she ran in slow motion. Nothing moved except a slowly spinning front wheel. The rear tire on the passenger side was gone. The smell of burned rubber stung her nostrils, hot despite the cold rain. The car listed toward the road, the roof over the driver's side mostly intact. *He always wears his seat belt. He's okay. He's got to be okay.* But raindrops splashed into her eyes and shadows blocked her view through the windshield. She couldn't convince herself.

Nick sped past her. "Sam!" He slid onto the ground like a batter to second base, looking into the car. "Sam! Sam, buddy, can you hear me?"

Quinn landed on her knees in the sharp gravel next to him, desperate to hear Sam's voice. But it didn't come. He hung upside down in the car, his seat belt locking him in place. His hands lay limp on the ceiling and his forehead bled. "Sam!" She reached in through the smashed side window to touch his face. He didn't respond. "God, Sammy. Please."

"Let me brace him." Nick grabbed Sam's shoulders. "See if you can undo his seat belt."

Panic fading, doused by action, Quinn flipped onto her back, squinting against the droplets splattering her face. Glass bit into her back as she dragged herself into the vehicle, trying not to brush against Sam in case he had a neck injury. They shouldn't move him out of there until they knew what kind of damage had been done.

"Sam." She touched his face again. His skin was reassuringly warm, his breath even against her hand. The flashes of panic stilled. "Sam. Can you hear me? Come on, sweetie." She fought not to tap him harder or shake him to try to wake him up. The cut on his head wasn't deep, but it had already purpled, and head injuries were so dangerous. She tried not to think about that, to focus instead on what to do. Sam moaned and moved his arms but didn't open his eyes.

"Quinn, we've got to get him out." There were sirens in the distance, but they didn't sound like they were getting closer. "We're sitting ducks out here."

Which meant Nick thought someone had deliberately caused this accident. Maybe he was only being the protector again, but she trusted his judgment. With gentle hands, she palpated Sam's neck a little. It felt normal, but she was no medical professional. If she had power, she could identify an injury—but she didn't. Helpless, and aware that the longer she waited, the more at risk they were, she pulled herself deeper into the car and reached for the seat belt.

"Brace him good, Nick." She swallowed against queasiness. If they hurt him worse…she felt Nick shift, and his arms moved past her legs to wrap around Sam's shoulders.

"When you release the latch," Nick said, "we'll maneuver him in your way. You can support his head and shoulders while I get his legs out."

Quinn looked up at where Sam's long legs were wedged under the dash. It bowed inward in the center, away from the partially crushed passenger side.

"It looks like they might be trapped," she warned.

"I know. I don't think they're busted, though, just maybe wedged."

"Should you get them out first? I don't want to break his leg when he falls off the seat."

"We've got to reverse his circulation. If he has a head injury…"

Pooling blood in his brain could cause further damage.

"Okay, here goes." She reached up, held her breath, and pressed hard on the seat belt latch.

She'd expected it to be jammed from Sam's weight on it, so when it gave way she wasn't ready. Nick didn't have a good angle or the strength to hold all Sam's weight against gravity. Quinn barely kept Sam's head straight as he came down on top of her, shoving the air out of her lungs. She wheezed and curled her fists into his jacket to drag him up her torso, trying to straighten his body. Nick cursed and pushed himself into the foot well. One of Sam's legs came free, then the other, his boot heels thudding onto Quinn's knees.

She struggled for air but kept Sam's head cradled on her chest while Nick backed out of the car, coughing. Her lungs recovered and filled, and she tightened her hold on Sam, praying she wasn't doing it wrong. Nick straightened Sam's legs along hers, then gripped her ankles and dragged them out of the car. When they were clear, he eased Sam off Quinn and onto the gravel shoulder.

The rain hitting his face roused him, and he jerked his arm up to block it. Quinn struggled upright, weak with relief, her back and thighs throbbing from being dragged across the hard metal edge of the roof. Cuts on her back and shoulders stung, but she ignored them and bent over Sam, trying to block the rain.

"Sam." She touched his face, her fingers trembling. "Are you okay?"

Nick pulled off his coat and draped it over her to shelter them both.

Sam sighed and blinked blearily up at Quinn. "What the fuck?"

"Oh, thank god." The pain in her chest receded, leaving her feeling raw but whole. She fisted her hands in his jacket and bent her face to his solid chest. His hand cupped the back of her head, and she stifled a sob. Leave it to Sam to try to comfort her when he'd been smashed up.

She pulled back. "I don't know." Her hands shook as she released him.

"No, seriously." He tried to roll to his side, but Quinn pressed him back down. "What the fuck happened?"

"Your car flipped. What do you remember?"

Sam frowned. The movement pulled at his cut, releasing a tiny trickle of blood, and turned his expression into a wince. He touched his forehead. "Something rolled me. Is the car…?"

"Yeah. Can you move your legs?"

His boots scraped on the gravel. "Yeah. I think I'm okay. Hurts. But not bad." He made to sit up and Quinn backed off to give him room. She watched his movements carefully. He wouldn't tell the truth about his injuries. Only once she got to her feet so she could hold the jacket over his head did she become aware of all the people standing around the Camaro. A state police car sat several yards behind them, lights flashing. The trooper stood next to his vehicle, talking urgently on the radio he'd pulled through the window, probably reporting in before approaching the wreck. She could see the top of an ambulance winding through the gridlock. They weren't getting out of here anytime soon.

A man in the crowd made eye contact with her. Her heart skipped, but he turned to talk to the woman beside him, his body language unthreatening. Maybe Quinn was paranoid to think someone could have caused the accident on purpose, but given everything that had happened lately, it was safer to assume so.

"Nick." Sam's voice was weak.

Nick crouched next to him. Quinn couldn't hear what he said, but Nick nodded, then crawled inside the car. He backed out with a laptop case and a huge canvas duffel that almost didn't fit through the bent window. He carried them toward the Charger as the trooper approached.

"How's he doin', ma'am?" The trooper touched the brim of his hat and settled on his heels at Sam's feet.

"I'm not sure. He seems okay."

"I'm fine." Sam pulled his feet under him to rise but wobbled on the hand braced on the ground and sat back down. He pressed his fingers to his eyes.

"Lightheaded?" Quinn asked. He nodded. She put her hand on the back of his neck, wishing she could *do* something.

"You know him?" The trooper stood.

"Yes, sir, we were a short ways back. We were on the phone with him, as a matter of fact, when it happened."

The officer looked disapproving. "You hear it?"

"No. It was on speaker, and we were talking on our side."

"You see anything?"

Nick joined them on the shoulder. "The wheel flying by, that's it. Doesn't look like any other car was involved."

"It wasn't." Sam braced himself again. Nick bent to help him up and steadied him when he swayed. Quinn slipped under his other arm to take some of his weight. His T-shirt was soaked through, and fine tremors shook his torso.

"What happened, son?"

Sam squeezed his eyes shut and blinked them back open, as if his vision were fuzzy. "I'm not sure, Officer."

The ambulance had made its way to the crowded shoulder, and paramedics hustled over. Sam threw Quinn a pleading look as they led him to the ambulance, but she didn't know what she could do. He was hurt, and she had no power to heal him. They would be safe here with paramedics and state police around.

The trooper asked Nick and Quinn a few more questions. When he seemed to have all the answers they could give, he moved on to canvass the onlookers for eyewitnesses. As soon as Sam was taken to the ambulance, though, the people who'd stopped to help or watch thinned out. Traffic streamed by at a faster rate now, and in minutes a tow truck appeared.

"Crap," Nick muttered. "Sam's gonna freak about them towing his car."

"I'll take care of it." Quinn walked over as the driver climbed down from the tow truck's cab and eyed the flipped Camaro.

"That's my friend's car," she told him. "Where are you going to take it?"

"Garage in Angola." He handed her a business card. "Where's the driver?"

"He's in the ambulance. I can fill out any paperwork you have."

"Here." He harrumphed and handed her a clipboard and pen. "I gotta talk to the cop." He lumbered off. Quinn quickly filled out the form and signed it, then left it on the seat and hurried back to Nick, who leaned against the Charger, waiting for her.

He looked grim and pocketed the business card she handed him. "Every record created from this thing is going to flash a trail."

"I know. Police report, tow, ambulance, hospital." She looked back to where Sam sat on the ambulance bumper. "At least it happened here, not right outside of Benton Harbor." They were far enough away that whoever had done this—still assuming it had been deliberate—wouldn't be able to guess their destination.

"Whatever. We'll deal." Nick gave the back of her neck a little squeeze and left his hand there as they watched the paramedics take care of Sam. The warmth could only counter the rain where he made contact, but it was enough to ease Quinn's worry. One thing at a time, and right now, the one thing had to be Sam.

"Could this have been deliberate?" she asked Nick. "How could someone flip a car without being on the road?"

"We have to find out what Sam saw." Nick pointed up the slight rise at the side of the road. "There's a vantage point that could have given enough visual notice, and you know how it could be done."

"A goddess again," Quinn agreed miserably. "Just like the hotel room."

"Let's not jump to conclusions until we talk to Sam. It might have been an accident."

But what if it hadn't been? She eyed the crowd with fresh eyes, worried now about an innocent being hurt if the attacker tried again. They had to wrap this up as soon as possible.

When the paramedics seemed to be finishing up with Sam, Nick and Quinn walked over. The woman smoothing a butterfly bandage over his cut looked up at them curiously.

"We're with him," Nick said. "How's he doing?"

The other paramedic climbed into the back to stow equipment.

The woman said, "He lost consciousness, so we're taking him to Cameron Memorial in Angola for additional testing."

"I don't—"

Quinn cut Sam off. Nothing mattered but making sure he was okay. "We'll be right behind you. Don't worry."

"I'm going to check with the trooper to make sure he doesn't need anything else," Nick said. Quinn nodded and watched the EMTs helping Sam onto a stretcher. As soon as they'd closed the door, she headed to the Charger.

Nick climbed in a few seconds later and frowned at her. "You're hurt again."

"What?" She'd been concentrating so hard on Sam, she hadn't even realized she was avoiding pressure on her back. Now the stings became throbs, the scrapes and bruises from being pulled out of the car clamoring for attention. "It's minor," she assured him. "We'll take care of it after we make sure Sam's okay."

• • •

The ambulance was still in the bay when Nick pulled into the hospital parking lot. They hurried into the surprisingly quiet ER, where Sam was just being processed. Quinn went through the triage, registration, and preliminary exam with him. At each step the staff response was more positive about his condition, easing her concerns.

Nick went back to the car and brought in dry clothes for them to change into, and Quinn used paper towels to absorb some of the water from her hair and Sam's.

"How you feeling, dude?" Nick asked Sam, who shrugged.

"Not bad. Tired of waiting. I want to sleep, but they think I've got a concussion so that's not a good idea for a while. They're going to do a CT of my head."

"Everything else okay? No broken bones?"

Sam shook his head very slightly. "No, just bruises."

"Okay. I'll wait in the lobby," Nick told Quinn. "I want to watch the news reports, see if it comes up."

"All right."

When the door soughed closed, Sam managed a small smile.

"Who gave him a niceness transplant?"

"Stop that," Quinn scolded. "He appreciates you."

Sam made a noncommittal grunt and stretched his neck gingerly. "Whatever." He winced while he stretched his back, then slouched again. "I'm glad you're back. I missed you."

Quinn rubbed her hand across his shoulders. "I missed you, too."

He met her gaze. "*Me* me, or assistant me?"

She smirked. "Both. So what happened? You do remember, don't you? Even if you didn't want to tell the cop?"

"Of course I do. The more I think about it, the more mundane it seems, but there's still a possibility…" He glanced at her, then away. "I don't know. My lane was clear for about six car lengths. I hit a patch of…something. Water, oil? It wasn't cold enough for ice, and the road is well drained, but there might have been a dip in the pavement or something. I spun away and rolled over."

Quinn let out a long breath. "It sounds mundane to me."

He compressed his mouth and shook his head. "There was a flash, or a splash, or—something that moved in that patch. After that it happened too fast—except the roll went so slowly. I don't know. My perception was off. How could someone have done it on purpose?"

Oh, she knew how. "With a great view of the road and enough time to see you coming and prepare? A goddess could do it." She swallowed her anger. "The hill next to where you crashed was high enough. But I'd think the rain would erase any visual advantage."

"And the timing had to be perfect. My tire had to hit that spot at the exact moment they did…whatever they did." He waved his hands. "And assuming they'd go to that much trouble and be that good or that lucky for it to work—"

"Why didn't they follow through?" she finished.

The door opened and a technician wheeled in a gurney. "Time

to go for a ride! Swing over here." He lowered the gurney and helped Sam transition from the exam table to the wheeled bed. The look on Sam's face told Quinn how much he hated this.

The tech smiled at Quinn. "I'll have him back in a jiffy."

It wasn't exactly a jiffy, but eventually they returned, and the physician's assistant came in and told them Sam's scan was okay. He offered a few sheets of information with treatment instructions and symptoms to watch for, as well as a prescription for painkillers, which Sam crumpled up as soon as the PA left.

"I'm muzzy enough without adding these. I'll be okay."

His face wasn't exactly etched in pain, but tightness around his mouth and eyes still telegraphed it. Quinn retrieved the script and put it in her pocket. "You might change your mind," she said in response to his glower. "Don't do that. You'll make it worse."

They met Nick in the waiting area. Quinn raised an eyebrow at the TV. Nick shook his head.

"I think we're good."

"Yeah, we are. My car is totaled," Sam griped.

"We'll get it back." Nick clapped him on the shoulder. "You okay?"

"Fine. Stop being so solicitous." He shrugged off Nick's hand.

Nick grinned at Quinn, relief obvious in his eyes. "I would, if I knew what 'solicitous' meant. Come on, the rain's let up. We should make good time now."

They did, though it was far too late once they reached Quinn's cabin to stop for provisions. Nick went through a fast food drive-thru instead and offered to go to the store early in the morning.

"Tonight, let's crash and regroup," he said as he parked the car in front of the traditional-style cabin, hunkered in a clearing carved out of overgrown woods. "Tomorrow, we'll figure everything out."

"Sounds fine to me." Sam trudged up the steps to the cabin, then stopped and turned. "Maybe someone should search the place, make sure no one's been here."

"No one has," Quinn said. She pointed to the top step, one above Sam's. "Look at your feet."

The car's headlights showed light gray dust coating his boots, and dark footprints marred the steps he'd climbed. The top step was unmarked.

"They could have gotten in another way, and how did you keep that from washing off?" Nick asked.

"Trade secret," Quinn replied. "I'll do a perimeter check, but I'm sure no one's been here. I'd feel it." As much as the bar was home, this cabin was her heart. It had been in her mother's family for generations, and the two of them had come up here for what her mother called their goddess weekends. They talked about things every mother and daughter needed to discuss, but here was also where Quinn learned how to be a goddess, even long before she came into her power. It was also the last place she'd been with her mother after her father died, before her mother caught the infection that killed her.

She only needed normal instinct to know it was fine, but Nick didn't operate that way. So she walked around the building with him on her heels, his flashlight flicking at the ground, then the windows, then back to the woods surrounding them. The rear porch, which overlooked the Paw Paw River, held the same layer of untouched gray dust, as did all the windowsills. No one could have gotten to the back doors or windows without evidence. Even goddesses couldn't fly.

"Could they booby-trap it?" Nick asked. "You know, do the kind of stuff they did in the hotel?"

"I don't know, Nick," Quinn said wearily. "All I can tell you is that I don't sense any use of power."

"Would you? Without having power yourself?"

"Yes. Like you'd sense a presence in the room even if you

couldn't see or hear them." She was exaggerating her sixth sense, but they could stand here all night playing the what-if game. They were exhausted and hurt and needed rest.

"All right." Nick led her to the front and unlocked the door, letting the other two go in while he unloaded the car.

The cabin was small and square, with a central living/dining/ kitchen area and two bedrooms, one on either side, with one bathroom next to the smaller bedroom. It had plank walls and large windows framed in plaid curtains that matched the rugged, squishy sofa and side chairs. Shelves held hundreds of books, old videocassettes and DVDs for the small TV/video combo unit, and bins full of old board and card games from Quinn's childhood. It smelled slightly stale from being closed up and a bit musty from the rain, with a hint of gardenia that Quinn knew had to be her imagination after all this time.

"You can have the first shower," she told Sam. She was desperate for one, so Sam had to be twice as much. She got a stack of big, fluffy towels out of the linen closet and handed them to him. "There should be shampoo and soap and everything in the shower stall."

"Thanks, Quinn." He disappeared into the little room, and she gathered sheets to make the beds. Nick joined her in the main bedroom a few minutes later.

"This is a nice place." He shook out the top sheet for the double bed, then bent to tuck it in on his side. "How come I've never seen it?"

"It was my mother's." She tossed him a pillowcase and bunched up another to put on the second pillow. "We used to come up here together. You and Sam are the first men to be here in decades. Since my parents first got married, I guess."

"I'm honored." He dropped the cased pillow against the headboard. "Sleeping arrangements? I notice there are only two bedrooms."

"You and Sam can share."

Nick stared in horror at the bed. "No way! I'm not—"

"In the other room, Nick." She laughed. "There are twin beds in there."

He groaned. "Twins? Come on. My feet will hang off. Geez, half Sam's body will hang off, and he was just flipped on his head."

"I'm sorry—that's all I have. Unless you want to share with Sam in here." Those weren't the only alternatives. They could let Sam have this slightly bigger bed, but all of Quinn's defenses were down, and sharing a room with Nick would be too dangerous. And sharing a room with Sam, after she'd pushed him away, would be cruel.

She smoothed the comforter over the sheets and left the room. Nick followed. "I already did the beds in there. Towels are in the bathroom. You can go after Sam." Again she felt a pang of longing, but hospitality won out. Not to mention, if she went last, she could stay in as long as she wanted to.

A few minutes later, as she washed dusty dishes in the kitchen area—she had to keep moving or she'd never start again—Sam limped out of the bathroom clad in only a towel he clutched closed in one fist. Bruises had blossomed on his right ribcage and left shoulder, probably from the seat belt. Another showed above the edge of the towel on his right hip.

Quinn must have made a noise because both men turned toward her. Sam looked down at himself and rubbed a hand across his chest.

"It's not as bad as it looks." His head came back up, and his eyes met hers, glinting with humor and memory.

Nick rolled his eyes and shoved to his feet. "For god's sake. Get dressed, Sam." He slammed into the bathroom without looking at Quinn.

Sam's mouth quirked smugly. She didn't know how he mustered the energy to give Nick a hard time, but gratitude soothed the shredded areas of her heart. He'd accepted the change in their relationship, and was even trying to make Nick jealous.

"I'm so sorry," she murmured.

"There's nothing to be sorry for." He sank onto the couch. "This wasn't your fault."

"If it was deliberate, it was. No one would be after you unless they were after me." She laughed bitterly. "If it *wasn't* deliberate, it was still my fault. I was talking to you on the phone. I should never have done that in this kind of weather."

"You're not responsible for my bad judgment." He pressed his thumb against his temple, his face contorting.

"Here." Quinn set down a freshly dried plate and filled a glass with water. "I think the first-aid kit we bought has some over-the-counter stuff."

"When did you buy a first-aid kit?" He scanned her, but the sweatshirt she wore hid her cut arm and the injuries on her back.

"In Boston. Lucky we did, huh?" She handed him the glass, then searched the kit on the picnic-style dining table. There was a packet of ibuprofen right on top. She tore it open and tapped the pills into his hand. "They should help without making you muzzy. But you should go to sleep anyway. It's late."

He caught her hand. "Thanks. You sleeping with me to wake me every hour, make sure I'm not in a coma?" His smile now was mischievous.

"Not this time, big guy." She ran her free hand gently over his unruly hair. "Nick will watch over you."

"That'll be fun." He pulled himself to his feet but didn't release her. "Make sure he doesn't have an air horn before you go to bed, okay?"

She smiled. "Okay." She squeezed his hand. "Thanks for

everything, Sam."

After he'd gone into the smaller bedroom and closed the door, she finished cleaning dishes and wiped down all the cabinet shelves. There were a few canned goods in one corner, but nothing that appealed. If Nick was hungry, he could heat something while she was in the bathtub.

She was putting away the last pots and pans when the bathroom door opened. Steam billowed out ahead of Nick, a navy blue towel around his waist and a pale blue towel turban-style around his head. Quinn laughed with a surge of affection. He was competing with Sam—and doing very well, with his powerful arms and shoulders, solid chest, and flat abdomen—but cutting the threat of such a competition by being goofy.

"It's all yours," he said, giving her the complicated version of his smile. It resembled the one he flashed at women in the bar, flirtatious and inviting, but it also had an element of the goof wearing the turban. His eyes, though, gave her the undercurrents. He was worried, conflicted, needy. All things he didn't want her to see, things he tried to mask with the lip part of the smile. "I hope we left you some hot water," he added.

"It's a big tank." She draped the wet dishtowel over the edge of the sink and walked to Sam's giant duffel, which he'd left between the doors to the two bedrooms. She found her own soft cotton pajamas on top and pulled those out, including a pair of comfortable underwear she didn't let Nick see. Under the clothes Sam had packed for her—a small quantity but everything she would need up here—were myriad guns and electronics, all set into two layers of foam that filled the bag and were the reason Nick had had trouble getting it out of the car.

Nick peered over her shoulder and whistled. "No wonder he wanted me to get that bag. Looks like the trunk of the Charger."

"Not quite." She'd been in that trunk. It rivaled an armory. "But yeah, it wouldn't have been so good for him to get caught with this stuff. He has permits for all of it, but still. Questions."

"What does an admin assistant have all that weaponry for?"

Quinn zipped the bag and straightened. "Same reason you do."

Nick frowned. "What's been happening that you haven't told me about?"

She sighed. "Nothing, Nick. Sam plans ahead and considers every possibility. Just like you," she added.

He nodded, eyeing the bag again. "I didn't know he took it that seriously."

"Took what seriously?" Quinn folded her arms and stared at him. Way back when she first started recharging with Sam, Nick had taken her assistant aside for a not-so-furtive conversation. Neither one would ever tell her what they discussed, but it didn't take a mind reader to figure out. Nick had decided there was something between them and had tasked Sam with Quinn's protection when he wasn't there.

But instead of 'fessing up, he ignored the question and cupped the back of her head with his palm. "Go get cleaned up. When you come out I'll take care of your cuts."

She didn't argue. She craved that bath now almost as much as she craved sex from moon lust. She filled the deep claw-footed tub in the little bathroom while she brushed her teeth, then eased herself into the steaming water, hissing as it touched the dozens of scratches from her hips to her neck. So much for safety glass.

She soaked until she started to fall asleep, then washed her hair, ducking under the water to rinse it. When she sat up, she noticed tendrils of red in the water. Some of her cuts must have opened after the water soaked away the initial clots. She finished washing and chose a red towel from the pile on the shelf over the toilet. After drying her back carefully, she pulled on the underwear and pajama bottoms, then tucked the top against the front of her and opened the door.

Nick, wearing cotton drawstring pants and a thin white T-shirt, sat at the table. He'd laid out gauze, cotton balls, ointment, bandages, a bowl of water, and a small towel. He straddled one picnic bench and motioned for Quinn to sit in front of him.

"You look flat out. Let me take care of you so you can get some sleep."

"You, too." He was heavy-lidded, which made Quinn think about the double bed in her room.

"Arm first." He held out a hand to cradle her wrist and examine the slice before stroking on antibiotic ointment and taping a wide bandage across it.

She swiveled on the bench to put her back to him and leaned against the table. "How's it look?"

His fingertips stroked from the nape of her neck, across her back, and down her spine to her hips. He nudged her pants lower and touched a spot at the base of her spine.

"Not too bad. A couple are bleeding, but none seem deep." His touch was gentle as he spread ointment on the little cuts and scratches, then paid more attention to the worse ones. Quinn sat still, her eyes closed, absorbing the tingles his fingers left behind. Her muscles became languid, soothed more by his touch than the warm water in her bath.

Sounds in the small room seemed amplified. Soft taps as he set things on the table. The rasp of medical tape being pulled off the roll. His bare feet sliding across the wood floor. His breathing.

He smoothed the last bandage on her hip. Then his hand rested on the side of her neck. Stroked down to where it met her shoulder. His thumb swept across her skin. She felt his mouth on the nape of her neck, hot and gentle. She held her breath, not wanting to break the spell. Nick had never allowed himself to touch her like that before.

Then there was only coldness where he'd been.

"All set," he said, his voice coming from several feet behind her. "Need some help with your shirt?"

"No." She sounded hoarse and fought not to clear her throat. "I've got it." She carefully pulled the long-sleeved cotton top over her head and down to her waist, then stood and turned to face him.

He looked normal. Until she examined his face, and a flicker of muscle in his jaw indicated how difficult it was for him to keep his expression clear. His hands shook a little as he folded a towel.

"Thank you."

He smiled. "You're welcome." He jerked his head toward her door. "Go get some sleep."

"You, too."

"I will."

Quinn hesitated, but she didn't know what else she could say. She went into the bedroom, closed the door, and climbed into the soft bed with a moan of gratitude.

And fell asleep wishing she wasn't alone.

Chapter Six

While you are exploring your abilities and your role in goddess and global society, please consider serving the community in a voluntary capacity. Board and committee service is an enriching experience for both yourself and those with whom you serve. The more you give, the more you receive in return.

—The Society for Goddess Education and Defense,
Election Notice

Quinn awoke to the scent of nirvana—bacon and coffee. She stretched, lying in bed for a few minutes, imagining the scene outside her door. Sam would be at the stove, flipping pancakes and draining bacon. Nick would be at the table, drinking coffee and reading the paper. She bet they argued about what to do next. The problem was that they didn't know who the enemy was or where to find him.

Her contentment erased, she sighed and climbed out of bed into the chilly air. She dressed in jeans and a cable-knit sweater over a T-shirt, then emerged into the main room.

And stopped dead at the scene before her.

Nick stood at the stove, the sleeves of his dark green Henley pushed up, a plaid apron tied over his jeans. He held a spatula in one hand and a frying pan full of pancakes in the other. Sam, about four inches taller, turned bacon next to him, while coffee bubbled in the old percolator on a back burner. He wore a blue long-sleeved T-shirt, and his apron was plain white with a ruffle around the bottom. The girlie-ness of the scene only served to make them both look more masculine.

Quinn could have stood there watching them all day.

"Mornin', sleepyhead." Nick smiled over his shoulder, the sun glinting off his dark blond hair and turning his green eyes pale. "Have a seat."

Sam finished transferring the bacon to a paper towel-covered plate and set it on the table. He glanced up and frowned. "What's the matter?"

"Nothing." Quinn smiled and moved to the table. "Just admiring the view."

Nick snorted and turned back to the stove, and Sam shook his head at her.

"How are you feeling?" She sat and inhaled deeply. Her stomach growled.

Sam shrugged and nudged the bacon with the tongs. "Sore. Stiff. But mostly okay. How about you?"

"I'm fine. I can't even feel the cuts." Surprisingly true. She didn't want to test it by leaning against anything, but regular movement didn't hurt much.

"That's my fine doctorin'." Nick slapped pancakes onto the platter on the table. "Soup's up."

"Hey, Quinn." Sam opened the back door, bent to reach something on the porch, and came back in holding a large silver dish. "What's this?"

"Oh." She blushed. "Sometimes people release dogs and cats that they don't want anymore into the woods. When I'm up here, I try to leave food out. I kind of forgot."

"Is there any food left? I saw a cat slinking around this

morning."

"In the bin behind the door."

Nick crossed to the door. "I'll get it. If you bend over too many times, you might pass out."

Sam shoved him but came inside and sat down with Quinn at the table. Nick joined them a minute later, and they ate without discussion except for Quinn's compliments on the food. When they were done, she cleaned up while Sam retrieved his laptop.

Nick, pacing, laid out the information they had so far. "The leech has hit two goddesses, maybe three. Someone says I've gone rogue—which hasn't hit the Protectorate, by the way, since I've talked to a couple of people and they haven't acted any differently." He stopped next to his bag on the couch and dug around in it. "In the meantime, the Society is acting like Quinn is the one who's rogue." He pulled out a baseball and circled the table, now rolling the ball from hand to hand. "Alana alluded to a family tie, and Jennifer's e-mail didn't appear on the Society loop. Neither has anything else since the leech hit."

"As if the Society is trying to contain it," Sam said. He typed something on the computer. "They work hard to keep public perception positive and not overblown. If people found out goddesses can bestow power..." He shook his head at the implications.

"So it could have been the Society at the hotel and on the highway," Quinn offered from the sink. She rinsed the silverware in her hand and dumped it in the drainer. "If they think our efforts to find the leech are going to endanger everyone."

Sam scowled. "You mean like trying to deter us but not kill us."

"Right. I mean, we don't know what the security team knows and is already doing. Because they won't tell us." She threw a spatula into the drainer. "Or it could be the Protectorate," she suggested, watching Nick's expression darken. "They don't have the manpower to protect every goddess, do they?"

He shook his head. "But they're not going to violate everything they were created for just to cover their asses."

Neither would the Society, but instead of bickering, Quinn focused on scrubbing scorched butter out of the pancake pan. "None of that factors in the family-tie thing, anyway."

"So maybe..."

Quinn whirled on Sam when he trailed off. "Go ahead, say it. That's where this is going. I can't hide from it forever."

He sighed and closed the laptop. "Maybe the goddess who created the leech is related to you."

Quinn squeezed the sponge in her fist, heedless of the water dripping to the floor. "Yeah. That seems most logical, right? Good thing I never tried to become part of the family."

Sam moved away from the personal. "Why doesn't it happen more? Goddesses giving other people power."

Nick shrugged. "It's hard, and damages her. It would upset the balance, both in the goddess and between her and the source of her power. And the result wouldn't be worth it. No recipient would be able to hold on to the ability for very long."

"Unless he started leeching," Sam said.

"Wouldn't that be almost inevitable?" Quinn asked. "I don't know what would happen to him if he didn't acquire more power, but it seems like it would be addictive."

"So why would one of you do this?" Nick threw the ball against the wall between the bathroom and bedroom doors and caught it.

Quinn didn't bother to scold him. She did *not* want to put herself in the head of someone related to her who would do something so awful. She pulled the drain on the sink and ran some water in the bacon pan to soak, keeping her head down so she wouldn't see the silent communication Nick and Sam had to be exchanging.

Sam cleared his throat. "Let's move on to Nick being rogue. You think of any connection between you and this Jennifer Hollinger?" he asked Nick.

Quinn hung up the hand towel and sat on the picnic bench, this time glaring at Nick when he raised his arm to throw the ball again. He scowled but gripped it in one hand.

"None," he said. "I never heard the name before Quinn showed me her e-mail. I've never even been in Mississippi." Quinn raised an eyebrow at him, and he lifted his arms in a shrug. "Well, I haven't stopped. I've driven through."

"Let's see if we can find a picture of her." Sam slid his wireless broadband card into the laptop. "Can we get a signal out here?"

"It's not exactly wilderness. Should be a strong signal." While they waited for the computer to connect, she added, "My property backs up on Sarett Nature Center. They own hundreds of acres, and there's a good buffer of flood plain between us and the main educational area. But a few miles the other way is normal civilization."

Sam clicked and typed for a minute, then turned the laptop to face Nick. "She look familiar?"

He leaned over. "Not a bit."

Quinn moved closer. "You sure it's the right Jennifer Hollinger?"

"You tell me." Sam pointed at the caption under the photo. "'Jennifer Hollinger of Vicksburg, MS, is a hero after saving four people from drowning.' Some idiot drove through what he thought was a puddle and was really a flooded creek. She diverted the water so they could get out of the car before it filled."

"That's her. She looks different, but I think she dyed her hair. I've only seen her a couple of times, though." She pulled her cell phone from her jacket pocket and turned it on. "I'm going to see if Alana found out anything."

The guys talked quietly at the table while she called Alana. Her tone was guarded, but at least she hadn't sent her to voice mail.

"You didn't call me back," Alana accused.

"I totally forgot. I'm sorry. Sam was in an accident."

"Oh! Is he okay?"

"Yes, we all are. Thank you for calling to check. The thing at the hotel must have happened after we left." After Alana made appropriate commiserating sounds, Quinn asked about Jennifer.

"She wasn't at home. They're still looking," Alana admitted.

That was not a good answer. Quinn had the dreadful sense that it was too late. "What about the leech?"

"Nothing I can report." Alana's tone had grown progressively colder.

"How are Tanda and Chloe?"

"How do you think they are?" she snapped. "I have work to do." She hung up.

Quinn sighed. The guys stopped talking.

"Nothing." Except ever-worsening relations with the Society. She kept her head bent as she tried Tanda's number. It still went to voice mail without ringing. This time, she left a lame message asking how she was and tried Chloe, whose phone rang half a dozen times and disconnected. Not even voice mail.

She'd never been in a situation like this. She'd been a part of things in some capacity—from committee member to board member—going all the way back to high school, before she got her power. More than shut out, she felt discarded. It was almost worse than being left by her birth parents, because this time she'd belonged before they rejected her.

She shoved the phone back into her pocket and tuned in to Sam asking Nick how else they could investigate the rogue accusation.

"We're at a dead end," Nick insisted. "Until we can get

something from Jennifer, there's nada."

"All right. Moving back to you." Sam turned to Quinn. "Family ties."

She shifted to her right as Nick joined them at the table. He sat on her left, his right leg bouncing so fast it shook the floorboards. She touched his knee, and he stopped.

"It has to be my birth family." She straightened her spine and her heart. Enough avoidance and hand-wringing. Those people weren't hers, both by their choice and her own. If one of them was stupid or evil or deluded or whatever she'd have to be to create a leech, so what? It just meant Quinn—with Sam's brain and Nick's badass-ness—had more reason than anyone to track them down and put an end to this, before they got to any other goddess.

"I don't know anything about them, besides the little they left for me when I was eight."

"So Alana could have been referring to your mother," Sam said.

"Or aunts, cousins, siblings. I have no idea."

"Okay then." He flexed his fingers, his expression intent. "Let's find out who's out there."

He looked at Quinn expectantly, but she had nothing to offer. No names, not even physical descriptions because her memories were too vague. She didn't know what her mother had done with her original adoption paperwork. She hadn't found anything naming her birth parents when she went through her mother's things after the funeral. The realization set her adrift, and the loneliness that permeated her twelve years ago threatened to swamp her again.

Nick's hand rested on her knee, tethering her, reminding her that she wasn't alone and never had been. She rested her hand on his for a second before he withdrew it.

"Nick can get you started," she told Sam. "He apparently

researched me before we even met."

Nick shifted and grimaced. "I told you, it was a training assignment."

"But you did it, right?"

"Yeah."

"And did you compare all your other training assignments to your family tree?"

His cheekbones went dusky red. "Uh, no."

"I rest my case."

"What case is that, exactly?" His eyes sparkled at her, as much gold as green now. Quinn smiled at him.

Sam snickered. "Give me what you've got." He tossed a pad and pen across the table. Nick scribbled a few things down and tossed it back, along with a look of warning that Sam ignored.

"It was a long time ago," Nick said. "Most of what I know is outdated."

"It's a start." Sam squinted at the paper. "Is this a Z?"

"Is your vision fuzzy again?" Quinn asked, worried.

But Sam scowled at Nick. "No. His handwriting sucks."

"You've gone soft," Nick shot back at him. "Too much word processing. Have you reached Tanda or Chloe?" he asked Quinn, who shook her head. "I think we should go see Tanda. Talk to her in person, find out what happened, what she knows."

"I'd like to check on her," Quinn agreed. "We can get a flight out of Kalamazoo—"

"You're leaving again?" Sam asked.

"It's just for a couple of days," Quinn said.

"More than that." Nick stood. "That's a couple thousand miles."

"We're not going to *drive*." She laughed.

"Oh, yes, we are. It's not negotiable. Driving, we're off the grid and have room to maneuver." He grabbed his coat off the wall peg and shrugged it on. "We're past last quarter—"

"Which makes me as safe from the leech as I'm going to be." Quinn stood.

"—and *someone* wants you neutralized. We don't know who. I'm not taking chances." He straightened his collar and looked at Sam. "You can come with us."

"Oh, gee, can I?"

"You have a wireless card, right? You can do all that mumbo jumbo"—Nick waved a finger at the computer—"on the road."

Quinn gave in. Add Nick's valid points to Sam's ability to do nonstop research, and she didn't stand a chance.

Sam printed maps of their route as backup to Nick's road knowledge and the unreliability of GPS—enduring with stoic silence Nick's harassment for packing a printer. Quinn and Nick gathered their things and loaded the car. When they were ready to go, Sam handed the folder of printouts to Quinn and his duffel to Nick to put in the trunk, before lowering his computer satchel through the window into the backseat.

"I plotted a route that detours south. It'll take us longer, but we need cash, and ATMs have transaction limits. There's a branch of the bar's bank right off the highway, and we can go to the teller. We'll come back north to I-80."

"Sounds like a plan." Nick slid into the car. Quinn held the seat forward for Sam, who crawled into the back. She settled into the front and looked back at the cabin as they rolled down the needle-strewn driveway to the street.

There was nothing wrong with their plan, and she was not the type to hole up while events surged on without her. But something in her wished she could go back inside and curl up under her quilt for a few more days.

It's just the new moon, she told herself, but she called bullshit right away. Yeah, she was as close to normal as she could get during the new moon, and powerless longer than most other goddesses who had control over access to their source, but she'd dealt with that for seventeen years, for cripes sake. But if the moon were full, they could draw the leech to them, instead of chasing a phantom. She grinned, picturing Nick's reaction if she suggested such a thing.

Nick slipped a CD into the console and hit the main road, settling on his spine for the long drive. Quinn glanced back to find Sam already plugged in to the broadband and engrossed in his research. She sighed and slid down in her seat, closing her eyes. This was going to be a long trip.

• • •

They reached Portland midafternoon on Tuesday and drove to the address listed for Tanda in the Society directory. Nick parked at a meter across the street and examined the entrance to the high-rise apartment building.

"Doorman, security desk inside, elevators recessed—no way to get to them without being seen by security." He squinted. "Or cameras."

"We planning to sneak in?" Sam asked from the front seat. He'd been testy for the last four hundred miles, a combination of confinement and his inability to reliably access the Internet.

"No," Nick replied, "but someone did. Unless she knew him. Or is unusually trusting."

"Maybe it didn't happened here," Quinn countered. "She has an office. Rainy Day Investigations." Tanda's source was rain, so she only worked on rainy days, and her strongest ability was reading human energies. She could follow the trail of a person's energy if they were missing or help them find a lost object. Or more frivolous things, like matching a type of car or home or jewelry to a person's needs. She could often tell if someone was lying or hiding something. Or…that was what she *used* to be able to do. To have it taken from her—she must feel like Quinn did during the new moon, only with no hope of becoming whole again. How much despair must she be feeling? Quinn wished it hadn't taken her so long to get here.

"Let's go find out." Nick and Sam opened their doors. Quinn climbed out, then tried to push Sam back inside.

"You can't come in with me."

"What? Why not?"

"Tanda might still be freaked. She won't want a crowd invading her home. She might not even want me." She had never responded to Quinn's calls or voice mails. "But you're big and looming and that could be too scary for her."

Sam scowled but got back into the car. Nick slammed his door.

"You either, Nick."

He braced his forearms on top of the car and dropped his head between them, then lifted it again. "We gonna do this every time, Quinn? Not to leave my sight, remember?"

"I know." She didn't want to go in alone, but she was trying to put herself in Tanda's shoes. She'd been betrayed, and a place she felt safe had been invaded. She might not want a whole bunch of people overrunning her. "But why would he be here? He's already taken everything he can."

"What about the goddess who's already attacked us at least once?"

"How would she know we're here?"

Nick shook his head. "She could have someone waiting for you in case you did come here. But it doesn't matter. It's my job. She'll be okay—she's met me before."

Quinn was skeptical but didn't argue anymore.

The doorman nodded and opened the door for them as they approached, but the security officer at the desk was less accommodating. He addressed them as soon as they walked in, giving them no choice but to approach the station. He nudged the sign-in book and lifted a telephone handset.

"Resident?"

"Tanda Wilcox," Quinn told him and picked up the pen.

"Don't—" Nick blew out a breath when she put her name in the book. She gave him a pointed look and handed over the pen. He glared and shook his head but scribbled something under her name.

The officer relayed their names to whomever answered his call and then told them, "You may go up. Ms. Wilcox is present." He settled the phone onto its cradle.

Quinn's shoulders relaxed, and she realized how worried she'd been that Tanda would turn them away. "Which apartment, please?"

"Twenty-two thirteen."

"Thank you."

He watched them all the way to the elevator and continued while they waited for it to arrive. Once they were inside Quinn breathed a sigh of relief.

"You didn't put your own name, did you?" she said. She hadn't clearly heard the officer's mumbled conversation with Tanda.

"Of course not. I put Edward Halen."

"I don't know how you get away with that stuff." She tilted her head to check the numbers flashing at the top of the car.

"It's less obvious without the Van. You shouldn't have signed your real name."

"I had to. One, it's forgery."

Nick snorted.

"Two, how would Tanda let us up if she didn't know it was us? *One* of us had to give our real name. It's not going into a database," she tried to reassure him. "Someone might find out later that I was here, but they're not getting a signal now."

"Unless the guard's dirty and was watching for you."

He had an answer for everything, and each one felt more like a shackle. "I suppose that's possible."

"Of course it's possible!" Nick drove his hand through his hair, spiking it even more than usual. "You make it damned hard to protect you."

Quinn's eyelids prickled. She watched the numbers changing on the display at the top of the panel. "I'm sorry. That's not my intent." It wasn't like she wasn't afraid. Losing her power would be as bad as losing Sam or Nick. "It just feels more and more like imprisonment."

Nick stared at her. "What are you talking about?"

She turned to face him. "It's never been this way. Someone else—you—dictating my every move. Going to extremes."

"The threat's never been this strong."

She understood that, and she also understood, deep down, that not all of the way she felt was about restrictions. She had no space. Nick was always right there, both closer and further away than ever. She was letting it get to her.

"I'm sorry," she said again, softly. "I don't want to make your job harder. I just want to comfort a friend and do what I can to stop the leech from doing this to others. Those are worth the small risks."

The elevator dinged and slowed, putting an end to the conversation. The doors opened on a green-carpeted hallway with walls papered in textured ivory. The off-white apartment doors sported gold number plaques.

Nick glanced at the ceiling at both ends of the corridors, noting the camera domes. "Can't see the angles of those cameras. Might be suspicious, my hanging around out here in the hallway."

"We'll see what Tanda says." Quinn stopped in front of 2213. Nick rolled his eyes and leaned against the wall next to the door while she knocked.

Tanda opened it immediately, her eyes warm, her smile sincere. But her appearance took Quinn aback. Her brown hair hung lank on either side of her face, which was pale except for the very dark circles around her eyes. Her extremely light blue eyes. They looked bleached, and for a second Quinn couldn't stop looking at them.

When she did, she realized Tanda's shirt hung loose, though it was clear it wasn't meant to be that way, and her jeans were cinched with a belt, bunching them around her hips. *Oh, Tanda.*

"Quinn." She stepped out into the hall and hugged her with surprising strength. "I can't believe you came."

"I had to see you." Quinn hugged her back, feeling guilty that it had taken them so long to get here, when Tanda obviously needed a friend. "I've been calling, but you haven't answered. I was worried."

"Bastard stole my cell phone." Tanda pulled back and caught sight of Nick. Her face lit up, and suddenly she didn't look so haggard.

"Nick, you scoundrel!" She tugged at his sleeve.

"Tanda." He hugged her, too, and Quinn stopped worrying. Tanda had obviously had enough time alone, and she knew Nick better than he'd let on.

"Come in, both of you!" Tanda closed the door behind them, then engaged six deadbolts before leading them into the living room.

"You always have that many locks?" Nick asked her.

"Yeah, fat lot of good it did me, huh?" She motioned to the plum-colored love seat and plush chairs grouped around a cherry coffee table in a sitting area two steps down from the foyer. The grouping faced an expanse of windows and a sliding glass door to a concrete balcony and was lit with both tall black floor lamps and flickering white candles placed on small tables.

"Can I get you drinks?" Tanda offered.

"Water's fine, thanks," Quinn said.

"I'll be right back."

"Told you so," Nick muttered as soon as she was out of sight.

"Shush." But she couldn't help asking, "How does she know you so well?"

Nick shook his head and sat in a fussy chintz overstuffed chair next to the love seat. "I've protected others at conferences or whatever, and she was there."

Tanda returned and sat on the love seat next to Quinn, setting a pitcher of water and some glasses on the glossy coffee table. Nick leaned forward to pour for them.

"How are you?" Quinn asked Tanda, taking her hand.

"Oh, about how you'd expect." Tears welled in her eyes, but she didn't try to hide or suppress them. "It's like losing a limb, I guess, or a sense. My life is completely different." She blinked and met Quinn's eyes. "Steve left me."

Quinn gasped. "No way!"

She nodded and sniffled. "About a week ago. He doesn't like the way I'm handling this, he said. Like I'm whining and feeling sorry for myself."

"How dare he!" Quinn wanted to say the very essence of who Tanda was had been taken from her, but that would make her feel worse. "It's not like being a goddess is just a job and being leeched gives you an opportunity to try something new. It's not a layoff."

"Exactly." She took a deep breath and got herself under control. "Anyway, he blamed me for letting it happen and for how it changed our lives, and now he's gone and good riddance." She eyed Nick, her lips quirking in a sad smile. "You in the market, cowboy?"

Uncharacteristically serious, he said quietly, "No." He didn't look at Quinn, but a frisson went up her spine.

Then Tanda made it worse by patting Quinn's hand and saying, "I know." What the hell did that mean?

"Can you tell us what happened?" Nick asked. "Were you

here?"

"Yes, which is why it's so bizarre. Levon—the guy at the desk—was on duty but he never saw anyone. He doesn't leave the desk unless his partner is there, and he didn't see anything, either. It was a quiet night."

Quinn looked at the glass doors. "What about the balcony?"

"We're twenty-two floors up."

Nick rose to look outside, but Tanda waved him down and said, "Don't bother. It's about two feet deep, just an observation spot. It's not wide enough for someone to have jumped onto, and the way the apartments are structured, all the balconies are staggered about twenty feet apart."

"They could have rappelled down."

"Maybe, but again, unlikely. The couple with the balcony right above me was outside when it happened. They love the city in the rain. They said they saw the flashes of light down here, but before that, nothing. They would have spotted someone rappelling. Plus, if he came down the side of the building, he'd be wet. He wasn't."

"Okay." Nick sat back in the puffy chair and crossed one ankle over his leg. "When did you know he was in here?"

"I was making myself some dinner in the kitchen. I remembered my cell phone needed charging, so I came out to get it and he was standing right there." She turned and pointed to the center of the room. "The locks were still engaged. I could see them."

"Only option left was that he was here before you got home." Nick stood and went back to the foyer, opening the closet door to peer inside. "He could have slipped in when the guard was occupied or said he was visiting someone else in the building, then broke in here—those locks would be easy for him, right?" He looked at Quinn, who lifted one shoulder. He was probably right.

"Thanks," Tanda said. "Like that doesn't creep me out even more."

"Did you know him?" Quinn asked.

"I don't think so. He wore a cloak with a deep hood. The lights were off in here, except an accent lamp in the corner." She pointed to the platform running along the side of the room, where a tall bookcase would have cast shadows from the lamp she indicated. "I didn't recognize his voice, but he struck so fast I can't be sure I've never seen him before."

Quinn wanted to ask how he'd done it, but the words stuck in her throat. Nick somehow knew and did it for her.

"I don't know." The tears welled again. "He said something in Latin, I think, and there was a flash of brilliant white light. I fell back, then it was like he was pulling string out through my abdomen. It hurt a little, but even worse was the paralysis. I couldn't move or yell or even think. There was more light, then blackness. I think I passed out. Next thing I knew, I was lying here in the dark, and I couldn't do a damned thing." The tears turned into sobs that she tried to muffle with her hand. Quinn moved closer and gathered her friend in, her heart breaking for her. Nick handed over a box of tissues.

Quinn imagined the scene, the sensations Tanda had described, and wished with all her heart there was some way to reverse the leeching, to drain the power from the leech back into Tanda. But she had never heard of such a thing.

"You said he took your cell phone?" Nick asked when he returned from prowling the rest of the apartment.

"Yes." Tanda eased away from Quinn and accepted the clean tissues she handed her. "It was my only phone. I got a new one, but all my contacts are on the old one, and the backup is on my work computer in the office." She smiled sheepishly. "I haven't wanted to, you know, leave."

"How come you didn't cancel the old number?"

"The security team asked me not to. They want to monitor the phone, I guess, and try to track him through it or something."

"Why would he take it?" Quinn turned to Nick. "That seems stupid."

"He probably ditched it," Nick guessed. "Took it to cut Tanda off, to delay the word getting out and stuff."

The setting sun blazed through a break in the clouds, filling the room with golden light.

"Oh!" Tanda checked her watch. "It's dinner time. You should stay."

"That sounds great," Nick said, imploring Quinn with his hand over his stomach.

"We'd love to, but—"

"Really, Quinn, I want you to stay. It's been so nice having you here, and you need to rest before you hit the road again, don't you?" She flashed a smile at Nick. "I know he won't fly."

"I would like to, but Sam's waiting downstairs in the car—"

"What!" Tanda leapt toward the phone. "Why didn't you say so? Oh, the poor boy. Where's the car?" Nick told her as she hit some buttons on the keypad. "Levon, can you please have Beau do me a favor? Can you send him across the street to the black Charger sitting there and have the man inside the car, Sam Remington, come upstairs? Thanks, Levon. You're the best."

So the three of them stayed for a wonderful spaghetti dinner and conversation that avoided anything to do with goddesses. They left much later, after turning down Tanda's offer to stay overnight. Quinn had been tempted to accept, wished she could stay for a while and help Tanda figure out what to do next, but two things made her say no. If the leech did target Quinn, it would be awful to have it happen here. And the best way they could help Tanda was to find the leech, so she could stop being scared.

They didn't speak until they were in the elevator.

"Well, that wasn't much help." Nick sighed.

"We don't seem closer to answers." Sam leaned against the back of the elevator, his face pinched. "I know one thing, though." His eyebrows came together over worried eyes as he looked at Quinn. "I don't want that to happen to you."

"Me neither."

"Don't even go there." Nick pounded on the lobby button a few times, though they were descending smoothly. "It's not going to happen."

The problem was, if it came down to it, Quinn didn't know how they could stop it.

CHAPTER SEVEN

*The Society's annual meeting is not merely a tool of governance.
All members are encouraged to take advantage of the opportunities
for networking, education, and even socialization with members
they may not otherwise have an opportunity to meet due to distance
or circumstance. The stronger our relationships individually, the
stronger our community.*

— The Society for Goddess Education and Defense,
Notice of Meeting

They found a cheesy motel about an hour down the road, a run-down one-story affair off the highway. Sam registered them, paying cash for two rooms and convincing the not-so-savvy female clerk that she didn't need their IDs. Then ensued a boredom- and fatigue-induced argument about who would sleep where.

"I don't know how many times I have to say it," Nick said. "Not letting her out of my sight."

"You're not the only one who can protect her," Sam argued. "We have business to take care of, and it doesn't make sense for me to be in a different room. Of the three of us, you've gotten the least sleep. Since you won't let either of us drive—"

"Guys." Quinn leaned forward.

"Dude. I've been crisscrossing this country for years. I drive alone all. The. Time."

"Boys!"

"That's not relevant. You don't normally drive this long, this far, in such a short time. Don't try to tell me you do."

Quinn gave up. Their rooms were at the end of the building, and there were no cars between here and the office. Their debate hadn't drawn attention that she could see, and they weren't listening to her. So she gathered up her stuff, plucked a keycard from Sam's back pocket, and went into her room.

The voices outside halted abruptly when she kicked her door closed. She surveyed the tiny, dingy room and its double beds. "Damn." She'd gotten the wrong card. The room next door had the king bed.

Oh well. Served them right for acting like ten-year-olds. She wasn't in the mood to switch. After she washed up and brushed her teeth, she unlocked her side of the connecting door and cracked it open. That would be good enough for Nick. Without bothering to undress, she collapsed on the multicolored nylon bedspread and fell instantly asleep.

For a while she slept soundly, dreamlessly. But then she emerged into a world of flickering, changing light and colors. Flashes of brilliant white accompanied screams she recognized, screams of other goddesses she knew, people she called friends. She tried to find them, to get to them, a solid, warm presence at her back that she knew was Sam. But every time she thought she was getting close, there was that light, the screaming, and it was too late.

Then she saw a shadow, a lumbering shape ahead of her. It was him. The leech. He paused, turned to his right. She gasped. She recognized his profile. She knew him! She opened her mouth to call out his name, but no sound emerged from her throat. He turned anyway, and she realized she wouldn't be able to scream if he leeched her. *Sam.* She reached behind, but he was gone. She was alone now, in the dark, except for the leech. She didn't fall, but she was suddenly on the ground. Breathing came hard. The leech loomed over her, his face the only thing she could see.

"Good morning," Nick said.

Quinn startled awake so violently she knocked a cup out of Nick's hand. It went flying, hit the table near the window, and splashed all over the drapes, chair, and floor.

Nick, sitting on the edge of the bed dressed in jeans and an open button-down over a white T-shirt, nothing like what he'd worn in the dream, stared at the mess. "Bad dream?"

"Very." She rubbed her face and pushed herself up to lean against the headboard. The brightness of the room disoriented her and failed to banish the lingering terror. She had to fight not to scramble off the bed, away from Nick.

Quinn concentrated on her surroundings, feeling sick at her inability to conquer the dream. She was under the covers now, her clothes twisted and bunched around her body. The sweat drying on the back of her neck chilled her, and she hunched into herself.

The connecting door next to the bed was open wide, and Sam's keyboard clicked on the other side of the doorway. She grabbed the little electric clock on the nightstand and tilted it toward her to double-check the time, the dream disturbing her so much she didn't trust her internal clock. Eight thirty. "I'm sorry," she told Nick, motioning to the mess.

"Better the mocha than me." He handed her the other to-go cup and stood. "You can have mine. It's not frou-frou, though. Just black." He disappeared into the bathroom and came back out with an off-white hand towel.

"I can't take your coffee."

"It's fine, I'll get some down the road." He bent to mop the spill off the warped laminate table. "Hey, this splotch look like a bunny to you?"

Quinn smiled a little. "I dreamed about the leech," she told him.

"It was you." She watched him carefully, hating herself for it. But he didn't freeze, or jerk his head around to look at her, or slow his movements.

"Yeah, that sounds very bad." He swiped at the curtains, then half sat on the table and looked at her. "Is that something you're afraid of?"

"No." She didn't hesitate, and the realization snapped whatever remaining hold the dream had on her.

But Nick continued. "It's logical. I don't have alibis for Tanda and Chloe. With the stuff we're hearing—"

"It's not logical. Not to me." Dreams weren't based on logic, no matter what part of a person's subconscious fed them. And maybe a dream could have enough emotional power to influence her for a moment, but her conviction that Nick was not a threat, and never would be, came from something beyond influence.

Nick's eyes had gone golden in the sunlight, and she could see the gratitude in them. Had he been afraid that she'd turn on him since this whole thing started? She wanted to get up and hug him, but it felt too awkward with Sam only feet away.

"So." She slid off the bed and headed for the bathroom. "How did you and Sam do last night?"

"That wasn't very nice, you know!" Nick called after her. She left the door cracked a little so she could hear him. "Sam snores!"

"I do not!" came from the other room.

"Do so. Like a hibernating bear with a deviated septum. And he sprawls. I had to sleep on the floor."

"I'm a big guy!"

Quinn grinned. "You could have come in here," she called out. "There was an extra bed."

"Too scared!" came back in stereo, making her laugh.

"What's the plan for today?" she asked around her toothbrush.

"Sam wants to do that business stuff he was whining about last night."

Payroll was due, and they needed to upload a file to the bank so the deposits would be in her employees' accounts on Friday. Plus, Sam was concerned about some of the cancellations for the next full moon. Two of her clients were cancer patients for whom all other treatments had failed before they came to her. She could heal, but cancer was more than just healing. If she skipped a month it might progress again, undoing all the good she'd done in past treatments. She'd suggested trying to hook them up with another goddess, but they had to find one who had the experience and lived close enough to cover for her.

"I'll be in after I shower," she told them. "Need to wake up."

"Don't take too long," Nick warned. "I want to get back on the road by noon. And we'll pay for an extra day if we're not out by then."

"No problem." She took a quick, cool shower and changed clothes before packing the few things she'd used and meeting them in the other room.

"Here are the goddesses we can try." Sam handed her a sheet of paper covered in his neat handwriting. "I'm almost done prepping payroll." He raised an eyebrow at her. "What do you want to do about the Society meeting?"

Quinn accepted the paper and picked up the garlic-and-cream-cheese bagel sitting on a paper bag next to his computer. "This mine?"

Sam grimaced. "It is now."

"She's a big moocher this morning," Nick said from the corner. He tapped something out on his cell phone.

"Yep, that's me. Quinn 'Moocher' Caldwell. I guess we should send Alana an e-mail that I won't make it. I don't think anyone will be surprised. Assuming they're still holding the meeting." Nonprofit laws required them to, but they could reschedule, and with everything going on, it didn't seem prudent to put all those goddesses in one place. But it wasn't her call, of course. The sense of estrangement didn't feel as strong as it had mere days ago. Reconnecting with Tanda had helped, she supposed. Maybe reducing her involvement in Society politics would be good for her in the long run.

She settled onto the bed with the list and her phone to make calls. It took half an hour to find someone to cover for her. But she'd also gained some information.

"File's almost done uploading," Sam said when she clapped her phone shut for the last time. "I got a response from Alana." He looked concerned. "She said it's for the best that you don't attend."

"Great." Quinn wanted to reassure him that she was okay with it, but it was time to move on. "I got Holly to cover for me."

"Good. Mrs. Calebas and Mr. Dalini will be relieved. I'll let them know once we're on the road." He glanced at his watch.

"But listen. That's not all I got."

Nick, who'd spent a little time watching the NFL Network and a lot of time pacing while they worked, perked up. "You got something from Holly? About what?"

"Jennifer. I asked everyone I talked to. No one's heard from her and no one saw her e-mail."

"That's weird." Sam frowned. His computer beeped to signal the file was done, and he started shutting it down. "Are you sure it came through on the loop and not privately?"

"Yeah, we've checked it three times," Nick confirmed. "Goddess voodoo?"

Quinn ignored his quip. "Holly might be the last one who spoke with Jennifer. It was five days ago, and she said she'd sounded fine. But get this: She had a new boyfriend."

"So?" said Nick.

But Sam got the implication. "The leech?" He slid his laptop into the case.

"Could be." She gathered up her own things and slung her bag over her shoulder as Nick hefted her duffel with his. Sam glanced around the room as he followed them out.

"Holly said the guy sounded like the one Chloe had been seeing before she was leeched," Quinn said when they'd reached the car.

Sam paused while setting his stuff in the trunk. "It can't be the same person, can it? There wasn't time between Tanda and Chloe to establish a relationship."

"No, but remember, Tanda had a live-in boyfriend already. Holly said this guy Chloe dated traveled for work all the time, so he could have been in Oregon when Tanda got leeched. And he could have been prepping for Chloe a lot longer than we thought."

Nick leaned against the car. "Want to head for Mississippi?"

"I think we should." Quinn tossed her stuff in the trunk, and Sam dropped it closed. "Did they send a protector down there?" she asked Nick.

"We're shorthanded. This situation has elevated the threat for everyone. They didn't have anyone available."

"Then we should definitely go," Quinn decided, energized by the idea of action. "I don't know for sure, but I'm afraid no one at the Society is doing anything, either. If she's not already leeched, she might be in trouble. I tried calling her again, but she still didn't answer. If the leech is stealing phones…"

"All right, let's go, then." Sam slapped his hand on the roof of the car. "I'll go check out."

"We need gas," Nick told him. "Meet us across the street."

Sam waved in agreement. Quinn got in the front passenger side and said, "Can I run in and get you coffee?"

"I would kiss you for it." He rolled down his window and breathed deep. "I was going insane in there. But let me check it out first." He started the car and pulled out to the road, letting two cars go by before roaring across to the gas station.

"You could have taken a nap," Quinn pointed out. "Or come over to get another coffee while you waited."

He gave her a "yeah right" look and peered past her to study the store, like he had before. "Don't flirt with anyone in there this time, all right? I don't need to break up a catfight. I'll be right in."

Quinn laughed and went inside. This time there were no lines. She filled three cups and pressed them into a cardboard carrier. The bell at the door tinkled. She glanced over her shoulder but saw only the clerk, slouched on a stool behind the counter, engrossed in what she'd bet was a skin mag.

She lifted the coffee carrier but froze when someone gripped her elbow tight enough to make her gasp.

"Set it down," a deep voice growled.

She started to turn her head, but someone else grabbed her around the neck and squeezed. Before she could even think about fighting back, her vision went black from the edges in.

• • •

Quinn came to four minutes later, her head pounding and her mouth dry. There was so much pain in her neck she didn't know how they'd knocked her out—if they'd cut off her air or used some kind of drug. She forced her eyes to stay closed, despite the desperate need to open them. Wherever she was, she wasn't alone. Not in a vehicle, or at least not one that was moving. She was horizontal on a hard, flat surface. Something low, because the murmurs above her seemed high up. She inhaled slowly to try to calm her racing heart and smelled dryness, like dusty concrete, and motor oil. An impression tried to coalesce…tang like metal, stuffy heat…cars. The convenience store had a repair bay attached. She was probably on the floor in there. That was good. They hadn't taken her far.

So where the hell was Nick?

"Not until she wakes up," someone said. Her head had cleared enough to discern the words, though they were said quietly. "We gotta make sure she's all right. I'm not takin' her to the boss damaged. She'd have our asses."

Another voice came from farther away, but louder. "Shit, that guy she's with is looking around."

Relief flooded her, but it was short-lived. If he was looking around, he hadn't seen them take her. Knowing he was near, but not near enough, left her feeling more vulnerable than she'd felt since she came into her power. Even the friend's abusive boyfriend who broke her arm hadn't left her feeling like this. He'd been a known threat. Who knew what these guys were planning to do?

"Of course he is," came yet another voice. "That's Nick Jarrett. He's her protector."

"Oh, ma-a-n-n-n. This has not gone down right. We're in big trouble."

Unless her brain was seriously oxygen-deprived, Quinn had just counted four voices. That was bad odds, even for Nick. Especially if…

"If he comes in here, pop him."

Especially if they were willing to kill him.

Suddenly, she was less afraid for herself than for Nick. One of the men had said they couldn't hurt her, so that gave her some control back. Steely calm coated her fear, and strength returned to her body. She was *not* helpless, and they would *not* harm Nick.

She opened her eyes. She lay in front of a workbench at the back of the shadowy garage. A massive pickup truck filled one side, a smaller SUV the other. No one stood by her, but figures moved near the windows at the front of the bays.

Quinn moved her legs so they'd rasp across the concrete floor.

"She's awake," said the second voice.

"No duh."

"So let's go."

"Not yet." A big shape, dressed in black and wearing a hat pulled low over his face, hunkered down in front of Quinn. He dangled a huge black pistol in front of his knees. "How you doin'?"

The gun chilled her more than a vague threat to "pop him." They had the ability to shoot Nick. If she stalled, pretending to be woozy, that would give Nick time to find her, and he'd be ambushed and maybe killed. Better she was clearheaded and ready to be moved. At least she could get off the floor, figure out her situation. She couldn't see anything from where she was. Taking a chance, she sat up. Nausea swept over her, but she swallowed hard and willed the coffee and bagel to stay down. "I'm okay."

The guy with the gun nodded to someone and a hood came over her head. Damn it. Someone pulled her arms behind her and wrapped her wrists in a zip tie. So much for strength and steely calm.

"All right, load her up. Jarrett's gone back inside. We gotta move now."

Quinn didn't fight or even scream. Nick would kill her for letting them haul her to her feet and maneuver her into the SUV, but they didn't want to hurt her, and he couldn't save her if he was dead.

If the SUV had tinted rear windows, Nick wouldn't be able to see her. But if he saw the vehicle leave the garage, maybe he'd guess she was in it. *If* he saw the truck.

The heavy cloth over her head muffled the few words her abductors said to one another and kept her from asking what they wanted with her or who they were. Not that she expected them to answer. They guided her onto the bench seat in the back of the

SUV. Someone put on her seat belt, as insufficient as it would be with her arms tied behind her back. Uncomfortable, too. Her shoulders ached already.

An overhead door rumbled in front of them, and the truck rolled forward. They paused outside—Quinn could tell by the sun hitting her body. The door rumbled again, then the truck rocked sideways as someone got into the front and shut the door. Then they were on the road, and no one said a word.

Nick hadn't seen them. They'd have watched for him, to make sure he didn't follow. Despair swept over her for an instant before she banished it. It was up to her to get out of this, and she had to pay attention, not stew in her own fear. At least Nick was safe.

They drove without turning for an hour and twelve minutes, stopping in some stretches for what she assumed were stoplights. Then they accelerated and merged onto a highway, judging by their speed and the *whoosh* of the tires on pavement. They followed the highway for twenty minutes before she spoke.

"Can someone—" The hood muffled her voice so much she started over, louder. "Can someone please tie my hands in front of me? This is really uncomfortable, and I assume we've got a ways to go."

No one answered, but chilled metal touched her wrist before the tie gave way with a snap. She sighed and moved her burning shoulders around for a second, but the men didn't give her much room or time. They re-zipped her hands in front of her, more tightly than they needed to.

At least her seat belt was on properly now.

They drove for hours. Quinn started out marking time whenever they got off or onto a highway or made a turn, but it didn't take long for her to lose track. She sensed the sun going down, the moon rising, and wished like hell it wasn't nearly a new moon but a full one. Adrenaline had kept her alert for a while, but hours passed with nothing happening but the soothing movement of the car, and though she could breathe fine through the fabric of the hood, it was warm and moist inside. Her head still throbbed, her bruised neck was stiff and tender, and thirst gave her a sore throat. Eventually, staying awake became more and more difficult.

The men didn't talk, and that was eerie. There were at least four of them, maybe more, and in six hours and thirty-three minutes they'd had nothing to say?

"Bladders of camels, too," she muttered, squirming. She thanked god she hadn't had time to drink the second coffee and had used the bathroom right before they left. Still, six hours was a long time not to pee. She'd tried to wait them out but was getting desperate.

"When are we going to take a bathroom break?" she called out. No one answered, but a few minutes later the truck slowed. Gravel crunched under the tires, and they stopped. The guy on her right stood, cut her hands free, unbuckled her seat belt, and pulled her over to the right side of the seat. Then he wrapped her hands again as the door opened, and he guided her out.

Her stiff legs protested her weight, and her knees buckled when she stepped down to the ground. The man caught her and steadied her until she could take a step. He led her across a wide expanse of gravel, then stopped her. A spring creaked, like on an old-fashioned screen door. He urged her forward. Her toe thudded against thick plastic. She lifted her foot and found a step up. And caught a whiff of a urinal cake.

"You've got to be kidding me."

"Beggars can't be choosers, ma'am."

What kind of kidnapper called his victim *ma'am*? This one had a New England accent. The others didn't, though, so it was a meaningless detail. His manners calmed her and she reached for the hood, but he stopped her. "Not until you're inside."

Quinn held out her wrists. "Can you at least cut my hands free?"

"No."

"Come on. My fingers are numb! How am I supposed to—"

"You just are."

She would have stared at him incredulously if he could see her face. Manners apparently only went so far. She heaved a put-upon sigh. "If I get anything on my hands, I'm using *you* as a towel." She stepped up into the Porta-Potty and waited while the door slammed closed. Then she pulled off her hood and looked around. The dim light from the rest area lamp poles showed that the conditions weren't too bad. It was a larger unit with an indoor sink and a small pump for water. She draped the hood over the spring and locked the door, then struggled to get her jeans down with her tightly bound hands. It took forever and she didn't think she'd make it. But her distended bladder held, and she suppressed a moan of relief as she emptied it. Then more struggles to fix her clothes while the guy outside pounded on the door.

"You're the one who wouldn't undo my hands!" she yelled. "Go find a tree!"

He grunted and then, incredibly, his footsteps crunched away across the gravel. She rushed to get her jeans fastened, then slowly, quietly, unlatched the door and eased it open.

The unit was positioned sideways to the parking area, with the door opening on the left. When she cracked it, it blocked her from where the truck was parked. No one stood nearby. She slipped out and toward the left side, closest to the woods, and held the door so it didn't bang closed. Plastic slapped softly on plastic, and then she was behind the john.

She pressed her back to the wall for a second, well hidden in the shadows, and struggled to keep her breathing steady and silent. She checked to her left and right. No sign of her tree-seeking friend.

About fifteen feet of lit, open space lay between her and the woods, but if she could get in there, she might be able to get away. She had to act fast before they realized she was done going to the bathroom.

Taking a deep breath, she tensed, then took off as fast and as lightly as she could, trying not to make any sound on the stones. That was impossible, and halfway to the woods someone cursed, then shouted. Footsteps pounded behind her. She dashed full-tilt into the woods, her bound hands slowing her down, but she made it into the darkness before they closed on her.

She darted to the right, hoping they'd think she charged ahead. She needed to get some distance and find a place to hide, then somehow dig her cell phone out of her jacket pocket and call Nick.

She couldn't hear them behind her anymore, but she made a racket of her own that would cover up their noise. She could barely see and was moving so fast—relatively speaking—that she had several near-misses with trees, only dodging at the last second.

Then her foot landed in a hole below the leaves. Her right ankle snapped sideways. She cried out as she went down hard on her side, the nausea welling much more strongly this time. Pain flowed up her leg and dispersed through her entire body. She lay on the ground, holding her breath against the sharp agony in her ankle for way too long before it subsided.

Now she could hear her abductors crashing through the woods. Farther away than she thought, but still too close. She couldn't just lie here. Panting slightly, she rolled up to her knees, then pushed to her feet on the left side, slowly putting her weight on her right. To her relief, the ankle felt okay. When she rotated it, the ligaments and tendons shrieked, but it wasn't so bad she couldn't walk.

She worked her way up to a trot again, relieved when the ankle continued to hold, but moving much slower now so she didn't injure it again. A beam flashed ahead—headlights on the highway. She was almost out of the woods.

A body stepped in front of her and caught her upper arms as she slammed into him. A scream gathered in her throat, but she managed to hold it in. She balled her hands into fists as best she could and swung them right, then with all her force spun into a two-fisted punch that connected with the side of the guy's head. He cursed and lost his grip. She'd run half a dozen more steps before she realized she recognized his voice.

"Nick?" she whispered, peering back at him. He leaned against a tree, his hand to the side of his head.

"Yeah. Jesus Christ, Quinn, I'm trying to save you."

Oh, thank god.

"Then save me." She held out her hands. He stepped toward her, his hand in his pocket. With the snick of his switchblade and a quick tug, she was free.

"Thank you," she breathed, rubbing her wrists. She'd never felt anything so good. Except maybe a few minutes ago in the Porta-Potty.

"Keep running. Charger's on the road a couple hundred feet back."

Quinn didn't need further urging. Her pursuers had gained on her since she fell. But with her hands free she could at least push obstacles out of the way before they hit her in the face. In minutes they burst onto the shoulder of a four-lane highway. She hobbled to the Charger, parked in a small emergency pull-off. Nick slid across the hood and got inside at the same time she did. She looked back toward the woods that lined the road as he started the car. No movement, no light, but she still sensed them pursuing her. Her foot pressed on an invisible accelerator, and she braced against the dash, willing the car to start moving.

"They might have run back to the truck," she said. If Nick drove ahead, they'd pass the kidnappers, and as fast as the Charger was, the SUV had a powerful engine.

"Don't worry." Nick pulled onto the road but did an immediate U-turn across the grassy median. His tires spun once in the soft earth, then caught and flung them onto the far side of the highway. He slammed his foot on the accelerator, and they flew.

Quinn wondered where Sam was, but every fiber concentrated on watching through the rear window for pursuit. She saw no headlights and no flashes of streetlamps off a vehicle running dark. Slowly, her body relaxed.

After a few minutes, she said, "I think we're clear." She turned back, grinning with the euphoria of freedom, and saw Nick's face. His jaw was clenched so tight it pulsed. His hands and arms were stiff enough to rip the steering wheel off its column if he turned it, and his eyes bore so hard into the road in front of them, Quinn was amazed it didn't explode.

"Thank you, Nick," she said softly, hoping to defuse him. He was furious with her. Even though he'd cleared her to go into the store, she'd been too complacent and let them sneak up on her. Nick never had a chance to stop them from taking her.

"Don't," he bit out, and she knew he meant more than don't thank him. She didn't talk the rest of the short drive. Nick got off the dark highway at the next exit and followed even darker, more deserted back roads to the edge of what appeared to be a small lake. He skidded to a stop outside a tiny cabin, one of a few dotting the shoreline, and pushed his door open, leaving the headlights on to illuminate the pitch black.

Quinn climbed out slowly, wary. Nick stalked toward the cabin, spun around halfway there, and stalked back to her. He met Quinn at the front of the car, yanked her into his arms, and slammed his mouth down on hers. Fury burned into instant passion, and instead of bruising her, Nick plundered.

Heat swept over Quinn, chased by his desperation and the power of something that had been bottled up far too long. She shuddered and arched into him, her hands clenched hard on his shoulders, her body burning and aching. Part of her protested, *This is Nick*! But the rest of her sighed, *This is* Nick. He drove one hand up under her hair to hold her head and bent her backward over his other arm while his mouth devoured hers and his tongue plunged, over and over.

Quinn hadn't been kissed, or kissed anyone else, in years. Not even Sam. Not since the first time she'd kissed Nick, and that had ended in disaster. Part of her despaired that this would end the same way, but before she had time to really react, he broke away and stared down at her, panting. "We've got to get inside."

"Okay," she whispered, pushing away from him. But he didn't let go. He held her and crossed the dozen feet to the door of the cabin, up the steps, and inside. The door closed, and he shoved her backward with his body to press her against the hard wood. This time, the kiss was all hunger. He laced the fingers of his left hand through her right and held it over her head, against the door. His other hand found her waist, under her coat and shirt, and stroked her skin in time to the rhythm of his tongue.

Quinn didn't care what this meant. She wanted to scream, to laugh. Her body acknowledged how *right* this was, how necessary. Not because of channeling power or moon lust, but because this was Nick, and she wanted him. She tugged at his leather coat, trying to get it off. He barely let go long enough for it to drop to the floor. When she pushed his T-shirt up his body, he grabbed the back of it with one hand and yanked it over his head, then threw it aside and pulled Quinn against him again. A sob escaped her throat when her mouth met his skin for the first time. It was silk to her fingertips, his back and shoulders hard beneath her hands. Need thundered through her, and she welcomed it, even embraced it.

But then he stopped. He buried his face in her neck, his heaving chest crushing her against the rough wood. He brought one hand back and slammed it against the door but didn't release her where his other arm wrapped around her waist. Then he didn't move for long minutes.

Quinn's passion subsided along with Nick's tension. She stroked her hands through his short, almost prickly hair and then across his shoulders, soothing. He still didn't move, wouldn't look at her, even when she tried to tug him back so she could see his face.

"When I couldn't find you"—his voice rumbled in her ear—"it was pure terror. I saw that truck leave the garage, and I knew you had to be in it, and if I lost it for a *second*, you'd be gone forever."

"It's all right," Quinn murmured. "You didn't lose me."

He leaned away from her now, far enough to brace his forehead against hers. "Never out of my sight, Quinn." His voice cracked. "How many—"

"Times do you have to say it, I know." She traced her fingertips along his jaw and didn't remind him that he'd okayed the short distance. It wasn't his fault. "Thank you for saving me."

"You saved yourself. I couldn't get close enough to the damned truck to stop it, and even if I could have, I had no idea how many were in there, what I was up against." His voice was rough, anguished, and Quinn's chest hurt with the pain of it. "In all my years as a protector, I've never lost a goddess. And then you—" His voice cracked again, and Quinn shushed him.

"It's okay, Nick. I'm safe. You got me."

"Only because you were smart enough to stall until I got in position."

She had to chuckle. "That wasn't intentional. They didn't untie my hands. I had no choice but to be slow."

"Thank god for that." He pressed his lips to her forehead, then eased away until her feet touched the ground. Everything shifted when he let go of her, and they became separate entities again.

The air thickened with the apology on its way. This was the part where he regretted what he'd let happen. He'd compromised his integrity as a protector, had forced himself on her, had jeopardized her safety because he was focused on what they were doing instead of on whether or not they'd been found.

She didn't want to hear any of it.

"Where's Sam?" she asked.

Nick backed away and bent to get his shirt.

"I left him at the hotel." He sounded normal now, less tormented. "Called him a few times. He found this place when the truck first slowed down, like they were looking for something, and I thought I might be able to get you out."

"We'd better let him know you did." She smoothed her hair and clothes, then turned away rather than watch Nick put himself to rights. He was way too sexy with rumpled hair, half dressed, his mouth heavy from their kisses. If she looked too long she'd want him again, and he wouldn't be able to pass it off as simple relief.

Which she had to let him do, if he was going to remain in her life. He'd leave her with another protector rather than let this compromise everything he stood for. He had a job to do, a job that was more important to him, and to the Society, than any personal needs. He couldn't have a normal life, so he wouldn't prevent her from having one, too. Grief swelled her throat and rose up, making her eyes sting.

She pulled out her cell phone and hit the button for Sam's. He answered immediately, and hearing his voice was like reconnecting with the mother ship. The urge to cry receded.

"Quinn."

"Yeah, Sam. I'm safe."

"Thank god. Where are you?"

"The camp you told Nick about. No one's found us. We'll wait another half hour or so, then head back to get you."

"No, go straight on to your place, if you're sure you've lost them. You'd be backtracking too much to come get me, so I called for a rental car. I'll meet you at the cabin. Are you okay?" he added. "You sound okay, but—"

"I'm fine. They didn't hurt me."

"Good." He cleared his throat.

"We'll meet you soon."

"Wait, Quinn." She waited, hearing the rustle of papers. "I did some more digging on your birth family while I was waiting. It shouldn't have taken so long, but Nick had the fucking last name wrong."

She didn't want to hear about Nick's shortcomings right now. "You found something?" Her heart pounded in escalating rhythm.

"I sure as hell did." He paused. "Quinn, you have a sister."

CHAPTER EIGHT

Goddess lineage is maternal and almost never dormant. The Society keeps careful track of its members, registering a new goddess upon her birth and offering educational support when she turns twenty-one and discovers both the source and manifestation of her power.

— The Society for Goddess Education and Defense,
New Member Brochure

Quinn's phone beeped. Low battery.

"I have a what?"

"A sister. She's—"

Another beep. *Shit*. "Sam, I'm going to lose you. I'll call you back." The call dropped and the screen went dark. She whirled on Nick, her ankle protesting. "Let me use your phone."

He shook his head. "It's almost out of juice. I was on with Sam for a lot of the last six hours."

"You have a charger, don't you?"

"Car charger broke. Haven't had time to get a new one."

"What about a regular charger?"

Nick waved a hand. "No electricity."

She turned, studying the room she hadn't noticed when they first came in. The tiny, warp-planked cabin was bare bones, with an empty steel bed frame in one corner and a bent Formica table in another. No outlets, no lamps, only the glow of the headlights outside. "What is this place?"

"Private campground. Sam figured it would be deserted this time of year. The sign out by the highway is damaged, too. They won't find us."

"Shit." She shoved a hand through her hair, realizing how wild it must look between the hood, her run through the woods, and Nick's hands in it. "Okay, let's get going as soon as possible."

"Give it a few more minutes." He picked up his coat from the floor and shrugged it on. "You warm enough?"

"Fine." She limped to the bed and lowered herself to the edge of the frame. "Should you turn off the headlights?"

"It'll be okay for a minute." He didn't come closer, but she could feel his frown in the darkness. "Are you okay?"

She nodded. "Sam just told me I have a sister."

The distance Nick had been trying to maintain disappeared. He snapped back to his usual self and sat beside her.

"I meant you were limping, but we'll come back to that. He didn't have time to tell you anything else, did he?"

"No."

He took her hand. "Only a few more hours."

"You really need to get a car charger for your phone."

His teeth flashed white in the darkness as he smiled. "Or maybe one of those battery-powered instant chargers?"

"Yeah." She wished she could shut off her brain until they got to Michigan and she could get answers from Sam, but it persisted in spinning questions and theories. At least, if she concentrated on those, she could ignore the indecipherable swirl of emotions inside her.

After a moment of silence, Nick joined the what-if game. "You think the family ties Alana mentioned mean your sister?"

A foreign sensation zipped over Quinn's skin at the word. "It's the likely assumption. But how do they know? She might not even be a goddess."

"She's gotta be. Dormancy's rare, you know that."

Quinn wanted to feel joy and excitement about the prospect of a sister, but the men in the truck had made that impossible. "The guys who abducted me?"

"Yeah." His voice went deep, gruff. "What about them?"

"They were careful with me. They wanted me neutralized but not harmed. Because 'she' would have their asses."

"Oh, man." He straightened and let go of her hand to check his watch, pressing a button to illuminate the face. "Why were you limping? Twisted ankle?"

"Yeah, it's okay. I'm sure it's swollen and it'll be sore for a while, but I can walk."

"The first-aid kit had a chemical cold pack. You can put your foot up on the backseat and ice the ankle."

"Okay, let's go."

They drove nonstop. For a while, Nick left Quinn to her thoughts, reclining on the seat behind him. She focused on the mundane. What would a sister look like? Was she older or younger? Was she adopted, too? Quinn didn't want to be jealous if she wasn't, if their parents had kept her sister when they hadn't keep her. She reminded herself of their visit when she was eight, of how glad they had been that she was with people who loved her. She thought her mother—her birth mother—had had tears in her eyes when she smoothed Quinn's hair and told her to be happy. And she *had* been happy. She couldn't lose sight of that. But when she let her imagination go, it spun daydreams of pushing her little sister on the swings, playing tag in a big sunlit park, teaching her to tie her shoes.

Fanciful crap, she thought, squinting as the sun broke on the horizon. She hadn't had that and never could. Her sister was an adult, and whether she knew about Quinn or not, welcomed her or not, they'd have to build a relationship from scratch, like any grown strangers who met…under extreme circumstances.

The dread flowing quietly under her thoughts rose. For a while, she'd forgotten her sister could have orchestrated her abduction. Maybe she'd also flipped Sam's car and attacked her and Nick in Boston. Maybe she was a psychopath.

That was when Quinn forced herself to stop thinking.

Nick actually let her drive when he got tired, and whenever they stopped for gas she woke him up and stayed with him almost every minute. He was in and out so fast when it was his turn to use the restroom, she wasn't sure he did anything.

They got back to Benton Harbor in record time. The car hadn't even stopped next to the green sedan in front of the cabin before Sam barreled out the door. He swept Quinn into his arms, her feet dangling, and hugged her tight.

"Thank god."

She rested her head on his shoulder and squeezed him, grateful to have him to come back to. Who needed blood family? "Thank Nick."

"I know." He set her down but kept an arm around her. "He didn't give up. You should have heard him when he followed those guys. Thank you, Nick."

Nick gave him an inscrutable look while he lifted the bags out of the trunk. Quinn knew why. Sam sounded like a grateful husband. She slipped out from under his arm and went to the car for her bag.

"They weren't trying very hard to hide," Nick said. "And she escaped on her own. I was just the pickup."

"Still." Sam stepped forward to take some of Nick's load, but Nick sidestepped him and went into the cabin.

Sam looked down at Quinn. "What's with him?"

"I don't know." Fear and relief might have driven Nick to kiss her, but she had no idea what he was thinking now. When he'd first been assigned as her protector and they'd grown close, Quinn tried to talk about the "something more" that filled the air when they were together. Nick had blocked her so sharply he'd left no room for discussion. He was a protector, right to the bone, and protectors did not get involved with goddesses. Even as young and inexperienced as she was then, Quinn understood his conviction came from the heart, not an externally imposed rule. His personal feelings didn't matter. He would never tell her what he wanted.

She'd accepted it then and hadn't ever tried to change it, never mind what Nick had come to mean to her. She didn't think she could change it now, despite his lapse the other night. And if that were so, Nick didn't have much right to jealousy.

The front door yawned open, the flickering light inside beckoning. Sam watched her, then turned his speculative gaze on the house.

"Tell me about my sister," Quinn said to head him off as she led him inside.

Sam picked up a sheaf of papers lying on the table. "Her name is Marley Canton and she lives in Maine."

"Never heard of her," Nick called from the bedroom.

Neither had Quinn, so did that mean she wasn't a goddess? *Marley*. Quinn let the name roll through her head. If Marley wasn't a goddess, that could mean she wasn't the attacker. But it also gave a potential motive, if she was jealous of Quinn's power or considered it demonic or something. Quinn scoffed at a prick of hurt. It was far too early to be thinking of building family relationships.

"How did you find her?" she asked Sam.

"Birth certificate with your birth parents' names on it. The *correct* names." Sam shot Nick a dirty look as he came out into the main room.

"You must have read it wrong," Nick said.

"If your handwriting was better, I wouldn't have." Sam settled at the table in his usual position in front of the laptop. Today he wore a snug T-shirt, and his arms flexed as he worked the keyboard. Quinn sat on the couch and glanced up at Nick. He looked back at her, then at Sam, and chose a chair far from either of them.

Quinn took a deep breath against the far larger ache that didn't care how much she understood Nick and his motivations. A rejection was a rejection.

Concentrate. She considered what Sam had said about the birth certificate. "Both my birth parents were listed?"

"They're still married, as far as I can tell." Sam looked apologetic.

"Did they keep her? Marley?" She couldn't help asking the question but wasn't surprised when he nodded. It was what she'd always feared. They hadn't wanted her, not even enough to find her after she'd grown up.

"She's a registered goddess, but inactive." Sam picked up the folder with the database information and stretched to hand it to her.

"What's her power source?" Quinn flipped open the folder to scan the roster. She didn't know what she expected. Some kind of *zing* of recognition when she saw her name in black and white, maybe. An invisible weight pressed on her, and she glanced up to meet Nick's eyes. Instead of distant and reserved, they were warm, encouraging. Quinn flushed and looked back down, flustered. She wasn't sure how to interpret that, and she was too raw to try right now.

She forced herself to concentrate on the roster. Sam had highlighted Marley's listing, the word "crystals" circled as her power source.

"She can pretty much bring her power anywhere she goes," Sam said.

"Son of a bitch," Nick growled, clearly taking that as evidence against Marley.

Sam frowned at him. "I don't know what level her power is. Crystals have been used as a focusing medium for centuries, so—"

"It could be limitless," Quinn finished. She set the folder down and covered her face with her hands, resting her burning eyes.

"You're not reacting like I expected," Sam said. "What's wrong?"

"She's not overjoyed that she has a powerful goddess sister who might be evil." Nick moved to sit next to her and rubbed his hand up and down her back. It went far to negate the pain of his rejection a few minutes ago.

"What are you talking about?" Sam demanded.

Quinn shrugged at Nick to bring him up to date.

"The goons who kidnapped—"

"Abducted," she corrected from behind her hands. "I'm not a child."

"The goons who took her from the convenience store said a woman was in charge. They were under orders not to hurt Quinn."

"That's weird."

"She could also have been behind the hotel attack and your car accident."

"The flash I saw could have been a crystal set in a puddle," Sam agreed. "She could have been watching and focused her energy through it to flip my car."

"And used the same energy to control the flip so you didn't get killed."

Quinn raised her head to see Sam nodding. "It makes sense. Endanger me, then make Quinn afraid to pursue whatever trail we were on. I thought I imagined the slow motion of the Camaro's roll, but maybe it actually was."

"Same thing with the hotel," Nick said. "The noise and tossing stuff around? Amateurish. But instead of someone who didn't have control over their power, like the leech…"

Quinn stood and walked to the stainless steel sink. "It could have been someone holding back, giving us time to get out. It would be frightening enough to make us think it was real, without intending to hurt us." She took a short glass from the plastic drainer and filled it with water, then drank it without turning. Every movement was a struggle against the heavy awareness that her flesh and blood could be working against her. Not simply ignoring her existence but willfully acting, maybe even trying to harm her. They assumed the lack of physical damage was intentional, but maybe it was luck.

"There's something else, Quinn. Not about your sister," Sam said, "but I got an e-mail while I was on the road. From Alana."

Quinn turned. "She e-mailed *you*? Like she knew I wouldn't get it?" God, she'd become suspicious of everything.

He shrugged. "No, she copied me on it. Everyone knows I do all your work for you."

She managed a small smile.

"They found Jennifer Hollinger."

Her breath caught in her throat. "Alive?"

"Barely. She was on an island in the river. Dehydrated, undernourished, scratched, and wearing torn clothes, like she'd been wandering for a few days. Disoriented, too, but one thing was clear."

"She'd been leeched."

"Yeah."

"Dammit." Poor Jennifer. She didn't know her, but tears stung her eyelids anyway. If they'd moved faster, she might have prevented this. Where the hell had the Society and their security team been? What was the Protectorate doing to keep this from happening? "Not much point in going to Mississippi now."

"Nope," Sam said.

"There's only one thing to do, then."

"No, Quinn," Nick warned.

Sam leaned over his laptop, fingers flying over the keys. "You want to go to Maine."

"I said no." Nick stood, his hands in fists. "You don't know enough. She endangered you, whether or not she intended to hurt you. She could be working with the leech. *Someone* created him."

Quinn's stomach lurched. She hadn't taken her thoughts all the way there. "I know." As much as she wanted to rush to Maine, and prove them wrong, she wasn't a fool. "But there's no way to learn much about Marley from here."

"I got some more data," Sam said, "but it's meager at best. Like I said, she's not a very active member of the Society."

"So we'll go to the next best place," Quinn decided, hope and a little girl's optimism dictating her choice as much as logic and determination. "Sam, where are my parents?"

• • •

No matter how Quinn argued, Nick refused to fly to Connecticut.

"It's faster, Nick. Time is important here!"

"Less important than your safety is. With the security since 9/11, there is no way we can get on that plane without leaving a blinking neon sign saying, 'Here I am! Come and get me!'"

"Right. *Security*. No one will get to me, and I'm frickin' sick of driving!" And it obviously wasn't any safer. Not that she'd say that aloud. Nick would think she blamed him, and she didn't. But she didn't argue because she was right and he was wrong, since they both had valid points. She argued because she couldn't help herself.

Too many things crowded into her mind and heart, and she was venting unfairly.

Nick rocked back on his heels, a satisfied smile tugging at his mouth. "Fine. We'll stay here a few more days. You should recuperate anyway."

"From what?" She dropped onto the sofa, aware of how long it had been since she had a shower or real rest. Since any of them had. "I'm fine," she lied.

He ticked off her injuries on his fingers. "Cut arm, cuts on your back, bruises, possible concussion from being knocked out, sprained ankle. Did I miss anything?"

She didn't mention her sore back from awkward positions in the car and bad motel-room beds.

"Right. And I could use a break, too." He stalked toward his room. "So you just chill for a while."

"High-handed tyrant," Quinn muttered. Nick slammed the door.

Sam, pouring coffee at the stove, turned to grin at her. "You guys fight like siblings."

Quinn scowled, remembering their last "fight," and how non-sibling-like it had been. "Well, we're not."

"I know." He brought her coffee in a plain ceramic mug. "He's right, though. Driving is safer."

"How? You were in a crash, I was abducted—she has some way to track us. If she's not trying to kill us, then flying is the best way to get to her quickly, without giving her days' worth of warning."

"There's another reason to wait." Sam stretched his legs in front of him. They seemed to go halfway across the room. He leaned his head back, looking for all the world like a frat boy whose only concern was tonight's kegger.

"What, oh wise one?"

He grinned. "'Bout time you recognized it."

Quinn finally smiled back, her frustration fading. "Brat."

"I know. Anyway, I think it would be *wise*"—he emphasized the word—"to wait until full moon."

Nick's door opened. He carried a pile of folded clothes and had a towel slung over his shoulder. "Sam's right. Going in powerless is stupid."

"Waiting two weeks could be stupider." It was just new moon now. "The leech could strike how many times by then." And she didn't want to wait anymore, dammit. After twelve years of being alone, she wanted to meet her family *now*. Answer all the questions crowding into her, including whether her parents were her enemies or if she could maybe start relationships that weren't freaking hopeless and painful.

But all the guys cared about was her physical safety.

"You think seeing your parents won't threaten Marley?" Nick shook his head. "You can't be objective about this. Let us—" He cut himself off, and he was lucky, because Quinn knew his words would have been arrogant and pissed her off. She took a deep breath and gave in. They had to compromise.

"We'll wait a few days, then drive. It will be first quarter by the time we get to Connecticut, and I'll start to have a feed."

"Only when the moon is up," Sam cautioned, "and it'll deplete quickly."

She pushed to her feet, annoyed again. "I know my limits better than you do, Samuel. Don't patronize me. And you." She pointed at Nick. "Get your ass in the shower so I can take my turn. I'm filthy."

"Aye, aye, captain," the men said in unison. Quinn took a turn slamming the door of her bedroom, but amusement slowly overcame anger.

"God." She sighed and threw herself on her bed, the little

room's walls tilting toward her, feeding her urgency to leave, to surge forward. As frightening as it was to face her birth family, it was going to be more difficult to stay here.

As soon as she closed her eyes, she was up against that tiny cabin door again, Nick's entire body touching hers. His skin smooth and hot under her hands, his scent filling her up, lifting her to joy independent of the desire he'd ignited in a scant second. Quinn would have let him take her up against the door and rejoiced in it—again, not because of uncontrollable moon lust, but because of passion driven by the love she'd buried for so long.

She rolled to press her face into her mother's old quilt, her fist closing around the cool fabric. Damn him for breaking open that vault! Sam's revelation about Marley had given Quinn something to focus on, but now they had a plan in place and no action to take for several days. The need to go to Nick, to make him talk to her, twisted with the fear that he'd reject her again, this time blatantly and maybe even forever. After all this time, after so much mutual denial and silent, deep growth of their friendship, why had he crossed that line? Protectors were loyal to the powerless goddesses they protected but committed to none. What would have happened if they hadn't stopped and someone found out? Would he be barred from the Protectorate? It was all he'd known his whole life. If he was stripped of it…she wasn't worth that loss, and whatever relationship they might salvage in the aftermath wouldn't last for long.

How could she survive losing Nick, especially when she also faced losing Sam? Their relationship had already changed. She could tell he'd finally accepted it, and it was only a matter of time before he moved on. Either the way she wanted him to, by finding someone to love who could love him the way he deserved, or because he couldn't work for her anymore, knowing he couldn't have her. In the meantime, she didn't want Sam to know what had happened between her and Nick. That would be salting the wound, even if it had begun to heal.

If Sam did decide to quit, Quinn could hire another assistant, maybe even someone who'd run her business as well as he did. But no one would understand her like Sam or be the kind of friend he was. He was her rock, her only family, even if best-case scenario brought parents and a sister into her life. They'd stay friends, no matter what he decided to do.

But Nick had infiltrated her soul. If he left, he'd rip a hole in her so dark and deep it could never be repaired.

She closed her eyes and let her mind drift into random memories. Sam working at his desk, a groove carved between his eyebrows when he concentrated. Nick shooting the shit with Quinn's waitresses, who flirted while Nick kept a subtle eye on everyone in the bar. Shooting pool with the guys after hours, Quinn cleaning their clocks. Nick, very young, lounging on her couch, complaining about the romantic drama she'd put in the DVD player, a movie she couldn't remember because all she knew was her racing heart and the press of his shoulder against hers.

Then Sam, interrupting her negotiations with one of the bar regulars, leading her upstairs to one of the empty rooms, and encouraging her to recharge with him because it was safer and easier.

Nick, cold and hard, erecting the wall that had always been impenetrable. Instead of shutting down, Quinn's feelings had intensified behind that wall, concentrated and simmered until two nights ago, when he'd unlocked a door she'd never known was there.

Hard knuckles rapped her bedroom door. Quinn's eyes flew open. Her breath rasped at the abrupt leap from deep in her thoughts to full consciousness. She had to clear her throat before she said, "Yeah."

"Your turn." Nick's voice was normal, but it still scraped across all Quinn's nerve endings.

She rolled to her side and stared at the door. "Thanks. I'll be out in a minute."

She gave Nick time to retreat to his bedroom, but Sam would still be out there. A few minutes later, her door rattled under another knock.

"Quinn?" Sam sounded tentative.

"Yes?"

"I'm going to the store for supplies for the next few days. You want anything in particular?"

"No, thanks. You know what I like. Ask Nick, though."

"Already did."

"Thanks."

His boots thumped across the floorboards. The front door creaked open and closed. There was silence for a few seconds before the rental car door thudded and the engine whined down the driveway. Quinn figured it was safe to flee into the bathroom now.

But she had no idea how she was going to get through the next few days.

• • •

She slept a lot. The new moon didn't do anything to her but make her as normal as any non-goddess, but she still used it as an excuse to go to bed early, sleep late, and take naps. She didn't realize how exhausted she was until a few days of that routine, and she felt better than she had in months.

Nick enlisted Sam's help in cleaning weapons and working on the car, and when they weren't doing that, Sam helped Quinn with research. It ensured Nick and Quinn were never alone together, a fact Sam clearly noticed but never commented on. Quinn caught him eyeing them speculatively more than once, but he kept his mouth shut. At least, around her. She had no idea what he said to Nick when they were beyond her hearing.

The research gave them a solid base of information. Quinn's mother, Tess, was a member of the Society but like Marley, not a very active one. Quinn checked all the records the organization posted online, and meeting minutes and lists of attendees never mentioned her mother or sister. Neither did newsletters or e-mail loops, regional chapter notes and websites, or individual goddess sites.

But normal records did, and Sam was a whiz at digging into those. Tess and her husband Ned lived in Fairfield, Connecticut, a top-dollar suburb on Long Island Sound, where Ned was an executive for a software company. Tess ran a greenhouse, which Quinn found ironic, considering her adoptive mother's power source was plants. But the database listed Tess's source as mineral, and a lot of minerals were found in soil, so the affinity for gardening made sense.

Marley was their only other child. She'd lived her whole life from birth to college in Fairfield and attended Fairfield University before moving to Maine seven years ago, when she was twenty-three.

That part bothered Quinn. Her sister was thirty now, only eight years younger than Quinn. Which meant the last time she saw her birth parents, when she was eight years old, Marley had been either on the way or an infant. Their parents had been willing, or able, to keep her. But they hadn't wanted Quinn, even then.

It was unfair to cast blame. Her adoptive parents had already given her a good home for eight years, and undoing that would be a legal mess. And of course Quinn would have resented Tess and Ned and longed to be back with Mom and Dad. That long ago, adoptions weren't open the way they were now. Birth parents didn't stay in touch with the kids they'd given away. There was no way to make everything "right." That was life. Except logic rarely had an effect on emotion. Quinn could spin it all day long, and she still wouldn't banish that eight-year-old's sense of abandonment.

Tess did modest business in the greenhouse but appeared to have a significant income from personal consultation. It took Sam a while, but eventually he figured out that she made subtle adjustments to a person's appearance. She didn't seem able to do major changes, like underlying bone structure or body sculpting. Or at least, she chose not to. But frizzy hair—like Quinn's had been—acne, eyes that were maybe a bit too hooded or lashes that were sparse and thin, spider veins and blemishes and unsightly growths were all fair game. Quinn wondered what drove Tess—vanity or a desire to help people. Or greed, since she charged a lot of money for what she did.

Ned was, on the surface, a typical executive. The local newspaper featured him regularly. He won golf tournaments, dined with members of the board of selectmen, was a past trustee of the university and associated prep school, and was photographed with his wife at country club events every few months.

They came from a world Quinn had never been a part of, but one she understood. Her adopted father had preferred not to climb so high on the corporate ladder in the years he'd worked for someone else before opening the bar when she was a preteen. He hadn't been willing to make family sacrifices to get ahead professionally. So they'd lived modestly and out of the public eye, and they'd been happy. All in all, Quinn couldn't regret the life she'd lived, despite that stubborn ache over the fork in her road and the one she hadn't been given a chance to take. She hoped things would feel different once she met them and could get out of this never-ending circle of thoughts.

One afternoon the boys clattered into the cabin, shirtless and gleaming with sweat from doing chin-ups on the tree outside. Her mouth went dry over Nick's sculpted torso, narrow waist, and powerful arms.

"I did six more than you!" Nick shoved Sam, who stumbled sideways, laughing.

"This time. But that's only because I was tired from doing ten more than you yesterday." He shoved Nick back and pulled his shirt on.

"Bullshit. You only did ten more because your feet touch the ground, you freak."

They spotted Quinn at the table and sauntered over. Nick caught her eyeing his abs and slapped his shirt onto his shoulder with a grin.

"Hey, bright eyes. What're you up to?" He spun a chair and straddled it. He flexed the arm closest to her, and she burst out laughing.

"You guys are unbelievable. Macho men with teenage maturity."

"What?" Nick pretended to be affronted, and when Sam laughed, he threw his shirt at him. "She's talking about you, too, bozo. Now seriously." He sobered and motioned to her pad. "You've been planning."

"Yep." She pulled off the top page and stood. "It's a day past first quarter, and it's time to go."

• • •

"You're sure this is the place?" Nick peered through the Charger's windshield at the one-story Cape-style house across the winding road. He'd pulled off as far as he could, but the almost nonexistent shoulder and semideep ditch next to it discouraged on-street parking. The houses in this neighborhood all sat on huge lots, with great distances and tall tree lines between them.

"Positive," Sam answered. "This is the address listed in public records as the residence of Tess and Ned Canton."

Quinn didn't share Nick's skepticism. Though the house was on the small side, with a two-car garage and a sunroom visible at the back, the land was vast. Wide lawns had been carved out of the surrounding woods, a few maples towering on either side of the house. She spotted embedded wires in the long driveway, the kind that heated it in the winter so snow blowing or plowing was mostly unnecessary. That took money. And peeking over the top of the house was the unmistakable roofline of a greenhouse. It wasn't where Tess did her work—she had a separate site for that—but it was evidence enough for Quinn.

And now that she was here, she couldn't wait another minute. "I have to see her," she said.

"That wasn't the plan." Sam, in the backseat, put his hand on her shoulder.

She smiled, unable to curb her anticipation. "I know I said I'd call and schedule a meeting, but that doesn't feel right now. I want to meet my mother."

"Sam, you go in with her," Nick decided. "I'll stay out here and keep watch." He made a call on his cell phone. Sam's rang and he answered, looking quizzical. "Keep that line open. You can alert me if you need me in there. She's probably not a threat, and no one knew we were coming here, but no sense taking chances."

"And you want to listen to everything we say," Sam said with a smirk. Nick didn't respond, but Quinn saw his silent laughter.

"You ready?" Nick asked Quinn, hand on the ignition. She nodded, and he started the car to glide up the driveway to the house. Her heartbeat seemed to keep pace with the car's acceleration. He parked outside the garage and twisted the key to off. "I'm out here if you need me."

"I know." But she stared at the house in front of her and made no move to get out of the car. Fear, resentment, and hope all paralyzed her. She couldn't even visualize what kind of reception she'd get. How would Tess feel when Quinn showed up on her doorstep? Would her daughter's presence threaten the very nice life she appeared to have built? Or had they been waiting all this time, as Quinn had for them? *This isn't all about you*, she reminded herself. This morning they'd gotten word of a new leeching in South Carolina. Quinn didn't know the leeched goddess, but the database file showed her power source as wind. The leech had kept moving, and the Society seemed incapable of stopping him. They'd sent out new, more urgent warnings, but there was no way to be certain every goddess received them. No one had a photo of him, and Quinn wasn't sure she'd be able to identify him from the generic sketch they'd attached .

Nick said the Protectorate was working overtime, but she suspected he wasn't calling in because he was afraid they'd pull him and assign him elsewhere. She was selfish enough to be grateful. She didn't want to say good-bye, though if anyone asked, she'd have said that the approaching full moon had given everything a new urgency. She couldn't argue that she wasn't a potential target anymore.

Which meant she needed to grow a set and get moving. She took a deep breath and shoved open her door to climb out, straightening her ivory wool pants and cotton sweater.

Sam pulled on a navy sport coat over his khakis and blue button-down shirt and adjusted the collar. "Chilly out here today."

"It's November." The leaves were spectacular, flaming reds and brilliant yellows and oranges that were almost peach. The lawn was still a lush green, and the contrast made her think of jewels, which made her think of money, which tapped into additional insecurities she refused to acknowledge. It was stupid to guess at her parents' motivations. "You ready?" she asked Sam.

"Whenever you are." He stood patiently, god love him, letting her take all the time she needed.

They walked up the flagstone walkway to the black front door. Deep breaths temporarily stilled nerves that insisted on jangling. The doorbell rang the Westminster chimes, and they hadn't died before the door opened, a pleasant smile on the face of the short, curly-haired woman on the other side.

Small as she was, she blocked out the chilly fall air and brilliant foliage and even, for a frightening few seconds, Sam. Quinn was eight years old again, looking up with a trembling smile and tears in her eyes, yet she towered over her mother, whose expression was politely inquiring. *She looks nothing like me*, Quinn thought, and the world came rushing back.

"Can I help you?" Tess's gaze landed on Sam first, then swung to Quinn. She held the smile for a few beats before it faded into shock.

CHAPTER NINE

As a goddess approaches age twenty-one and discovers her power's source and manifestation, emotions and hormonal changes wreak as much havoc as during puberty. Though responsibility for training new goddesses has traditionally lain with mothers and grandmothers, remember that support and educational materials are available through your local chapter or the national office.

— *The Society for Goddess Education and Defense* *booklet,*
"Educating Your Young Goddess"

Quinn's voice was steady when she said, "Tess Canton?"

The woman nodded. "Are you—?"

"My name is Quinn Caldwell. This is my assistant, Sam Remington. I'm your daughter."

"Daughter," Tess said at the same time. "Oh my god. Come in. Please, come in." She spotted the Charger in her driveway and hesitated. "There's someone— Is he with you? I mean…goodness, I'm all flustered." She smoothed her hands down her pants. "Does your friend want to join us?"

"No, thank you. He's fine out here."

"I can't believe—I never expected— Oh my Lord, I've got to call Ned."

"Not yet, please." Quinn reached out in panic, catching her arm. "I'd like to spend some time with you alone first. If that's okay. And if this is a good time." She closed her mouth before she crossed the line into babble. Had she felt steady a moment ago? It was gone already.

Tess's eyes flicked to Sam, as if he belied Quinn's request to talk alone, but she nodded without mentioning it. "Let me fix some tea. It's nice in the sunroom now." She led them to the room at the rear, through elegant, comfortable living space and past a formal dining room with a gleaming mahogany table. The sunroom was insulated and warmed by the rays coming through the skylights and glass walls. Quinn and Sam sat side by side on a cushioned wicker love seat, and Tess excused herself to make the tea. The tension snapped, and Quinn closed her eyes for a moment, knowing it would return with her mother.

"She's pleased to see you," Sam murmured. "And not very cautious. We could be anyone."

"I wonder if she's even aware of the leech." Quinn glanced out the doorway to make sure she wasn't coming back yet. "She wasn't wary of you."

"No," Sam agreed.

But then, even if Tess knew about the leech, what mother would suspect her daughter, or the man with her daughter, even if she hadn't seen her in thirty years?

Quinn looked around the room, focusing on the framed floral watercolors on the one non-glass wall; the smooth, expensive fabrics of the furniture and rugs; and the solid wood and glass coffee tables. Tess returned a few minutes later, carrying a porcelain-inlaid tray that matched the china teapot and three cups, as well as the small plate holding lemon cookies.

"I can't believe you're here. It's been so long." Tess set the tray down and sat in a matching wicker chair at a right angle to them. "Please, help yourselves. My hands are shaking." She couldn't seem to take her eyes off Quinn, and they shone with emotion. "How did you find me?"

Sam shifted forward to pour tea as Quinn answered. "Sam did. Computers can do anything, but you know that, right? Your husband is in software."

"Yes, your father." She looked stricken. "Oh, I don't mean...I know your adoptive father was important to you. I'm so sorry about his death. And your...your mother's."

Taken aback, Quinn stuttered when she said, "Th-thank you. It's okay. I think of you both as my parents, as well as the ones who raised me." They'd been following her. They knew she was close to her father. That her parents had died, leaving her alone. So why hadn't they ever contacted her? She couldn't ask. That would reveal the twisting hurt in her chest.

"Do you remember when we came to visit you?" Tess asked.

"Acutely."

"You were so beautiful, and so earnest, and I've regretted every day since then."

Quinn's lungs loosened. "Regretted what?"

Tess laughed uncomfortably. "Everything. Leaving you eight years before that, leaving you then, confusing you by showing up in your life and then not staying. But they loved you so much, we couldn't even consider taking you away, and I knew staying in your life would make things too difficult." She took a deep breath. "We found out the next day that I was pregnant."

That answer eased the ache even more. They hadn't chosen Marley over Quinn. They'd already decided to leave her where she was, where they thought she was happy and well cared for. And, of course, she had been. She couldn't believe how much lighter she felt, having confirmation of what she'd always hoped.

"I just learned I have a sister," she offered.

Tess nodded. "Yes. She turned thirty a few weeks ago. She lives in Maine."

"Is she married?"

"No, much to my regret." Tess looked uncertain. "Are you? Is he—" She focused on Sam, seemed to remember Quinn had introduced him as her assistant, and glanced outside. "Or—"

"No, I'm not married, either. I run my father's bar in Ohio," she began, and for half an hour, they talked business—Quinn's, Tess's, Ned's, and Marley's.

"You two make me look like a greedy old hag." Tess laughed when Quinn mentioned that much of her work was pro bono or barter. "Marley is the same. She runs an inn and uses the crystals for so many different things. She can do only minor healing, but she's got such a welcoming soul. She draws people to her and helps them find their path. She's like a life coach."

"Do you see her often?" Quinn poured them all a third round of tea. When she handed Sam's to him, she smiled gratefully. He'd been a solid, reassuring support even though he hadn't said a word.

"Not as often as we'd like, of course. She's too many hours away, and the inn makes it hard for her to take a vacation or anything. We go up in the off-season, which is the same for both of us. Even Ned manages to get away then," she added wryly, in obvious reference to his workaholism. She'd mentioned it twice.

"What's she like?" Quinn asked. She held her breath, waiting for the answer. That was foolish, because of course Tess's response would be biased. But she wanted Marley to be good, with an agenda that did *not* include overturned cars and hotel attacks. Or leeches.

Tess's smile was proudly maternal. "She's the sweetest thing most of the time, but so stubborn! When she was a little girl, she kept trying and trying to 'get her goddess in her,' as she phrased it. She collected everything, trying to find out what her power source was, which of course she couldn't learn until she turned twenty-one. She nearly burned her room down when she tried fire. Flooded the kitchen hoping it was water. Piled rocks under her bed and crushed flowers all over her room. She even collected insects." Tess rattled on, describing Marley's affinity for horses and disappearing into a bedroom to retrieve the show ribbons Marley had earned in high school.

"She wanted to go away to college. Ohio State, in fact." A cloud passed over Tess's face, as if she'd thought of something she'd never considered before. "But…her father thought it best she go to Fairfield U for management—she always wanted to run a hotel." Tess paused, her brows knitted.

It was the opening Quinn had been looking for. "Does she know about me?"

Tess refocused on her and looked worried. "Well…"

Quinn tried to hide her anger. She wasn't here for a confrontation but for answers. "It's okay if she doesn't. I mean, I didn't know about her."

"We never told her. We thought it would be confusing and difficult…" She trailed off. Quinn guessed it would have been confusing and difficult for *them*, not Marley, and they hadn't wanted their daughter to resent them for their secrets. Then, as time went on, it got harder and harder. She inferred it was the reason they hadn't sought Quinn in her adult years, though she didn't quite have the courage to ask. But she wondered if Marley had discovered it somehow. If she wanted to go to Ohio State to be near her big sister. What would be different now if she had, and they'd made contact in normal circumstances instead of suspicious ones?

Tess changed the subject, which drifted to her greenhouse and cosmetic work. "It's mostly little things. I don't advocate major changes. But sometimes the simplest adjustment can make life so much easier, especially for teenagers or people who make a living on their appearance. Like smoothing hair." She smiled fondly at Quinn. "Not that I'd do anything for you now. You're beautiful just as you are."

Quinn didn't care about stuff like that, but she flushed anyway. "Thank you."

"How about me?" Sam spoke up for the first time. He fingered a small mole next to his mouth. "Can you get rid of this?"

Tess laughed. "As if you don't know how much women love it. Don't be silly. Those kinds of things add character and uniqueness to a person. We shouldn't strive for some uniform concept of beauty. Here." She rose and disappeared into the house, coming back a moment later with a photo album. "This is the kind of thing I mean." She showed them a young woman with a major scar across her face. The before picture showed it puckered and reddened. In the after picture it was shorter and silvery, faint but still present.

"You couldn't get rid of it completely?" Sam asked.

"I could have, yes, but we discussed it and she didn't want to. I thought it was brave of her. A lot of people would have pushed for me to make it perfect. But she said it was something she had learned from and was an important part of her." She flipped the page. A port wine stain covering a man's shoulder, upper arm, and shoulder blade had been rendered almost invisible. A third photo showed a tattoo where he'd made the rippled edge of the stain a shoreline with a crab and seagull. She flipped again to a boy with a wartlike growth on the side of his neck, gone in the after picture.

"Some are purely cosmetic," Tess admitted, showing them a girl with uneven earlobes. "But most are about self-esteem. Of course, a lot of what I do can also be done surgically." She touched the wart photo. "But this is non-invasive so almost risk free."

Quinn nodded, pleased that her mother had found balance between philosophy and commerce. She checked her watch, stunned at how much time had gone by. She'd learned a lot and enjoyed the meeting, but staying longer would waste time they didn't have. Tess would still be here when everything was over. "I'm sorry," she said. "We've kept you from work all morning."

"Please don't worry. I wasn't going in until later, anyway." For the first time in hours, Tess looked uncertain. "Will you…I mean, I really don't have a right— But I'd like to know if you plan to contact your sister. Marley." She didn't give Quinn a chance to answer, rushing to add, "It's up to you, of course. I want to be ready when she, you know." Her smile was half wince.

"I do," Quinn admitted. "But I have a feeling she already knows."

Tess nodded with resignation and didn't ask Quinn why she thought so, which meant her mother had been content to live in denial until now.

"I can call Ned," Tess offered, "and see if he's available to have lunch with you. If you'd like. I know he'd want to see you."

"That would be nice, thank you." Quinn stood, Sam coming to his feet behind her, and reached to hug her mother. "It's been wonderful talking to you."

Tess held her hard. "Oh, for me, too. Will you be in town long?"

Not if she was going to confront her sister before any other goddess was harmed. Not that she could say so, but thinking about it reminded her that Tess was vulnerable.

"I'm not sure," she finally said. "I'll let you know. Be careful, okay?"

Tess frowned, her fingers tightening around Quinn's. "Of what?"

"Didn't you hear about the leech?" Hopefully that sounded neutral enough. She didn't want Tess to worry or ask questions that Quinn didn't want to answer.

"Oh." Her face cleared. "That. Don't worry. the Society will track him down. Everything will be fine."

That was a stupidly naive attitude. "Be careful," Quinn said again. "I'm sure he's charismatic and well-bred. Like Sam here."

Tess's trilling laugh tapered off as she crossed to the phone.

"You're probably right. And you're sweet to worry. I'll be careful."

It wasn't enough to reassure her, but Quinn didn't know what more she could do. They waited while Tess called Ned at work and arranged for him to meet them at a restaurant in downtown Fairfield. Tess remained in the doorway, waving as they got in the car and left.

"That took a long time," Nick griped as they turned onto the road. Quinn gave him quick directions to the center of town.

Sam leaned on the back of the seats. "If Marley has anything to do with the leech, her mother doesn't know it. She's kind of—" He broke off, shooting a look at Quinn.

"Naive," she agreed. "She thought I was there to meet her, so I didn't want to push too hard."

"What's your take on what she said about your sister?" Nick asked.

"She sounds…well, like she said, stubborn. Willful. Overly sympathetic to the fringe element."

"Do you think she sounds like the kind of woman who'd create a leech?" Nick asked.

Since Sam's jaw was close to Quinn's ear, she heard his teeth grind together. She knew he thought the answer was yes but didn't want to say it because she was related to Quinn. "From a neutral perspective? I'd think a woman who would disregard or dismiss the dangers of doing so would have to be stubborn and rebellious. So, yeah. Definitely the kind of woman who'd create a leech."

Nick raised his eyebrows at her. "And?"

"And what?"

"How do you feel about that?"

Quinn sighed. "I didn't even know she existed, and if she did this, created this *monster* who's hurting people I care about and taking apart a life I've built—" She stopped herself and continued more calmly, despite the anger roiling in her gut. "My reputation has been damaged, and I've put my work on hold." Not to mention the changes in her relationship with Nick, though it remained to be seen whether those could be considered damage or not. "I know no one forced me to investigate this, but even if I hadn't, it affected me. I'm pissed."

A Lexus pulled out in front of them, and Nick nosed the Charger into the narrowly marked space the other car had vacated. The big, silver-haired man who had to be her father already paced the walkway of the panel-fronted restaurant squeezed next to a tiny jewelry store. He peered down the street one way, then the other, then scanned the cars lining the curb. In a trench coat over a dark gray suit, he was exactly what Quinn expected after reading Sam's report and hearing Tess talk about him.

"He looks nervous," Nick observed, turning off the ignition.

"Wouldn't you be, seeing your daughter for the first time in over thirty years?" Sam responded. "Want us to bring you a doggie bag?" he teased.

Nick didn't joke back. "Fuck that. I'm coming in this time. I was going insane when you were in that house."

They all climbed out of the car and crossed the street. Ned focused on them as they approached, and his expression lightened.

"Quinn." He held his arms out to the sides, then enveloped her in a bear hug, sweeping her back to the last time she'd seen him. He'd done the same thing then. A little less heavy and a lot less well dressed, he'd smelled the same as he did now, and amazingly like her adoptive father. She blinked back foolish moisture and let him hold her at arm's length.

"You're beautiful. So beautiful. I knew you would be. And what's this?" He let go of her with his right hand to offer Sam a shake. "Two boyfriends?" He laughed heartily. Sam's chuckle was strained, and Nick didn't even bother to smile when Ned offered him his hand.

"No, sir, this is Sam Remington, my assistant, and Nick Jarrett. He's—"

"A protector." Her father's face went stern, but he shook Nick's hand nonetheless. "I'm familiar with the name."

"Oh. Good." Nick raised his eyebrows at Quinn as they passed him to enter the restaurant. She shrugged. She had no idea if that was good recognition or bad.

The hostess seated them and they ordered sodas before perusing the menu, making small talk until the server returned. Once she'd taken their orders, the conversation went much as it had with Tess.

But Quinn had a much different feel with her father. The man clearly suffered no regret or reservation. He talked openly about everything and offered details normal adopted kids might want but that Quinn hadn't thought of, like medical and family histories. She had cousins on his side of the family.

Those were all things she'd like to explore someday, but not now. The longer the afternoon wore on, the heavier the weight of awareness grew. She couldn't indulge in the reunion any longer. So during a break in the conversation, she said, "Can I ask you something, Dad?"

The "Dad" was calculated but surprisingly natural. It didn't feel like a betrayal of the man who'd raised her—he'd have encouraged it—and it put Ned even further at ease.

"Of course. You can ask me anything."

"How come Tess isn't more involved in the Society? I'm the board secretary, and I never saw her at meetings. We might have connected sooner if she had been."

His groomed silver brows came together above his nose.

"I can't say I know too much about that goddess stuff. I think maybe she didn't want it to overshadow my career."

A typical male-executive-type response. Quinn tamped down

annoyance on Tess's behalf. "What about Marley?"

"Oh, now, Marley is a different story!" His voice boomed around them. "She's a rebel, that girl. Learned everything she could from her mother and her teachers but didn't stick around long. Doesn't like to be told what to do, is her problem."

"Is it a problem?" Quinn asked, taking a bite of her excellent crab Alfredo.

"No, no, she's a good girl. Likes to do her thing and doesn't much care what others think about it. She runs an inn up in Maine—I'm sure Tess told you—but she probably didn't mention that Marley collects misfits."

Quinn stopped chewing, but because her mouth was full Sam was the one who asked what kind of misfits.

"You know, people who don't 'fit in' to normal society."

"Like goddesses?" Nick said.

Ned chuckled. "Some, but those who don't fit into mainstream goddessing, either. But all kinds of misfits. Male, female, flighty, fruity, anal-retentive to the point of obsession. Anyone who doesn't fit can find a place at Marley's inn." He set his fork and knife across each other on his plate and waved at the waitress to order coffee.

"How about a boyfriend?" Quinn asked.

"She wouldn't tell me. I don't have a great track record," he admitted with a sheepish smile. "I chased away all her high school beaux."

"I can see how you would be intimidating." Quinn laughed. "I can't help being curious about her life."

"Of course, of course. Actually," he said, pressing his finger across his lips, "now that I think about it, there was one guy last time we visited who seemed to hang around her a lot. More than any of the others. She didn't treat him like a boyfriend, exactly, but he sure seemed enamored of her." He gave a proud-father nod. "I wouldn't be surprised if he courted her."

He seemed kind of young to use such old-fashioned words, but maybe the corporate world had bred it into him.

"Do you remember his name?" Nick asked, and if Ned thought it an odd question, he didn't say so.

"Arthur or Anthony…no, something stranger. Archie, Andre—something like that. It began with A." He thanked the waitress for the coffees she set down beside him and Quinn—Sam had declined and Nick opted for a Samuel Adams. Then Ned frowned at Nick, and Quinn suspected the conversation was about to flip on them.

"You mind telling me what a notorious protector is doing with my daughter?"

"Notorious?" Nick laughed. "I don't know about that. I've always been Quinn's protector."

"Why does she need one? And why you?" He eyed Sam. "He looks capable enough."

Quinn only said, "I have a history."

"I see." The furrows in Ned's forehead deepened, but he remained focused on Nick. "Why should I trust you?"

Nick thumped his beer on the table. "There's no reason why you shouldn't."

"What other goddesses have you protected?"

"More than half of them." His tone had grown testy. "And there hasn't been a single one of them harmed in my fifteen years of protection."

"Impressive." But he didn't sound impressed. The waitress approached with the check and he reached out, but Nick intercepted it.

"I'll take it, thank you."

Quinn frowned at her father, unhappy with his attitude and not liking how close "notorious" was to "rogue."

"Why do you say Nick is notorious?"

He shook his head, all his earlier affability gone. "We've heard rumors."

"How? You said both Tess and Marley aren't involved with the Society."

Ned harrumphed and wouldn't look at her.

"Where would you have heard rumors about Nick?" she demanded.

Ned muttered and evaded, but in the face of three unwavering stares, he admitted he paid attention to things.

"My daughter is up there in the woods with god knows what kind of people. I want to know who does what in her world."

"Nick's not part of her world," Quinn pointed out.

Ned looked sheepish. "I have two daughters."

Quinn sat, uncertain what to say. Both her parents had been keeping tabs on her. Tess understood about her adoptive father. Ned knew about Nick. But they had never contacted her, never tried to form a relationship. It soured what had started as a pleasant reunion—and Quinn no longer wished to push it further. For the first time, she considered that their lack of contact reflected a flaw in them, not her.

As they made their way outside, Ned patted her shoulder, ignored Nick, and shook Sam's hand with his other one already in the air, flagging down a cab. The three of them stood on the sidewalk, watching his taxi drive away.

"I don't like him." Nick stalked across the street to his car.

Sam looked sympathetic but said, "I have to admit, I think you've been better off, Quinn." He followed Nick.

She waited until he was halfway across the street before following. She agreed with them but for some reason felt compelled to defend her family. That wouldn't make either of them change their minds, and the truth was…she would never know.

• • •

They were silent as they climbed into the car and buckled up. Quinn's positive feelings of a few hours ago were gone, leaving a sharper loneliness than usual.

Nick waited for a trolley on wheels to go past, then peeled out into traffic. "Where we goin'?"

Quinn sighed and let her head drop to the back of the seat. "Let's find a hotel for tonight. We can head to Maine tomorrow."

"Not a chance."

"Nick—"

"No, Quinn. There's something weird going on here, and we're not charging in blind."

The need to do so burned fiercely, but she knew better than to react without planning. "So what do you propose?"

He pulled into the parking lot of a Fairfield Inn. "I need to scout Marley's place first. Problem with doing that is leaving you alone. Daddy Warbucks had a point back there." He stared out the windshield for a couple of minutes, clearly lost in thought, before heaving a frustrated sigh. "I need to do whatever's going to keep you safest. Instinct tells me Marley's deeply involved in all this, and she's your sister." He looked at Quinn. "I don't suppose I can convince you to leave it alone at this point? Go back to the cabin?"

She smiled.

"Didn't think so. I can't be in two places at once." His eyes met Sam's in the rearview mirror. "You can protect her here. You've been doing my job three-quarters of the time anyway, but at a different level. And the moon's nearly full."

"Which will make her a more tempting target," Sam reminded him.

"And more badass. I never had to protect her when she was freeing women from their abusers. Only later, when she didn't have the power to use against them." He shifted to face the backseat. "You don't think you can do this?"

Sam's jaw tightened and his eyes blazed. "Of course I can." He leaned over the seat. "The local chapter of the Society is Chloe's chapter. I think there's a meeting in two days. Maybe she can take us. We can try to gather more information, see what everyone's saying about you two."

"That's a good idea," Nick agreed. "The leech would be stupid to go near Chloe's at this point. The heat's higher, even if to us the Society doesn't seem to be doing much. He's got to assume they're watching her. Be alert, though," he told Sam. "Whoever sent those guys to snatch Quinn aren't as high profile."

Quinn didn't want to let Nick go. It didn't make sense because he'd already been around far longer than she was used to. She knew how to say good-bye to him, for cripes sake. But it wasn't just that. She was afraid—not for herself, but for him.

For no good reason. When he said no one had ever been harmed on his watch, he didn't mean there hadn't been attempts. He was a powerful protector, and no matter what someone was trying to do to his reputation, he was the least vulnerable of the three of them right now. Still, dread flared at the thought of him driving alone to Maine, where the culprit in all of this could be.

Nick's hand landed reassuringly on her thigh. Quinn looked at him, and the intensity of his gaze locked her in place.

Sam looked back and forth between them. "I'll go register us for a suite," he said, climbing out of the car and striding into the lobby office without looking back.

Quinn put her hand on Nick's. "Be careful." The dread intensified into nausea.

"I will." He tilted toward her, hesitated, then leaned over the rest of the way. His lips met hers with warmth and tenderness, a far cry from his last kiss. Quinn whimpered, a sound she couldn't ever remember making before. He didn't leave it at that but moved his mouth, tasting her, telling her what he still wouldn't say, and her head spun. She felt like she was falling, but the world righted when he straightened. "I'll call you."

Moments later, after unloading Quinn's and Sam's things from the Charger, Nick was gone.

• • •

Their room was light and airy, a welcome contrast to the dim heaviness of the cabin and all the cheap, ugly motels they'd stayed in over the last few weeks. Once they were situated, Quinn needed things to be normal. She could still taste Nick's mouth, smell his skin and leather jacket, recall the sensation of falling that was far too symbolic.

She hooked up her computer to the wireless network to download her e-mail. Sam set up his own laptop on the opposite side of the wide desk. Despite the decor, it was enough like their work routine to let her relax a little. She focused on the mundane routine of the Internet. Most of her mail was spam or short check-ins from Under the Moon's staff. She skimmed vendor solicitations, a Liquor Control Commission newsletter, and a couple of client inquiries. Then one return address made her perk up.

"We might not have to track Chloe down." She clicked on the message. "She e-mailed…" She trailed off when she saw the content.

> *Quinn:*
> *I spoke to Tanda, who said you might be heading my way. I'd love to see you—everyone seems to be avoiding me. And I have to tell you something weird that happened, but only in person. Call me.*
> *Chloe*

She reread it aloud to Sam, who whistled. "Better call her."

Quinn already had her phone out. "She gave me a new

number. The leech probably took her phone, too." She programmed the number into her phone and hit send. It was late afternoon, but the call went straight to voice mail.

"Chloe, it's Quinn. I just got your e-mail." Which she realized had been sent two days ago. "I'm in Connecticut now. I can be there in less than two hours. Call me back."

"I wonder what she has to tell you," Sam said. "'Weird' makes me nervous."

"Me, too." She scrolled through to make sure she didn't have any missed calls on her phone. "I hope she gets the message. I'm worried about her."

"I'm worried about you," he came back quietly.

Quinn stood, leaving the phone on the desk. Any worry was unproductive. "I'm no more vulnerable than all the other goddesses and less than many, with both you guys on me all the time."

"When we're not, things happen," Sam pointed out.

Quinn had to smile at that. "You're not wrong." She felt much better having both of them around until this thing was over. She had power, confidence, and the ability to take care of herself. But Tanda and Chloe had all those things, too, and it hadn't protected them.

She turned and sat on the sofa, thinking. "Tanda said it was raining the day the leech came, right?"

"Yeah."

"That makes sense, because he can't leech power that isn't there. But her power is much less predictable than a lot of ours. Why didn't she have a regular protector?"

"I asked Nick. He doesn't know much about anyone else's schedule, unless a goddess is going to be left uncovered because of conflicts or something. There aren't enough of them to assign one fulltime to any particular goddess, though. The ones whose power comes and goes most frequently and unpredictably don't always have a protector when they should—like on a sunny day in Oregon. Too unpredictable, and without evidence of a threat, she might never get one."

"And Chloe lives by the ocean, so she'd only need a protector if she traveled."

"Right."

"Same with Jennifer, with the river."

"As far as we can tell, no one with a protector has been leeched, and vice versa. Where are you going with this?"

She didn't know. It seemed like it should connect to the accusation that Nick had gone rogue, but how? Nick kept insisting it wasn't important, but it had to be. And there had to be *someone* out there who could fill in the blanks. It frustrated her not to have anyone in the Protectorate she could ask but Nick.

Then she remembered. "Toss me my cell phone, will you?"

Sam obliged, and Quinn paged through the phone book. Somewhere in here was the name and number of a guy Nick had told her to contact if she ever couldn't reach him. There. John W. She paused to consider what she was going to say, then hit send.

"Yo."

"John?"

"Yeah, who's this?"

"Quinn Caldwell. I'm one of Nick Jarrett's—"

"Yeah, yeah, one of his goddesses. I know who you are." He sounded cold, and she cringed.

"Nick gave me your number a long time ago, and I thought maybe you could help me."

"With what? Nick hurt?"

"No. I hope not." There hadn't been time for him to get hurt. But the foreboding deepened. "Are you with the Protectorate?"

"You could say that."

"I'm trying to get a handle on this rogue thing. He's obviously not rogue, and I want to know why someone would say he is."

"What are you talking about?"

Oh, shit. She thought Nick had talked to them about this, or at least that other protectors would have heard about the accusation. She thought fast. "I just met my birth father," she tried. "My birth mother is a goddess, but she's not really part of the Society. But my father called Nick 'notorious' and was pretty hostile to him. I don't know why he'd think such things."

Whatever John assumed her subtext was, it seemed to ease his suspicions.

"Nick's the best protector there is. You should know that, he's been yours for, what, fifteen years?"

"I know, but in all that time, nothing's ever happened. He sits in my bar and drinks beer."

John laughed. "You only know about what you saw. His presence is exactly why nothing happened. Goddesses like you are constant targets, Quinn. He's saved you and a dozen others more times than I can count on both my hands and feet. Twice."

She'd had no idea, and it floored her to realize it. One day, she'd make Nick tell her about them. "So why would someone try to malign his reputation now?"

"Dunno. They'd have a hard time doing it."

"Could it be a distraction?"

"Not a good one, since I don't know what you're talking about. The best way to distract Nick from his job would be to go through me."

"Would saying he'd gone rogue do that?"

His voice tightened. "It would. I wouldn't believe it, but I'd sure as hell recall him to find out why they were saying it. That's the second time you've used that word. Why?"

If Nick hadn't told his boss about it, she wasn't going to. "My father's reaction, that's all. I think he was being protective, like he thinks Nick's my boyfriend or something." Across the room, Sam snorted but didn't look up. "Thanks, John."

"Let me talk to Nick."

Shit again. "He's not available. I'll have him call you." She hung up before he could argue with her and bent, pressing the phone to her forehead. God, she hoped that hadn't been stupid. If John did a little asking around, he'd find out she lied about the rogue thing, and he'd recall Nick, and…she felt sick.

"Well?"

She sat up and sighed. "If someone's trying to get Nick off the job or blamed for the leechings, they're doing a poor job of it."

"Unless they're just getting started. We need—"

Quinn's phone rang. She looked at the display. "It's Chloe."

"That's what we need." He smiled, but it was tense.

"Hello?"

"Hey, it's Chloe!" Her voice was full of relief and excitement.

"It's so good to hear from you! I tried to call but—"

"I know, Tanda told me. Asshole took my phone, too. The Society's monitoring calls, but I don't think they're getting anywhere." She laughed, a brittle sound. "So, what are you doing? Do you have time to come see me? Or I could come to you."

The last part sounded reluctant, so Quinn hurried to reassure her. "No, we'll come there. I have plenty of time. Tomorrow morning?"

"Perfect. I know it's silly." She paused, and Quinn could hear the rush of waves in the background. "It doesn't work for me now, but I don't want to leave the shore."

"It's not silly. It makes perfect sense." Even during the new moon, Quinn sensed it rising. Even when she was close to normal, she never felt like anything but a goddess. The idea of losing that froze her insides. It would be the worst kind of torture. "I wouldn't dream of taking you away from it."

"I'll see you tomorrow, then."

"Great! Hey, is it okay if I bring Sam?"

"Of course. He's always good for my ego. Thanks, Quinn."

"You're welcome."

She quirked a smile at Sam when she'd hung up. "You'll need to lay on the charm tomorrow. She can't wait to see you."

He didn't smile back. When he closed the lid of his laptop and pushed his chair back to lean over his knees, she braced herself.

"What's between you and Nick?"

Nothing stuck in her throat. She swallowed hard, then admitted, "I don't know."

He dropped his head. Quinn bit her lip, unsure what to say or why he was asking. She couldn't measure the silence and like a fool, filled it.

"He's always been my friend. My security. He somehow knows me without explanation, understands what I need and what I don't. He's fiercely loyal and defensive." She stopped, struck by the realization that she could also be describing Sam.

He raised his head when she didn't continue. "What happened that night?"

"When I was abducted?"

He nodded, and she studied him, again wondering why he was asking. But the pain she'd seen behind his eyes in the first couple of months after she stopped recharging with him wasn't apparent now.

"Um…let's say he was…upset."

Sam's brows lowered. "He didn't hit you, did he?"

"No! God, no!" She laughed and passed a hand across her face. She never talked about Nick like this. "We…reacted… unprofessionally."

He rose to his feet and stood inches away. Confused, Quinn didn't move. He slid his hand along the side of her jaw, cupping her face and neck and stroking his thumb across her cheek.

"You never kissed me, Quinn."

"I know," she whispered. "I never kissed anyone else, either."

"Because of the intimacy." It wasn't a question, and it wasn't wrong. "Is it more than you can give?"

"No. It's more than I can take."

Sam nodded. "But you kissed Nick."

Quinn opened her mouth but had no response. He must have seen them from the hotel office. Sam framed her face in both his palms, tilted his head, and lowered his mouth to hers. The kiss was tender, loving, but nothing like Nick's kiss earlier. A tear slipped out from beneath her lashes and slid down her cheek, then along Sam's finger. A matching tear leaked from the other side. Sam released her mouth but not her face, and his eyes shone. Not with need or competition, but with regret.

"I love you, Quinn."

She buried her face in his chest. "I love you, too, Sam," she whispered, knowing he'd understand how she meant it. Sam's arms came around her, comforting. Pure friendship. Quinn's heart thrummed with her relief.

"Don't give up on him," he said. "It's not the same. He loves you, too."

Quinn backed up and palmed away the moisture on her cheeks. Nick's story wasn't hers to tell, but despite his recent lapses, she didn't believe anything was going to change.

"I don't deserve you," she said instead.

He smiled crookedly. "Nope. But you do deserve to be happy." He sat back at his computer. "Let's talk about Chloe."

Later that night, as Quinn lay in bed staring at the ceiling, her entire being seemed lighter. Freed from the burden of guilt over rejecting Sam, yes, but also hopeful. Which was stupid, because nothing had *really* changed for her and Nick.

They'd never discussed the soul-deep connection they'd made

the first time Nick was assigned to her or the friendship that had deepened with every new moon. The heat between them had always been there, too, but never acknowledged or acted upon. The strength of his duty had always been apparent. But Quinn had yearned for Nick like a fish yearned for water. When she needed to recharge she chose men who reminded her of him, and the encounters always ended in disappointment. Sometimes, when she chose unwisely, they ended in something worse. Nick never knew.

One night about ten years ago, Quinn had built up the courage to make a move. Tension in the bar had been high, and a fight broke out at closing time. It was one of the few times she witnessed Nick in action. She wasn't afraid to carry a bat into the fray, but Nick had beaten her there, landing enough blows to break it up and haul the main offenders outside. Then he'd cleared the bar and returned to her, fired up and eyes blazing with the strength of emotions neither one of them had ever acknowledged out loud.

And Quinn had taken a chance. She dragged him behind the bar and kissed him. He kissed her back at first, his hands tightening on her hips hard enough to leave bruises and ignite five years of banked passion. But when Quinn tried to take it further, he pushed her away. She stumbled against the liquor shelves hard enough to rattle the bottles. He flinched, but Quinn ignored the flare of pain, both where the hard shelves dug into her back and in her rejected heart.

"It can't happen, Quinn." His tone was raw and harsh, but she believed it was because he *wanted* it to happen, not because he didn't.

"No other man measures up to you, Nick." She stepped forward, and this time, when he lurched back, her heart broke open and bled. She didn't move again, but she couldn't stop talking. Couldn't give up, though bitterness coated her tongue and her words. "Believe me, I've tried to find one."

He flinched again, to her gratification.

"I want you as more than this. I want to be more than a job to you."

"You are," he growled. "But I don't have a job, Quinn, I have a duty, a responsibility that goes far deeper than a little bit of lust."

Quinn gasped and backed away, raising a hand to stop him from saying any more. But he didn't stop.

"You're important to me. It would kill me to leave you to another protector."

She sobbed a laugh. "Don't say stuff like that. You're making this worse." She wished he'd come to her, hold her, reassure her somehow. But he either didn't trust himself or didn't trust her, so he stayed where he was.

"I'm being as honest as I can be. You—" He shoved a hand through his hair and gritted his teeth enough to make his jaw muscles flex. "You are incredible. The stuff you do, the people you help—you validate every choice I've made. Which puts me in an impossible situation. I can't do it, Quinn. I'm sorry."

It was the apology that hammered home the nails of his words. No more harshness, no raw pain, just conviction. And that was it.

Quinn hadn't bothered trying to convince him that twelve weeks a year was better than nothing, or that she'd never find a man she could have a normal life with. She suspected Nick had hoped she'd find it with Sam when he came to work for her, and maybe at first she'd thought that, too. Instead she'd used him and risked the best friendship she'd ever had.

She rolled over and watched her ivory curtain go from glowing red to glowing green as the stoplight outside changed. A lone car drove up the road, engine whining slightly when the automatic transmission changed gears. She remembered listening to cars outside her apartment even when Nick wasn't expected, hoping to hear the familiar purr. She didn't know when that had changed.

Maybe soon after she hired Sam.

Who had just told her not to give up on Nick, even as he finally gave up on her. Damn both of them for making her hope, anyway, after a decade of pining silently. No. Forget hope. Forget kisses and crumbling walls and the sense that freedom and love were attainable. No matter what, it wouldn't happen.

She couldn't handle that kind of pain again.

Chapter Ten

While our abilities are generally accompanied by compassion and wisdom, goddesses are as human as anyone else. Jealousies, rivalries, and split loyalties are all threats to the balanced dynamic of the Society. However, the truest friendships can also be formed between members, and these often begin at chapter meetings.

— The Society for Goddess Education and Defense,
Special Session on Relationships

Sam, missing his Camaro, insisted on renting a sports car, then complained that men who drove late-model Mustangs were pussies.

"You're the one who didn't want another sedan," Quinn said.

"This is a chick car."

"They didn't have Camaros."

He shot her a pitying look. "Like a modern Camaro compares to my '84, anyway. But that's not the point."

"What is the point?"

He set his jaw and looked sullen for the next thirty miles.

Chloe lived in a small cottage on stilts right on the beach near Westerly, Rhode Island. Her little place was crammed between two larger homes but set closer to the water than most of the houses on the street. The ten-foot yard held wild-looking rosebushes and sea grass, and a crushed-shell path led from the rocky driveway to the steps up to the porch.

Sam parked behind the Prius that was under the building, and Quinn got out and strode toward the steps, pausing to inhale the deliciousness of the salt air. The temperature was still mild for November, a light breeze off the water complementing the hazy sunlight. The rolling rhythm of the waves drew Quinn past the cottage and down onto the sand. The moon wouldn't rise until afternoon, but its tug on the tide echoed in her blood. Today her abilities would be meager, but maybe the energy between moon and ocean would amplify them.

"Quinn?"

She turned. Chloe stood on the cottage's wraparound porch, shading her eyes against the still-low sun. Quinn smiled and waved, her heart contracting at Chloe's eyes. Even from this distance, the color was abnormal, bleached. An indicator of her loss that would be difficult to hide.

Chloe grinned and ran down a second set of stairs to the sand, hurrying to meet Quinn in a hug.

"It's so good to see you!" Chloe tilted Quinn side-to-side, squeezing. She seemed much more chipper and calm than Tanda had. If it weren't for her abnormally light gray eyes, Quinn wouldn't know anything had happened to her.

Chloe let go and tucked her arm through Quinn's elbow. "Where's Sam?"

"Probably standing at your front door." As she spoke he appeared around the side of the cottage. He wore jeans and a chocolate-colored V-neck sweater over a white T-shirt and looked very J. Crew with his hair blowing in the breeze off the water.

"Yum," Chloe said, and Quinn laughed.

"Quite."

"C'mon. I have breakfast all ready."

Visiting Chloe was far different from visiting Tanda. Tanda

was refined and serious and had still been grieving the loss of her goddess power. Chloe, however, was often described as "kooky," and her way of dealing with her loss fit the description.

The first thing Quinn saw when she walked into the kitchen was a big framed needlepoint sampler that said, "Once a Goddess, Always a Goddess...Unless You Date Leeches." She didn't know whether to laugh or cry. "You were dating the leech?" she asked, though Holly had already told her she was.

"Yep." Chloe pointed at herself. "Idiot."

"Was he dating all of you?" Sam asked, sounding incredulous.

Chloe raised her head. "All of us?" Her voice quavered, and Sam looked abashed.

"I'm sorry. I guess you didn't hear about the others."

Blinking fast, as if against tears, Chloe shook her head. "No, I haven't been in touch with many people. But he traveled a lot, so it's not surprising." She smiled when Sam took a basket of muffins from her to set on the table. "He wasn't dating Tanda. She had a boyfriend. The asshole," she added, already back to her normal demeanor. "Would make sense for *my* asshole to cozy up to whomever he wanted to steal from, though."

"Okay, right, I forgot that." Sam poured juice and laid napkins on the table, while Chloe removed warm croissants from the oven and butter from the refrigerator. Quinn stood back, knowing she'd just get in the way of their dance if she tried to help. Chloe basked in having someone to nurture, as well as Sam's solicitous attention.

"Chloe, I'm sorry," she began, but Chloe waved a hand at her.

"For what?"

She obviously meant it as a dismissal, but Quinn explained anyway. "For getting all wrapped up in myself and not trying harder to reach you."

Chloe rolled her eyes. "Oh, for goodness sake. You already apologized, and you know he took my phone. It's not like you were hanging in your bar. I know you." She eyed her out of the corner of her eye. "I know Nick, too. I expected him to be hanging all over you. Doesn't he think you're a target?"

Quinn wasn't sure how to respond. Sam helped her out.

"We do think she is. I'm the hanger today, while Nick checks out a couple of leads."

"Ahhhhhhh." Chloe nodded. She pulled the kettle off the stove and set it on a trivet, clearly done with the topic. Quinn's determination to catch this guy took on a new dimension. Not just protecting herself and the other unleeched goddesses, but getting justice for her friends.

"Tea, Quinn? Or coffee?"

"Tea sounds good, thanks."

"I'll take coffee." Sam held Quinn's chair for her, then waited to seat Chloe as well. "This is fabulous, Chloe, thanks."

"Oh, it's nothing. Since I can't do my usual stuff"—she waved a hand at the windows looking out on the ocean—"I've been spending a lot of time baking."

Quinn took a bite of an orange muffin. "Wow." It melted in her mouth, filling it with a blend of tang and spice. "This is incredible."

"Good!" She beamed some more. "I'm going to open a bakery. I always wanted to, but the goddess stuff took so much of my time, I couldn't. So maybe it's a blessing my power was taken from me."

"What did you do?" Sam asked, tearing a croissant.

"The usual. You know, a lot of the same stuff Quinn and everyone else does. Finding lost things, diagnosing problems. I wasn't very good at healing, but I could make adjustments. Like if a broken bone didn't fuse right, or if someone had a birth defect. It's a never-ending stream." She scooped some sugar into her teacup and stirred it vigorously.

"I think you're amazing," Quinn said. "Your attitude is very healthy." She wouldn't be so positive if it happened to her.

"Oh, no, it's not!" Chloe hooted. "I'm sick of helping everyone else all the time. I want to be selfish for a while. Don't you ever feel that way?"

"She's plenty selfish," Sam said. Quinn smacked him on the arm with the back of her hand.

"It's not always about selflessness," she told Chloe. "Sometimes it's fun. There was a woman in Columbus a couple of years back. A guy she dated once and refused to sleep with wouldn't leave her alone. She hired me to put the fear of goddesses into him."

"That was one of the fun ones," Sam agreed. "You made his Eminem CDs play Neil Diamond."

Chloe laughed in delight. "No way!"

"Not exactly," Quinn corrected. "I twisted the path in his CD player so it played a different disk than he thought he was playing."

"She also turned his shower water blue, which turned him blue. Then she set his dog on fire."

Chloe gasped.

"Don't worry," Quinn said. "It didn't touch the dog. But since the dog sounded like he was roaring something like, 'Leave her alone or the wrath of Khan will crash upon you!' it was quite effective."

"I didn't know you were so much fun!" Chloe reached to spear a slice of pineapple from a plate. "Tell me more."

They swapped stories for hours, laughing until they cried. At dinnertime, they ordered pizza for a late lunch and sat in chaise recliners on the back porch to wait for the delivery.

"In your e-mail, you said something weird happened," Quinn reminded Chloe. It had been in the back of her mind all day, but they'd both needed the interlude, and she'd instinctively known asking would ruin their happiness, however momentary it was. She was sorry to bring it up now, especially when a frown replaced Chloe's relaxed expression.

"A security team came to interview me after I was leeched. A few times. I guess as they compiled more information, there was always more to find."

"That's logical," Quinn said.

"Yeah, but the last time, a few days ago, they sent one guy to talk to me, and he asked a bunch of questions about *you*."

Quinn wished she felt more surprised. The dread their interlude had held at bay came creeping back.

"What kind of questions?" Sam asked.

"Weird ones. Like, how long have I known you, have I met your family, do you have a boyfriend, stuff that made no sense."

Sam looked grim. Quinn figured he was thinking the same thing she was—the Society's suspicions went beyond "family ties." It sounded like they thought she'd created the leech. Had they sent the security team after her yet? They'd been on the road, and therefore hard to find. She had to get to Maine before they caught up to her. She checked her watch, a little shocked at how many hours had passed. They hadn't heard from Nick all day.

A horn honked out front, and Sam got up. "I'll go pay the driver."

"You're so lucky," Chloe said as he rounded the corner of the house. "He's so devoted to you."

Quinn nodded sadly. "I know."

Chloe leaned forward and put her hand on Quinn's arm. "Sweetie, I'm sorry. I said something wrong, didn't I?"

"Not really. It's true."

"But there's Nick."

Quinn sighed. "There's always Nick."

"Always, and yet never."

"That about sums it up." She stared out over the water. Amazing how she'd thought her feelings for Nick were buried so deep no one else could ever have discerned them, yet everyone she talked to nailed their relationship in a few words.

"You know, not to put any blame on you or anything, but being jealous of you and Nick was part of the reason I hooked up with Adrian in the first place."

Quinn jolted with recognition. "Adrian?" Ned said Marley was with a guy whose name began with an A.

"The leech. I have no idea if that's his real name."

"And you were—"

"Jealous of you and Nick, yeah."

Quinn stifled a quick burst of resentment. From inside, she couldn't see what there was to be jealous of. But someone on the outside might only see the friendship and assume it was more. And as complicated and painful as things were right now, it beat being betrayed and damaged by someone you cared about.

"I saw you at the last board meeting," Chloe continued. "July, right, in Chicago? It was new moon, and he was with you. And you guys just *work* together. I was feeling lonely and spiteful and when this guy came up to me in the hotel bar—"

"Wait. You met him in the bar?" Quinn sat up, her feet hitting the floor. "At a Society board meeting?"

"Yeah. I saw him about once every two weeks after that, for a couple of days. He said he had to travel for work."

Sam's heavy tread sounded from the side of the cottage. As soon as he appeared, Quinn said, "Did you hear that?"

"Part of it." He set the two boxes on the small, square plastic table between the two chaises. "Paper plates?"

"Cabinet next to the fridge, with the napkins. Thanks, doll." Chloe flipped the first lid and the spicy aroma wafted out. She pried out a wedge of the broccoli-chicken pizza.

Sam went inside and came out a minute later with all the supplies. "So he was scouting at the meeting," he said to Quinn. "I wonder if he's been to other meetings. Chapters, maybe."

"Might have been. Did you see him with anyone else?"

Chloe shrugged. "Nope. He was alone in the bar. Until he came up to my room with me." She grinned. "It was a fun night."

"But not worth what came later," Sam said. "Was it?"

"Of course not, but I try not to think about that. I mean, you can only call yourself stupid for so long before it becomes true. I made a mistake, but I couldn't have known. Even if I hadn't slept with him that night, it would have happened." She lifted the slice of pizza to drop dangling cheese into her mouth.

Quinn ignored the pizza, energized by the new information. This was more than they'd had before. A name, a process. But not enough to help them find the leech, never mind stop him. Not even enough to confirm the connection to her family. "Chloe, do you know Marley Canton? She's in Maine."

Chloe shook her head. "I knew a Tess Canton. She came to the chapter meetings for a while. Not in years, though. Why?"

Sam's brow puckered, but Quinn didn't see why she shouldn't tell her. It was going to come out eventually.

"She's my sister. Marley is."

Chloe gaped. "No way!"

"Yeah. I didn't know until a couple of weeks ago."

"Wow. What a time to find out." She dropped her crust onto a plate. "Is Marley involved? Is that why security asked all those questions?"

Quinn reached for a piece of pizza. "Probably." *Hopefully.* Quinn being a suspect didn't seem to cross Chloe's mind. "I wonder if Marley knew the—knew Adrian."

Chloe shrugged. "I have no idea. But obviously, I've been clueless all across the board."

They sat in silence for a few minutes as they ate, not wanting to pursue the subject anymore. After a little while, the mood lightened, and they enjoyed the unusually mild weather and friendly conversation until four o'clock. The moon had reached the horizon, and the faint buzz that accompanied its power vibrated deep inside Quinn, familiar and comforting.

But then a blade of unease sharpened into fear for an instant before fading. All the hairs on her body rose. She shivered.

Nick.

She reached for her cell phone, mindless of the fact that Chloe was midsentence. Sam, who'd been using Chloe's wireless connection to go online, leaned toward Quinn.

"What's the matter?" he murmured.

"I don't know," she whispered back. "Can you call Nick, please? Check in with him?"

"Sure." He stood and set the computer on the chair, then walked several feet away to make the call.

"So you should come to the chapter meeting!" Chloe said, not paying any attention to their exchange. "Since you missed the big one last week. Everyone will be glad to see you."

Quinn wasn't so sure about that. "What happened at the Society meeting?" *Did anyone talk about me?* But she hadn't told Chloe that the board cut her off, and Chloe hadn't mentioned it, so she didn't voice the question out loud.

"The usual, only more boring."

"They didn't talk about the leech?" Quinn couldn't believe that.

"Oh, sure. The board gave their official statement and some security tips, handed around the sketch of Adrian, weak as it was. His charisma doesn't come through. But they said the security team was handling it, anyone with information should call the office, blah blah blah. If they heard anyone talking about it, they forced the conversation to something else."

"That's unbelievable." Quinn shook her head. "Why are they being so stupid?"

Chloe shrugged. "I don't think they're being stupid. I think they're trying to keep people from panicking. Can you imagine if we started seeing the leech in any random guy? PR nightmare, not to mention maybe people getting hurt."

"I guess you're right," Quinn said. "Hey, do you have a copy of that sketch? Or any pictures?"

"Nope, sorry. We never took photos, and there was no reason for me to get a copy of the sketch."

Sam returned to his chair and shook his head at Quinn. He looked worried. Panic squeezed Quinn's lungs. *It might not be anything. His battery died again. I told him to get another charger. Or maybe he turned the phone off so it wouldn't ring and give him away or something.*

Or something. Her attempt to stave off the panic was only partially successful, but what the hell could she do about it now? Nick was hundreds of miles away.

"I'd love to come to the meeting with you," she told Chloe, forcing herself back to the subject. "Is there a nearby hotel you recommend?"

"You can stay here. I only have the sofa bed, but it's just one night. You don't mind, do you, Sam?"

Quinn cringed. The rising moon only provided a trickle of power, and if she didn't use it, she should be able to avoid the moon lust for one night. It would be disastrous to have to deal with it now, after their conversation last night.

She managed to stop herself from building a barrier of pillows down the center of the barely double-size sofa bed later that night. She had already claimed a side and was in bed with the lights off when Sam joined her.

"How many times did you try to reach Nick?" she asked him.

"Four."

"I tried three. It's not like him, Sam."

"I know. And the last time…" He lowered his voice. "The last time I called, a minute ago, it picked up. There was static and some yelling before it cut off."

Panic fluttered through her again. "What kind of yelling?"

Sam slid his long legs under the covers and sighed when his feet poked out the bottom. He hitched himself higher against the back of the sofa and adjusted the pillows. "Could have been radio yelling. Maybe one of those vintage rock cassette tapes he has."

"Or?"

"Or it could have been real people. I didn't hear enough to know if it was Nick."

She sat up. "We have to go after him."

"Quinn, he'd kill me if I let you anywhere near there if we think there's trouble."

"I know, but we can't leave him." She swung her legs over the side of the bed and dug underneath for her shoes. "We shouldn't have let it go this long."

Sam caught her elbow and tugged her upright. "It hasn't been long. It takes hours to get to Maine, and I think Marley's place is rural. Maybe he can't get a signal again."

She was tired of that excuse. For all the bragging of the various mobile phone companies, none of them seemed to have the coverage they needed, when they needed it most.

"He's probably fine," he tried, but she could tell he wasn't certain of it himself. "I'm supposed to keep you safe. Here is safe. There—we don't know."

"All the more reason to go after him." She pulled her arm away and got down on the floor. Where the hell was her shoe? She spotted it, an arm's length under the bed, and caught it as Sam climbed off the bed and pulled her to her feet.

"No one has gotten the better of Nick Jarrett in fifteen years," he reminded her, rubbing his hands up and down her arms as if to soothe, but too briskly to have the intended effect. "What if the yelling was nothing?"

"What if it's not?"

"What if it's a trap?"

His earnestness penetrated. He was trying to protect her, like Nick had demanded, and he was right. If it were a trap, running into it would hasten any harm that could come to Nick. Her brain started working rationally again. "Someone could have taken Nick's phone."

Sam's hands relaxed their grip. "Right. There are a hundred things it could be."

Sighing, she dropped back onto the bed. "I don't know what to do."

"Sleep." He sat beside her. "If he hasn't called by morning, I'll drive up there while you're at the meeting. You'll have more power tomorrow and will be around a dozen goddesses. This guy would have to be insane to show up there. Plus, you might get some information. You've been cut off for weeks. We don't know what else is going on."

"Morning is too far away." But Sam had convinced her, so she lay back down with another sigh. Sam slid under the sheets next to her, and his hand found hers in the dark, his thumb stroking over the back of her knuckles before he let her go and rolled over.

He snored softly a few minutes later, but Quinn couldn't shut off her brain. She forced it to work through possible scenarios at the meeting, who would be there, how they'd act toward her. When she started to drift off, she caught herself listening for the cell phone, sure that despite its ear-shattering volume, she wouldn't hear it.

She finally succumbed and managed three hours and forty-two minutes of sleep before waking to find Sam watching her, his light brown eyes clear and wide awake.

"Morning," he said.

"Hi." She covered a yawn with her hand. "Phone didn't ring. Did it?"

"No."

"What time is it?"

Sam gave her a look. He knew she knew what time it was. "Six."

"And you're still here?" With a groan she pushed upright and swung her legs over the side of the bed.

"You know Nick will kill me for leaving you," he said.

Quinn wanted to cry. Nothing mattered if something had happened to Nick. "Then we'll both go."

He sighed. "No, I'm out the door in ten minutes. I didn't want to leave without talking to you, but you didn't sleep well so I didn't want to wake you, either."

She looked over her shoulder. "How do you know I didn't sleep well? You were snoring all night."

"I always know, Quinn. How long?"

She ignored the question and headed for the bathroom. When she came out Sam stood by the door, dressed in a checked button-down shirt and jeans, his duffel slung over his shoulder. Humming and water running in the kitchen told her Chloe was awake, too.

"Call me, okay? No matter what you find. In fact, check in every two hours or I'm coming after you."

"Don't worry." He pinched her chin and gave a reassuring smile. "It'll be fine."

She didn't like that her mental response was "Famous last words."

• • •

Chloe cornered Quinn by the beverage table at the back of the meeting room. "What's wrong?"

The windowless room with its low drop ceiling closed in around Quinn. She stepped to the side to let a few other women get to the coffee urn. "It's been six hours since I heard from Sam."

"Oh."

She twisted the top off a bottle of water so hard it went flying. She didn't bother chasing it, despite the scolding look someone threw at her. "I haven't paid attention to a single thing that's been said since lunch. I'd have been on the road four hours ago if I had a car and some idea of where I was going."

"Quinn?"

She faced the young woman who'd appeared at her shoulder and bit back her irritation. "Yes?"

"I'm sorry to interrupt. I wanted to say I'm sorry."

"For?"

"For your loss."

Quinn's breath left her in a whoosh. Her heart paused, then thudded so hard it cramped. Her vision went dark. Then she inhaled deeply and forced her vision clear.

"I'm not sure what you mean," she managed to say.

"Um…at the Society meeting last week, the board said you were unable to attend because of a death in the family."

Quinn spun to Chloe, who spread her arms. "I didn't hear that."

Fed up, Quinn said, "Thank you, but there was no death in my family. That was the board's excuse for pushing me out of the loop on the leech." She stopped short of saying they suspected her. She didn't know that they did, and she didn't want to set *everyone* against her.

The young woman gasped. "Leech?"

"You heard about me but not about the leech?" Her tension overrode her manners. "There's a man out there leeching goddesses. Including Chloe, in case you didn't know of your chaptermate's tragedy." She looked around her. The six or seven goddesses in the room had frozen and now all stared at her. The young woman backed up until another put her arm around her shoulders and murmured into her ear.

"I get not wanting to cause a panic," Quinn continued, unable to help herself, "but every goddess is in danger until this guy is caught, and as far as I can tell, no one is working very hard to do that."

Most of the other goddesses had returned to the room. Some nodded, some frowned, and a couple who had never liked Quinn sneered. Her chest heaved with every breath, but she pulled herself back together. None of these people was responsible for what was happening.

"I'm sorry," she told the young woman. "That's not your fault. I appreciate your condolences, I do."

One of the sneering women muttered, "Who let the dog out without her leash?" Her friend laughed, and Quinn's anger, which hadn't receded very far, flared again.

"What's that supposed to mean?"

The snide-looking goddess didn't pretend she hadn't spoken. She looked around exaggeratedly. "You're here alone. No big strong man tagging along to keep you in check or bring you water. It must be so hard for you. Where's your 'assistant'?" She and her friend snickered. "Did he find someone more powerful? Or maybe he's leeching—"

Quinn didn't think. She snapped her fingers, and the cupcake in the woman's hand burst into flames and turned to ash. Another snap, and the bottle of juice she held shattered—no matter that it was plastic—and pink liquid cascaded over her white shirt. The woman gaped at Quinn, as did all the other watchers. Shame pierced her anger but didn't abate it. Sam could be hurt or dead while he tried to save these people, and they dared to *accuse* him? Behind the anger, a new fear flared. If the Society suspected her of creating the leech, maybe they did suspect Sam of being the leech.

She glared, her hand up, looking for an excuse to do more than mess up a nice shirt. She was tired of hiding, discreetly digging for information.

"Quinn Caldwell!" The president of the chapter pushed through the group. "What the hell are you doing?"

Quinn opened her mouth to retort but her cell phone rang, and suddenly nothing else mattered.

"Forget it. I'm leaving. Thank you for your hospitality." She snapped open the phone and stalked out into the hall of the community building. "Hello!"

"Quinn, it's me."

"Sam." Relief cascaded through her, and her knees buckled. She stopped to lean against the wall.

"I'm sorry I haven't called. I couldn't. Signal has been spotty up here."

But that wasn't the only reason. She could tell. "What's wrong? Are you okay?"

"I'm fine."

Her lungs compressed again, and she couldn't get any air out to talk. Sam didn't need her to ask, though.

"It's Nick. He's been shot."

CHAPTER ELEVEN

Historically, the Society deemed it wise to hide the abilities of our members from the general public. Though full secrecy is not practical or desired in modern society, caution should rule all goddess-related activities. In addition, interaction with non-goddess authorities is to be considered only under extreme circumstances, when all other options are exhausted.

—The Society for Goddess Education and Defense,
Public Relations Handbook

"I need to borrow your car." Quinn didn't wait for Chloe, who'd followed her into the hall, to answer. "Please," she added, but only because autopilot told her to. She strode down the hall, Chloe running to keep up with Quinn's longer legs and desperation.

"What's going on?"

"Nick's been shot, and it's serious."

"I'll come with you," Chloe said immediately, but instead of moving faster, her stride slowed. Quinn turned back, ready to protest. Her friend had said she didn't want to leave the ocean, and despite her positive attitude about the whole thing, Quinn doubted she was ready to come face to face with her leecher. Without power, she'd be vulnerable if it came to a fight. But the keys in Chloe's hand rattled before she closed her fist over them, and even then her hand still shook.

"Thank you, Chloe, but it's better if you stay."

"I can identify Adrian." Her voice cracked on his name, and despair slumped her shoulders.

"I don't even know if he's there." Quinn walked back to Chloe and hugged her. "Nick could have been shot for trespassing or something." Her throat clenched, and adrenaline surged again, driving her to leave, to get there *now*.

Chloe handed Quinn the keys to her Prius. "I'm sorry. Yes, take my car. I'll get a ride from someone."

Quinn took the keys but hesitated. "I'm sorry. I'm being—"

"What you need to be. Go." She turned Quinn toward the door and shoved.

Quinn ran. She jumped into the car and took off without familiarizing herself with any of the controls. At the first stoplight, she punched the coordinates Sam had given her into Chloe's GPS system. After that, she tapped what power she could to cast ahead and make sure every light was green when she reached it. When she got on the highway, she checked surrounding energies for radar, only slowing when she sensed its use. Then she did ninety up I-95, wishing she had enough power to jump herself to Nick's side. But even if it were possible—which it wasn't—it would require massive amounts of energy, and then she wouldn't have any left to help Nick.

And she knew he needed her help. Sam hadn't given her any details. Okay, she hadn't let him. She'd ordered him to give her their location and hung up on him, a stupid move. She was driving too fast to risk calling him back. The longer she drove, the harder it was not to notice that he hadn't called her back, either.

She didn't know if Nick was in a hospital, if he was dying or dead, who had shot him and why, or what he'd been doing to get shot in the first place.

"It was a simple scouting mission," she ground out to no one.

She wished telepathy was one of her abilities. She had to conserve her use as much as possible, which pretty much limited her to turning red lights green and avoiding cops. The quirk that allowed her to measure time passing was enhanced as the full moon approached, and she'd never hated it as much as she did now, when every minute, every second, passed in agonizing slowness.

The GPS beeped, and she slowed the car. An exit sign loomed ahead of her, and the unit told her to take the exit. She was near the New Hampshire/Maine border, and had set a land-speed record getting here. But "here" was nowhere, she realized as she coasted to the end of the ramp. She looked right and saw only darkness and trees. No signs. To the left was a sign for a town twenty miles away, and nothing else. The GPS flashed. She was here.

No one was behind her—and hadn't been for the last half hour—so she fished out her phone. Sam had called twice, and she hadn't even heard the ring. Dammit. She dialed him back.

"Are you okay?" he asked as soon as he answered.

"Fine. Drove fast. I'm here, but 'here' is nowhere."

"You're at the end of the ramp?"

"Yes."

"Okay, turn right and go about three miles. Then call me back." He hung up.

"Sam! Shit." She set the phone down and hit the trip meter as she turned right. Less than three minutes later, she called Sam back.

"Left on the dirt road. Go a little over a mile, and turn left again on the wagon track. We're a few hundred yards up. You'll see the Charger first." He hung up again.

Cursing more foully, Quinn did as Sam had instructed, trying not to bottom out the Prius on the rutted dirt road or the vegetation between faint double lines he called wagon track. Then there it was, the Charger, parked askew on the side of the road. There was no one there. She crept forward. The car hit a bump, jostling her, then glided across new macadam. She braked and stared at the brightly lit two-story building ahead of her and the three rows of parking containing a few cars between her and the building.

She pulled into an empty spot and looked for a sign or any kind of identification to tell her where she was, but she saw nothing. Uncomfortable with the whole scene, she charged ahead anyway. Sam came out the double glass doors as she approached the building.

"Thank god." He grabbed her hand and rushed her inside. "I'm sorry, Quinn. But thanks for hurrying."

"What's happening? Where's Nick? What is this place?" She caught glimpses of calming artwork on pastel walls as they dashed down corridors lined with handrails. "Is this a hospital?"

"Private psych facility. But it's the only place in a fifty-mile area, and I knew they had to have some medical supplies."

"Did they take care of him?"

He didn't look at her. "They bandaged it." He skidded to a halt outside a room. "He's in there."

Quinn abandoned her questions and pushed through the wide door, closing her eyes in gratitude as soon as she saw Nick, awake, lying on a hospital bed.

"Hey." It came out of his throat as a croak, and her worries flooded over the relief. He was in bad shape.

"Hey, yourself." She looked him over. He wore his own clothes rather than a hospital gown. The left leg of his jeans had been cut and torn up the seam, exposing a bandage-wrapped calf. Sweat stained the neck and armpits of his T-shirt, and his face shone with it. As Quinn stepped nearer, she saw wildness in his red-rimmed eyes.

Sam caught her arm before she got too close. "Don't touch him."

"What's going on? What happened?" She looked back at Nick, who swallowed and tried to talk. Sam spoke over him.

"I found him at the edge of Marley's property, about a quarter mile from the inn. He was hiding in a ditch—"

Nick made an angry noise.

"—doing surveillance. He had a scope trained on a window of the inn and wasn't moving. When I approached him, he flipped out for a minute." Sam looked down, as if giving Nick a chance to protest his phraseology. "When he calmed down, he figured out he'd been looking at that same empty window for hours. A lot of hours," he added. "Part of the reason he didn't take our calls. We decided to go closer—"

"You decided to go closer?" Quinn protested. "He's obviously in a trance or compulsion of some kind, and you go *closer*?"

Sam grimaced. "Yeah, well, I think compulsion is the right word. When we got about a hundred yards onto the property, he got shot in the leg."

"And then?"

He shrugged. "Nothing. We couldn't see anyone, and it's not a bad wound, but the bullet's inside and he was bleeding more than enough to need treatment. I found the nearest facility and brought him here." Despair came down over his face. "Quinn, there's something majorly wrong."

She barely registered his words. "Why didn't you call the police?" she demanded.

Sam thrust his hand through his hair. "You know the kinds of questions they'd ask. Might detain him or both of us. He wouldn't let me do it."

"I'm fine," Nick croaked. "Just need to rest a little."

"He's not. No one can touch him. When someone tries—"

Nick waved his hand toward a pitcher on the rolling table next to Quinn.

"He needs water." She grabbed the pitcher and held the straw toward Nick's mouth.

"Quinn, don't!"

She stopped, but Nick lurched forward and caught the straw in his mouth. He sucked hard on the water, his hand on hers where she held the pitcher, but his face turned red and pain filled his eyes. He drank fast, then fell back on the pillow, gasping.

"What the—" Sam moved closer to the other side of the bed, looking back and forth between them in bewilderment. "Why didn't—"

"She's a goddess, Sam," Nick rasped out. "Get the doctor."

"But—"

"Get the doctor." He reached for Sam's arm. Sam lurched back, but Nick's fingers wrapped around his wrist. Both men screamed in pain. Sam dropped to his knees on the worn tiles, his fingers scrabbling at Nick's hand. Nick writhed on the bed, arching, the tendons in his neck bulging.

Quinn ran around the bed and caught Sam as he collapsed onto his side, breaking Nick's grip. Both men panted. Quinn, torn between them, didn't know whom to help first. Nick lay on the bed, his eyes closed, chest heaving, but he didn't look like he was still in pain. She supported Sam as he sat up. He touched his wrist, wincing, but it looked normal.

"What the hell was that?" she asked.

"We don't know." Sam's voice was weak. "Every time someone touches him, he screams. That's why they couldn't get the bullet out."

"Sorry," Nick managed to mumble. "Not thinking."

"The bullet is still in there?" Quinn left Sam's side and went back around the bed. Careful not to touch Nick's skin, she unwrapped the gauze from his calf.

The wound was ugly. It oozed dark blood and had purple

edges. Worse, lines of purple extended from it, reminiscent of blood poisoning.

"We've got to get that bullet out. Sam, get the doctor."

"But—"

"Get him!"

"Quinn, he's a psychiatrist."

She turned to look up at him. "He's the only doctor here?"

"It's a small facility. He couldn't reach anyone to come in. I don't think he has the stomach for this."

Resolve took over. "Then we'll have to do it. Get him. We need supplies." For the moment, she'd forget the facility was required to report the gunshot wound. They'd deal with that later. All that mattered right now was that Nick was in pain, possibly dying, and they had no other options.

Sam didn't leave, but he didn't say anything, either. He was looking at Nick with compassion and regret, and Quinn assumed he didn't want to cause him more pain. Or maybe…

"Sam, when he touched you, you screamed, too."

He wrenched his gaze back to her. "Yeah, it's a shared thing. Like he's projecting what he's feeling. It's okay—if I wear gloves, it should block it. For me. That won't help him."

"God." She shoved her hair back and drew a long breath. "Okay. I'll take care of the pain. You extract the slug. Get the doctor and everything you'll need to do this."

Sam nodded and left. Quinn moved up to kneel next to the bed at Nick's side, masking her fear. This was beyond anything she'd ever done before, and she didn't understand what was causing it. "You okay?"

He looked exhausted, his eyes sunken and bruised, his lips white at the edges. But he nodded a little.

"What do you see when someone touches you?"

"Their demons," he whispered. "The doc was the worst. He's

dealt with some serious shit in here. It fades after the contact breaks, so I can't tell you what I saw, but the pain is worse than anything I've ever felt. And Sam." He opened his eyes and licked his lips. "It's all about you."

She winced. "You didn't scream when I touched you. But it hurt."

"Some. No demons, though."

Quinn didn't know why that would be, but maybe, as he'd said, being a goddess offered some protection. She had demons, of course, and if Nick could see them, he'd know they were mostly about him. She tried to smile reassuringly. "We'll take care of you."

Nick's eyes closed. "I know you will."

Sam returned, followed by a tall, thin man with equally thin hair pushing a steel cart laden with instruments and supplies. Sam pulled a plastic chair to the foot of the bed and positioned the cart.

"Ready?" he asked. Quinn nodded.

Nick managed a weak grin. "Go for it."

Sam pulled on a pair of latex gloves and stripped a set of forceps out of their sterile wrap. He nodded at Quinn, who sat on the edge of the bed and braced Nick's head between her hands. He kept his green eyes locked on hers, and she opened herself to the power of the moon, letting the cool surge of energy snap into place. She didn't know how much she could draw. The moon wasn't very high yet, and there were still two days before she reached full power.

The physical limits on her ability to draw and use what could be unlimited power had never bothered her before. Humanity was about strength and weakness, and goddesshood was another level of that. But now, for the first time, it affected someone she cared about.

And it sucked.

Quinn didn't watch Sam but knew when he first touched Nick,

who hissed through his teeth and grabbed her wrist as if fighting to keep still. His eyes skittered sideways.

"Keep looking at me, Nick." She reached into Nick, to feel what he felt, so she could interfere with the effect of Sam's touch. Her power wasn't strong enough to block it completely—she had to take some of the pain into herself. The sharpness made her gasp and she stopped as soon as Nick settled and locked his gaze back on hers. Taking in too much could make her lose contact with Nick, and the explosion of physical and psychological pain could kill him.

"I can feel the bullet," Sam said. "It's deep."

Quinn ignored him and focused intently on Nick's eyes, trying to draw all his attention so he wasn't aware of what was happening at the foot of the bed.

His body jerked. "Son of a bitch," he gritted out. His fingers tightened on her wrist, but he didn't look away from her again.

"That's it, Nick. Stay with me. It won't take long." She pressed her hands tighter, holding on.

"Nng. Naaarrrgh!" He strangled the yell, but the pain increased. Quinn let more of it in. Shards of glass tumbled through her bloodstream, but Nick screamed and she opened up even more. Her eyes watered with the effort of keeping contact, but Nick relaxed a tiny bit and his breathing became more gasp, less hiss.

Quinn tried to relax her body, to distance herself from the pain. She gritted her teeth to avoid screaming as Nick's grip tightened again and the shards sliced deeper into her. Sam cursed behind her. Nick's body bowed. She couldn't talk, couldn't see anything beyond the torment in his eyes, or feel anything but the agony spinning between them.

"I've got it."

There was a clink behind her, and Nick went limp. Quinn gulped in air as the glass seemed to melt and slide out of her body.

"I need to rinse it with saline, put some ointment on it, and rebandage it. I'm not going to try to stitch it or anything. Infection risk, besides keeping him in pain."

"Appreciate that," Nick managed to say. His hand slipped off of Quinn's wrist, but she didn't release him. She held on while Sam quickly medicated and bandaged the wound. Her fingers cramped and her back spasmed. Nick groaned a few times, but the worst of his agony had passed. When Sam declared himself done, Nick sank deeper into the pillow and patted Quinn's hand.

"Thank you," he whispered, his eyes boring into hers even more intensely than they had during the procedure. Then they closed, and he fell asleep.

And Quinn allowed herself to collapse.

• • •

"What the hell was it?"

A short while later Sam and Quinn huddled over the cart in the corner of Nick's room while he slept. Sam had gathered her off the floor and deposited her in a chair, then rushed out to find her a bottle of juice. She'd recovered enough within a few minutes that she could focus on what the hell was going on.

She held the bullet with the forceps Sam had used to retrieve it and studied it with both her senses and her power.

"It's been treated," she said.

"With what? And why?"

"Hard to say without knowing who did it, but there are some goddesses who combine their powers with other disciplines. Like healers who use herbs and homeopathic remedies and infuse them with power to enhance their properties."

"Or the opposite?"

She frowned. "So it would seem. This is strange, though. It's like a hallucinogenic, but it caused him pain and insight, not hallucinations." That rang a bell, but before she could figure out why, the tall psychiatrist returned with a baggie Sam had asked for, to contain the bullet he'd extracted.

"I'm sorry, but we are *not* equipped for this kind of thing," the doctor said with a nervous glance at Nick. "I must insist you move him to a proper facility. One that has the experience to…handle all the…requirements."

"We'll pay you for the room and supplies," Sam assured him. "And we'll leave in the morning. He needs rest now."

The doctor pursed his lips but nodded shortly. "If you're finished with this?" He backed out of the room, pulling the cart.

"He's got to call the police," Quinn said in a low voice, watching the door. "It's the law."

"Don't worry." Sam dragged over the vinyl chair he'd used and pressed Quinn's shoulder until she sat. He bent close to her ear. "I convinced him we'll move Nick to a regular hospital tomorrow, and they can handle the report. He's not made for this. He was eager to take that reprieve."

"Good." She stared at the plastic-encased bullet in her hand, her vision going lax from fatigue and post-adrenaline comedown, as well as from the use of power.

"Tell me again where you were." She forced her heavy eyelids open. She had to stay strong so they could figure this out.

"The inn is on a hill surrounded by open land. It's clear-cut at the back and carved with walkways and gardens and stuff. It's one of her draws, I guess. Peace, serenity…"

"Getting shot."

"It might not have had anything to do with her."

"Or with Nick specifically? Like they'd do this to just anyone who was there?"

Sam didn't answer, but she'd been speaking rhetorically. There was no way this didn't have anything to do with Marley or that Nick wasn't a deliberate target. Blame tried to settle on her shoulders. Nick wouldn't have been hurt if he hadn't come up here, if she hadn't been so insistent on this path.

But that was stupid. The only person responsible for this was the person who'd done it. They could run and hide, but that would only delay the inevitable. They had to keep going and stop the enemy before they harmed anyone else.

She held up the bullet, finally understanding the hallucinogeniclike properties. "Do you know who does things like this?"

"Who?"

"Jennifer Hollinger."

Sam scowled. "Like this? To hurt people?"

"No." She set the bag on the flat arm of the chair and let her head drop against the back. "She infuses objects. Fun stuff for souvenirs—infusing light or kinetic energy or the essence of certain compounds. There were rumors she did it for legal highs, too."

"But she's been leeched."

"Exactly."

Understanding dawned. "You think the leech did this."

"Or someone working with the leech." She didn't need to spell it out. The heaviness in her voice was obvious.

"Quinn."

"See if you can find another chair. We need a little sleep before tomorrow." She dragged herself to her feet and pulled the chair to the side of Nick's bed before collapsing into it.

She was asleep before Sam returned.

• • •

Quinn woke with degrees of awareness. First was the dishearteningly familiar churn of need. The moon lust usually took half the full moon period to manifest, but because she'd ignored it for so long, it surged much earlier.

Luckily, the crick in her neck and tingling up and down her left side were stronger discomforts. Sunlight poured through the window, making her blink. She realized the tingling was from the vibration of her cell phone, which *wasn't* also ringing. She must have hit the button to silence it at some point in her frantic scramble to get here. That explained why she hadn't heard it when Sam called last night. She tugged the phone out of her pants pocket and checked the display. The number wasn't familiar.

"Hello?"

"How's your boy?"

She sat up. The voice was disguised, neither male nor female, but whatever device the caller used to distort it didn't filter out the glee. Hatred made her voice shake when she answered.

"What boy?"

"Don't play coy. The legendary Nick Jarrett, taken down with a little of the magic he protects."

"It's not magic."

"Of course it is. Magic is just another word for things science can't explain."

"Who are you?"

"I think you call me 'the leech.' I'd capitalize it, though."

"Why disguise your voice? Do I know you?"

"No. You don't know me. But you will, and I don't want you to see me coming. Ta for now."

Her phone beeped the call summary, but she didn't look at it. It had been thirty-four seconds. Not enough time to trace the call, either electronically or with power. And dammit, she hadn't even thought of it.

And there wouldn't be a next time. He wanted to play games but wouldn't be stupid enough to repeat himself. She squeezed the phone in her hand, her jaw clenched, until the urge to roar her anger subsided.

"Who was that?" Sam unfolded himself from the chair he'd scrunched into on the far side of the bed and rubbed his eyes. Nick slept on between them, much more peaceful and rested than a few hours ago. The sunken look was gone, his color normal.

"The leech," she said, not taking her eyes off Nick. His chest rose and fell with a slow, natural rhythm. Watching it calmed her, and she unclenched her muscles, one by one.

Sam, on the other hand, lurched to his feet. "What?"

"The leech. Apparently Nick was right. He'll be coming after me." She told him about the conversation. "He's responsible for Nick's leg."

Before Sam could launch into the outburst that had built while she talked, the doctor appeared at the doorway. "It's time to check out," he said dourly. "If one of you would like to settle the charges?"

"I'll do it." Sam followed him.

So Nick had been right all along. She might not be the leech's endgame, but he was coming for her, and he was smart. He knew she wouldn't be as easy as the others had been, so he was targeting the people around her first. Trying to get them out of the way or to unbalance her, make her vulnerable emotionally? Maybe both. His motives didn't really matter. Now there was no doubt this was personal. So, okay. He'd learn what a mistake that was.

Quinn sat forward and touched her fingertips to the back of Nick's hand. He didn't move. Relieved, she stroked his fingers, then up his wrist and forearm to his elbow. Still no writhing or screaming. He rolled his head the other way but slept on.

"Nick." She pressed her thumb into the spot inside his elbow. "Wake up, hon."

He smiled. "I like the way you say that." His voice was sleep-rough, but not the croak it had been the night before. Rolling his head back toward her, he opened his eyes and twisted his arm to wrap his fingers around hers. "Not a bad sight to wake up to, either."

Quinn couldn't help it; she laughed, shoving her hair back with her free hand. Her relief that he was okay made her momentarily giddy. "I'm a mess."

"The gold light makes your skin glow. Your eyes, too. You're beautiful." His brows furrowed, as if he were remembering what had happened. He looked around at the hospital room, then lifted his left leg a little and flinched. "Ow."

"I'd better look at that before we leave." Quinn released his hand and moved to the end of the bed. She carefully peeled up the bandage. The flesh beneath was pink now and not bleeding. She smiled. "Much better." The wound was still severe, but she didn't want to try to heal it yet. She'd used so much power, she wasn't sure how much she could draw on right now, and the leech could attack at any time.

"If you say so." Nick frowned. "Man, he shredded my favorite jeans."

"You can thank him later. Can you get up? They're kicking us out."

"Yeah, no problem." He swung his legs around, started to push himself off the bed, and sank back down, raising his eyebrows and squeezing his eyes shut. "Okay, small problem."

"Here." Quinn reached for the pitcher. "Drink some water. I'll go see if I can find a vending machine, get you something to eat. Your blood sugar must be low."

Nick caught her hand as she rose. "Hey." He tugged, and she sat back down. "Thank you for what you did last night."

"You don't need to thank me."

"Yeah, I do. This is a pretty severe role reversal. It wasn't your job to come get me, and it put you at risk."

Quinn felt her face go stony. "It had nothing to do with a professional relationship. You're my friend. At some point, my own well-being has to stop being more important than anyone else's."

Nick held her gaze for a moment, then let her go. She stood, hesitated, and decided they'd said enough. He needed food, not a debate.

By the time she got back with a pack of peanut butter crackers and a bottle of apple juice, Sam had returned. He had Nick on his feet with his arm slung over Sam's shoulder, but they hadn't moved far from the bed.

"Are you having trouble walking on it?" She moved to Nick's other side and slid under his shoulder. His long, lean, hard body aligned with hers stoked her lust to a simmer.

"Nah. It's the dizziness thing. Dr. Scary was in here, though, looking like he was going to shoot me again if I didn't get my sorry carcass out of his bed."

They wobbled out of the room and down the hall to the rear entrance. Once outside, Quinn and Sam lowered Nick to a bench next to the door. As soon as she wasn't touching him, the simmer subsided but didn't go away completely.

Quinn swallowed hard and stepped back a few feet. "I'll get Chloe's car. We'll drive to the Charger. Sam, where's the rental?"

"Back on the road near Marley's inn."

"Can you call the rental company to come get it? We're not going to be able to take it with us."

"I can drive," Nick said. But he was blinking funny again, a lot like Sam had after his accident.

"No way," Quinn said.

"Fine, but you're not driving the Charger."

"Neither are you. Not until your head clears."

"Sam can do it."

Quinn snorted. "Obviously, you're out of your head." Both men gave her pained looks. "All right, fine. I'll be right back."

She brought Chloe's car to the sidewalk, then drove them to

the Charger on the side of the dirt track.

"Why is this road so dubious?" she asked.

"It's not the main way," Sam explained. "Just the fastest."

"How did you know that?"

His mouth quirked. "Google satellite maps."

She shook her head. "You're such a geek." But thank god for that.

"Thank you." He opened his door to get out. "What's the next step?"

"There's a truck stop about ten miles down the highway," Quinn said. "I think Nick probably wants a shower, after all that sweating last night."

"Hell, yeah."

"They'll have medical supplies in the store. And we need food. We can plan over breakfast."

"Sounds fan-freaking-tastic to me," Nick said. He hadn't moved. His eyes were closed, his head back against the headrest.

Sam hesitated. "Aren't you coming with me?"

"Nope. Don't crash her."

Quinn caught Sam's pleased smile before he stood and slammed his door.

Nick winced. "God, I feel hungover. All the crap without the fun."

"You didn't think that was fun? I'm crushed." She put the car into gear as Sam started the Charger with a roar and rolled down the wagon tracks.

Nick didn't open his eyes, but his voice went husky. "When we have fun together, Quinn, there won't be any hangover the next day."

• • •

Two days ago, Quinn might have confronted Nick after a statement like that. But she didn't dare risk it now. She'd been attracted to Nick forever but had never been with him when she was under the influence of the moon. She was very afraid the combined moon lust and natural desire for him would make her do something stupid. So she kept her eyes on the road, her hands on the steering wheel, and her mouth clamped shut for the next fifteen minutes.

The truck stop's multitude of tiny stores was mall-like, albeit not the kind Quinn usually shopped in. She managed to get a change of clothes for herself, since she'd left their things behind at Chloe's, and the supplies to redress Nick's wound after he showered. She hated leaving him in pain, but with the leech primed to attack any time, she had to be ready. It was a convenient excuse to keep her from using more power and increasing her cravings for him.

Quinn expected arguments from both guys about splitting up to take showers and change clothes, but Nick posted Sam on watch as she went into the women's locker room. When she emerged they'd switched places, and Nick stood outside, his weight on his right leg. His hair was damp and spiky and he hadn't shaved, but in a clean, soft-looking T-shirt and jeans, he looked delicious. When Quinn stopped next to him, she got a whiff of musky soap and barely stopped herself from leaning in to sniff his neck.

"Where's Sam?" she asked. "Already in the restaurant?"

"Hell, no. He's doing something with his hair. He's such a girl."

"Let's go sit down." She took Nick's elbow and started toward the diner side of the truck stop. "He'll find us." He wouldn't admit it, but she could tell even standing in one place took its toll on him. And she needed a table between them and lots more people around.

They got a booth and she told him about the leech calling while he was asleep, playing it down as he got more and more pissed the longer she talked. Sam joined them a few minutes later, sliding in next to Quinn. Her body sizzled, and she slid away as subtly as possible.

"I told you all along it was you." Nick's hand was in a fist on the table. "We'll go back to Benton Harbor."

"The hell we will!" Quinn leaned forward and worked to keep her voice down. "It's too late for that. All this time we've been operating under assumptions and running around blind, trying to ferret out information. Now we have something concrete. We're not backing off now. Especially," she ground out as the waitress approached, "when it's obvious my sister is involved *and* that Sam and I might be suspects."

"What?" the guys said in unison, staring at her.

The waitress interrupted, so after they'd ordered enough food to fuel them for a week, Quinn brought them up to speed on the conversations they'd missed. "I don't know that anyone actually thinks Sam is the leech, but it connects, doesn't it? With the questions the security team asked Chloe? Maybe they've suspected me all along, and the family ties thing was to keep me in the dark."

"But *why*?" Sam was incredulous. "There's no evidence, and I'm always at the bar. People can confirm that."

But Nick shrugged. "Not sure they could convincingly. And you two have always been beyond close. A lot of people wouldn't be surprised that you'd taken that step." He motioned to get more coffee.

"But Tanda and Chloe know me," Sam protested. "They know I'm not the leech."

Quinn heaved a sigh. "They'd argue that you concealed your identity or affected their memories or something. And we've been on the road since this started, so it looks like we're on the run."

"Except you went to the Society offices and to talk to Alana," Sam said.

"Maybe they didn't suspect me until after that. Or they didn't have enough to arrest me or something. I don't know!" Frustrated, she fell back against the booth while the waitress flirted with Nick over the coffeepot. By the time the woman sashayed off, Quinn had managed to calm down enough to redirect the conversation to something more productive. "That's all speculation and out of our control. Tell us everything you learned before you got shot."

Nick shifted to stretch his leg and leaned over the Formica-and-chrome table. "The inn looks like it does good business. There were a lot of cars out front, couples walking around in the back." He sipped his fresh coffee. "Everyone looked normal to me, not like the misfits Ned said she collects."

"Maybe they don't mingle with the regular guests," Sam suggested.

"That's what I thought. There's a compound on the other side of the property from where you found me. A few small cottages, a stable, a shed, and a larger building. No one was around there, but it might be where her friends collect."

"Did you get inside?" Sam asked.

Nick shook his head. "Didn't want to risk it. And I was trying to get a handle on Marley."

"Did you find her?" Quinn asked.

"No." He looked disgruntled. "My plan was to scope the place—literally—and then go in like a customer, you know, looking for a room. But I thought I saw something in a window. Next thing I know, Sam's breaking the spell, and I realize I've been staring at nothing for hours."

"I looked through the scope and there was nothing in the window," Sam said. "Not in any of the windows. I couldn't even see into the rooms."

The waitress appeared with a huge tray and set down their plates. Scrambled eggs, sausage, home fries, and toast for Nick. A western omelet and bacon for Sam. A raisin bagel and fresh fruit for Quinn, who gave in to temptation and swiped a piece of Sam's bacon. The waitress poured more coffee all around again, then left them alone.

"So why did you start to go closer?"

Nick and Sam exchanged a look. Then Sam said, "It was like being pulled."

"Or pushed," Nick said.

"We just got up and started walking across the lawn."

"What did you think you were going to do?"

They both shrugged and forked egg into their mouths.

Quinn sighed. "Yeah, that was helpful." She stabbed a strawberry, stared at it, and dropped her fork. "It makes no sense. None of the leeched goddesses have mind control power. It doesn't exist."

"Maybe the woman in South Carolina had something." Nick shoved a huge bite of sausage in his mouth.

"No, she couldn't have." Sam poked his fork at a chunk of pepper. "It was probably a form of telekinesis, moving our bodies rather than controlling our minds."

"So it could have been Marley, or the leech, which we already knew." Nick looked disgusted.

Talking was getting them nowhere. Quinn forced herself to eat the strawberry. Her appetite had disappeared, but she needed the fuel. "I'm going to call Marley and arrange a meeting."

Neither of the men offered an opinion on that, so she dug out her cell phone. She'd added Marley's number, listed in the Society directory, to her phone book when they were still in Michigan. She called it up and hit send. After four rings, a machine came on with a message stating she'd reached the Athena Inn.

"That's subtle," she muttered while she waited for the beep. "My name is Quinn Caldwell. I'd like to talk to someone about a room." She left her number and hung up.

"I called six times yesterday," Nick said. "Never got a person, and no one called me back."

"But you saw people walking around? Like, guests?"

"A few, yeah."

"Weird."

Sam chewed his last bite of omelet and picked up the check. "I'm going to pay. I got it," he said, waving away the money Quinn pulled out of her wallet. As soon as he slid out of the booth, she could breathe easier.

Nick concentrated on mopping up yolk with his last piece of toast.

"How's your leg?" She watched the tendons flex in his hand and wrist, her eyes traveling up his forearm, her palms itching to touch. "Did Sam help you redress it?"

"I did it. It's fine. Hurts like a son of a bitch, but it looks good."

"I can heal it now."

"Later." He swallowed and wiped his mouth with his napkin. "You're wiped out."

If he only knew. "I want to go to the inn and try to find Marley. I need to see her face to face." She hesitated, knowing it was fruitless, but she had to try. "I think I should go without you and Sam."

"No way."

"You'll be safer away from whoever's responsible for this," she argued, motioning to his leg. *And away from me.*

Nick smirked with no humor. "I think we know who's responsible."

Defending someone who might be related to her, share her blood, came automatically, even though she agreed with him. "We don't *know*—"

"It was on her land!"

"I know." She stuck her elbow on the table and rested her head on her palm, weary of it all. "She's my sister, Nick. I—"

"But she's not your family." He stabbed his toast at her then leaned over his plate, his voice going lower and more intense. "You don't know her or what she's capable of. And if you're going to take her side over me—" He stopped, leaning back abruptly, and flung his toast to the plate. "I've lost my appetite." He shoved out of the booth and stood. "I'll meet you outside."

Quinn sat, miserable, wishing he'd let her explain but thinking it might be better to let him stay angry.

She didn't trust her sister over her friends, for god's sake. She didn't want them hurt, she was pissed that they already had been, and she was afraid they were more vulnerable targets than she was. Any hope that Marley was innocent or that Quinn could have a real relationship with her family had been lost when Nick took that bullet. Being protected was well and good when all it meant was that no one harmed her. Letting others get hurt instead, or worse, was simply unacceptable.

Sam returned to the table as Nick swung out the door. "What was that all about?"

Quinn watched sadly after Nick. "Complication."

"What'd you do, say you were going to see Marley without us?"

She didn't respond.

"That's really what you said? What, are you stupid?"

Quinn shoved at him. "Get up."

"Quinn…"

"I'm not stupid, and contrary to what Nick believes, I'm not oblivious to the probability that my sister is responsible for his bullet wound or that she's got something to do with the leech or that she's dangerous to me. But I cannot keep circling around this and letting the people I care about get hurt. So move." She shoved him again and he slid out of the booth, wisely keeping silent as she stormed out to the parking lot.

Nick leaned against the Charger, parked three spaces from Chloe's Prius. Quinn stopped in front of him, the renewed flare of desire infuriating her.

"Let me heal your leg."

"No way."

"You were limping."

"So what? You're too drained. You pull that kind of power while the moon's on the other side of the planet, you'll kill yourself."

She snorted. "Hardly."

"You're not doing it." He looked past her and a satisfied smirk shaped his mouth. "You don't even want to try it."

Quinn turned. Sam stalked toward them, his expression thunderous. For a moment, she felt a hundred years old and ready to drop everything and go back to Ohio. But that wouldn't help any of them. Nor would another six hours of planning. She needed to act.

"Fine. I'll do it later." She spun away and strode to the car, got in, and took off before Nick could realize what she intended and stop her.

She knew she had no chance to outrun him, so she didn't try. She keyed the address for the inn into the GPS and followed the route. Her phone rang. She left it in her pocket. A few moments later the Charger appeared in her rearview mirror, Nick and Sam both glaring through the windshield.

So they were pissed. Good. She wanted enough of a head start that they wouldn't stop her, and maybe she could gain enough advantage to protect them for a change.

Chapter Twelve

Among goddesses, no ties are stronger than those of family.
Mothers, grandmothers, and sisters help a new goddess develop and
fine-tune her abilities and provide emotional support as she finds
her place in our world. However, as is the case outside the goddess
community, "family" is not always defined by blood.

—Society Annual Meeting,
Special Session on Relationships

Soon she was on the wooded, winding road to the inn, the driveway
a few hundred yards ahead. She searched the sides of the road,
looking for an opportunity, but didn't see it until she got to her turn.
A drainage ditch had been dug into the far corner. She turned right
past the one-way sign, whipping into the turn without warning.
When Nick followed she reached for the moon's energy, exhilarated
by the clean, cold surge, and sent the Charger into the ditch with a
thought. It was deep enough and wide enough to trap the front tires
so he couldn't get out.

The Prius sped past white pines lining the long, narrow
driveway, halting with a little screech in front of the large white
colonial house. Black shutters glistened in the sun, and a few hardy
fall flowers bloomed in the beds on either side of the wide porch
steps. Rocking chairs sat invitingly in front of sparkling windows

covered in sheer white curtains, and a grapevine wreath adorned the front door. All very picturesque and not telegraphing "evil lives here" in any way.

Mindful that Nick and Sam would be close behind her, Quinn got out of the car, her eyes on the building. Chirping birds pierced the serenity as she climbed the steps and approached the front door.

As she reached for the handle of the screen, the inner door opened and a woman, laughing at the man behind her rather than looking where she was going, swung the outer door at Quinn's face. She stepped back just in time.

The woman gasped. "Oh, I'm so sorry! I wasn't looking." She tilted her head. "Are you a new guest?"

"I hope to be. I'm looking for Marley Canton."

The woman clucked her tongue. "I'm afraid the inn is booked for the next several weeks. I know, because we were so lucky to get this week when a couple canceled. Called off the wedding, poor things. Anyway, Marley's in the kitchen. Fran at the counter can tell you when they can book you. Toodles!"

She and the man trotted down the steps to an SUV parked in a small, needle-strewn lot to the left. Quinn stepped into the warm lobby and glanced around. The square foyer was empty of both Fran and all furniture except a tall counter to the right of the central hallway. On the left, a staircase stretched upward, the carved banister gleaming as much as the polished floor, the dark wood contrasting with the bright white of the walls and check-in counter. The shivery feeling inside Quinn could be anticipation or apprehension, but it came from her, not from the environment. The foreboding she'd had before Nick left to come up here was absent. Still, she remained alert, prepared for anything.

The bell on the counter dinged when she tapped it, but it didn't bring footsteps or voices. It would be rude to walk into the back,

Quinn told herself, but did it anyway. She saw no one in the hall, nor in the spacious dining room she passed. Pots and pans clanked deeper into the building. Quinn followed the sound of running water to the very back of the house.

The kitchen door was open to the backyard, the room sunny and bright and clean except for the makings of bread dough scattered across several counters. A young woman stood at the center counter, digging her hands deep into the dough she kneaded. Quinn registered dark hair pulled back in a ponytail, the exact color of her own, and a wide face with high cheekbones and pointed chin that reminded her of Tess. She didn't move, waiting for a sense of…something. Family. Connection. Recognition. There was nothing. Then her sister looked up and froze, surprise and pleasure spreading over her face.

"Quinn!"

"Marley." It didn't shock her that Marley knew who she was—not as much as it did to see her pale lavender eyes. They couldn't be normal. Uncertainty drained her determination, and she began to hope again. Maybe Marley wasn't the threat after all. Maybe she was just another victim.

"How did you get in here?"

Reminding herself to assume nothing, Quinn said, "It wasn't hard."

"But the front door is—"

"A couple was coming out. They let me in. Said Fran would be at the front desk, but there wasn't anyone around."

Marley pursed her lips and shook her head. "Fran's in the laundry room." She manipulated the dough into a mound, dropped it into a bowl, and draped a towel over it. "Let me get cleaned up and we'll go in the other room." She turned to the sink to wash her hands. "Not exactly the—"

BwoooOOP. BwoooOOP. BwoooOOP.

Marley cursed over the loud alarm and quickly dried off her hands.

"What's that?" Quinn shouted.

Marley waved a hand toward one wall and the alarm stopped. Quinn saw a speaker up near the ceiling, then noticed the windowsills, backsplashes, and shelves high on the wall were all lined with different kinds of crystals. Marley's power source, and she'd just used it. So her eyes weren't the result of leeching. Quinn felt her expression twist with disgust, her hope short-lived. Marley had both light eyes and power, so the only possibility remaining was that she *had* created the leech.

"Someone's trying to get in." Marley squeezed past her and rushed down the hall toward the front door.

"They're probably with me!" Quinn hurried to follow, not wanting Marley to attack her friends. When she burst into the foyer lobby, two men held guns on Sam and Nick, who stood with their hands raised, looking disheveled and disgruntled. When they saw Quinn, Sam sagged in obvious relief while Nick tensed, his eyes flashing and his jaw tight.

"They *are* with me," Quinn said, stepping up next to Marley. "Call off your goons."

"They're not goons."

But neither were they typical security. The guy on the left, standing in the doorway of what appeared to be an old-fashioned parlor, had long, stringy hair and wore dirty jeans and a Metallica T-shirt. The older one on the right was beefier and held his rifle with more authority, but he looked farm-hardened rather than street-tough.

No one moved. Exasperated, Quinn stepped forward and introduced Nick and Sam. Then she pointed to Marley. "Marley Canton, my sister."

The two armed men lowered their weapons halfway, surprise

overtaking grim determination on their features.

Marley smiled slightly. "Bobby and Tim, two of my staff. You'll meet Fran in a little while. She's my assistant manager." She motioned to Nick's leg. "You're bleeding."

Quinn whirled and bent to check. Blood had seeped through the denim, which meant he'd torn open any slight healing he'd had overnight. She moved quickly to tuck herself under his arm. "I'm sorry," she murmured, wishing she'd healed him earlier. "I shouldn't have gotten so angry and taken off." She'd known he would come after her, but she hadn't thought about the impact on his injury.

Now that his adrenaline was wearing off, Nick looked pale and pinched with pain. "We need to work on our communication skills," he said.

Quinn helped him down the hall to the kitchen and noticed he barely put weight on his injured leg. He had to be hurting.

"Sam, do you mind getting the medical supplies from the car?"

"I have everything you'll need," Marley said. She nodded to Tim and Bobby. "We're good, guys. I'll call you if I need you."

They nodded and disappeared in opposite directions.

Sam trailed behind as Quinn and Nick followed Marley back to the kitchen. Quinn settled Nick at a large, heavy log table and sat in a matching chair, propping his leg on her lap. The moon lust had abated since she'd run from the truck stop, but heat seeped into her where his leg rested.

Marley brought over a first-aid kit, bowl of water, and scissors, then joined them at the table. Sam prowled the kitchen, not touching anything and being so unobtrusive that Marley didn't even flick him a glance.

"What happened to him?" Marley asked.

"I was shot by one of your thugs," Nick accused. He jerked his leg when Quinn removed the red-soaked bandage and a few of his leg hairs with it. "Ouch."

"Sorry. We don't know who shot him," Quinn corrected. She dampened a piece of gauze and mopped around the wound. "But it happened yesterday on your property."

"What was he doing on my property?" Marley's tone held more than a note of defensiveness.

"You tell me!" Nick didn't exactly yell, but he didn't moderate his voice, either. "I didn't intend to be there."

"Where?"

"Out back. Past the labyrinth."

Marley's brows knit together. "I don't have anyone out there with a gun."

"Sure. As evidenced by the quick response of the ones inside the house."

"I mean it. I've had guests. I'm not going to have amateurs with rifles roaming around in the common areas."

"Why do you have amateurs with rifles at all?"

Marley didn't answer right away. Quinn pressed a clean gauze pad coated with antibacterial ointment against the wound. Nick hissed and his hand jerked toward hers as if to pull it away, but he stopped himself.

"Damn, that hurts."

"Sorry." She raised her eyebrows at him, silently offering, once again, to heal the wound. He shook his head, but she couldn't let him go on hurting. It was her fault the wound had reopened. She closed her eyes and covered his calf with her hand, drawing on the limited pool of energy available to her, and focused on filling in the tissues, sealing blood vessels. His muscles relaxed, and she checked the hole. It looked as if it had happened weeks ago instead of yesterday, but it wasn't healed completely.

She took a deep breath but before she could try again, Nick folded his hand around hers. "Thanks." His look said *that's enough*, and Quinn was weak enough now to obey. She taped fresh gauze over the area to keep it clean and rested her hand on Nick's shin before turning her attention to her sister. "Well?"

Marley nibbled on her lower lip. "It's a long story."

"We're here for a long story," Sam said from behind Quinn. "You can start at the beginning. Like how long you've known about your sister."

Marley nodded. "I guess that's as good a place as any to start. I've known since I was ten."

Quinn absorbed the shock of that. So long, and Marley had never contacted her? She would have been about seventeen, a senior in high school. She'd decided by then that she didn't care about her "other" family and was focused on the future, but that would have changed in an instant if she'd learned she had a little sister.

"How did you find out?"

"I heard Mom and Dad talking. Nothing major. Dad said something about 'the baby,' and whatever else he said—I don't actually remember—made it clear he wasn't talking about me. I was nosy and went digging. I found a copy of your birth certificate and adoption papers in the safe in the back of their closet."

"Pretty good for a ten-year-old," Nick said. Quinn considered ripping off a few more hairs. Then she saw his face and she realized he wasn't impressed, but encouraging the conversation.

"Did you confront them?" Quinn didn't like the idea that Tess had lied to her. None of them could change the past, but how they acted now would affect any potential future relationships.

"Nope. My curiosity was satisfied. You were a lot older, and I figured you wouldn't be interested in me. Then a couple of years later Mom taught me more about the goddess thing, and that was a *lot* more interesting than a long-lost sister who couldn't be bothered to find out I exist."

Quinn suppressed a smile. "I never had a clue until about two weeks ago."

Hurt passed over Marley's face. "And you're just now finding me?"

"You knew, and you never came to find me! There's also the matter of a 'family ties' issue with the board of the Society."

Hurt turned to guilt. Marley was either terrible at hiding her emotions or wasn't trying. "Okay. We'll get to that. If you want this in order." She glanced up at Sam, who nodded.

"When I turned twenty-one I joined the Society. I didn't know if you were a goddess, but that was the first thing I checked when I got my directory. And there you were. Not only a goddess, but already a prominent member of an organization our mother wanted nothing to do with."

"Why not?" Tess hadn't seemed like the kind of person to remove herself from the structure and support of the Society.

"That's another long story."

"Marley, this is important. Tell me why Tess isn't part of the Society."

"She's part of it, kind of. She maintains her membership and adheres to its tenets. But she hates those women and isn't friends with any other goddesses. I found out that when she first joined, someone learned she'd been a teen mother and gave you up for adoption. The elders were appalled that she would remove a potential goddess from their midst."

"But I was adopted by a goddess."

"They didn't know that at the time." Marley stood and walked to her bowl of dough. She checked it, then dumped it onto the floured butcher-block surface and began kneading again. "She wouldn't talk about it at all. They treated her badly, so she removed herself from them."

"What about you? Is that why you're a rebel, too?"

She beat down the dough and folded it over. "The word fits me more than our mother. She conformed to Fairfield society so well, she could be a selectman's wife. Might still, if Dad runs again next year. Anyway, no, that's not why I retreated." She put the dough back in the bowl and washed her hands, then resumed her story when she returned to the table.

"The only thing I wanted to do at my first quarterly meeting was find you. You were on some committee, and everyone was talking about your business, Under the Moon. Some people were horrified that you'd taken over your father's bar. Others thought it was the perfect setup for your"—she made air quotes—"'real' job, using your powers as a goddess to help people."

Quinn had heard the murmurs. She'd had the bar for three years by then, but as she honed her control and her power "grew," for want of a better word, so had her business. Some people—like the goddess at the chapter meeting who'd made the snide remarks yesterday—hadn't hidden their jealousy.

"Did we meet?" Quinn couldn't remember if they had, but it wasn't like she was keeping an eye out for someone who looked like her.

"No. I hung out with a few other neophytes. I told myself my peers were more important, and that you wouldn't be interested in me and my fledgling, difficult powers. In reality, I was scared to try. So I did what I assume our parents did and put it off until it became too hard to even consider."

A few weeks ago, hearing her sister's story, Quinn would have lamented lost time and missed opportunities. Now, though, she dispassionately considered whether things would have been different if Marley had found the courage to contact her. If their relationship could have prevented any of this from happening.

"Why were your powers difficult?" she asked. Nick shifted his leg and winced. Quinn guessed he had some residual pain, even though he gave every appearance of being as interested in Marley's story as she was. She dug in the first-aid kit and found a packet of painkillers. Tearing it open, she poured the tablets into Nick's palm. He glanced down, then up at her with gratitude. Sam set a glass of water on the table next to him, and he murmured thanks and slapped the pills into his mouth.

Quinn realized Marley was watching them. Her smile was sad.

"You guys are quite a team."

"Yeah." Quinn didn't want Marley getting any ideas about joining that team. "So, why were your powers difficult?"

"I had a hard time figuring out my source. Mom had some of everything in the house, and we tried it all. But if I had, say, a hunk of amethyst in the room and tried herbs, and it was strong, and then later I was outside and tried the herbs again, it would be weak. It took months to figure out the crystals. After that, it got easier. More fun, anyway." She smiled and looked like the kid she would have been then, playing with her power. "What I focus through depends on what I want to do."

"Like flip a car?" Sam asked.

Marley looked stricken. "What?"

"You flipped my car, didn't you? And it was your men who abducted Quinn."

Marley shifted on her chair and avoided their eyes. Her fingers plucked at the fringe of a plaid placemat. She wasn't acting like someone who wanted to hurt them, and Quinn tried to keep her anger out of her voice, more concerned with getting answers than lashing out.

"Is Sam right?"

"I wanted us to know each other better before we got to that." Marley's voice shook. "I have very good reasons for both."

Even though she'd expected this, Quinn's heart sank into a disappointment unlike any she'd ever known. Some part of her had still wanted Marley to deny it all. At the least, she'd wanted her sister not to be a criminal.

"I'd really like to hear this." Nick dropped the foot of his injured leg to the floor and twisted in his chair to face Marley full on. His expression sarcastic, he said, "Do tell."

"I will but…I need to know what you know first." She looked at Quinn when she said it.

Quinn wasn't inclined to help her out. "About what, in particular?"

"Can you tell me what led you here? Why you found me?"

They ran through the basics of what they'd learned, ending with Alana's reference to family ties and their search for records that revealed their relationship.

"You're the most logical family she could be referring to. And the only thing that would make our relationship such a big deal to the board is the leech. So you have to be connected to him," she concluded, avoiding a direct accusation.

Marley's eyes filled with tears. "I don't know that I am. I don't want it to be true."

Quinn couldn't tell if Marley's distress was real or an attempt to play on her empathy. Not that she had any right now. "But it is."

Marley nodded. "It's got to be. Anson Tournado is my fiancé."

Fury surged and Quinn held herself very still against the urge to punish. Sam placed his hand on Quinn's shoulder, and Nick's head angled her way when Marley used the present tense—that he *is* her fiancé, not *was*. They hardly moved, but she felt them closing in around her. It was enough for her to control herself, though Marley shrank back at the look in her eyes.

"And?" She dreaded what came next, but what Marley said was no surprise now.

"I imbued him with the power of a goddess. And now someone's leeched three other goddesses."

"Four." Nick's voice was hard.

"I didn't know," Marley whispered. Her tears spilled over in silvery trails down her cheeks. "I don't want it to be him. It *can't* be him, but…"

"But who else could it be," Nick finished for her, tone granite-hard.

Marley nodded. "And if it *is* him, he isn't even close to done. I think he's coming after you, Quinn. I have no evidence or anything. I just feel it." Her tears flowed faster. "You're running out of time."

"Why?" Nick barked.

But Quinn knew. "Tomorrow's the full moon."

• • •

"Tell us everything you know about Anson," Nick demanded. "Everything."

"Wait." Sam's hand tightened on Quinn's shoulder. "Let her collect herself. There's time. He doesn't know where we are."

"Oh, no?" Nick's green eyes had darkened to emerald. "If Marley's guys didn't shoot me, who do you think did?"

Quinn pushed to her feet, knocking Sam's hand away. She was tired of good cop/bad cop, of coaxing Marley's story along. The closer they got to Anson, the more at risk her friends were. "If your boyfriend tried to kill my protector—"

"You don't know that he did!" Marley protested, leaning away to look up at Quinn. Her pale eyes were wide. "It could have been a hunter…or…or…anyone!"

"Hardly. That bullet was infused with a drug that induced intense pain." She didn't describe the demons thing. It was too personal.

Her sister slumped and nodded miserably. "That's a power he was interested in. He wants some of everything, but he has his favorites."

"Why would you do this?" Sam asked. "Why would you create

the biggest threat to goddesses in a hundred years?"

"I didn't mean to," Marley sobbed. "I didn't think— I didn't believe— He said it was just a transfer of power. That all the stories were fake, because powerful women didn't want powerful men."

"Where is he?" Quinn demanded. "Are you hiding him? So help me god…" She reached for Marley, the rage building so high she was only dimly aware of the energy following it, carving a path through her and coalescing in her hand, ready for use. But when Marley jerked away, Quinn froze. She took in her sister's extreme paleness, the terror in her eyes. Saw the white glow over her own skin, realized she could have hurt her, actually hurt her, and felt sick.

No one moved. She sensed Nick staring at her, Sam's concern emanating from behind her. Slowly, she released her draw on the energy and let it seep away, taking her anger with it. Marley's distress was sincere. She wasn't evil, only very, very stupid.

In the silence, Quinn's stomach growled.

"O-kay! That would be my cue." Nick eased to his feet and wrapped his hand around her arm. "It's been a while since breakfast. Let's go pick up some lunch, then we can all sit and work this out. M'kay?"

Marley jumped up. "Oh, no, you'll have lunch here. It won't take long to prepare." Her voice trembled, and tears still clung to her eyelashes. Quinn drew in an anguished breath. She wanted to believe her sister, to salvage shreds of possible friendship for the future. But she couldn't take her at face value. Nick was right. She needed a break, to get some perspective, but if they left the property Marley could disappear. Finding her again would be much more difficult and much more vital, especially if she went to Anson.

"I'll stay here," Sam said, standing close to Quinn, his eyes on Marley. "You two go pick something up and bring it back."

Quinn didn't want to leave him behind. Marley could do

irreparable harm to him in the short time they'd be gone, and she had those guys with the guns. But he watched her sister with an implacable expression. Marley huddled into herself, sniffing and wiping her eyes, not appearing to be much of a threat. When Sam reached under the table for his duffel and removed a handgun, never taking his eyes off Marley, Quinn finally agreed.

Nick limped outside, and Quinn followed. He got into the Prius without comment but stared longingly at his stranded Charger as they passed.

"You'd better not have damaged her," he said.

"She'll be fine. I can fix her like that." She snapped her fingers.

"I'll believe that when I see it." He pointed to the right. "There's a grinder place up here."

She cast him a glance, amused despite herself. "Grinder?"

He shrugged. "Speak the lingo, you blend in better."

She pulled into the rutted, wavy parking lot of Bruno's Grinders and turned off the car. They both sat for a moment, watching the few people inside the take-out restaurant. Quinn's head throbbed, her shoulders and neck so tight from tension there was no room for her body to recognize the proximity of the man in the car. Until she thought about it, and the yearning throbbed a few times before fading again.

"Thank you," she said.

"For?"

"Stopping me from doing something I couldn't take back."

He shrugged. "It wasn't difficult."

"So what do you think?" she asked after a few more minutes of silence.

"I don't know." He propped his elbow on the door and rubbed his forehead. "She seems sincere. I mean, sure, she did something colossally stupid, but I don't think she's lying about her intentions."

"I don't, either. But I can't—"

Nick didn't look at her. "How about we deal with the concrete stuff first? She still has a lot of questions to answer. Like, why did she say he is her fiancé, not was?"

"That one's easy." Quinn snorted. "She loves him and doesn't want him to be a bad guy. And if he is the leech—which he's got to be, no matter how deep her denial—then it's a subtle way of accepting responsibility."

"If she gave this guy his power, why hasn't she told anyone?"

"Maybe she has," Quinn countered, aware Nick was putting her in a position to defend her sister. "I mean, Alana knew something. Maybe that's why they didn't want me to be part of it."

"Okay, if they know, why don't they have her in custody or anything?"

"They're not the FBI. They may have someone watching her, either to make sure she's not in cahoots with Anson or to use her as bait. But he's probably done with her. He's obviously been elsewhere."

"He's here now though." Nick shifted his leg.

"We think. And the Society wouldn't know that."

"Unless they're tracking your movements and think he's coming after you at the full moon. Using *you* as bait."

Quinn stared at him, another shocking possibility filling her head. Her skin flushed. Nick stared back. Then, obviously reading her, he made a "what the hell?" face. "You think they're tracking you through *me*?"

"No. Not exactly."

"Then what?"

"I called John," she admitted. "Maybe that triggered— He didn't know about the rogue thing."

Nick groaned. "What the hell did you do that for?"

"I was worried. I don't know what's going on."

"Seems clear to me. This tornado guy—"

"Tournado."

"Whatever. He knows I'm your protector, and he made Hollinger send out that accusation hoping I'd be recalled. Leaving you vulnerable."

"I'm not vulnerable right now, so it didn't work."

"And I wanted to keep it that way. If John knew, he would recall me. So, what?" He returned to Quinn's concern. "You think Tournado's got John's phone tapped or something?"

"I don't know." She thought about Jennifer. "You know, we were wondering why that e-mail didn't get out. It was on the group mail. But if Jennifer hadn't been leeched yet, maybe she ensured it only came to me, instead of to the whole Society. You know, protecting you. Us."

"Goddess voodoo," he said. "You blew me off when I suggested it. Could she do that?"

"Not voodoo," Quinn insisted. "Hacking. Or something like that. She could have coded her e-mail so Anson wouldn't know what she was doing."

Nick's frown cleared. "That could explain why it stayed quiet. So when Tournado's attempt to discredit me or get me away from you didn't work, he came here and shot me. Trying to take me out or, what, lure you up here?" He shook his head, unconvinced. "How did he know I was coming?"

Quinn didn't have the answers, and she could tell they were about to go in circles again. She needed a break. "Let's get the food." She got out and went around the car, but Nick stood without her help and limped into the restaurant. The scent of spicy tomato sauce and toasting bread filled the air. Her stomach growled again, and Nick grinned.

"You always were a stress eater."

She smacked him on the arm. "I didn't finish breakfast." He smiled and rubbed the back of her neck, and both the muscles and inner tension loosened. How did he do that so effortlessly?

They sat at a tiny table while they waited for the food they'd ordered.

"Back to Marley," Nick said, leaning on his arms and putting his face inches from hers so they wouldn't be overheard.

It was too close, because in easing her tension, he'd attracted her body's attention. "Hang on." They'd been gone twenty minutes, and she wanted to check in. Get her equilibrium back somehow. And get a little distance from Nick. She pulled out her phone and dialed Sam, who answered right away.

"Everything's fine here."

"Okay." She let out a long breath and finally felt normal. "The food should be ready in ten. Then we'll be back."

"Got it."

"See anyone else?"

"I met Fran. She's as protective as Nick. Doesn't like me."

Quinn drew in a quick breath at the word. "Do you think she's a real protector?"

"Could be. Ask Nick."

"I will. See you soon." She closed the phone.

"Does he think who's a real protector?"

"Fran, Marley's assistant manager. Sam said she's very protective. It would be a good cover, right?"

Nick looked disgusted. "If she is, she's not a very good one. Marley was alone with us for way too long while Fran was doing laundry."

"Good point. Maybe she's not. We'll ask when we get back." She glanced up when the guy behind the counter rang a bell, but the number he called wasn't theirs.

The important question had to be asked. "Do you think Marley's still working with Anson? That all this was deliberate?"

"If she is, she's a good actress. I don't get a lying vibe off her."

"Me, neither. But my judgment is clouded."

Nick's face softened. "I didn't think you'd admit that."

"I thought I'd made it kind of obvious."

"Yeah, but your judgment is clouded." He smiled, and her heart rolled.

"Nick—"

He picked up her hand and held it between both of his. Her skin warmed, the sensation spreading up her arm and into her body, filling her. Natural attraction fed into her hunger, and she closed her eyes, trying to keep it at bay.

"Quinn, no one's judgment is less clouded than yours. You want her to be cool. That's normal. But you're not blind to the possibility that she's not. You're asking the question."

"Threatening her."

"You were scared."

"And mad." She grimaced. "I sent your car into a ditch."

"Yeah, that pissed me off." He smiled again. She wished he'd stop doing that. This time she felt like he'd sprinkled glitter in her chest. That was hardly compatible with her anger and suspicion.

"But you were doing what you felt you had to do," he continued. "You only slowed us down, and you knew it. I'm pretty commanding. You were tired of fighting me. I get that."

Her lips curved. "Fighting you? Rescuing you, maybe."

"About that." He turned serious. His eyes lightened to a golden green, and her heart panged.

"About what?"

"What you did last night."

"Oh." She looked down at the table, but only for a moment. His soft words, spoken intently, compelled her to meet his eyes again.

"I've never felt pain like that, Quinn. I thought I was going to die."

She whispered his name, her hand convulsing around his.

"You were amazing. Whatever you did, you kept me grounded. I didn't think until later that you probably hurt just as much."

"No, only a little," she lied. "It doesn't matter. I'd sacrifice anything for you." Afraid she'd ventured too far into off-limits territory, and afraid he'd push her away from it again, she sat back and glanced away.

The bell dinged again, and the Italian behind the counter called their number. She went up to take the bag, and a minute later they were heading back toward the inn.

"So how do you want to play the rest of this?" Nick asked.

Quinn forced herself to think unemotionally. "Let's find out what she can tell us about Anson. Then we'll get Sam set up with his laptop and he can try to match her story or find more that she doesn't know or doesn't want to tell us. I need to talk to her about our family some more, too."

"We need to prepare for tomorrow, Quinn."

For the leech. "I know. But we don't know how."

"Hell we don't. We pull the Charger out of the ditch and get the hell out of there, hole up somewhere he won't have allies."

"Nick—"

"Even if your sister isn't in cahoots with him, her so-called 'misfits' could be on his side. It's not safe to stay there."

"Cahoots?" She couldn't stop a giggle, which diffused Nick's intensity in turn.

"C'mon, give me a break. I'm trying to save your life here."

She sobered. "You're trying to save my life*style*. He doesn't kill. Having my powers taken away doesn't change who I am, it only changes how I live."

Like, if she were no longer a goddess, she wouldn't need Nick's protection anymore.

"Do you *want* him to leech you?" His tone was exasperated.

She didn't even need to think about it. "No."

"Then we get the hell outta here."

"My safety isn't important anymore."

"The hell it's not!"

"There are more important things."

She pulled up next to the Charger, which looked forlorn in its forward cant. "You could have died. I'd rather lose my abilities than lose you." Before the weight of her words could settle, she continued. "Marley may be working with him, or she could just be incredibly stupid. And she's my sister." Quinn held up a hand and closed her eyes for a second, the truth of the relationship coming home to her. "I don't have to like her or condone anything she's done. But I would never forgive myself if we left her and something happened."

Nick took a deep breath. Quinn knew he understood. Family was what drove him, wasn't it? And he'd dedicated his life to keeping others safe. He had to get that this was what she was trying to do now.

"All right. I'll consider it. After we hear the rest of what she has to say, we'll discuss our next move."

"Thank you." She nodded toward his car. "If I get that out of there, will you be able to drive it up?"

"Yeah, sure. Leg's fine now."

In three seconds, the car had risen up a few feet, spun on its rear wheels, and settled onto the gravel at the end of the drive. "I'll see you there."

Nick growled at her, but he switched cars and followed her up the drive to the house. Sam came out as they climbed the steps, and he stopped them on the porch.

"I've talked to Marley a little. All her guests have left except the one couple we met earlier. They're going on an overnight trip and will be gone within the hour."

"So she's been preparing for this," Quinn observed. "That woman said the inn was booked, but this means she hasn't been taking new guests."

Sam scowled. "So is she part of it, or did this guy manipulate her into getting you here? You know, let her know her sister was his main target. Those kidnappers were hers. She said they were under orders to keep you safe but not tell you anything." He peered into the bag and sniffed. "You got sausage?"

"With peppers." Quinn nudged Sam with her elbow. "What else did you find out?"

"Not much. She wanted to wait for you. Says she's worried about what's going to happen tomorrow."

"It's best if I meet him at my peak power. I know that's his best time to leech me," she said before Nick could open his mouth, "but it's also when I'm strongest, and he's not taking me by surprise like he did the others. I'm going to be a bitch to leech, and he might be cocky after the first ones were so easy. Plus, if Marley's telling the truth, she's vulnerable. If he comes here and I'm gone, he might do something major."

"Like what, killing Marley in rage?" Sam asked.

She nodded and repeated to him what she'd told Nick. "If she's part of this, we're better off keeping her with us, where we can see her. If she's not, she has all her power sources here, arranged for effectiveness. She knows the house and property, and if she's sorry for what she's done, she'll be an asset in a fight."

Nick clenched his jaw and tapped the foot of his bad leg. "I'll go for it. But I'm front line, and there are no arguments about that."

"Of course. Let's go eat."

CHAPTER THIRTEEN

But the goddess didn't believe her grandmother. The man was handsome and charming, and he'd even saved the goddess from falling into the pond. The first time he whispered her name and kissed her fingers, she fell in love. When he lamented that they could never be together because of her gifts and his lack, she eagerly bestowed upon him a portion of her ability. Thus began their tragedy.

— "The Goddess and the Leech,"
*from **Tales of the Descendants of Asgard***

They carried the food inside, where an older woman was now helping Marley form cinnamon rolls from the dough she'd worked with earlier.

"You're back!" Marley cried. "Quinn, this is my assistant manager, Fran. Fran, my sister."

Quinn stepped forward and shook the woman's hand, then had to wipe sticky dough off her fingers with a towel. "Pleased to meet you."

"Same, I suppose."

"Fran," Marley scolded.

"It's okay." Quinn studied her. "I've been told she's protective."

Fran glared at Sam, who held his hands up at his sides in an innocent gesture.

"Are you in the business?" Nick asked, moving next to Quinn

and snitching a bit of dough.

"What business?" Fran lifted her chin and looked down her nose at Nick, though he was a good six inches taller than she was. With her salt-and-pepper hair pulled into a clipped loop at the back of her neck and silver half-spectacles sitting on her nose, their chain dangling, she looked like a librarian. But something in her demeanor said she could kick all of their asses.

"Protection business."

"None of yours." She went back to rolling out the dough.

Nick mouthed, "She's in the business," to Quinn and filched another bit of dough.

"The food's getting cold." Quinn returned to the table and set out the grinders. Marley carried sealed bottles of water to the table and passed them around.

"You don't trust me yet," she said in response to Quinn's inquiring glance. "I know this is a minor thing…"

"It's fine. Thank you."

Nick didn't look convinced, but by now, Quinn was too tired of the strain of suspicion to care.

"Okay, Marley. Spill."

Marley swallowed hard, her eyes darting everywhere but at Quinn. "I have to go back a ways."

"To Anson."

"Yes." She grimaced at her sandwich and set it on the paper wrapper with only a few bites gone. "You met our father, right?"

Quinn nodded.

"He told you I collect misfits or something like that?"

Fran grunted, and Marley patted her hand almost absently.

"He did."

"I don't consider them misfits. But there's something about all of us that doesn't fit into society. Or *the* Society. A few years ago, I got tired of the politics and attitude of the goddesses in charge."

Quinn hid her annoyance and automatic need to defend her peers.

Marley continued. "Someone somewhere told someone else that I'd started this inn way up here, a getaway, and she came to work for me as a maid. She said she couldn't find a job anywhere else because of a felony conviction when she was seventeen and tried as an adult. She was an excellent employee, and she worked here for years before she decided to head south for college. She told some friends about me, who told other people, and soon I had a steady stream of workers and friends who were quirky in some way." She glanced at Fran. "The Protectorate didn't like the idea of so much in and out and sent Fran up here. She quit the official Protectorate a while ago but does the job anyway."

"I knew it," Nick muttered. When Fran glared at him, he grinned and crunched a potato chip.

"Anson?" Sam prompted.

"He came here three years ago, wanting to be my assistant."

Sam flinched. He looked at Quinn out of the corner of his eye, then back at Marley as if nothing had happened. Quinn wondered if he was reacting to the job title or something else.

"At the time I had a lull in active business but was going crazy trying to take and organize bookings, as well as the people who wanted appointments for goddess work. So I hired him. He was like a sponge, soaking up everything I taught him. He learned all he could about goddess history and ability, and he was whiz on the computer."

"How old is he?" Sam asked, his voice rough.

"Twenty-eight."

Sam closed his eyes, then pushed his chair back and walked out of the room. Quinn started to get up, but Nick put his hand on her thigh. "I'll go." He gave a chin-jerk to Marley. "You listen."

"So he's younger than you are," Quinn said. "But you guys fell in love?"

Marley seemed to shrink down into her shoulders. "We did. Or, I thought we did. We were having very passionate sex because I get so…you know, whenever I use a lot of power."

Boy, did she know. This was the first time she'd heard of anyone else suffering from it and wondered if it was a family trait. The similarities to Sam and herself creeped her out. She was glad that Sam had left the room, almost gladder that Nick had, though they hadn't gone far. Low voices drifted to her from down the hall.

"It grew from there. Last spring he proposed, and in July—" Marley swallowed hard. "In July, I did the stupidest thing in the world. I wanted him to be like me. We shared everything but that, and I knew he felt inferior because of it. I had to even the field or I was afraid that over time, it would kill our relationship."

How could she be so stupid? "So you just ignored everything we've been taught about leeches?"

Tears filled Marley's oddly pale eyes. "He said it wasn't true, that he'd done research and it was lies told to keep men from taking power from us. He told me how to focus power through a big quartz geode into him. I couldn't believe how easy it was. He sucked it right up and started moving things around. He found a rash on someone's leg and healed it in seconds. He was giddy with his abilities. That was the happiest night of my life." She swiped her fingers across her cheeks. "The next day, he was gone, and so was my geode."

Quinn understood how devastating that betrayal had to have been, but Marley's gullibility was hard to believe. "When did you hear about Tanda and Chloe?" she asked.

"A few days after Chloe was leeched. It was like being stabbed in the heart. I was already feeling used, and then to learn he might have done *this*. Someone I loved, that I thought I knew everything about. I called the Society, then went down to Boston to meet with them. I—" She faltered for the first time. "I told them about you. I'd talked to Anson about you and about how I wished I hadn't been so cowardly and had a relationship with you." She heaved a sigh. "And I told him how powerful you are, except you don't have constant access. I think he decided that if he leeched other goddesses and then you, he could have your level of power, or more, all the time."

Everything fell into place. "So that's why the Society marginalized me."

"They don't trust me now and probably extended it to you."

They sat in silence for a moment. Part of Quinn wanted to comfort Marley, but the rest of her held a futile fury. The two canceled each other out, leaving her with nothing to say.

Sam and Nick walked into the room, both looking grim. Quinn repeated what Marley had told her.

Nick scowled at Marley. "You used the present tense."

She sniffed and frowned at him. "What?"

"You said Anson *is* your fiancé."

"Oh." Her face reddened. "No matter what I hear, a part of me doesn't want it to be true. I love him." Her shoulders lifted in a hunch. "We still don't have proof…" Her voice grew faint and trailed off. No one bothered to point out how foolish that was.

"So now you get to the part about flipping Sam's car," Nick said.

Marley rested her head on her hands, elbows propped on the table. "I didn't know what to do. I knew you were a target, but I was even more scared to contact you when I found out. Tanda and Chloe are your friends, and your protector's the famous Nick Jarrett."

Nick smirked.

"I called Under the Moon, and the woman who answered said you were out of town indefinitely. So I flew to Ohio and traced your path. Then I projected where you might be going, found a place to watch, and set it up."

"To kill me," Sam accused.

"No! To deter you." She shook her head. "I hoped if it seemed someone was trying to hurt you, you'd back off."

"But…"

"But you didn't. One of my friends is a top-level hacker. He piggybacked on all your research, and it was obvious you weren't going to stop. So I sent some of my staff to get Quinn and bring you back here so we could talk. And you'd be safe."

"You don't believe I would have been safe from Anson here alone with you, do you?" Quinn asked.

Grief filled Marley's eyes. "I didn't know what else to do."

"All right," Quinn conceded. "When did you last see or hear from Anson?"

"The day I empowered him."

"Great. That's very helpful." Needing to move, Quinn stood and grabbed at the trash littering the table. Nick stopped her.

"I'll get this. Sam has to talk to you outside." He motioned to the back door onto a wood deck that overlooked the gardens and pathways. Sam nodded. He sat with his arms folded and his cheek pulsed. Something was wrong. Something more. Quinn left the trash, her hands stiff and cold. They headed outside, apprehension digging in where everything else had left toeholds. How much more could she face?

The day was overcast but still bright enough to make them squint. She would have leaned on the wall of the deck, under the shelter of the roof, but Sam continued down the steps and away from the building. Quinn followed a few paces behind.

"What's wrong?"

Sam shoved his hands into his pockets and hunched his shoulders. "All of this might be my fault."

"No way." Quinn shook her head. "You didn't even know Marley existed. How could you have caused her to do this?"

"Not that part." Sam's sigh was anvil heavy. "I think I know who Anson is."

"Okay." That should be a good thing, but the burn in Quinn's gut said it wasn't.

Sam stopped walking and leaned against the trunk of a tree. "I knew him as Tony. Short for Anton. Different last name. He was my freshman-year roommate in college."

"That was a long time ago, and that's all circumstantial. Coincidence."

He shook his head. "We kept in touch sporadically, but when I graduated and came to work for you, I lost track of him. He e-mailed me a couple of years ago. Around Christmas, I think." Sam blinked fast. "We did the catch-up thing. I told him all about you and my job and stuff." He glanced at her, then away. "I told him a lot."

"About the full extent of our relationship."

"Yeah."

"And you think he took that and decided to emulate you?"

"Maybe."

Quinn looked out across the grounds. "There's a lot about this that's uncomfortably parallel to us."

"What do you mean?"

She shrugged. "I could have done it. Made you a leech. It's easy to rationalize the way Marley did. Lies meant to hold us down, that kind of thing. If things had been…just a little different. I might have done it."

Sam shook his head. "Never."

He sounded so certain, Quinn smiled. "Why not? Because you wouldn't have wanted it?"

"No. I wanted it. You know the only reason I'm your assistant is because I couldn't be a goddess. God. Whatever." He made a face. "The consequences are too severe, and I'd have never risked becoming a leech. But you're way too conscientious to have tried it, anyway. You wouldn't go against the natural order."

He was right, and they were getting way off track. "We should confirm this. Do you have a photo or anything you can show Marley? Or does she have a picture? She's got to have a picture." Eager to find a target, some direction, she started back toward the house, but Sam caught her arm.

"I'm sorry, Quinn."

He was so not taking responsibility for this. "Sam, this guy used you. He knew about your mother, right?"

Sam nodded shortly.

"What was his major?"

"Mystic studies."

"See? He was heading this way long before he contacted you. I'll bet you anything he only did so he could set his path. Domination was always his goal, and he used you the same way he used Marley."

"If this guy harms you, it will be because of me."

She laughed, not feeling at all humorous. "Sam, if he succeeds in his plans, it will be because of a lot of people, not the least of whom is me. My ego."

"What are you talking about?"

"You know how Marley said everyone was talking about me and my power and how appalling it was that I was running a bar? I reveled in it. I did nothing to stop the talk. In fact, I ran for office to keep it going."

"I don't believe that."

Quinn hung her head for a moment. "Sam, your belief in me is so blind. I'm not the paragon you make me out to be."

"Maybe not, but that only means you're human. I have no

illusions about your flaws, believe me."

Now feeling a true spark of amusement, Quinn smiled at him. "Wanna list them?"

He ticked them off on his fingers. "You're ageist. You're bossy. You think your way is the best way and to hell with the rest of us if we don't agree. And you constantly overlook the best things in your life because you think you don't deserve them."

He'd managed to crush the spark. "I don't overlook anything, and it's not about what I deserve. It's about what you deserve."

"Yeah, that's the 'your way is the best way' part." He thudded his head back against the tree. "Forget it. That's an old argument, and we're done with it." He pushed away from the tree. "Let's see if Marley has a picture. I'll go back and pull all the info I can find on Tony, and we'll see if we can use any of it against him." He walked away, his long legs taking him far beyond the point where Quinn could catch up to him.

• • •

Quinn walked slowly up to the house, thinking. By the time she got there, Marley had found a picture and Sam confirmed that Anson was Anton. The picture resembled the sketch from Chloe's description, too. Quinn wondered why the Society hadn't sent the photo around instead of the sketch, but Nick figured it was to keep Anson from knowing how close they were to catching him.

Nothing anyone said convinced Sam he hadn't played a significant role in Anson's plans. He spent the rest of the afternoon moping over his computer while they discussed, argued, and planned.

By nine that night, Quinn was jumping out of her skin. The moon had been up for six hours and would be at peak full in the morning, right after setting. Since healing Nick's leg and rescuing the Charger, she'd let her ability to draw power build. She wanted to have as much capacity as possible when Anson attacked. None of them had any doubt he would.

Because her connection to the moon was so strong now, almost an open conduit throbbing with energy, her body's need to recharge had subsided. Quinn remained aware of Nick no matter what was going on, but not any more strongly than usual. Still, she kept several feet between them whenever possible.

Marley gave them all bedrooms upstairs so they could stay close and rotate watch through the night. Not that a watch was necessary, when no one seemed ready to go to bed. They lingered in the upstairs common room, the guys and Fran playing poker halfheartedly while Quinn and Marley curled up on the couch and talked.

In an attempt to maintain her sanity, Quinn decided to pretend none of this had happened. She had a million questions for her sister and couldn't think of a better distraction. For a couple of hours, they found common ground and got to know each other a bit. At two minutes past eleven, a little more settled and knowing she'd be better off tomorrow with rest, Quinn yawned and rose off the sofa.

"I'm going to bed."

Marley sighed but also stood. "I guess I will, too. Buffet breakfast will be out by seven, guys, but don't—"

A thud on the roof above them cut her off. Everyone froze, all looking upward, as if they could see anything through the ceiling. Nick, by the windows overlooking the back of the house, sidestepped behind the curtain and tried to peer out into the yard.

"Marley, kill the lights."

The room went dark. Quinn listened hard but couldn't hear any more movement.

"Are there any trees over the house?" Sam asked. "Maybe a

branch fell?"

"No." Marley had remained by the light switch near the stairs. Fran hurried over and tugged her back toward the center of the room. Everyone stood still, silent. Nothing happened. The tension in the room grew until Quinn imagined them all snapping in half like dry twigs.

Unable to stand it anymore, she opened herself up a little and used a bit of power to sense the presence on the roof, a human energy signature.

"It's one man," she told them, her voice low. "Down in the yard is too far for me to sense, but there's one man right above us."

"Anson," Marley guessed.

"No, a regular person. But there's…" She closed her eyes and pressed, trying to decipher the other energy she sensed. Not living energy, not just electricity, it was—*Holy shit.* "He's got explosives."

"Downstairs!" Nick barked.

Bobby and Tim dashed to the stairs, guns out. Fran dragged Marley away and Sam followed, but Quinn hung back, concentrating on putting up a shield behind them. If the guy above them blew up the roof before they were all downstairs, maybe she could keep the others from getting hurt.

The shield was only half formed when Nick snagged her arm and yanked her through the doorway. He pushed her ahead of him, but now he was closest to the danger and she didn't have time to shield him. She jumped to the landing and waited for him to reach her before starting down the last of the steps.

Ka-BOOM!

Quinn's ears rang with the blast, and she stumbled as the building shook. Dear god. This was much more than they'd expected. They couldn't fight this.

Nick caught her arm again and dragged her down into the central hall. "What else can you sense?" he growled, maintaining a constant visual sweep of the perimeter. Door, window, parlor, lobby, hall. All remained blank, empty.

Quinn closed her eyes and sensed around the building. It took more power to cast that wide, and she could only reach a short distance across the yard. "Four people right outside, plus two more with power." Her eyelids flew open and she met Marley's stunned look. "Either two goddesses," she said, "or Anson and one goddess."

"I can't believe someone would work with him," Marley protested.

"We don't have time to debate that," Quinn said. "They're coming. All sides."

Without a word the group gathered in a tight circle, facing out. Fran and the men all held guns. Crystals dangled from leather thongs at Marley's waist and adorned her hands and wrists as jewelry. Quinn tightened her awareness of the moon. They waited, the tension now so high it hummed.

A window broke somewhere out of Quinn's vision. A flinch went around the circle, but they held their positions. Two beats of silence later there was a tinkle of glass, then the roar of Tim's shotgun, a cry, and silence again.

"Got one," Tim said from the other side of the huddle, his tone implacable.

Movement in the hall to the kitchen. Black against blacker. Quinn tapped Nick's upper arm and felt him nod. He raised his gun. The shadow ducked. Nick held his fire, but he was closest to that hall, and he was vulnerable. Quinn reached out, connected with the shadow's energy, and dragged him out of the hall toward her. Before Nick could move, she thrust her foot behind the man's ankles, hit him in the chest with the heel of her hand, and slammed him to his back. She yanked off his black ski mask.

"It's not him." Rage poured into the hollow of her calm. She wanted the leech, dammit, not hired guns. The man tried to sweep her legs. She put a shield in the way, and his lower leg slammed into it and bounced off. He howled and grabbed his shin. Nick caught his wrist, flipped him over, and zip-tied his hands and feet.

But the man mumbled something, and Quinn saw that he was miked. She ripped it off his ear too late. More glass shattered and wind whipped through the room, whirling around them and knocking some of them off-balance. It wasn't a natural wind, clearly generated by one of the goddesses or the leech. Anson.

"What the fuck?" Nick yelled. The wind pushed him back, away from her, and he fought against it in vain. Quinn's hair lashed her face, blinding her. She fumbled in her pocket for a hair tie and tried to secure it. She had to see, but the effort occupied her hands. Another dark shape appeared out of the maelstrom, a gun aimed at Sam, and she panicked, her fingers tangling in her hair. She yelled and slammed her body into the man, using telekinesis to shove the gun sideways. He managed to fire, the round plowing into the wall behind the registration desk. Sam was on him almost before she'd regained her balance, wrenching the gun from the guy and ejecting the clip.

"You okay?" Sam called at her as the wind separated them, too. He reached out a hand and she tried to grab it but missed.

Dammit, she had to get to the goddess controlling not only the wind but now also a thick, swirling fog collecting from the misty grounds outside. The wind pushed her against the wall. She squinted. Papers from the front desk swirled around, making it even more difficult to see, never mind tell friend from foe. Bodies appeared here, disappeared there, the entire scene disorienting her so that if she hadn't had the wall at her back, she wouldn't know which way was up. A potpourri basket smacked her in the side of the head. Sparks shot through her vision. She couldn't stay here. Pushing off the wall, she stumbled toward the front door, which hung crookedly from one hinge. A woman stood there with her feet braced wide, sucking air from the outside to feed the maelstrom in the lobby.

Light flashing from the parlor drew Quinn's attention. Marley crouched there, a crystal held in her palm. Light flashed inside the crystal again, and this time there was a cry from someone beyond Quinn's vision. Marley jumped forward, and Quinn heard a crash like toppling furniture. More flashes, then her sister appeared in the doorway, her chest heaving and her hair wild, but otherwise whole.

Quinn turned back to the enemy goddess. The woman stood with her eyes closed, her arms wide as if she'd scooped the wind in front of her. Trying to counter that wind would do no good, but moving things—that Quinn was good at. She held up her hands in front of her body and pushed energy through them to get the woman out the door, onto the porch, then backward, down the steps, away from the fight inside the inn. The woman resisted but couldn't keep up the wind and fog at the same time. The roar of the rushing air subsided. Quinn stepped out on the porch, following the woman into the yard, intent on corralling her. Too late she realized her mistake.

Bodies surged around her, far more than the six she'd originally sensed. There were guns and knives and people who looked like they'd been well trained in hand-to-hand combat. Someone knocked her sideways as he ran around the side of the building, but he didn't seem to even notice.

As if obeying a single command—and judging by the earpiece the first guy had been wearing, they were—the enemies stopped moving and aimed their weapons at the front door. Quinn stood frozen in the center of the yard. She couldn't warn anyone inside without drawing attention to herself, and if they realized she wasn't there and came out after her, they'd be dead before they even saw what waited for them out here.

An inaudible hum, a rise in power vibrated on her left. She

whirled. Another woman built a ball of fire in her palm while she stared, focused, at the front door. Her intention was clear—she would heave the fire at the house and send the entire building into flames. Either trapping everyone inside an inferno or forcing them out to be gunned down. Quinn had barely registered the horror of those options when it clicked.

Two goddesses. Two people with power. The leech wasn't here.

Fuck.

A scream came from the porch. Quinn watched Fran fall to her knees, blood dark against her light-colored shirt. Gunshots sounded all around her, and the fireball grew. Marley. Sam. Nick. They would lose. Worse, they would die.

Quinn opened herself as wide as she could, imagining a giant conduit between her and the moon. She'd never done anything like this before, but she'd thought about it all day, visualizing scenarios, sensing the energy and planning how to use it. She closed her eyes and in seconds had pinpointed all the metal weapons within her range, all the enemies, and all her people. She shielded the latter and isolated the former and drew, harder than she ever had before. White light flooded her, overflowed her, and she tried to compress it, to force it into two streams. Her skin prickled and burned. With a yell she flashed the heat to all sources of metal, warping the gun barrels so the bullets would jam or explode and fusing the pins of grenades that hadn't yet been employed.

At the same time, she sent a concussion wave of energy sweeping across the lawn and driveway and into the house. She strengthened the shields around her people, Sam and Marley and Nick and Fran and Tim—lying motionless in front of the registration desk—and Bobby, standing on the stairs, facing down a man dressed in black. He collapsed under the force of the wave, as did all of her targets. All but one. The goddess nearby had set up her own shield of energy, protecting herself from Quinn.

The fireball rushed past Quinn and hit the front wall of the inn.

"*Nooooooooooo!*"

Quinn tried to run back to the building, but the effort she'd expended took an immediate toll. Her legs shook and numbed, and she fell at the bottom of the steps. She reached out, struggling to find a way to extinguish the flames, but a moment later, water streamed through the door, dousing the worst of them. Marley appeared behind the water, aiming a hose. Shadows enhanced gaunt hollows in her cheeks and under her eyes.

Quinn's sluggish mind churned. *The fireball goddess. Stop her.* But when Quinn looked back toward the spot where she'd been, it was empty. She cast feelers, trying to sense her, but the goddess was already out of range.

"Quinn!" Marley screamed. "Help me!" She now crouched over Fran, who lay on the porch, bleeding out.

Quinn hauled herself up the steps, stamping out small flames flickering across the porch floor as she went, and collapsed next to Fran. She closed her eyes and put her hand on the woman's chest. The bullet had gone through, low on her shoulder. The heart was okay, but a major vessel gushed blood. Quinn drew on her dwindling resources and focused her power into the injured protector. The vessel closed, then the smaller blood vessels. Flesh sealed over the wounds, front and back. Fran gasped and shuddered.

Lights flashed in blackness at the edges of Quinn's vision. She'd drawn too much, too fast. She closed the conduit she'd opened, and all awareness of their attackers blinked off. Her friends and Marley's remained residually connected to her, like a ghost image after closed eyes in bright light. They were all alive, if damaged, and the fading connection was reassuring.

The yard was silent now. No weapons discharging. No screams or shouts of anger. The fire died, and Marley went inside to Tim.

Quinn hoped her sister could heal him, because she was nearly tapped out. She wasn't even sure what was wrong with him.

She huddled next to Fran, drawing deep breaths as her vision cleared, but as it did she lost track of everything else. Nick stood in the driveway with his pistol, which she may have melted. But Sam…

She struggled to her feet and down the steps again. Nick sagged against the porch rail, looking haggard. He had a cut across one cheekbone and bruising on his jaw, and he held one arm against his body. Hurt ribs, maybe, or his shoulder.

"You okay?" they asked simultaneously. Then, together, "Barely."

"Where's Sam?" Quinn rasped.

Nick shook his head. "I don't know. He chased a guy through a window." He motioned toward the side of the house and grimaced as he straightened.

Quinn took a deep breath to brace herself and walked around the corner of the house. The grass was cold and damp against her dragging feet, and she realized for the first time that she was barefoot. Her left arch throbbed as if she'd stepped on a big stone, and her toes tingled in the chill. The air felt thick, not breathable, and her eyes didn't like the darkness. She kept flinching from phantom movement. Her voice resisted, too, and calling out for Sam was fruitless.

They rounded the corner and the moonlight shone down on the wide yard, empty except for two figures on the ground. One wore all black, ski mask still in place.

The other was Sam.

"No!" Quinn whispered, fear spiking her adrenaline. She stumble-ran to where he sprawled on the ground, eyes closed, one arm bent across his body. There was no sign of blood, but that didn't reassure her.

"Sam." Nick slid to a halt at Sam's far shoulder and patted his cheek. "Wake up, Sam."

"I'm so sorry," Quinn whispered.

Nick jerked his head up. "Stop it. He's not dead."

"No." She closed her eyes, opened herself to the moon, and assessed him. No bullet wounds. No head injury—at least, not from a blow. His electrical system was all messed up, his breathing shallow, his heartbeat erratic.

"He's been Tasered."

Nick dropped his head. "Jesus. Is that all?" He sat on the ground with a thud. "I guess that's what they need to take down a bull like him."

"They used too much juice for too long. He's tachy." She had to help him. There were no hospitals close by—they'd already established that—and she wasn't sure they could get paramedics here in time.

"Quinn, you're tapped out."

"No, I'm not." The energy was unlimited, even if she had few resources to access it. She put her hand on Sam's chest and opened herself wider again. Power came in a sluggish trickle, not the raging river it had been mere moments before. She nudged Sam's heart. It did three rapid beats before settling into a rhythm. Next she inflated his lungs deep. He pushed all the air out, then drew it in less shallowly than before.

Now the hard part. Static zigzagged through his nervous system, causing fibers to jump and vibrate. She imagined touching them, calming them like a finger on a guitar string stops the sound. His body relaxed under her hand, and with a short sigh, she passed out on the grass next to him.

CHAPTER FOURTEEN

Even when a goddess's power source seems unlimited, her own physical resources are finite. We encourage you to test your limits under controlled, safe circumstances.

— The Society for Goddess Education and Defense,
New Member Brochure

"…too much at once."

The soft voice was Marley's, Quinn thought, struggling up through fog. Then came Nick's, harsher, skeptical, shaking like he was running on caffeine and fear.

"I don't like this. That was too easy."

"Too easy? You're insane. Fran was shot, Tim has a broken arm, Quinn's unconscious—"

"Not anymore." Her voice croaked, and she didn't think anyone would hear her. But a second later Nick and Marley both bent over her.

"How you feelin'?" Nick asked. "I gotta tell you, this fainting shit isn't very impressive."

Marley gasped. "Nick!"

"It's okay." Quinn tried to sit up. Nick supported her with an arm around her back, and she saw she was on one of the stiff flowered sofas in the parlor. "He's right."

"He's a jerk. You saved us all and nearly killed yourself."

She shook her head. "He's right," she repeated. "It was too easy." When she swallowed, her throat grated like sandpaper. "Got anything to drink?"

Nick handed her a bottle of water. It was lukewarm, and she realized the lights were off.

"No electricity?"

"No. I think your energy wave knocked it out."

"How long was I unconscious?" She swung her legs off the cushion and shifted so Nick could lean back next to her. The water, warm as it was, felt like silk on her abused throat.

"You don't know?" Nick sounded incredulous.

"I—" She stopped. She didn't. That was bad. "No."

"Only about twenty minutes," Marley soothed.

"How are the others?"

"Fran will be okay. She's weak, but I don't think she needs a transfusion."

"Push fluids."

"We are. Tim broke his arm. Nick splinted it, but he'll need to see an orthopod. I don't think it's displaced." Her face tightened. "I don't have the healing power you do. I can't—"

"I'll take a look."

"No, you won't." Nick looked weird, and it took Quinn a minute to realize it was worry. He normally hid it well. But not tonight.

"If I can help him, I will."

"Quinn, you're completely drained."

"I'll be okay." That might be a lie. "I could at least check him, see how bad it is."

She could tell Nick didn't believe her. "What else?"

"Bobby's fine. The attackers are gone, every last one of them." Nick stood and paced a few feet away. "When I got you back to the house, they'd disappeared."

"How?"

He shrugged. "No idea. They all puddled onto the ground when you did your major goddess mind-meld thing or whatever it was."

"It must have been the goddess. The one who cast the flame."

"She what, teleported everyone?"

"No, but I think she cloaked them until she could get them out. Now please stop trying to divert me and tell me what's wrong with Sam."

Nick and Marley exchanged a look that said they knew how she'd react. Nick sighed and sank down next to her again.

"He's still out."

A sob welled in her chest, trapped. "Where is he?"

"Upstairs."

She raised her eyebrows. "How did you get him there?"

"Wasn't easy. Needed a Hoyer lift." The joke fell flat. "He hasn't moved. But it's only been half an hour."

"Let me see him."

She expected Nick to say no, but he bent and hauled her into his arms to carry her upstairs.

"I can walk."

"You need to rest."

"What about your ribs? I know they were hurt."

"Marley took the edge off. I'm fine."

He wasn't, of course. His legs shook, and his abs were rock hard against her side from his effort. She wasn't exactly petite. But he was halfway up the flight of stairs already, and struggling would send them tumbling back down, so she held him around the neck and tried to balance her weight for him. She was so exhausted her need to recharge was on hold, but she knew it would be intense once it hit.

Plaster dust and shattered wood fragments littered the hallway at the top of the stairs. Quinn glimpsed a small hole in the common room ceiling before Nick turned right and set her down at the doorway to the room Sam was in. He clearly tried to mask that he was out of breath. Quinn squeezed his shoulder in thanks, but her attention went to her assistant, lying ghostly pale in the moonlight. She sat on the edge of the bed and put her hand on his chest, but Nick grabbed her wrist.

"Don't, Quinn. You don't have the energy."

"I know." She felt his heart beat under her palm. "Even if I can check him, I can't fix him."

"He'll be okay."

But he didn't know, and neither did she.

"What I'm more concerned about," Nick said, "is what that attack was supposed to accomplish."

"I'm thinking the same thing." Anson hadn't been there. No one had tried to take Quinn or even harm her. The action had been peripheral, targeting the support team.

"I don't know what the purpose was or if they accomplished it," he stated. "But I know one thing for sure."

Quinn finished for him. "They'll be back."

• • •

"You need to rest, Quinn." Nick set his hand on her shoulder, but she didn't move.

"I'm not leaving Sam."

Marley spoke from the doorway. "Quinn, I'm not as depleted as you are. I can watch over him."

"You've got your own people to take care of."

"We'll manage. You're no good to anyone like this."

Quinn tried to turn her head to argue, but it hurt too much to look over her shoulder. Her entire body throbbed and ached from channeling so much energy through it, making their point for them.

Quinn didn't know what to do. She'd never felt so incapable in her entire adult life. Anson knew she was here, so her presence endangered everyone. Nick would never let her leave without him. He'd stand over her and fight to his last breath to keep her safe, but she'd rather lose her abilities to leeching than lose Nick forever. But the stakes were higher now. Anson obviously didn't care whom he hurt.

Sam would tell her the despair she felt, the enormous weight of responsibility, was so heavy because of her fatigue. She smiled a little, hearing his voice in her head, but then she wanted to cry, watching him lying so still.

Nick's cell phone buzzed. Frowning, he checked the display, then answered. "Yeah." He cursed. "When?" After a few more one-word queries and responses, he hung up and shook his head. "Dammit."

"Who was that?"

"John."

His boss. "What happened?"

"He hit again." Nick didn't look over when Marley gasped.

"Another goddess was leeched?" Quinn squeezed out. "Where?"

"Boston."

She stared at him for a few seconds, not getting it. "When?"

"Half an hour ago." He walked stiffly to the wall and leaned against it, as if too tired to stand on his own anymore. "Which means he wasn't even close to this battle. I don't know if this was supposed to be a distraction or if he just wanted a shortened timeline, or maybe more juice to come after you himself."

"Who did he get?" Quinn managed to ask. Her voice was barely audible, her body shutting down despite her struggles to focus on what Nick was telling them.

He named a goddess she didn't know. "He didn't drain her

completely. He'd barely started when her protector stopped him, doing some damage he'll have to recover from, according to John. Protector couldn't hold on to him, though, and apparently he has a concussion and a busted hand. Goddess has been pulled in to the Society offices."

"We have to get down there." Quinn lurched to her feet, but her head swam and she hit the floor with a thud. She was barely aware of hands helping her down the hall to another bedroom, where she collapsed on the bed. *No. Have to go. Can't let him…*

And then she was out.

The first couple of hours were dreamless. She woke briefly, struggling to calculate what time it was based on how long she'd been asleep. It was still scarily difficult, and her eyes closed against her will.

This time, though, she dreamed. The unprecedented amount of power she'd channeled that night had overloaded her system. Now, with a little rest, she was rebounding, and her body clamored to recharge, desperate when it had been denied for so many cycles. First, it hummed, an engine driving a clawing hunger. Her pulse throbbed in her neck, her groin. She rolled onto her side and squeezed her thighs together. Her bra constricted around her heavy, swollen breasts. She ached—her throat, her nipples, between her legs.

There was no one here to address the need, so her subconscious punished her for it.

She dreamed of Sam, standing by the river back in Ohio. His bare toes curled into the silt at the water's edge. The light was early-morning dim, so the green leaves and grass and water were dark while his skin looked like carved marble. His naked legs, ass, back, shoulders were all achingly familiar and daring her to touch. He shook back his shaggy dark hair, then dove into the water. He surfaced facing her, an abandoned grin on his face.

"C'mon, Quinn. Have some fun." His tone left no doubt what kind of fun she should have.

Her body craved what had so often nourished it. Even as she stood unmoving on the bank she could feel the cool, silky water on her bare skin, then Sam's strong, hard arms and legs around her. His penis inside her, stroking and pumping until she bit his neck, cut into his back with her fingernails, and exploded in a shower of light.

"You don't kiss me," he said, annoyed, and it was like the orgasm hadn't happened, like the dream reset.

"I'm sorry, Sam. I can't. It's wrong." Wrong to accept from him what she really wanted from someone else.

"It's never wrong." But he threw her away from him. She sank deep into the water, caught by the current that dragged her along, whirling and spinning up against rocks and surfacing only long enough to get a breath before being sucked under again. The maelstrom didn't scare her, though. Even asleep, she knew the drowning was metaphorical, punishment for not slaking her lust. Drowning in need, not water.

She washed up onto shore on a bed. Everything was dry, but she was still naked. Silk bound her wrists to the bedposts and Nick sat next to her, fully dressed. His hands rested on his lap and she arched toward him, her body begging. He shook his head.

This was *her* dream. She could have what she wanted here, guilt free. The restraints disappeared and she grabbed the sides of Nick's open flannel shirt and yanked him to her.

The woods and river vanished, and she was in her room at Marley's inn, dimly lit with moonlight. She was naked and panting…

And she held Nick over her, his shirt fisted in her hands.

"Are you awake?" he murmured, his lips brushing hers.

She nodded, shocked.

"Good."

His mouth crossed the last centimeter between them and closed over hers. At first it was simple, welcoming, but after a few seconds Nick opened his lips, parting hers, and dipped his tongue inside, just a touch. Quinn tightened her grip and pulled him closer, but he'd braced his arms on either side and held his weight off her. He concentrated on the kiss—the slow, devouring, savoring kiss.

Quinn had never been kissed like this before. It was as if that was all Nick wanted from her, all he would give. Yet the bold stroke of his tongue and the slight moan in the back of his throat told her there was going to be much, much more.

His right hand came off the bed and cupped the side of her face. His fingers stroked her hair behind her ear. He backed off a little, nipping at her mouth now while his hand caressed the side of her neck and top of her shoulder. Then he slipped it under her shoulder blade and lifted her against his chest.

He was so warm. Smelled so good. Need subsided into want, a low, rhythmic hum instead of a driving scream. Quinn loosened her grip on his shirt and pushed it back. He sat up and stripped it off, then pulled his T-shirt over his head before bending back to her.

Now she had flesh to touch, smooth skin rippling over powerful muscle. The low-burning embers caught. Her hands roamed across his chest, around to his back, where she gripped muscles and dug her nails in next to his spine.

"Nick," she whispered, lost in him. Emotion trumped irrational hunger, and she wanted him because it was *him*, not because she couldn't control her body.

"Quinn." He came back for more kisses, their bodies rocking against each other. Nick rolled across her to lie at her side, his arms circling her. Quinn's legs tangled in the sheet and she cursed. His mouth curved in a smile against her lips. She'd never felt anything so erotic. Need flared higher again, hotter, and she fought to get the sheet away, to unbutton his jeans, eliminate anything that kept them from being skin to skin.

"Slow down, baby." He held her head with both hands now. "We've got time."

"I can't." She stripped off his jeans and the briefs underneath, but when she would have taken him into her hand, he caught her wrist.

"I'm not a tool, Quinn." His voice was hard and cut right into her. She stilled.

"Then maybe you don't want to be here."

"The hell I don't. This is the only place I want to be." He let her push him onto his back, but when she moved to straddle him he blocked her. "I want more than your body."

He already had more. He had everything. How could he not know it? Her throat tightened. She wanted to tell him, to explain that years of pent-up longing combined with the moon lust were driving her insane, but the words wouldn't squeeze through. She ran her hands across his broad chest and down his abs, watching the moonlight paint his skin with flickers. She raised her head to meet his eyes, letting him see everything she couldn't say. This time, when she swung her leg across his hips, he didn't stop her. His lips parted as he drew in a sharp breath, and his fingers tightened on her hips, his thumbs in the creases of her thighs.

Then he grabbed the back of her neck and pulled her down to him, meeting her mouth with a hot, plunging kiss. Quinn moaned and straightened her legs so she lay fully on top of him, touching everywhere. His arms wrapped around her back, his hand tunneling up into her hair.

Quinn bent her head to his collarbone, inhaling as she tasted him. Leather, musk, salt, and sin. She slid down, running her tongue along ridges and nipping with her teeth, reveling in the harshness of his breathing. His fingers tangled in her hair, massaged her scalp, then wrapped her hair tight around them. He tensed as she went lower and jerked when her hand brushed his cock.

It was longer than her hand, hot and silky, and hard as stone when she squeezed it. When she wrapped her lips around the head, he stopped breathing and froze. She licked as much as she could reach, then pushed her mouth down. Licked again, took him deeper, as low as she could go. She sucked hard as she moved back up.

"Fuck." Nick grabbed her shoulders, pulled her up, and flipped her onto her back. "I knew you were going to have your way." But he didn't sound angry about it anymore.

Quinn bent her legs and lifted her hips. Nick ripped open a packet with his teeth, used one hand to cover himself, and then dropped his head into her neck and thrust deep with a long, low groan. She let out half a scream, her joy and ecstasy overwhelming her.

Nick's mouth moved against her neck, his breath hot, as he pulled out and sank deep again. Pleasure sizzled, white-cold and red-hot, all the way to the tips of her fingers and toes. Quinn squeezed him as hard as she could, and he gasped.

"Jesus, Quinn." With his arm under her back, that hand gripping her neck again, and his other hand clutching her hip, he began thrusting. She held on to his sides with her knees and his back with her arms and sobbed into his shoulder while her vision went black and she lost herself in him, in the tension he built inside her.

"Oh god, Nick." She pressed upward against him and he moved faster, thrusting harder, more frantically. "Please, Nick, now."

With a shout he threw his head back, his hips hard against her. Everything tightened into a point, then burst out to the edges of her existence. Pure white light, moonlight, filled her body and her vision. She couldn't breathe, the pleasure and the beauty were so exquisite. They lay, still holding each other tightly, still tensed against each other's bodies, as their world expanded again.

Nick sighed and rolled to his side without letting go of her. He tucked her against his chest, but said nothing.

"We should go," she murmured, "before Anson leaves Boston again."

"John said he was hurt. You need some more sleep. We'll go in a couple of hours."

Quinn tried not to sink, but it was a losing battle. This time, when the darkness overtook her, she healed.

• • •

She woke a few minutes after dawn, snuggled in blankets and laying across the backseat of Nick's car. She stretched, pleased to find her body fully recovered from the battle. Her outlook, too, was a full one-eighty from where it had been the night before. She'd been ready to leave, to try to face Anson alone so no one else would be hurt, but now she realized how backward her thinking had been. Her safety wasn't more important than anyone else's, but she wasn't the only one with a stake in stopping Anson.

Marley and her friends had fought hard last night, and Quinn could no longer question her motives. They'd all worked well as a team, and that was the only way they were going to win this. It was time to go on a full offensive.

She sat up, catching Nick's attention. "Morning," he said.

"Apparently." She freed herself from the tangle of blankets and climbed over the seat. "Where are we?"

"Halfway to Boston." He handed her a large cup of coffee. She sniffed it and smiled. French vanilla. It was still hot.

"How did you get me into the car without waking me?"

Nick snorted. "You were out deeper than Sam. Who's fine, by

the way."

She perked up. "He's awake?"

"Just. Marley says he's still a little fuzzy, but she's feeding him energy drinks and as soon as he can walk without toppling over, they'll come down to meet us."

"Good." She sighed and settled more comfortably on the seat, watching the woods they sped past and wondering what, if anything, she should say about last night. Nick would probably tell her he knew she needed to recharge and he was the only one available, but there had been an intensity he couldn't deny, an intimacy that terrified her. Everything had changed between them, but nothing had changed in the outside world, not yet. She couldn't face Nick rebuilding the wall.

"How do we know Anson is still in Boston?" she asked.

"We don't. But even if he's on his way to Maine, we won't be there." He glanced at her. "We should go to the Society."

Her first reaction was refusal. "You really think they'd help us?"

"Not necessarily, but they may have information we don't. It could help us find him."

"I doubt we'll have any trouble with that." When Nick cocked an eyebrow at her, she said, "He'll find me."

Nick scowled, but he seemed to have accepted the inevitable. "Then it could help us battle him. It's worth trying."

"Okay." She looked down at herself and grimaced. "I look horrendous."

"Sorry. I just put on you what was available."

She blushed, remembering why he'd had to dress her. The jeans held grass stains from when she fell to the ground during the battle, and her green T-shirt, while cleaner, was faded and thin in spots.

"We can stop for you to change," Nick offered.

"I don't have anything to change into," she said. "It's all at

Chloe's."

"Marley sent some stuff. Nothing fancy, but clean, at least." He pulled into the parking lot of a fast food restaurant. "This okay?"

"I'll make it work." She leaned into the back for the bag behind his seat.

"You want anything?"

"No, thanks." She couldn't handle food right now.

The bathroom wasn't the cleanest one she'd ever been in, but it wasn't horrifying, either. She found a pair of khakis and a yellow button-down shirt and cleaned up as best she could at the sink. Marley had included a brush, but Quinn wished she had a little makeup to combat how washed out she looked.

Especially when she emerged from the restroom. Nick had changed into clean jeans and a white collared shirt, and his hair was damp. He leaned against the wall only a foot away from her and smelled marvelous, like bay rum.

Quinn squinted at his face. "Did you shave?"

He tilted his head a little, sheepish. "I was getting pretty scruffy. Thought if we were going in to convince the Society to help us, I'd better not look like the rogue they claim I am."

"Good thinking." She rose up on tiptoe and kissed his cheek. His eyes bore into hers with an emotion she couldn't define if she tried. After last night, she had no remaining moon lust to battle, but the magnetism between them had nothing to do with goddess/protector and everything to do with woman/man. It took effort to break eye contact and back away.

Traffic into Boston moved smoothly, and soon Nick parked across the street from the Society building. He stayed at her side through the lobby, up the elevator, and into the Society's offices, a solid strength that kept Quinn calm as she walked into the reception area.

Alana sat at the reception desk. Worry lines creased her

forehead and held tension around her mouth, but when she looked up to greet them, shock smoothed her features. "Wha-what are you doing here?"

"I'd like to talk to Barbara."

Alana looked ready to argue but then seemed to change her mind. She hurried down the hallway without another word and returned less than a minute later, motioning them back.

Barbara Valiant rose behind her desk as they walked in. She was an imposing woman, tall and straight, her lightly lined skin not betraying her advanced age. She didn't invite them to sit, nor did she bother with polite greetings.

"I've been apprised of the events of last evening," she said without preamble.

"She was incredible," Nick responded immediately. He stood with his feet braced, his hands at his sides, a battle position.

"So I hear." She focused on Quinn. "Why do you think he has targeted you with such intensity?"

She and Nick had talked about this on the drive, and she knew it would be easier to get what she needed if she gave a little first. "We think he might have marked me from the beginning." She briefly explained Sam's college connection and the things Marley had told them, but her resentment grew as she spoke. "You know, if you hadn't been so determined to keep me sidelined, maybe we could have put all the pieces together weeks ago."

Barbara sighed and sat, finally motioning for them to do the same. Quinn accepted the invitation, but Nick stood at her shoulder.

"We were trying to protect the Society. Your relationship to a goddess with ties to a suspected leech—the most heinous of all criminals associated with our world—put us in danger."

Part of Quinn, the rational board member, understood that. The rest of her was still angry. "Why couldn't you just tell me that?

I didn't even know I *had* a sister. When this started, all I knew was that goddesses were in danger, and I wanted to help stop it. But you ignored me."

"Much to our regret, I assure you." Suddenly, she looked closer to her age than Quinn had ever seen her. "Why are you here?"

Quinn cleared her throat. "If Anson wants me, he'll be coming after me soon. The moon is at its peak. We want to be ready for him. To stop him. But we don't have enough information."

Barbara didn't hesitate. She picked up a folder from her desk and handed it over. "This is all the information we have on Anson Tournado. The security team—"

"No, thank you." Quinn took the folder but didn't let Barbara complete the offer Quinn knew she was about to make. She didn't have any reason to trust the security team or time to become comfortable with working with them. "We'll handle it."

Barbara nodded, and then her face went tight and slightly cold. "Please understand that you're not being given license to act outside the regulations of the Society. Should you be deemed to have caused harm or broken any other edicts, you shall be punished. Regardless of the final result of your actions."

Her jaw tense, Quinn said, "Understood." She wasn't promising to place a priority on Society regulations, only acknowledging what she'd been told. She'd deal with any consequences later.

"Your sister is another matter we should discuss."

Quinn tensed again. "In what regard?"

"She will have to answer for her role in the leech's creation."

"I understand that, but I need her. She knows Anson better than any of us, and we'll need her help taking him down."

Barbara nodded. "No sanctions will be made until this is over, but at that time, we must take into consideration the contributions of all involved in the leech's creation."

Quinn went cold. She might mean Sam, too, since Anson was

his old college roommate. "Including the Society? Because we all believed leeches to be legends. The Society of Goddess Education and Defense failed in both halves of its mission. Marley may have made a terrible error in judgment, but she's not evil, and the Society is as complicit in all of this as she is."

Since Barbara didn't seem inclined to respond to that, Quinn stood and indicated the folder. "Thank you for this."

"Good luck."

As they headed back to the elevator, Quinn took a deep, slow breath to dissipate her tension. "That was both harder and easier than I expected."

"Hopefully there's something in there that will help." Nick's phone beeped, and he checked the text message. "They're here. Parking."

Quinn willed the elevator to go faster and then hurried outside, looking both ways. She smiled when she saw Sam striding up the sidewalk, looking whole and healthy, Marley walking beside him.

"How are you?" Sam and Quinn asked at the same time, and laughed.

"I'm fine," Sam said. "Everyone is. Or will be." He looked down at Marley. "She fed me, like, six energy drinks since I woke up. I'm ready to go." He took Quinn's elbow and steered her a few feet away from the others, lowering his voice. "How are you really doing?" he asked.

"I'm fine. I'm more worried about you. I was so scared." She skimmed a hand over his head and checked, using a small stream of energy. No trauma that she could find. When she dropped her hand to his chest to examine his body, he caught her fingers and wrapped his hand around hers.

"I told Nick before, I'm back to normal. But you tapped into a lot of power last night. I can't believe you're still standing."

"Oh." She understood where he was going and tried hard not

to look at Nick. "I'm fine, really. I got a good night's sleep." If he thought she was evading, he didn't pursue it, either, simply pulled her into a tight hug, her head against his chest. His heartbeat was slow and steady under her ear. He pressed his lips to her head and murmured something she couldn't hear, then let her go, shifting to bring the other two back into the conversation.

Quinn passed him the file folder. "This is everything the Society has on Anson. See if there's anything that can help us."

"What's the plan?" he asked.

"We need showers and food and then we have to find a safe location to face him," Quinn said. "The moon's up and he'll be coming soon. I want to be prepared, and I want control. We won't get that unless we draw him to us, on our terms."

"I know a hotel," Sam said. "From the research I did before you guys came out here before."

"Okay, we'll follow you."

They split up, Sam and Marley turning around to go back to Chloe's Prius that Quinn spotted a couple of blocks up the street. Her throat swelled a little. It was so like Sam to think of that, rather than leaving her car all the way up in Maine. Now it would be easier to get it back to her when this was all over.

"How are you feeling?" Nick settled his hand on her waist, his arm a solid support against her back as they crossed the street to the Charger.

Quinn shivered, remembering the night before, drawing in a slow breath full of his leathery scent. "I'm good. Except for road fatigue, I feel the best I've felt in months." They walked in silence, and she tried not to think about what would be next for them. After this was all over, she had no doubt it would go back to the way it was before. Or worse. She didn't know what the Protectorate would do if they found out they'd slept together. John might have someone else assigned to her and keep Nick away.

A few minutes later, they pulled to the valet behind the Prius. Quinn smiled at the hotel staffer who took their disreputable duffels, mild distaste curling his mouth until she handed him a hefty tip.

"Quinn."

Marley's soft entreaty stopped Quinn inside the doors to the marbled lobby. Nick shot her an inscrutable look, then a commanding one at Sam before heading to the check-in desk. Sam took up a stance a few feet away, facing the doors.

"I'm sorry," Marley said.

Quinn sighed. "I know you are."

Marley shook her head. "I know you don't understand. Why I did this. How someone could fool me so easily." She stared out the etched glass doors, blinking fast. "Not all of us are as confident as you are. Or lucky enough to have two guys who love you and would do anything for you." Bitterness colored her tone now, jealousy that might have been a driving force in her bad decisions. Not necessarily jealousy of Quinn, but of anyone who had what she didn't.

But she was right. Quinn *didn't* understand. "You have Tim and Bobby and Fran and a whole compound full of people."

"Pfft. They don't care about me. You know how many people come to my place because they hear I can help them get back on their feet, and then leave and never contact me again? No one stays. Fran, yes, but…" Her eyes filled with tears and she shook her head again. "Sam would do anything for you. That's clear after talking to him for five minutes."

Quinn watched Sam's shoulders tighten and knew he was listening.

"I thought I had that with Anson," Marley lamented. "I just wanted—"

"You wanted to keep him," Quinn interrupted. "You got

desperate and let him talk you into something you knew was wrong. We all do that." Her circumstances had been different, but how could she condemn Marley when Quinn had held on to Sam just as tightly? "But we can't control other people's feelings."

Marley nodded and walked to the counter where Nick still stood.

"You let me go."

Quinn turned to Sam, who watched her sadly. "What?"

"You're not like her. You let me go."

It was Quinn's turn to blink back stinging tears as Sam, too, walked away. She had a new empathy for her sister. Of course people would do anything to avoid being alone. The crushing loneliness her relationship with Sam had held at bay threatened to descend on her, and now was the worst possible time to let it. She had to be strong. There was work to do.

Chapter Fifteen

*The goddess visited the dungeon after her love had been
sealed away, where he could steal no more power from other,
innocent goddesses. "If you leave me here, I'll die," he pleaded
with her through the iron bars in his door. "I can no longer survive
without access to the energy of life." Tears dripped down the
goddess's face, for she knew the truth of his words, and it was her
fault. She knew it was wrong, but there was no way to fix all the
damage she had done, and she deserved no mercy. She laid her
fingers on his. "Take mine."*

— "The Goddess and the Leech,"
*from **Tales of the Descendants of Asgard***

Nick had obtained a two-bedroom suite, by far the nicest accommodations they'd shared this month. Quinn's shoes sank into the plush ivory carpeting when they entered. The center room held dark, fancy antique tables flanking a beautiful but hard-looking love seat and two chairs in earth tones. Doors on either side of the room led to bedrooms with double beds visible. Nick went to the bay window to check the latch and peer out. "Fire escape here. No bedroom access, though."

"Duly noted." Quinn went to the French-style phone to order room service.

Sam had his laptop open already and scribbled down the

research Quinn wanted him to do. Once that was all done, she grabbed her bag and headed to a bathroom to shower. The bedroom was small, with only a few inches between the gold-comforter-covered double beds, a walnut armoire against one wall instead of a closet. The marble bathroom was tiny, too, but luxurious, with a plush rug and thick white towels. The hotel's gold logo filled the center of the white shower curtain—a real curtain, not an industrial-strength, mildew-resistant plastic liner like in most hotel bathrooms.

She lingered under the water, letting the soft spray wash away tears she couldn't attach to anything in particular. Fatigue, fear, the burden Barbara had placed on her, which was no more than she'd taken on herself but which weighed more heavily now, regardless. She pretended none of the tears were related to the loneliness Marley had reminded her of and that she could now feel looming at the other side of this.

When she came out of the steamy bathroom, Sam sat on the end of her bed. He looked fine, with no residual effects from his injuries, but guilt twisted her heart anyway. He'd endured so much for her. *From* her. She couldn't look at him as she reached for the plush robe on the bed.

"Is the food here yet?" She turned her back to pull the robe over her towel, then let the towel fall to the floor.

"No."

After belting the robe, she drew the other towel off her head and squeezed it around her hair. "I'm so sorry I let you get hurt."

He rolled his eyes. "That wasn't your fault." He shifted away when Quinn sat on the bed next to him. It was a small movement that likely meant nothing, but it felt much bigger. His demeanor had changed. Somehow, in the short time they were separated, he'd made a decision.

Afraid of the inevitable, she started talking. "Anson's

completely on our shoulders now. Even if I was his big goal all along, what he did here while we were in Maine shows he's not likely to be satisfied with leeching me. If he gets that much power, he could be unstoppable." The magnitude of it hit her anew. Failure just wasn't possible now.

Sam put his arm around her shoulders. "We can do this. We won't let him get to anyone else."

He'd barely finished the sentence when Quinn heard the hall door opening. "That can't be room service. I didn't hear a knock." She pushed to her feet and reached for the bedroom door. She'd almost reached it when it blew inward, knocking her off her feet. A white flash blinded her, mixing with stars from smacking her head on the floor.

"Quinn!" Sam bent, his hand going behind her head, but she shoved him away and launched herself up and into the main room. She instinctively knew what that flash was. What it had to be. She threw up her hands against another flash of light, glimpsing her sister in a heap on the floor, a dark figure looming over her with a hand on her chest.

She didn't have time to think. She opened herself wide to the moon and shoved at the figure, trying to get him off Marley. The photonegative effect of the light faded, but a hum rose around them. Glasses on the bar and vases on tables rattled, as did the door of the other bedroom. Nick shouted her name and banged on the door, trapped inside.

"Nooooo*oooo*O*OOOO!*" She pushed harder, desperate to free her sister. The figure—it had to be Anson—didn't budge, despite Quinn's efforts. Sam shouted behind her, and Anson lifted his head. There was a loud thud, and Quinn whipped around to see Sam sliding down the wall, unconscious. Fury took over. She scanned the room for weapons and used telekinesis to fling a heavy vase, books, and decorative bowls through the air at the leech. Marley shuddered and jerked under his hand, while he had taken on a faint amethyst glow. Everything Quinn threw bounced harmlessly to the carpet. He was powerful enough to deflect the missiles even while leeching her sister. She tried to render him unconscious like she had his people at the inn, but nothing happened.

Pressure built into a bloodcurdling scream of rage. She ran across the room, her hands in front of her, sending energy in waves, trying to knock him off or interrupt his pull of Marley's power. In slow motion Anson raised his free hand. Quinn slammed full-speed into an invisible wall and fell to the floor again. Her vision erupted in cracked lines of pain and her nose gushed warm blood.

She touched her face to heal the injury. Haphazardly, but well enough for the pain to fade and her vision to clear. But it was too late. Anson now loomed over Quinn.

She couldn't defend herself, couldn't affect him. Fear flooded her, but she wasn't helpless. Or alone. She unlocked Nick's door with a thought. It flew open so hard it cracked the drywall behind it. Nick charged out, his pistol leading, and fired three times. The first bullet soared off course. The second stopped before it got to Anson. But the third hit him in the hand. He yelped and stared at it, going white with shock. Then, fury contorting his face, he stretched a hand toward Nick. Nick's gun flew out of his hand and crashed through the window.

Nick didn't hesitate. He pulled another weapon from his rear waistband and kept firing, hitting Anson twice before the leech threw a chair at Nick, knocking him to the floor.

Quinn lashed out with her feet as Anson stepped closer to her, still distracted by her protector. She slammed her heel into his knee, then scissored her legs around his. He landed on his back hard enough to shake the floor but was on his feet as quickly as she was.

Sirens outside stopped everything. Quinn recovered first and lunged, but she managed only to catch Anson's long coat, which he slipped out of and ran through the doorway. By the time she reached the hall, he'd disappeared.

She hesitated, not wanting to let him go, but also afraid to leave the others here alone to face the police and the management. She wasn't ready for another fight, not when he was so damned strong. Plus, racing through the streets of Boston in a bathrobe, trying to engage an enemy she was not at all sure she could conquer…well, that would be stupid.

She cursed and went back inside. Marley and Sam lay on the floor, both unconscious. Nick stumbled across the room, bleeding from a gash on his temple and another on his upper arm, right below the sleeve of his T-shirt. But Quinn looked at the coat in her hand and smiled.

Anson didn't know it, but he'd just handed her victory.

• • •

The rush didn't last long. Keeping Anson's coat over her arm, Quinn closed the door and fastened the chain and privacy lock. Nick reached her and propped himself against the wall, leaning to peer through the peephole.

"He's gone?"

"Yeah. You okay?" She touched the gash on his head, wincing at the rawness. The injuries were getting worse every time—but no more.

"*Sonofabitch.*" He jerked away. "I'm fine. Get your sister." He wove his way back into the sitting room and over to Sam, still crumpled in a heap on the floor. Quinn saw he was covered in glass from a shattered picture frame. She told herself he'd be okay, that they'd all be okay, but even with the advantage Anson had unknowingly given her, victory wasn't at hand yet. It wouldn't be if she didn't have her team intact.

Later. Deal with this now, that later.

"Don't move him," she told Nick. "I'll be right there." She knelt next to Marley, who was as still and pale as a wax figure. Quinn skimmed her hands over her sister, checking for injury, but there wasn't one.

There was, however, a definite lack of power.

"Oh, no." A sob escaped her. "I'm so sorry, Marley. It's my fault," she whispered, stroking her sister's dark hair off her forehead. "Come on, sweetie," she said louder. "Wake up."

Marley's eyelids fluttered. Her eyes, pale lavender before from the initial bestowment, were now almost white, the darker purple flecks in the irises reminding Quinn of Easter eggs. She groaned and rolled to her side. "Oh, Quinn, I'm such an idiot."

"Take it easy."

"I'm okay. Just weak." She let Quinn help her to her feet. "I didn't let him in, I swear."

Quinn wondered why Marley would assume that was what she thought. "What happened?"

"I heard the elevator and was going to check through the peephole to see if it was room service. But the door opened by itself." She stared at Quinn, eyes wide, disconcerting in their lack of color combined with fear and anxiety. "I didn't let him in," she repeated. "I didn't tell him where we are."

The elevator dinged, and adrenaline rushed through Quinn. "We don't have time to be sorry. Go get our stuff. Get to the window with the fire escape." She watched through the peephole as police officers and what looked like the hotel manager dashed past. They hadn't pinpointed the gunshots yet.

"We've got to get out of here." Hurrying across the room, she swept her hand over Sam to remove all the glass covering him, then checked his spine first. Nothing was broken, so she nodded to Nick to pick him up.

"Are you shittin' me? The guy weighs more than I do. He's four inches taller." He shut up when Quinn dropped her bathrobe and pulled on Anson's coat, buttoning it and tightening the belt.

"Just go, Nick."

Without another word he bent and lifted Sam in a fireman's carry. Marley beckoned from the open window, and he staggered over. Quinn grabbed Sam's computer bag and Nick's weapon-filled duffel from the love seat on her way to the fire escape. They were heavy enough that she had to drag them across the floor. She bent to crisscross the straps across her body. That balanced the weight, but only if she stood upright.

Voices in the hall grew louder. The police were coming. Too quickly, someone pounded on their door. She gripped the sides of the window and pushed one leg through—careful to keep the coat between her naked body and the cold, hard-edged windowsill— then heaved herself onto the fire escape to follow the others to the alley below. She cursed as the bags kept catching between the rails, but she didn't have time to stop and levitate the bags to the ground. By the time she reached the bottom of the ladder, she was sweating.

"Any clue where valet parking is in this place?" Nick asked her. He'd let Sam down onto his feet but supported his full weight with Sam's arm across his shoulder and his own arm around Sam's waist. They'd never be able to drag him into the underground parking area unseen, even if she cloaked them.

She dropped the bags to the ground. "Give me the keys. You wait here."

Nick scowled but complied. Marley made to follow Quinn, who put up her hand to stop her.

"No," Quinn said. "Stay here. Help Nick support Sam and make it look like he's drunk if anyone shows up."

"You doing okay?" Nick asked her.

She'd used a lot of power, but adrenaline seemed to be making up for it. She had energy, even if she couldn't draw as easily as she had in the apartment. As for the rest—well, if she kept them moving, she could keep from wallowing in guilt long enough to rectify everything.

"Yep," she told Nick.

"You got a plan?"

"Nick, let me *go!* But yes, I have a plan." She hurried down the alley to the rear of the building. The dim, dingy entrance to the concrete garage was a far cry from the elegant front entryway. Quinn kept to the shadows on the far side of the entrance from the booth, where two attendants bent over something below the Plexiglas windows. A valet walking up the incline toward the front of the building bounced in time to the music on his headphones and never turned her way.

Quinn circled three levels, cursing the whole time, until she found Nick's car. She didn't bother trying to mask the growl of the engine, hoping the booth attendants would think a valet was retrieving it.

The back exit had a gate, and she didn't want to damage it or the car, nor did she have ID on her or any proof that she owned the vehicle, since she didn't. So she zoomed out the open front entrance and turned right into traffic, then right again, the wrong way down the alley, before anyone could approach or stop her. Nick stood as she'd left him, Sam slung across his shoulders—except he was on his other side. Marley stood looking down at a prone figure, rolling something in her hand. A crystal?

Quinn stopped with a screech next to them and jumped out.

"What happened?"

"He came out of nowhere." Nick dragged Sam toward the passenger side. Quinn hurried around to open the door and pull the seat forward. While Nick shoved Sam into the back, she dashed around again and got back behind the wheel. Marley crawled in after Sam and tried to straighten out his legs. Her movements were jerky, and Quinn saw tear tracks on her face. The crystal, or whatever had been in her hand, was gone.

"Who is he? The guy on the ground?"

"Anson's friend," Marley answered without looking up at her. "He came to the inn a few times. He ran down the alley with a gun. I tried…I tried…"

Nick slammed the door and Quinn took off. He gave her a significant look and said, "I saw him coming, dropped Sam, and popped him before he could get a shot off."

Marley whimpered. "He leeched me. I couldn't stop the guy in the alley. Oh, Quinn." She buried her face in her hands and sobbed.

Quinn didn't know what to do. She hadn't realized Marley wasn't aware of what Anson had done to her. They were in the middle of heavy downtown traffic now and she couldn't stop, especially when Anson was still sending people after them. Not to mention the police, who'd find the aftermath of their fight and maybe even the slugs Nick had shot at Anson. Even if Quinn was in a position to comfort her sister right now, there was nothing to say that would help.

Still, she had to try. "I'm sorry, Marley. It's my fault. I should have anticipated he'd be able to track us that easily."

"No." Marley straightened. "I'm the one who gave him the ability to do this. I've been afraid it would happen. But it's my punishment. I'll accept it. Eventually," she added in a whisper. "Now tell us your plan."

Quinn gained more respect for Marley. Finally, she was accepting the truth and acting like more than a victim—ironically just as she had become a real one.

"Okay, first we need an empty building. Something in a deserted area, if we can find one."

Sam groaned and shifted in the backseat. "Oh, man. I'm sick of being knocked unconscious."

Nick twisted in his seat. "Double vision, headache, nausea?"

"No. I don't know. Give me a minute."

Stopped at a light, Quinn watched in the rearview mirror as Sam squeezed his eyes closed, then opened them wide. But when those eyes met hers in the mirror, they were clear and even. He winced, stretching his neck and shoulders, but his movements became more limber and controlled.

"I feel like I've been hauled down a fire escape or something."

The silence rang in the car.

"Seriously? You hauled me down a fire escape?" He lifted his pant leg and touched something on his shin. "Weren't very gentle about it, were you?" he accused Nick, who faced forward.

"You're welcome. Go on with your plan," he said to Quinn.

"Sam, did you get to do any of the research I wanted?"

"Yeah, um, empty building. I found a warehouse that's been for sale for three years. Looks like a pretty dilapidated area."

"Remember where it was? How to get there?"

"You got a map?"

Nick dug around in the glove compartment until he found a city map of Boston. "It's a few years old." He handed it back to Sam, who opened it and examined the markings, then ducked his head to check the street signs they passed.

"Okay, yeah. Turn left up ahead." He directed Quinn's driving as she relayed the rest of her plan in pieces. They pulled up in front of rusty overhead doors in a battered brick building that had maybe half its glass windows intact. The tension in the car, made up of probably equal parts disapproval and fear, seemed to crawl over her skin.

Nick got out and tried to open the overhead door. It didn't budge. He tried the one next to it, and it, too, stayed firm. He held up a finger and went around the side of the building before Quinn could point out that she could unlock the door herself. They waited. She tried not to be aware of the minutes as they ticked by, but she noted them automatically. She'd hit eleven when, with a bang and a rattle followed by the hum of mechanics, the door rose.

As soon as she could, she pulled into the building, hoping she had a clear field and debris wouldn't puncture a tire or something. Nick would kill her.

But no, the cavernous space was empty. The weak light from outside penetrated the grime on the windows better than she'd expected.

They climbed out of the car and stood in a cluster by the wall, Quinn feeling vulnerable and skittish and sensing her friends felt the same.

"How long do you think it will take him to track us down?" Sam moved to set up his laptop on an empty mechanic's bin.

"Not long. He's got something of Marley's or mine—probably Marley's—to track us." She rubbed her forehead both to ease the headache building there and to hide her thoughts. Anson had an exceptional level of power now. He'd done so many things at once, so easily. Leeching Marley alone should have taken all his effort. Obviously, the collection of capacity from four goddesses was far more than she'd anticipated. Stupid.

Nick stopped walking the perimeter of the room, where he'd examined the few remaining items for anything they could use. "You're wearing his coat. Can't he track that even better?"

"No." Quinn should have been repulsed by the jacket, by the man's scent on it, but glee made that impossible. She had to stop thinking negatively. *I can do this.* We *can do this.* "Let's split up and search the building for the things we can use. No more than five minutes. Be back here before then."

Five minutes later, they reassembled. Quinn took inventory of the bits and pieces they'd collected. It wasn't much, but they'd make do. She went into action, telling Marley to change into some of Quinn's clothes and pulling on some herself, though she left her torso bare under Anson's coat for maximum contact with his energy. Then she fixed Marley's hair so it was more like hers and placed a chair with a bent leg in a shadowy area in the center of the room.

"You're a little shorter than I am, so sitting is better."

Marley did so without hesitation but said, "Won't he know it's me? I'm powerless. He can sense that, probably from a distance now."

"All we need is a few seconds of distraction. Here, turn to face this door." Nick had broken into a regular door on the building's south wall. Quinn had left it hanging open an inch and secured the other, bigger doors. Anson would be able to open them, but she was gambling that he'd go for the easier, quieter route. Even if he didn't, the noise would alert them, and they would have time to adjust.

Nick and Sam took up positions on either side of the door, while Quinn backed into the darkest shadows along one wall and intensified them to cloak herself. She used a little more power to concentrate on sensing Anson's approach and determining how many people he brought with him.

Then they waited.

The net she'd cast vibrated, indicating a presence. The timbre of the vibration told her it was definitely him, his personal energy matching the residue on his coat. By wearing it, Quinn had connected herself to him and taken a slight advantage.

"He's here," she said quietly. "Three people with him, no goddesses." She focused, struggling to keep her power under control, not use too much at once. "He's last. Wait for the others to come in."

That was all she could do except watch these first few steps. The door swung inward, creaking a little. A hulking shape loomed against the bright security light outside. His head rotated back and forth before he zeroed in on Marley. She'd dropped her head so it looked like she was unconscious. There was no reason for her to be, and Anson might detect a trap, but again, they only needed seconds.

A second shadow appeared at the first one's right shoulder. "What are you waiting for?" it whispered, not nearly as smart or as cautious as the first. "There she is." The two moved a few steps forward, and the third entered the building. This guy, shorter and wirier than the first two, headed straight for Marley. Quinn held her breath, sensing Sam going rigid. She knew if the guy tried to harm her sister, Sam would abandon the plan and go after him. Never mind that Quinn could take these guys and would, long before they got anywhere. But they weren't her prey.

The air seemed to shimmer a moment later as Anson stepped through the doorway.

Now! Quinn yelled only in her head, for fear of alerting Anson. She released the hook holding a net full of boxes of rusted metal scrap, which cascaded down onto the three shadows. At the same time, Sam and Nick jerked the rope they'd strung across the doorway. When Anson started forward, either to help or skirt his men, he tripped and fell flat with a yell.

Nick and Sam pounced, holding him down. One of the shadows struggled out from under the boxes and scrambled on hands and toes toward Marley, who he still seemed to think was Quinn. But Marley had leaped to her feet when the boxes came down, running halfway across the room to put a safe distance between herself and the attackers. Quinn zipped energy at the man, a short, sharp burst that knocked him out. The other two were already unconscious, as planned.

Anson was another story. Quinn knew she'd be ineffective fighting directly against him—he'd become too powerful. In the few seconds since Sam and Nick had jumped him, he'd managed to fling

Sam off to the side. Nick hung on, though with the power behind Anson's efforts to dislodge him, he'd be dead in moments.

Unless Quinn helped him. Instead of attacking Anson, she infused Nick's muscles with energy. His grip on Anson's arm and the back of his neck tightened, and he threw his leg across the smaller man's to hold him down.

Sam snatched at the rope they'd used to trip him and tried to wrap it around Anson's legs. The leech obviously worked against him, because the rope didn't want to stay wrapped. Quinn shielded it so Anson's power couldn't reach it. Sam got his ankles tied, then wrapped the other end around his wrists, jerking them to his back with force despite the wind that now whipped at them all. It swirled into a funnel, lifting the three of them off the cracked concrete floor as Nick and Sam clung to the rope around Anson. Quinn tried to form a sphere of calm inside the funnel, but she had little affinity for air and only managed to slow it. Sam pulled at Anson's shoulder, flipping him over, then hauled back and slammed his fist into Anson's jaw.

Everything stopped. The wind and unseen forces disappeared. The three men fell to the ground, Nick and Sam grunting at the impact. Anson thudded, limp, underneath them.

Quinn flipped on overhead lights and hurried to the men. Nick lay on his back, gasping for air. Sam sprawled next to him, supporting himself on one arm. They were rumpled but okay, thank god. She allowed herself a grin.

"Nice job, boys."

"Asshole," Sam muttered, his expression thunderous.

Marley joined them with a wary look at the thugs in the center of the room. "What about them?"

"Help Sam secure them. I don't need them interrupting me if they come to." Quinn took deep breaths, trying to prepare herself for what she had to do. At Marley's, the need to fight had drawn something out of her she hadn't ever had to use before, though she'd always known, somewhere inside, that it existed. But this—this was not only bigger and more difficult than anything she'd ever *heard* of, she wasn't even sure how to do it. "Nick, you might want to stand back."

"No way. I'm ready in case he wakes up partway through." Nick dragged himself to one knee next to Anson, his fist cocked. Quinn knew he would awaken, and if he did, it was doubtful Nick would get a punch in. She had to hurry.

But she stood straddling the man and studied him for a moment first. His eyes were closed, but she remembered their vivid blue. It contrasted with his dark, carefully cut hair and matched the tie that had been neatly knotted around his throat before the tussle. He was a well-built man, though much smaller and more refined than either Nick or Sam. She could see why women would fall for him and how he'd used charm to get as close as he needed. Marley had to love him so she'd bestow power. For Chloe and Jennifer he'd only needed proximity and opportunity.

"No more," she said aloud. Determination filled her and she crouched to put her hand on his chest. Before she could start, Marley grabbed her arm.

"Are you sure about this, Quinn? You know what the consequences will be."

"I know." The board would punish her for this. They had to. But it also had to be done. Anson was too powerful to be taken any other way.

"I'm not just talking about the board."

Quinn knew that, too. No goddess had ever done this in recorded history. So when Marley said she knew the consequences, what she meant was they had no idea what to expect. Maybe it would kill her, but whether it did or not, she'd have made her world safe for the innocents and the people she loved. That alone gave her the strength to try.

"I have to do this, Marley. Give me room."

She did, slowly. "I'm sorry."

Okay. Now. Quinn bunched Anson's coat in her fist so it tightened against her skin. His essence swirled around her—the essence she'd felt as soon as she touched it, that gave her a connection to Anson in a way she'd never anticipated. She tapped into it, drawing it inside herself, then opened up a conduit through her arm and hand on Anson's chest. Like went to like. She found the power inside him, now tainted, part of him. Marked as his. She drew on it, like sucking a milkshake through a straw.

It resisted, surprising her. He'd made it seem easy when he leeched Marley. But then, she didn't know how he'd done it, or what he'd done to prepare or aid the process. She mentally tightened her grip on the power she wanted and pulled hard. It seeped out of Anson and up into her, burning a whiskey-like trail. Like an infant tasting squash for the first time, her body revolted, tried to reject the foreignness of it. The flow slowed, burning more intensely the more she pulled. She gritted her teeth. Light flashed on the other side of her closed eyelids, then again.

Nick shouted, distracting her, and she opened her eyes. Anson's brilliant blue eyes stared back at her, and he'd wrapped one hand around her wrist. She hadn't even felt it. For a moment they stared at each other, his eyes almost glowing, a vibrant contrast to Marley's bleached irises. Then he bared his teeth. Quinn heard a wheeze beside them and realized Anson's other hand squeezed Nick's throat. Nick was already turning red, struggling to pull Anson's fingers away. She couldn't see Sam and Marley in her peripheral vision.

She bore down on Anson's chest, both to hold him in place and to increase the contact. His power flowed freely toward her now, but she had to concentrate harder to make her body accept it, and

Anson fought the draw until it slowed. He shoved at her, both with power and with his hand, and raised his legs to try to wrap them around her body. She blocked them with her free arm, but his efforts distracted her, and the power reduced to a trickle. With a roar Anson shoved Nick away, pushed Quinn back, and struggled to his feet. She tried to grab him, but her stiff fingers wouldn't grasp. He ran.

Nick fell to his side, clutching his neck and gasping.

"Nick." Quinn knelt next to him, touched him, but then Sam was there, lifting her to her feet.

"I've got him. Go after that asshole."

Sparks flew from the giant round overhead lights, which swung wildly and sent shadows soaring across the walls and floor. He still had plenty of power, and catching him now would be difficult. But she had to do it. He couldn't be allowed to leave here—he'd just start over.

The energy she'd taken surged and swirled inside her. Her body crackled, electrified and hot, like if she touched anything she'd set it on fire, and euphoria sang in her. She could do anything without draining herself. An urge to try it, to do something astonishing, warred with terror that Anson was going to get away.

When Quinn paused and drew a deep breath to stave off panic, she detected a thread between them. She knew exactly where Anson was. He'd found the set of stairs leading to the offices that overlooked the main warehouse floor. She ran to them, moving faster than a normal person. Her feet barely touched the metal steps she climbed, nearly levitating in her effort at speed and quiet.

He'd ambush her. He wouldn't just want to get away. He'd want to disable her and try to get his power back, as well as to leech hers. The office door at the top of the stairs was half open. Quinn stopped a few steps from the landing and pushed the door open without touching it. As she'd expected, a metal trashcan flew through the empty space where her head would have been. Anson cursed from inside the room, then ran out the far door. Quinn followed, her hand up, ready to bounce away anything that came at her.

The office was surrounded by glass, so she darkened the room. Anson probably sensed her as she sensed him, but if he couldn't see, he would be less effective in attacking her. She crossed the dark, empty space cautiously. When she got to the other entrance, which opened onto office space that still held random cubicles and therefore many hiding spaces, she ducked and ran along the wall to her right. Anson was somewhere in the middle, not moving. Getting to him would be tricky with the cubicle walls in the way. She paused, considering her options.

"You're a worthy opponent, Quinn Caldwell." Anson's voice was smooth, cultured, though marred by a ragged edge of fear. "I didn't expect you to use my methods against me."

Quinn didn't respond. She tried to pinpoint Anson's location, but his voice echoed and seemed to move. Which cubicle he was in was important. If she guessed wrong, he'd gain the upper hand.

"You only delayed the inevitable, though. And this time, I'll have to kill you."

Yeah, like you didn't intend that before. She moved a few steps to her right and peered around the cubicle wall. This block was three cubes by three. The three on this side were empty. And there were no openings down the perpendicular wall, so there had to be an aisle down the middle on the left, and three openings on the opposite side.

"You know, I never would have leeched Marley. That's all your fault. If you'd left her in Maine it wouldn't have happened."

"Liar," Quinn said under her breath. He was trying to bait her, determine where she was. She moved back to her left and around the end of the cubicle block.

"I'm not lying. I had no intention of harming the woman who gave me my start. I care about her, you know." His tone was regretful and almost sounded sincere, but Quinn ignored it.

This wasn't working. The thread between them wasn't enough to pinpoint his exact spot, and she couldn't see into any of the center cubicles. She stood slowly to make sure Anson wasn't visible above the tops of the cubicles. Then she grasped the top of the narrow wall next to her and launched herself upward.

It happened just like she visualized. Her body flew up and landed on the cubicle wall, feet balanced on the two-inch-wide metal strip, hands gripping the wall so she was ready to swing right back down if she needed to.

But Anson hadn't noticed, too intent on his monologue. "Can you believe the fuss everyone's making, anyway? I mean, it's not like I raped or murdered anyone. I made them normal. Millions of people would give anything to be normal. Even some goddesses."

His words barely penetrated. The four nearest cubicles were also empty. His voice still echoed and played games with her ears, but she could tell he was in front of her. She crawled forward, looking down onto dusty, empty desks and shelves.

And then there he was. Crouched in the center cubicle, protected on three sides by other cubes and half under the desk. He was doing something with his hands that Quinn couldn't see. She shifted her weight, preparing to jump down on him, when he held out his palm. In the center spun a piece of cloth, what looked like a rolled-up sock—her sock? One end was pointed and as she watched, it rotated upward to point at her. Anson jerked his head up, and Quinn pounced.

He had enough power to shield himself, so instead of landing on him she slid to the ground a few inches away. With a thought, she swept away his shield. Then she caught him by the shoulders and tried to wrestle him down.

He struggled, but she ignored the blows on her face and torso and concentrated on connecting again with his power core. It was easier this time to make the connection. Frighteningly easy. She craved the power, scrabbling for it like an addict, but when she drew on it, the resistance was stronger.

Anson yelled and twisted and punched and tried to get away from her. She maintained her hold but couldn't focus enough to draw. She thought of Marley and Sam and Nick and even her birth mother, as vulnerable as all the other goddesses, but it didn't bolster her strength. A desperate need welled in her, a silent keening when the power eluded her draw.

Anson dropped to the floor. His weight wrenched her shoulders, and she almost lost her grip, but she followed him down and tried to stay on top. He managed to roll, then caught her wrists and jerked her hands off him. His knees pressed down onto her arms, pinning her to the dirty floor. Darkness pushed in around her.

"Got you," he growled. He slammed his palm down on her chest, bare between the lapels of his coat. He connected with her core with a click she felt deep inside, then started to draw the power out of her. She gasped at the icy abrasion and for a minute she could do nothing. Her arms ached where he pinned them. The cold pain of the leeching numbed her ability to think. Her vision narrowed so all she could see was his face—lips pulled back in a gleeful grimace, hair flopping—he didn't look remotely attractive anymore, except for those brilliant, glowing eyes.

Now she understood how completely helpless the others had been, having no way to stop this from happening. Despair squeezed her lungs, darkening into a grief she could never have imagined. She almost gave up, unable to see past it. But then she gasped for air, and the movement shifted her awareness. Anson wasn't only connected to her. *She* was connected to *him*. She didn't need to touch him in any certain way to draw his power.

Taking a deep breath, she closed her eyes and found the thread of light that connected them. She blocked out everything else and pulled, again like sucking on a straw, only with her soul.

As soon as the process reversed, as soon as what remained in him began to enter her, what she'd already taken seemed to reach eagerly for the rest. Overall, Quinn had more power than Anson, and even as he pulled against her, the solid connection he'd made went both ways. She realized that even though the power he'd leeched had been marked as his, it *wasn't* his. It didn't belong to him. Her lungs screamed for breath and lights danced behind her closed eyelids, but she didn't move, only concentrated everything she had on collecting that power. The more she took, the easier it was, and she pulled harder, the conduit strengthening, the power filling her, until she'd drained Anson almost completely.

The rest of the world rushed back in when Nick, roaring, knocked Anson off her. The two of them slammed into the desk of the cubicle, Nick on top, drawing back his fist. Sam pulled Quinn out of the cube and collapsed against the cloth-covered wall opposite, cradling her against his chest.

Everything froze. Anson lay still under Nick, his eyes open but vacant. Nick held his shirt in his fist, the other arm still cocked, but Anson didn't move.

"Is he dead?" Sam panted.

"No." Nick let go, and Anson settled to the ground. "He's breathing."

Quinn felt as limp as Anson looked. She closed her eyes, unable to move. It was over.

Everything was.

CHAPTER SIXTEEN

Goddesshood is a legacy, passed down for innumerable generations, a gift to be cherished and honored. No matter how your source and abilities manifest, they will be a part of you forever. It is a goddess's responsibility to handle her power with care, respecting what came before, what is now, and what will always be. Celebrate, because your life will never be the same.

—The Society for Goddess Education and Defense,
Welcome Letter

"You leeched him?" Nick rose to his feet and winced, his hand on his side where he'd hit the desktop, no doubt the same ribs he'd bruised before.

"Mostly." She could detect a tiny glimmer of power still in Anson. "He's got enough to regret his loss. Not enough to do anything with it."

Nick looked skeptical. He nudged Anson with his toe. The body rocked, but the man didn't react.

"And he won't be able to leech anyone again?" Sam asked. His arms tightened protectively around her. She ducked her head a bit and burrowed, not to get closer to Sam, but in an attempt to ground herself. She didn't feel right. Her vision was crystal clear, yet colors seemed to swirl, not in front of her, but...behind her eyes? And inside her, deep, the place where she used to gather energy. Power swirled, but it was different. No longer the ability to draw energy by connecting with the moon, but power by itself. Filling her. Making her…whole. Her head swam, and when Sam said her name and she lifted her head, it seemed to take flight.

This must be what being high was like. She didn't care for it, but when she tried to release the energy, let it flow through her and away, it did nothing but sink deeper, as if settling in.

Not exactly what she'd been hoping for.

She forced herself to remember Sam's question. "No, he won't be able to leech again. We're safe now." The "we" made her realize Marley wasn't with them. "Where's my sister?"

"She's downstairs, guarding the goons." Nick limped over to them and reached a hand down to help Quinn up. "I gave her a gun."

Quinn took his hand, surprised when electric-like shock zinged up her arm and into her chest. Nick's startled eyes met hers, then shuttered. He tugged, and she stood on wobbly legs. He let go of her and reached to help up Sam up.

As soon as Sam was on his feet, he put his arm around Quinn's shoulders. "Can you handle him?" he asked Nick, already walking Quinn toward the stairs.

"Sure. He's half your size."

Nick grunted as he hefted Anson, and they made their way back downstairs. Marley leaned on her chair, Nick's pistol held firmly and correctly, aimed at the still-unconscious men on the floor.

Nick dropped Anson on top of his goons with a sneer of disgust. Then he peeled off the flannel shirt he'd put on over his T-shirt and carried it to Quinn. "Put this on." He blocked the others' view of her while she turned her back and shrugged out of Anson's coat. It seemed to take twenty pounds with it, and she felt a little more like herself.

Nick held his shirt while she put her arms in the sleeves. She couldn't help herself—she wrapped the collar around her face and lifted it to her nose, inhaling deeply to replace Anson's scent with Nick's. He still smelled like bay rum.

"What do we do now?" Sam asked.

Quinn did up the buttons and turned around. Nick had moved away and taken the gun from Marley. The growing distance between them caused an ache in Quinn's chest, different from all of today's pains and weirdness.

She tried to shove it away. There was more to be done. She could deal with the emotional aftermath later, when all the important things were taken care of. But the ache wouldn't go, and tears pricked at her eyes. When she drew a breath, her chin trembled.

Not now. She couldn't fall apart. She spun and walked away to press her face against her arm propped on the wall. She held herself tightly, so tightly she'd break if someone touched her, and she didn't breathe until she had to. *Keep it together.* She had hours before it would be safe to cry.

Finally, her muscles eased, and the tears receded. Resolve overtook the ache, though it hadn't faded. She was just able to put it in the background now. She turned. Nick stood a few feet away. She wondered why he hadn't come closer. But then she realized she'd set up a shield, without even thinking about it, to keep him from doing so. It had hurt him, she could tell by the look in his eyes, but she didn't know how to apologize. He shook his head a little—she didn't need to.

Gratitude threatened to drag her under again, so she dropped the shield and strode back to the group.

"Sam, call the Society and have them send their so-called security team over here. Marley—" She hesitated, then decided to damn the consequences. "You might want to leave or they'll take you into custody, too."

Marley sighed. "I need to face the charges. Don't worry," she added, seeing Quinn's reaction. "I'll be okay. This is my price to pay."

"We'll talk after. We need— I want to be your sister." As she said the words, Quinn was certain of their truth. For the first time since she learned of Marley's existence, she could think about her as family rather than a problem.

Sam snapped his phone closed. "They're on their way."

A few moments later the side door burst open, and the security team flooded in. Hostility came off them in waves. Quinn and her friends had accomplished in hours what the security people had been unable to do for weeks. Quinn raised her arms, ready to defend her friends, and the power inside her swirled excitedly. Her entire body began to buzz and she immediately shut down, frightened. This was so strange, so different from what she understood goddesshood to be. She created another shield, an easy task that took very little effort, and wrapped it around her center, closing it and sealing the energy inside. She could still sense it, even the different "flavors" that had come from the different goddesses, but now she didn't fear bringing the building down on their heads.

As angry and resentful as the security team was, they did their jobs with efficiency and professionalism.

Then one of them approached Marley. "I'm sorry, Ms. Canton, but you'll have to come in with me."

"She's been leeched," Quinn protested, unable to help herself. "Isn't that punishment enough?"

The man didn't bother turning her way. "That's not up to me." He wrapped a zip tie around Marley's hands and led her out the door.

The three unknown men and Anson had already been collected. The tall, dark-haired man who'd directed the team approached Quinn and handed her a card. "This is when the board expects to see you. Come alone."

Quinn looked at the card. It was a simple appointment card, like you got at the doctor, but was embossed with the Society seal and the words "Hearing Date and Time." Tomorrow morning, nine o'clock. Not even giving her Monday to rest.

"I'll be there."

"We've taken care of the police issue at the hotel." He didn't look happy about helping them. "It's safe to return there tonight."

"Thank you."

A moment later, she was alone with Nick and Sam in the cavernous warehouse.

She couldn't believe it was over. No more running or chasing. No more fear.

No more life the way it was before. In any way.

Her knees began to shake, then her thighs. They wouldn't hold her. She started to collapse.

"Whoa, there." Nick caught one side, Sam the other. She thought for a minute Nick would pick her up, but Sam somehow took control and lifted her into his arms. The world tilted in a few different directions, and her head swam. She couldn't focus.

"Get the car door. No, the back." The voice was muffled but she heard the door creak open and the seat squeak. Sam gently deposited her on the backseat, then slung himself in after her.

Nick hit the overhead door control before climbing into the driver's seat. The metal clanked and screeched, the noise pounding in Quinn's head.

"Take us back to the hotel," Sam ordered. "She's overtaxed. She needs rest. You got any water in here?"

Nick tossed back a half-empty bottle of water. Sam unscrewed the top and held it to her mouth.

She drank, but it wasn't overtaxing that had sidelined her. She wasn't drained like usual but buzzed, as if she'd had three shots on an empty stomach.

"What time is it?" she asked Sam, frowning. She should know.

"You've got to be exhausted to ask me that." He glanced at his watch. Quinn noticed his strong wrist and fingers, lightly curled, and the cords of muscle in his forearm. Something twisted in her abdomen. Something physical and familiar. *Oh, no.*

"It's a few minutes after midnight," Sam said.

"Moon's cresting," she murmured, rolling her head across the seat. The back of Nick's neck was exposed. She bared her teeth a little, remembering the taste of him, the texture of his skin under her mouth. Desire began a slow burn. She arched. Her nipples, unbound, abraded against Nick's shirt and tingled. "Oh, god."

"Quinn? What's wrong?" Sam shifted closer to her and put his hand on the side of her head. "Are you hurt?" His examining gaze met her wild one, and he stilled. "Oh."

"Sammy." Quinn clenched her hand around his shirt, fighting not to pull him closer. He smelled familiar and felt strong. Her hands shook with the effort to keep them from roaming. She'd never experienced this before. She couldn't think, struggled to get her body to obey.

"Quinn." He tried to pry her hand off his shirt and ended up pulling it over his head so he could slide back across the seat, as far away from her as possible. "Nick, get us to that hotel, fast."

"What the hell is going on back there?"

Quinn barely heard the exchange. All she could focus on was the desperate *need* filling her. It had never been so bad. Why was she holding Sam's shirt? She squinted at his bare torso and almost flung herself across the car to attack him. A groan slid out of her throat. She pressed her feet to the floorboards, forcing herself back into the corner of the seat. She couldn't do this. Sam wasn't hers. But her body didn't seem to care. The power surged behind its barrier, hunger cramping her insides.

"What the fuck?" Nick slammed on the brakes at a light and spun around, his arm over the back of the seat. Quinn caught the fire in Nick's eyes. She knew it was anger, but it fed hers anyway. She lunged for him, catching the back of his head with one hand and landing on his mouth in an open, carnal kiss. Her tongue dueled with his until someone behind them honked and he wrenched away.

"Jesus Christ. Get her under control." He slid back into his seat and drove, weaving between cars to get down the street faster. Quinn stretched her arms over the seat and into his shirt, her palms rubbing over his nipples. She purred in the back of her throat.

"How?" Sam demanded. "She drew on a hell of a lot of power tonight, Nick. She's always like this."

"Always?" Nick's voice went a little high. He squirmed but couldn't get out of her reach.

"Not like *this*, this." Sam tugged on Quinn's arms and managed to pull her back. She slid on the slick seat until she was lying on her back, Sam somehow over her. Her hips lifted to rub against him. Her nails sliced into the leather seat under her, her grip so tight, trying to keep herself from grabbing Sam. He was a body—a hot, hard, familiar body that hers knew what to do with, and Quinn was losing the battle to stop it. The burning ache grew until she whimpered and rolled, trying to get to the floor, the only place away from Sam.

He cursed. "She gets horny," he managed to say, holding her in place. "I always thought it was the moon, but it must be the amount of power she draws. She drew more power than usual. A lot more."

It was so much more than that. He didn't know the power was still there, inside her, craving. Demanding. It swelled, threatening to rip her apart if she didn't feed it. Nick's voice filled the car, profanity-laced frustration, but the growl burrowed deep into her. Quinn closed her eyes and rode the wave, so lost now she barely noticed when the Charger screeched to a halt at the hotel valet.

Nick leaped out, shoved his seat forward, and pulled Quinn out of Sam's arms and into his. She sucked in air, desperate to force down the clawing need, but when Nick pulled her tight against him, no doubt to keep her in control, her tongue traced his collarbone. This time when he cursed, his voice was lower, more intimate. It slid inside, marking her. When she inhaled, it wasn't exhaust-laden city air filling her lungs, but Nick's scent. The desperation dimmed a little. This was okay. She didn't have to fight so hard against this.

"She shredded my shirt!" Sam cried from inside the car. The valet stood at the driver's door, staring at Quinn and Nick, then at Sam.

"Embrace your inner stud and let's get her upstairs, dude." Nick kept a tight grip on Quinn as they went inside. It made her hotter, but she couldn't form words to tell him so.

They wrestled her to the elevator, casting a simultaneous "She's drunk" look at the reception desk. She thought she should be annoyed at that but couldn't think past the haze to care. If Nick wasn't inside her soon, she'd scream.

As soon as the elevator door closed, she slammed Nick against the wall and plunged her tongue into his mouth again. He held her rigidly, but his erection was hot against her abdomen. In seconds, she had his belt unbuckled and was unbuttoning his jeans when he stopped her.

"God damn it!" she said.

Sam pulled her away from Nick. Quinn struggled and they fell sideways, against the other wall. Nick hit their floor button again, hard. His short hair stood on end, his mouth was swollen, and dear lord, Quinn wanted him. She reached out and snagged the collar of his shirt, pulling him off balance. His stagger sandwiched her between his hard body and the wall. The rail digging in to the back of her hips would leave bruises, but the pain sent a bolt of pleasure up her spine. She rubbed her body up against him.

The elevator dinged. Nick wrenched away as Sam leaned out to check the hall.

"Coast's clear. Come on." He ran down the hall and opened the suite door.

Nick maneuvered Quinn into the room. Sam slammed the door and slumped against it.

"What do we do?" Nick asked Sam. "Lock her in the bedroom?"

"We can't leave her like this. It won't abate. She needs to have sex. Besides, even if we *could* lock the door from the outside, it wouldn't hold her. If we left her here, she'd find someone else."

"She's not goddamned having anyone else," Nick growled. "I'll take her to her room."

Silence rang between them. Quinn managed to hold herself still, though she panted a little, held up to Nick's chest by one solid arm. She couldn't see either man's face, but tension crackled, Sam's unspoken protest a challenge in the air.

Then the tension disappeared. A door closed. Sam had gone into one of the bedrooms.

"Come on, sweetheart." Nick maneuvered Quinn into the room she was supposed to share with Marley and closed the door. "What am I—"

But Quinn had stopped fighting, meager though her efforts had been up to now. She could have what she so desperately needed. Wanted. She bunched the soft cotton of Nick's T-shirt in her palms and drew it up over his head. It drifted to the floor. Nick braced her hips between his hands while she dug hers into his hair and swept her mouth up over his neck to his ear.

"Fuck me, Nick."

With a groan he pulled her tight against him, his feet spread wide as he plundered her mouth. She soared, but she was riding desperation, not pleasure. This wasn't even close to enough. She yanked at the shirt Nick had given her, fabric tearing, then her jeans and his. Nick didn't help, as if his slower movements could calm her. But her throat squeezed until she couldn't swallow, only the taste of his skin under her open mouth easing the tightness. He lifted her and laid her on the bed, where she sank into the plush mattress, silky pillows supporting her head and shoulders. The fabric soothed her burning skin. She wriggled her body deeper and tilted her head back, gasping for air. She cried out, wordless begging, the ache tightening into a piercing pain. She couldn't see again, everything a haze of swirling gold and white and pearlescent color, until she wasn't sure what was real and outside of her, and what was inside, trying to force its way out.

Then Nick's warm hands touched her thighs, giving her something to center herself with. His shoulders moved beneath her knees, and then his tongue was on her, gliding, stroking. She did scream then, ecstasy rocketing through her, gone too fast and leaving behind the same hunger, though now the world had solidified. He tongued her again, a long, hard finger sliding into her wetness at the same time, sending her up and over with a long, low moan. When the wave passed, her body had relaxed into the comforter, and Nick propped himself over her, his green eyes dark, intense.

"You okay?" he murmured.

Quinn managed a nod. She lifted her arms around him to stroke the skin of his back. "I'm sorry," she whispered, but already the hunger had doubled again. She raised her head and bit down on his shoulder. He grunted and pulled away, but his cock had flexed against the inside of her thigh.

"Fill me, Nick." She closed her hand around him and squeezed. Nick's rough hand stroked her breast, and electric flame flickered into her. "God. I need— Nick, please. I need you. *Now*."

"I need a condom." He nuzzled her ear, her throat, and went

lower to nip her other nipple with his teeth before rising back up and pressing her entire body into the bed. Quinn couldn't get a grip on the meaning of his words. She wrapped her legs around his hips, pulled him harder onto her body, though he was already crushing her so she couldn't breathe. His cock nudged her opening and she sobbed.

"Hold on, Quinn."

He was gone only seconds, but the abandonment set loose the scream that had threatened since the lust took over. He landed on her, his mouth covering hers, tongue filling her mouth, taking the scream as he finally, *finally* pushed into her, so deep her body convulsed before loosening and drawing him in even farther. She tightened around his cock, her whole body tense beneath him. He rocked upward, pressing hard against her clit, then rocked again. His hands clutched her head and he kissed her, his mouth clinging, devouring, hot and hungry.

The orgasm pierced Quinn but caught, going nowhere, imprisoning her. She ripped her mouth from Nick's so she could tip her head back and arch. Her nails dug into his ass while he pulled out and stroked deep again, then again, harder and faster each time. The sweet agony tightened until Quinn couldn't bear it any more. She clutched Nick's shoulders, turned her head toward him, and whispered, "I love you."

He'd just murmured the words back when Quinn exploded. In the fiery shower of light, she lost all sense of herself, all awareness of anything but the ecstasy pouring through her, endlessly throbbing, emotion and power intertwined and overcoming her entire being, until at last it cast her into darkness.

CHAPTER SEVENTEEN

Romantic relationships are more complicated when one of the partners is a goddess. It takes a strong man to adapt to the extraordinary abilities of women like us, and we face the difficulty of discerning whether they want us for who we are, or for what we can do.

—Society Annual Meeting,
Special Session on Relationships

The hotel room was silent when Quinn left the next morning for her hearing at the Society. Nick hadn't moved the entire time she showered and dressed. He slept heavily, clearly as exhausted as Quinn had been. She'd slept a deep, healing sleep that settled the power into a slow churn inside its shield. Her rested body seemed to accommodate the foreign energy more willingly, her head clear, the overwhelming, biting lust sated.

The sitting room had been dark, Sam's door stayed closed, and Quinn didn't try to wake either of them to go with her to the hearing. She needed to get used to being on her own.

The cab let her off in front of the Society building ten minutes before nine. Alana led her to the conference room, where the board sat waiting for her.

"Before we begin," Quinn said after Barbara had greeted her,

"I'd like to know what happened to Marley."

"She's not being detained. We agreed that the leeching she endured is far more personal punishment than any we can exact. However, she is required to remain in Boston and work for the Society as an educator and counselor for the next two years. After that, she will be free to move on."

Quinn nodded. It was a fair decision, and she believed Marley would embrace her role, to help ensure no other goddess fell into the trap she had.

"Shall we begin?" Barbara motioned for Quinn to sit. She didn't want to, but after the fight with Anson and her night with Nick, she was sore and tired.

Barbara nodded at the vice president, who read off a sheet of parchment-like paper. "The purpose of this hearing is to clarify the events of November fifth relating to Anson Tournado and the goddess Quinn Caldwell. Alleged transgressions on the part of Ms. Caldwell include doing harm to non-powerful humans and draining of power from the opposite." She set the paper down and looked at Quinn.

She swallowed and got her thoughts in order. "The harm to non-powerful humans was self-defense. They were armed and had attacked us before. They entered the premises—"

"Which premises were those?"

"An empty warehouse we'd found. I wanted a facility that would eliminate potential collateral damage, after Anson had penetrated hotel security and leeched Marley Canton in our suite."

Barbara inclined her head. "We will take the self-defense argument under advisement. Please address the draining of power."

"I watched Anson leech my sister, and I was powerless to stop it. I knew there was only one way to defeat him." She remembered the despair when she'd almost failed, and rasped out, "I fully believe draining the power he'd stolen from those to whom it rightfully belongs was the only recourse available."

After a moment of silence, Barbara asked, "Do you have anything to add?"

"No."

"Do the members of the board have any further questions?"

They shook their heads.

"Alana will show you to my office. I'll speak to you there after our deliberations."

They all stood, and the door opened. Quinn followed Alana into the hall, relieved no one had thought—or been brave enough—to ask her what had happened to the power she'd taken from Anson.

Alana led Quinn down the hall to the president's office, her demeanor stiff and awkward. When they sat in the guest chairs in front of the desk, the executive director folded her arms and wouldn't meet Quinn's eyes.

At first, Quinn didn't understand the change from Alana's earlier animosity. But then a possible reason came to her. "Does she know Anson got to you, too?"

It was a guess, and Quinn wasn't sure what she'd do if Alana admitted he had, but the other woman scowled and tightened her arms against herself. "He didn't get to me."

Quinn raised her eyebrows.

"He tried," she admitted. "And, well, yes, I liked him. But I never gave him anything."

The way she said it made Quinn narrow her eyes. "So he took it."

Alana jerked a nod.

"The database? He got access. That's how he targeted everyone."

"Yes," Alana said. "And believe me, it haunts me."

Quinn nodded, understanding. It would haunt all of them for a long time. "So Barbara plans to talk to me in here? Why not call me back to the conference room?"

"I think they made their decision before you came in. They just need to confirm it."

Quinn would be upset if she didn't think it was going to go in her favor. "What does she want?"

"I don't know."

The tall door opened and Barbara entered. "Thank you for waiting, Quinn. Alana, you can go back to work."

"Yes, ma'am." Alana left, and Barbara circled her desk to sit with a sigh.

"Quite a month we've had."

"Yes."

"I'm sure you can tell the board has decided not to sanction or punish you for crossing the line. I'm sorry to put you through that, but we have to follow procedure." She sighed and looked very tired and very old. "This has been a horribly trying situation, I don't need to tell you, and I'm afraid it's not going to be the last."

Quinn frowned. "What do you mean?"

"The mainstream media is digging at the story, at the rumor that goddess power is transferrable. Half of them are taking a skeptical approach, which won't cast goddesses in a positive light but will help suppress the truth. If the half who are treating it seriously prevail, however, it's possible others will try to take power."

"But they can't just take it," Quinn protested. "It doesn't work like that."

Barbara laughed, the sound more cynical than Quinn thought her capable. "That doesn't matter. They'll still try. The Protectorate is already working to increase its staff and alter its methods, as now in-power goddesses will be vulnerable, as well. The board will need to provide a whole new range of services for our members, from the educational programs Marley will start to a much larger, more effective security team."

"It sounds like a good plan." But the sentiment was hollow. Quinn no longer felt part of the board, or even the Society as a whole. Right now, she wasn't sure she cared.

"I want you to consider running for president next year."

"No way." She didn't hesitate. Politics had become her enemy, and she desperately wanted home. "You have a successor, anyway." The vice president wasn't as old or as experienced as Barbara, but she wasn't incompetent.

"We need someone who's been in the trenches, Quinn, who has experienced what's out there and knows how to survive it. This is a new age. It needs a new leader."

"It doesn't have to be me."

"But it should be. You're now the most powerful goddess on earth."

Quinn couldn't suppress her shock. She wanted to protest but couldn't bring herself to lie. The power of five other goddesses swirled and danced inside her, and though she hadn't tried to use it, her old limitations didn't seem to exist anymore.

Which meant her old needs didn't exist anymore.

Yanking her thoughts away from that familiar yet way too new and raw pain, Quinn waited for Barbara to ask her about that power. How much she had now, how it manifested, what Quinn was going to do about it. But none of those questions seemed to even occur to the older woman. Uneasy as she was about hiding it, Quinn was too afraid of what they'd do to her if they had any inkling how foreign and dangerous it felt.

So she turned to the mundane and asked about the goddesses who'd helped Anson. "He said something about people wanting to be normal. Is that why they worked with him?"

Barbara sighed and nodded. "I'm afraid so. We were able to track them last night, after the team took Anson into custody. He'd promised them that if they did what he needed, he'd give them the way to live normal lives. That's another aspect we'll need to address in the counseling program. No goddess should ever feel she has to turn to outsiders like that."

"No." Quinn couldn't imagine wanting to *not* be a goddess anymore. What had their lives been like, that they'd resorted to attacking other goddesses?

Barbara checked her watch and stood. "Please think about running for president," she urged. "I know you have a business in Ohio, but it's not like you'd start immediately. Jeannine will still serve her term next year, but we plan to change the structure of the board with new bylaws next spring, and pending the acceptance of the membership, you would be the ideal leadership for the new Society."

Quinn agreed to consider it, but only to end the conversation. She had too much to do, too many other changes to adjust to, and the presidency would require more time and attention than she wanted to give right now. Maybe at some point in the future she could think about it.

When she emerged from the elevator in the lobby a few minutes later, Marley waited for her. She crossed the marble floor tentatively, wiping her hands on her jeans.

"How did it go?"

"Fine. No problems." She studied her sister, taking note of the circles under her eerie eyes, her sallow complexion. Quinn understood now the soul-deep scars the leeching had left on her sister. "You okay? Get any sleep?"

"Not really. But it's okay, I will. Did they tell you my punishment?"

"Yeah. It sounds like a good plan. You'll be great at it."

"I'm happy. Barbara seems determined to make changes, and I'm all for that." She laughed, a hint of unease still apparent. "I have to start next week."

"What will you do with the inn?"

She sighed. "Fran's going to run it until I get home." She took a deep breath. "Quinn, I have something to ask you." Unease was an understatement now. Marley shoved her hands deep into her pockets, her shoulders rising to meet her ears. "It's about Sam."

Sorrow splintered in Quinn's heart. "What about him?"

"What's between you?"

Quinn thought about all the years of recharging, all the ways Sam made her life easier, both in the bar and with her other clients, and how much he meant to her, even now. She couldn't explain something so complex. "He's my assistant," she finally said, as inadequate as the description was.

"You don't have a…relationship with him?"

"I'm sorry. I can't talk about this." It hurt too much, knowing she was probably about to lose her best friend. She crossed the lobby toward the exit, her hand coming up to press against her chest, as if she could touch the pain there.

"Wait, Quinn."

She sighed and stopped. Marley came around to face her. "When we were at the inn, after you left and he woke up, we talked a little. He said he might be looking for a new job. It would be great if he could come work for me for a while. But I want a relationship with you. If you feel like I've stolen him…"

"You couldn't if you tried," she said before she could stop herself, pain making her lash out. He'd made plans even before telling her he was going. "It's Sam's choice. If he wants to lea—to quit working for me and come to Boston, that's for him to decide. I promise I won't hold anything against you." She cleared her throat. "I want a relationship with you, too."

"Okay." Marley stepped forward and wrapped her arms around Quinn, who hugged her back. "I'm so glad you found me,"

Marley whispered. Quinn squeezed her tighter. Her sister had lost a lot but was already trying to rebuild her life.

The shield she'd maintained around the power inside her suddenly rent. The part of it that had been Marley's seemed to recognize its origination, and it churned and surged, dragging with it the other powers, intertwined and irrevocably bound. The same headiness Quinn felt after pulling it from Anson made her sway, a euphoria climbing up through her.

Normally, with the full moon waning and moving away from her, using power would take considerable effort. But now, it was easier than it had ever been. The energy wanted to be used, and Quinn knew she could do anything she wanted to, with only a thought.

Almost anything.

She opened a conduit to her sister, attempting to bestow power back to her. But Marley was too damaged and couldn't accept it. It rolled back into Quinn, shrinking from the dim grayness that was Marley's capacity.

"It won't work," Marley choked out as she pulled away. "You're generous to try, but I can't take it."

Generosity had little to do with it. Quinn didn't want this. It was too dangerous, too damaging. "Why?"

"I want it. I crave it like a junkie." The tears flowed down her face now. "But I'm like a cracked vase. I can't hold it."

It was an accurate description. Tears welled in Quinn's eyes, too. "I'm sorry, Marley. I don't want it. I'd do anything to transfer it."

"No, you wouldn't. It would do harm, and you won't let that happen anymore."

Marley was right. Maybe Quinn could force it, but if the vessel couldn't hold it, if Marley couldn't control it, she'd be even more broken, especially if Quinn couldn't separate the energies and return only what was taken. She'd have to find out if all the goddesses were damaged the way Marley was, but even if they weren't, would bestowing power back on them turn *them* into leeches? How could she research something that had never happened before?

It didn't matter. She wouldn't rest until she found a way to make everything right again.

"I'm sorry," Quinn repeated.

"It's okay. It's my punishment." Marley shrugged. "I have to accept that." She squeezed her sister's hand, then backed away. "Thanks for everything."

"I'll be in touch."

"Me, too. I already intend to tap you for this educational program." Marley sniffed and rubbed her face on her sleeve. "Take care of yourself."

"You, too."

Quinn went outside and hailed a cab, which promptly got caught in traffic. She closed her eyes and tried not to think, but that proved impossible.

She was on her way to end her life as she'd known it. In truth, it had ended the moment Nick showed up early and told her about the leech. Before that, even, when she and Sam stopped being lovers.

She had to let him go. Really, truly, completely go. Even if he'd resigned himself to not having her, she knew he couldn't live his own life if he kept serving hers. It would kill her to fire him. She would if she had to, but she knew, deep down, that he wouldn't make her.

Nick would leave, too. The power she held would always be there, strong enough to make her invulnerable. No matter what the new global reality was going to be, she would be one goddess who didn't need a protector. And there were so many more Nick could help.

The cab rolled forward, but when Quinn opened her eyes she spotted a tiny park off to the right. A copse of trees called to her.

"Let me off here, please."

When she entered the shade, everything else seemed to disappear. The traffic noise faded enough to sound like wind. A robin sang on a branch above her, and a real breeze caressed her face. She sank down on the plush grass, buried her face in her arms, and wept.

She sobbed for Jennifer and the goddess in South Carolina, for Tanda's and Chloe's losses and her inability to make things right, even if she'd brought them justice. She wept for Marley and the relationship that had been broken before they could even start building it. From there, it was easy to cry for her birth parents, who'd never wanted to know her, and her real parents, who'd died too young.

She sobbed for Sam and all he'd meant to her, and for Nick and everything he'd almost become.

When she was empty and could cry no more, the loneliness that had hovered over her for so long crept in, ready to fill the space. But she wasn't going to let it. She'd wallowed in her longing for Nick, let things go too far with Sam, because it ruled her life after her parents died. It was long past time for her to grow up.

The sun had moved past its zenith when her phone rang. She stretched out on the grass and stared up through the trees, letting the rhythm of their sway soothe her rawness. On the fourth ring, right before it would have gone to voice mail, she answered.

It was Sam. Quinn's eyes filled with tears again, and she cursed. She had to be stronger than this.

"We're getting worried about you," he said. "How did the hearing go?"

"Fine." She told him about the board's decision and Barbara's request.

"Are you going to do it?"

"I don't know yet." She didn't want to tell him about the power issue she had to deal with first. It wouldn't be a clean break if he thought she still needed him, even if only for his research skills.

"It would give you a chance to work with Marley," he pointed out.

"You talked to her, then."

"Yeah, she called when they released her. She sounded okay. Sad. But strong."

"She is strong."

"It runs in the family."

She listened to his breathing for a minute, taking every last drop of time she had with him.

"Are you coming back?"

"Soon."

"I'll meet you in the coffee shop. We need to talk."

"Okay. I'll be there in a few minutes."

She sighed and lay there for a while longer, not wanting to give up the minute peace of the trees and cool air. Resolve was a lot easier than action. But eventually, she struggled to her feet and trudged the few blocks to the hotel, finding Sam in the coffee shop, as he'd said.

He stood as she approached and enfolded her in his arms, resting his chin on top of her head. They stood like that for a while, and Quinn knew they were on the same page. It was a relief to know he was ready, that he wouldn't argue, but it didn't help repair the tear in her heart.

They sat, Sam not releasing her hand. "I think you know what I'm going to say."

She drew a deep breath. "You're resigning and moving to Boston. Marley needs an assistant, and you can't work for me anymore." Her voice broke at the end, belying the confidence she'd tried to project.

"I don't want to leave you, Quinn. But last night—"

"Was too horrifying to bear?"

His lips curved. "Not exactly. But I know it wasn't just taking care of a physical need."

"Sam—"

"It's okay, Quinn. You've been trying to say good-bye for a long time." He absently rubbed his breastbone. "And now I know…well, I already knew," he admitted. "You only love me. You've been in love with Nick for years."

She couldn't speak. The stupid tears started again. Sam cupped her cheek and wiped them away with his thumb. "Quinn, a lot of people live their entire lives without loving someone like I've loved you. But I understand why it can't work. You belong with Nick. But I can't handle watching it."

A sob broke through. Quinn choked it back. "Nick's not going to stay, Sam." She didn't want to say this. If he knew, he might not be willing to move on. But she couldn't help herself. It hurt so much she had to let it out. "He can't protect me anymore. His job will take him all over the country and he won't have time for me."

Sam shook his head wonderingly. "You are the biggest fool I've ever met."

"Hey!"

He cupped her face in both his hands and bent to kiss her softly on the mouth. "I love you. Now get your ass upstairs."

She hesitated. "Are you coming back to Ohio?"

"I'm going to help Marley get started down here, move her things from Maine. She's a mess, organizationally. She needs my mad skillz." Quinn smiled, and Sam looked pleased with himself. "I'll come out to get my stuff in a few weeks, if that's okay."

"I can ship it if you want."

"No, I want to see everyone at the bar, say good-bye to the

clients. But I think it's best if I wait a little."

She nodded and stood to hug him again. "Good-bye, Sam."

"See you later, Quinn."

He walked her to the elevator, and Quinn wondered if he thought she wouldn't go upstairs if he didn't. She might be an emotional wreck but as he'd said, she was strong. She'd get through this all at once, like ripping off a bandage, and move on without regret. Or rather, with tons of regret but equal amounts of determination.

When she got upstairs, though, and let herself into the suite, it was empty. Cleaning services had been in, and there was no evidence of their night together, nor of the attack by Anson prior to that.

He'd done it. Nick had left her, and he hadn't bothered to say good-bye.

At a knock on the door Quinn spun to open it. Her heart pounded with foolish hope, though she knew damned well it wouldn't be Nick.

The bellhop motioned behind her. "I came up to get your bags? Your friend is retrieving the car."

Relief flooded her. He hadn't left. He might be trying to move things along at top speed, but he wasn't gone yet.

"I don't have any bags, but please tell him I'll be right down."

The bellhop nodded and backed out. She went into the bathroom to splash water on her face and eradicate the evidence of all her crying. Her eyes were puffy and red, but as she stared at herself in the mirror, she realized they didn't have to stay that way. With a glimmer of power, they became normal. She ran her fingers through her hair, and it looked freshly brushed. She smiled. Maybe there were some benefits to her new status, however insignificant and hopefully temporary.

She headed back downstairs and turned in her keycard at the

desk, then went out through the automatic doors at the front of the building. The Charger, freshly washed in her absence, gleamed in the sunlight. Nick leaned against it, his jeans-clad legs crossed, his leather coat looking even more beat-up and disreputable than ever. But his posture was open, the look on his face enough to stop her breath.

Quinn stepped forward, not sure what was about to happen and afraid of being crushed.

"Hi," she said.

"Hi."

"The hearing went okay."

"Sam told me. You going to run for president?"

"Maybe."

He nodded.

"Barbara told me the need for protectors will be bigger than ever. I suppose you'll be traveling more. You won't need to come to Ohio, at least." She was the only goddess in the state now.

"Why not?"

"Since I leeched Anson, my power won't wane."

"Yeah, so?"

"So I won't need a protector during the new moon."

"Is that all I am?"

Her heart skipped a beat. Hope came back to dig a furrow though the sorrow. "Isn't it?"

He blew out a breath and shook his head. "Come on, Quinn. You know I've been more than that for a very long time."

She took a step closer, her entire being lighter, even the uncomfortable power inside flipping joyfully. "I know, but—"

"Do you think I spent as much time with any other goddess as I spent with you?"

"I don't know."

He took a deep breath. "My parents didn't want to retire. My mother insisted they could have it all. They took turns protecting, or left us with our grandmother, and came back to tell us all stories about the noble goddesses who were able to do such amazing things because we let our parents help them. And then they got hurt."

Quinn swallowed and nodded, confused about what was happening. Nick stared at the cobblestones at their feet, hiding his expression from her.

"My dad could have continued. But my mom was just... so broken." He straightened and focused his gaze over Quinn's shoulder now, remembered anguish filling his eyes. "He decided to stay with her, with us. It killed him, so my mother told him to go, but that was worse. So they stopped, and as we grew up and my brothers chased other dreams, it was clear I was going to have to carry on that legacy."

"It sounds—" She paused to clear her throat. "That was a big burden for a little kid."

He shook his head. "Not for a second. Until I met you." Now his green eyes burned into hers. "I swore I'd never do that to someone. Let them do that to me."

Tears spilled over Quinn's lashes. She tightened her hands on her elbows to hold herself together. The more agitated her emotions got, the more the power in her swirled and flipped, making her nauseous. "I get it."

"No, you don't. Come here." He raised his arm, wrapping it around her back as she stepped still closer. All the anguish was gone. "I love you, Quinn. I always have, but I wasn't going to trap you, or be trapped."

"I wouldn't have done that to you," she said fiercely, anger that he thought she would drying up the tears. "I never would have pinned you down, taken you away from the Protectorate."

"I know. I know. Shh." He stroked his thumb across her

cheekbone, though no more tears had fallen. "It took the leech, the threat against you, to understand what I was doing. I didn't want you to live that way, but you were anyway. It hurt us both just as much." His brows dipped low. "I thought Sam would give you what you needed. But—"

Quinn sighed. "You are such an idiot." So was she, of course, but she wasn't going to say it out loud.

"But?" A smile flickered at the corners of his mouth, the rest of his features relaxing.

"But I love you."

"Good." He breached the inches between their mouths and kissed her with promise. "Partners?"

"What about your job?"

"We'll work it out." He tightened his arms around her. "Partners?"

"Partners." She buried her face in his neck as he held her tightly to him and sighed when he let go.

"I hope you don't mind driving back to Ohio." He pulled open the passenger door for her.

"Of course not." She slid into the car and watched him round the hood and climb in beside her. "You'll have to fly sometimes."

"Yeah, yeah." He put the key in the ignition. "If you say so." He started the car with a roar and hit the on button for the radio. As he pulled out of the valet circle, the opening strains of AC/DC's "Back in Black" pounded through the speakers. He turned right onto the main road and headed home.

Acknowledgements

First and most importantly, thank you to my Mini Boot Squad, for all the magic you have brought me since we started back in June 2006. M1, M2, Bix, and Smith, you help me make everything better and, in sharing my journey, enhanced the joy. I don't want to be a writer without you.

Additional thanks to Lisa Mondello, Ava Quinn, and Jody Wallace for helping me in ways I can never repay. And even greater thanks to Tracy Madison, for reading chapter one over and over (and then the rest of the book!), nursing me through my neuroses, and gushing like a fangirl at appropriate moments. You are a complete gem.

Liz Pelletier has the honor of being the first publisher to ever offer me a contract by phone. Thank you, Liz, for staying up to 3:30 a.m. to read *Under the Moon* and giving me the opportunity to be part of an amazing company like Entangled Publishing. Thanks, too, for assigning me to Kerri-Leigh Grady. Starting work with a new editor is frightening, but KL, you've made this one of the best experiences of my career. Thank you for your insights, your confidence, and your support. You rock.

To Eric Kripke, for helming a television show that sparked my imagination and helped me remember both the new feeling of being in love and the despair of choices too hard to make, so that I could pour them into this book. And finally, to Jason Manns, whose music I discovered when this book was first born, so many years ago. I will always think of honeyed clouds and motorcycles when I listen to you sing.